THE AVON ROMANCE

Kathleen E. Woodiwiss, Johanna Lindsey, Laurie McBain, Shirlee Busbee...these are just a few of the romance superstars that Avon Books has been proud to present in the past.

Since 1982, Avon has been continuing a different sort of romance tradition—a program that has been launching new writers of exceptional promise. Called "The Avon Romance," these books are distinguished by a ribbon motif on the front cover—in fact, you readers quickly discovered them and dubbed them "the ribbon books"!

Month after month, "The Avon Romance" has continued to deliver the best in historical romance, offering sensual, exciting stories by new writers (and some favorite repeats!) *without* the predictable characters and plots of formula romances.

"The Avon Romance." Our promise of superior, unforgettable historical romance...month after dazzling month!

FELA DAWSON SCOTT

SHADOW OF DESIRE

AVON
PUBLISHERS OF BARD, CAMELOT, DISCUS AND FLARE BOOKS

SHADOW OF DESIRE is an original publication of Avon Books.
This work has never before appeared in book form. This work is
a novel. Any similarity to actual persons or events is purely co-
incidental.

AVON BOOKS
A division of
The Hearst Corporation
1790 Broadway
New York, New York 10019

First Avon Printing, January 1986

AVON TRADEMARK REG. U. S. PAT. OFF. AND IN
OTHER COUNTRIES, MARCA REGISTRADA, HECHO EN
U. S. A.

Printed in the U. S. A.

WFH   10   9   8   7   6   5   4   3   2   1

To my parents,
Bill and Shirley Dawson.
For your love and support.
No one believed
More than you two did.
I love you both
So very much.
So this one's for you.

Prologue

England 1782

It was the most wonderful day of her life, her eleventh birthday. Edward and Mary Campbell, friends of the family, gave Katrina the best party a little girl could ask for. All her friends were there to help celebrate. They played games that left them all laughing, and danced until they were flushed and breathless with exuberance. It was a perfect day, but best of all was the present Katrina received from her mother and father—a delicate sapphire pendant surrounded by small perfect diamonds with a pair of matching earbobs. Her blue eyes widened with surprise at the beauty of the gift, and tears slipped down her soft cheeks as she ran to her father's open arms, unable to find words to express her feelings. William Easton hugged away his daughter's tears and claimed the jewels had reminded him of his little girl's sapphire-blue eyes that always sparkled so gaily with laughter.

They were all to spend the night at the Campbells' estate, but Lord Easton received word that he was needed back at Camray. Her father carried the tired birthday girl to their coach and they started for home. The hour was late and Katrina instantly fell asleep on her mother's lap.

Katrina was suddenly awakened as the coach made a wild lurch. Shots echoed in the still night, and she heard

1

the driver's anguished scream as he fell to the ground. The horses came to an abrupt halt. William Easton grabbed his pistol and sprang from the coach to defend his family, but his attempt to fight was quickly ended as a lead ball ripped through his chest. Virginia Easton screamed in horror as her husband slowly crumpled to the ground, his life flowing from him in a scarlet torrent. As the small guard bravely fought the highwaymen, Lady Easton fearfully grabbed Katrina and crawled from the conveyance. She spoke to the frightened child in desperation, her voice trembling from fear and grief.

"You must run into the woods and hide! No matter what happens, you must not stop! Do you understand me, Katrina?"

"I . . . I under-stand," whispered Katrina, her mind numb with confusion.

With tears streaming down her pale cheeks, Lady Easton whispered harshly, "Promise me! . . . Promise!"

Sensing her mother's urgency, Katrina nodded. Wide-eyed and filled with terror, she ran. Her mother followed but was quickly spotted by one of the highwaymen. Spurring his horse to a gallop, he swiftly overtook the fleeing woman and, without hesitation, ran his sword through her back. As she fell to the ground in a pile of satin and silk Lady Easton's last sight was Katrina disappearing into the dense foliage; her last breath, a sigh of relief.

Katrina did not look back but kept running, fear and her promise pushing her blindly into the blackness ahead. Branches reached out like a hundred clawing fingers, grabbing and scratching, tearing at her clothes and face. Deeper and deeper she fled, her feet stumbling over the rough, untamed ground, until she could go no further. She tripped and fell to her knees, painfully scraping them raw on the rocky ground. Trembling, she gasped for air that burned her lungs. The pain in her side was unbearable. Unable to get up, weakness shaking her frail body, the child crawled into the brush to hide and wait.

As the last man was slain, the leader of the group paused to examine the bloody carnage strewn all around. He slowly removed his hood, an evil, triumphant smile curling back his lips, a cruel, sinister delight filling his dark eyes. His satisfaction soon turned into a scowl and he barked angrily at his men.

"Where is the little girl?"

"She must have run into the trees," the man nearest him replied.

"Then get her!" he ordered through clenched teeth. "That brat must not live, you fool! Do not come back until she is found and killed! Do you understand me?"

A cold chill passed over the man as he stared into his master's crazed eyes. A strange foreboding descended on him, but fear outweighed his doubt and greed added fuel to his courage. Murder had always come easily to him, and he quickly shook off his qualms and crashed into the forest to hunt down the child. He easily spotted and followed the frantic girl's trail, covering the distance she had put between them in a very short time. He stopped when the trail abruptly ended, his senses alert, his nerves strung tight by the night's hunting. Like an animal, he knew instinctively she was near. Excitement, fear, and greed churned inside him.

Slowly, he began his search, knowing she could not escape him . . . knowing she had nowhere to go. He finally came upon Katrina and, grabbing her by the hair, cruelly dragged her from her hiding place. Suddenly, he found himself looking into the most startling blue eyes he had ever seen. Katrina was staring at him in horror and pain, tears streaming down her scratched and bruised face. He slowly raised his ominous sword, the words "Kill her! Kill her!" clouding his fevered mind. The child's eyes never left his and in them he saw fear and confusion combined with the very beginnings of hatred. Her lower lip trembled slightly from the dread of what was to come, but she did not turn away. The man's hand quivered as he stood, unable to move, unexpected indecision pulsing through him. A tremendous pounding rang loudly in his ears. He broke into a heated, nervous sweat, perspiration dampening his palms. Could it be his own heart he heard? Perhaps it was hers!

Fear clung heavily in the air. He could smell it around him, taste its bitterness, and hear its eerie sounds in his foggy mind. It fed on his confusion, gnawing at his innards, drawing the breath from his body.

Then suddenly, the blade's deadly edge fell. Katrina's scream of terror rent the night, its sound reaching out to the other men, touching a strange chord in all. A shiver passed through them, and their blood ran cold as they looked about nervously, suddenly very much aware of the presence of death.

Katrina never knew why the man had not killed her. He had slashed the ground beside her, then, without a word, had returned to the others. No longer afraid, Katrina followed the puzzling man back to the road and hid in the trees, watching the men prepare to leave.

"Is the brat dead?" the leader asked harshly.

"Yes," the man lied, quickly reigning his mount to a halt. "You need not worry about her. She is dead!"

"Excellent! Everything has gone perfectly!" exulted his sinister master. "Be sure to remove all the valuables so it will look like highwaymen killed them!" Then, riding over to the inert body of William Easton, he muttered, "Well . . . dear brother, it looks like Camray will finally be mine! All mine! The bastard son has finally triumphed!"

His chilling laughter filled the air, and as he turned to ride off with his men, Katrina saw his face. It was her uncle . . . Lawrence Langsford! A cold dread descended upon her like a heavy weight. Stumbling from the cover of the dense foliage, Katrina went over to the still body of her mother. Virginia Easton lay facedown on the hard ground, dark red blood staining her beautiful gown. Shedding tears of sorrow, unable to comprehend fully the pain inside her, Katrina knelt by the silent form and reached out with shaking fingers to caress her mother's silken hair.

"Mother?" she pleaded. "M-Mother . . . please don't leave me now! I . . . I . . . need you!"

Katrina's petite shoulders shook as sobs wracked her. With blurry, red-rimmed eyes, she looked for her father and crawled on her hands and knees to the bloodied figure. When she touched him, a moan escaped William Easton, and slowly his eyes fluttered open.

"Papa?" cried Katrina unbelievingly, fearing her mind was playing tricks on her.

"Kat! I . . . I heard them say they had killed you!" he whispered as tears of joy slid down his cheek.

"No, Papa . . . I'm fine. B-but you're hurt!" Katrina exclaimed, trying to stand. "I'll go for help!"

"No!" he muttered, grabbing her arm tightly. "No, stay with me, Kat. . . . Where is your mother?"

Bursting into tears again, she answered, "S-she's dead! They killed her, Papa! It was Lawrence . . . I saw him! I don't understand. Why would he do this? Why does he want us dead?"

Katrina began to cry uncontrollably, sobs distorting her pretty face. Reaching out, William Easton grabbed his child's quivering chin, gently but firmly, the movement causing him tremendous agony.

"Kat, you must listen to me! It's too late for your mother and me, but you must save yourself! So . . . stop your crying and listen carefully to what I say!"

Trembling with exhaustion, Katrina did as her father asked.

"That's my girl," he said weakly. "Lawrence . . . he wants Camray and will do anything to get it . . . he has proven that tonight. You must do exactly what I say, Katrina. He thinks you are dead and must not find out otherwise. Remember, for your own protection, you must stay dead. Is that clear, Katrina?" William Easton's body shook as a spasm of coughing overtook him.

"Please . . . I must go for help. I won't let you die!" Katrina pleaded, but her father continued to hold her tightly, refusing to let her go.

"You must listen! I haven't much time!"

Katrina hesitated. Part of her demanded she go for help, yet years of obedience to her father made her stay. Even more dominant was a deep, undeniable instinct that told her Lord Easton was near death. Settling down on the cold ground, she cradled her father's head in her lap and listened intently to his strained words.

"You must not return to Camray, Katrina. Go only to Father Murray in Tattershall. . . . He will help you. The good

Father will take care of you and protect you from Lawrence, so do as he says. Do not go to the authorities, for it would be your word against Langsford's, and they would not believe you. It is your very life you are protecting, child. . . . Always remember this night. Remember everything that he has taken from you. Never, never forget! When you are older and more prepared, then and only then must you take back what is rightfully yours. You must get Camray back! It is your birthright, Kat!"

Lord Easton's chest rattled, each breath a struggle, as he continued. "Learn all you can in the years to come, until you are old enough to take over the estate. You must always be strong and learn to fight for what is yours. You are the heir to Camray and a true Easton, so I must place this responsibility upon your shoulders; there is no one else. Take this ring, Kat, our family crest. Keep it always. Now, you must promise me you will do as I say and wait. Then, when the time is right, you will get Camray back. Promise me!"

Her father's hand was covered with blood, and the ring had gone unnoticed by the highwaymen. Pulling it from his finger, Katrina answered, her voice determined and strong. "I will, Father, I promise I will!" Placing the bloodied ring on her own smaller finger, she wiped the tears from her eyes and squared her shoulders. Kissing her father's cheek lovingly, she looked sadly into his faded blue eyes. "I love you, Papa."

William Easton shuddered in pain and gazed weakly upon his dearest Katrina. "That's my girl. . . . Kat . . . always remember your mother and I . . . love you very much. You . . . must be . . . brave."

Katrina felt her father's body go limp as death finally took him from her, leaving her alone and empty. Dry-eyed now, she loosened his hand from hers and gently placed it on his chest. At that moment, fury began to burn within her, giving her a reason to go on, to seek revenge for all she had suffered at the hand of one man.

"I will keep my promise, Papa. Lawrence Langsford has taken everything precious to me in this world. I will see him dead for his deeds and Camray will be mine as you wish."

There were no more tears in the young girl's heart, only a cold deadly anger.

Katrina's grim promises were her only future, and hatred and rage would guide her through the years to come.

Chapter 1

Summer 1790

Katrina Easton lay tossing and turning on her bumpy, narrow cot, disturbed by the visions that haunted her sleep. She awoke with a start, stifling the scream that threatened to break the silence of the peaceful, sleeping village, her small body trembling from the emotions the dream had aroused. Breathing heavily, her heart beating erratically, Rina looked about the tiny attic room, and once again was brought back to the present. Soon the terror in her deep, blue eyes disappeared as she recognized the familiar rickety bed she was lying on and the old chair next to it that doubled as a night table. A neat row of nails along the wall held the few faded and patched clothes she possessed and an equally shabby cape for the cold winter months hung beside them. Rina glanced at her dressing table with its cracked mirror, and a sad, bitter smile crossed her lips as she remembered the beautiful, richly decorated bedroom she had had as a child at Camray. Camray . . . would it ever be hers?

Once again, the nightmare had interrupted her much-needed rest, just as it had nearly every night for the past eight years. Rina stood and crossed the rough-hewn floor to the open window. A mass of golden curls fell to her waist in wild disarray, strands of silver, gold, bronze, and copper mingling in rich, velvety tresses. As she gazed at the coal-colored sky, a soft cooling breeze molded her nightgown to her body, revealing the firm, full breasts that accented her petite figure. Her waist was so tiny a man could easily span it with his hands, and the gentle curve of her hips flowed seductively into luscious, slender legs. Her delicate heart-shaped face was graced by beautiful almond-shaped eyes the color of sparkling, blue sapphires, fringed by long, sooty lashes.

Rina sighed wearily, staring thoughtfully at the moon, a pale, golden sliver hanging low in the sky. She began to think of another time . . . another night. The nightmares made it so real, so terrifying, as if it had happened yesterday and not eight long years ago. Only, the moon had been full that night, brightening the heavens with its soft, yellow light. Rina remembered it well, too well.

Katrina had done exactly as her father asked, going immediately to Father Murray in the village outside Camray. After she'd told him her story, the priest had prayed for guidance. And his prayers were answered that very same day.

Jake and Jenny Tidwell had traveled to Tattershall specifically to see Father Murray, an old friend. As they explained the reasons for their visit, an idea began to form in the elderly priest's mind. Many years before, the couple had lived in Tattershall but had moved away to care for an ailing sister. Recently, Jenny's sister had passed on and they wanted to move back to the small village. They hoped the Father would help them find a place to live before they made the move.

Father Murray knew the Tidwells had worked for William Easton long ago, before Katrina was born, and had been very fond of their employer. So he told them of Lawrence Langford's treachery and asked if they would consider taking the young girl into their home. Jake and Jenny never hesitated, for they had always longed for children. So Katrina became "Rina," the only child of Jenny's late sister.

For Rina's safety, the Tidwells almost decided not to make the move back to Tattershall, but Katrina insisted, wanting to be close to Camray, even if that also meant being near Lawrence Langsford. Unable to resist her earnest pleas, Jake and Jenny went through with their original plan.

Tattershall was a small, peaceful village about fifteen miles from the east coast, along the North Sea. The cluster of small cottages that lined the cobbled lane were rough in appearance, but clean and neat. Being far off the main roads, Tattershall saw few strangers. For generations, the villagers had worked the fields surrounding Camray, their lives happy and content under Lord Easton's fair hand. But that changed when his half brother took over the management of the vast estates.

When Katrina moved into the small cottage with Jake and Jenny, she saw the uncertainty and fear in the villagers' faces. Two months had passed, and already they were realizing what life was to be like with Camray's new lord. Those who had someplace to go soon left, but most remained, fearing the uncertainty of leaving more than the hardships of staying.

Grimly, Rina thought about the last eight years of her life—the back-breaking work, savagely cold winters, and the grueling poverty. She had faced it all with an unbelievable strength that grew from the constant, bitter hatred that gnawed at her mind and heart.

So far she had kept all promises she'd made that dreadful night. She'd struggled to be strong and learned to fight for herself. Jake taught her everything a man would teach his son. Rina could use a pistol, sword, and knife expertly. She could ride and fight as well as any man, but Jenny made certain she was also primed in the arts of being a lady, never letting Katrina forget her position in life. Father Murray had seen to Rina's complete education, including math, history, literature, French and Italian. She also learned the rudiments of medicine and healing, never forgetting the pain of being unable to help her father as he lay bleeding to death in her arms.

Life in Tattershall had been hard for Katrina, as it was for most commoners, but no one ever heard her complain. Though her strength and independence were nurtured by anger, there was also an inborn love and gentleness within her that provided a delicate balance to her world. This love drove her as strongly as her hate, making her unselfish and kind to those she cared for. Whether she ruled Camray or not, she felt an overwhelming obligation to see to the people she had grown to love. In return, she had earned their devotion and loyalty, even though they knew her only as Rina, the Tidwells' niece.

Rina was brought out of her reverie as a burst of red and orange streaked across the pink horizon and, gloriously, the sun peeked over the mountains. Sighing, Rina watched as it brightened the sky with the announcement of morning. She grasped the chain around her neck and, touching the ring her father had given her, whispered, "Papa, I promise, Camray will be ours again."

Chapter 2

Blake Roberts leaned casually against the ship's rail, deep in thought. He savored the glass of fine brandy he held in his hand and watched as the sun began its slow descent toward the horizon, casting a golden haze over the water, turning the world into a gilded mirage. Blake knew he would never tire of the magnificence of a sunset at sea. At that moment the whole universe seemed to stand still, and a comforting peacefulness would seep into his being as the fiery sphere dropped from the sky, leaving him in semi-darkness. The waves gently lapped against the side of the hull, lulling and soothing, and the moon seemed to appear miraculously, lying low, cradled by the sea's dark arms. Stars glittered and blinked across the sky in the age-old patterns that had guided many men before him in their adventures.

This was one of the many ships that Lord Blake Roberts owned, and his ships were only one small part of the vast empire he had built in the twelve years since he had left Windsong.

Standing alone in the peaceful night, Blake remembered how proud he had been when his grandfather had turned over the running of their estates to him and his younger brother, Ryon. Blake was twenty-one at the time—young, cocky, and so damn naive. Eager to experience the glamour of society, he'd spent much of the first year at their town-house in London. It was there, at court, that he met Cath-erine Ramsey, a red-haired beauty with emerald-green eyes.

Blake winced as he remembered how quickly he'd been ensnared by her flirtatious charm. In his youthful foolish-ness, Blake believed he loved Catherine, was certain he couldn't continue to exist without her by his side as his wife. Blinded by her beauty, he could not see the kind of scheming tramp she truly was. He'd learned soon enough, though, when she spurned him for an elderly nobleman with twice his wealth. The shock and pain of his beloved's be-trayal had stunned him. Never again would he play the fool for a woman. The Blake Roberts who made that vow was a wiser and harder man.

Blake took another sip of brandy and forced his mind away from Catherine. He should be grateful to her, actu-ally—if it hadn't been for his need to escape the very thought of her, he'd never have turned to the sea, never have established the trading and shipping company that had brought him such wealth and satisfaction. He would have never known the peace of sunsets such as this one.

A soft, gentle breeze ruffled Blake's hair, and his eyes once again focused on the darkness about him. The ship's gentle rocking brought him back to the present, his mem-ories receding to their proper places in the past.

The following day he would be docking in London. It had been too long since he had been home to see his grand-father and brother. Now the old man lay ill, perhaps dying. The thought brought tears to Blake's eyes, and he found it difficult to imagine Windsong without his grandfather's presence.

Blake's mother had died after giving birth to his younger brother, Ryon, and their grief-stricken father died a year later. Their grandfather had raised the two boys as best he could, giving them the love and guidance they needed. Blake's heart ached as he thought of all the years he had been away. Why hadn't he spent more time at home, es-pecially during these last years, when his grandfather had become so weak? The knowledge that Ryon had remained at Windsong brought some comfort to Blake. He also knew the joy his grandfather must have felt when Ryon married a year ago. The young couple were now expecting their first child. Perhaps the babe was already born. Blake smiled as he thought of being an uncle. Certainly being a great-grandfather would delight Jason Roberts tremendously.

Taking one last look at the stars, Blake turned and went below deck to his cabin. Thinking of his family and Windsong made him realize how very much he had missed them. It certainly would be nice to be home once again and enjoy the peace that love could bring.

Chapter 3

The sun shone brightly down on the small group of workers. The unusual warm spell combined with the humidity gave them no relief from the heat. Rina straightened her aching back, resting one hand on her hip while her fingers massaged her sore muscles. She glanced around the never-ending field of wheat, the sweat rolling down her back and between her breasts, causing the coarse, cotton dress to cling to her skin and reveal her slender but unmistakably feminine figure. Her thick hair was pulled back in a long braid with a few unruly, wild strands curling around her damp face and neck.

The others began to leave the field to seek a short rest and a bite to eat, so Rina grabbed her bundle and crossed to a nearby oak tree. Its giant limbs spread out like a canopy, providing shade from the warm sun. As she thoughtfully nibbled a piece of bread, Rina did not notice the young man who came up beside her.

"You shouldn't be so serious all the time. It makes you frown. You're so much prettier when you smile, Kat." John grinned at Katrina as he plopped on the ground beside her.

"John! You startled me! You really shouldn't sneak up on people like that," Rina scolded, pretending to be mad. Despite her efforts, her frown quickly turned into a stunning smile that brightened her whole face becomingly, adding a mischievous sparkle to her large eyes.

"If you weren't so involved in what you were thinking, you would have heard me." John pulled Rina's hat down over her eyes playfully, then tugged gently on her long braid. Giggling, Rina pulled the hat off and started hitting him over the head with it in a barrage of painless blows.

"Okay! Okay! I give up, Kat. You win!" Groaning in defeat, the young man stretched out his long, lean frame, his broad shoulders resting against the trunk of the tree. John's strong, stocky build and tremendously powerful arms and shoulders caused most men to be wary and women to sigh in admiration, but he seemed quite unaware of both reactions. He casually raked a big hand through his unruly blond hair. A look of love and tenderness filled his dark brown eyes as he watched Rina. God, how beautiful she was. Even with sweat and dirt streaking her face and all that gorgeous hair pulled back into a confining braid, she was pretty.

They'd been inseparable since she'd moved in to the cottage next door eight years before. They'd fought and played like brother and sister, but somehow lately John found it disturbing that she was so damned lovely.

"Why the frown, John?" Katrina asked, unaware of the path his thoughts had taken.

"Damn it, Kat. You get prettier every day!" John muttered suddenly.

"You shouldn't call me Kat. It would be better if you called me Rina like everyone else does," she snapped, blushing under his probing gaze.

"I only call you Kat when no one is around . . . and you know that. So don't change the subject."

Much to John's amusement, Katrina glanced away, anger glimmering in her eyes as her color darkened even further. But, determined not to be undone by him, she forced herself to meet his look calmly. As he gazed into those deep pools of blue John knew that she had no idea what effect she had on men, and how dangerous her beauty could be.

"You know every unattached man in the village is madly in love with you. It's innocent enough, and I know they'd do nothing to harm you. It's the strangers that pass through that I fear. Watching out for you has become a full-time job lately." John paused a moment, then voiced his next thought. "You know, Kat, sometimes I wish that we hadn't grown up together."

Touched by his concern for her well-being, Rina reached over and tenderly caressed his cheek. "John, I don't understand. You're the brother I never had. Why would you want to change that?"

Hearing the hurt in her words, he sighed unhappily. John had watched Rina grow from a scrawny little girl into a strong, beautiful woman. He had seen the way men looked at Rina and heard the ribald comments, and he felt totally helpless to stop what he saw happening around him.

"If I hadn't grown to love you as my sister, we could marry and I wouldn't have to worry about you anymore. Most men would respect a married woman, and those that don't . . . well, I could take care of them easily enough. Rina, you can't trust men! Not when they want a woman. I'm afraid that one day I won't be around and someone will hurt you."

Just thinking about such things made John see red. He would kill anyone who even thought of harming one hair on her head! The fact that she was really Katrina Easton had never mattered to them. When she first came to the village she was so frail and alone. John had sensed her fear, and his heart reached out to the sad and lonely girl. From their friendship grew a strong binding trust. John shared Rina's secrets and knew of her promise to get Camray back and destroy the vile man who had usurped her birthright.

"Johnny," Katrina broke into his thoughts, "you're being quite silly. You know I can take care of myself. You, of all people, should know that!"

"Yeah," he agreed grudgingly, "I suppose you're right."

Rina was petite but very strong from years of hard work and many hours spent with Jake learning how to defend herself. With her quickness and agility, Kat was a formidable opponent.

Grinning, he teased, "I should be worried about the poor bloke who would be stupid enough to try anything!"

"Right," laughed Rina in agreement. "He would be in sad shape, so no more of this big-brother talk. Understood?"

Taking another bite of cheese, she shoved the rest in John's mouth and let out a shriek when he bit her finger. He grabbed her and started to tickle unmercifully, making her roll with laughter, begging him to stop. Her laughter died suddenly when Rina spotted a cloud of dust approaching them.

A black carriage drawn by a pair of matching black horses pulled up to the field. A shadow passed over Rina's face, leaving it solemn and unreadable. She watched closely as the two men sat smugly in the fancy barouche and looked over the field.

"It looks like His Highness is out to inspect his lands, making sure we peasants are doing our job right," John growled, his eyes following the men warily.

Lawrence and Randolph Langsford looked very much alike, and the similarity in their personalities was frightening. They were thin and not extremely tall, but their muscular strength was apparent beneath their finely tailored clothing. Fair skin made their raven hair look even blacker, their features more sharp and distinct. But it was their eyes that caused people to notice them, unreadable ebony spheres that seemed to see things others could not. Their thin, unappealing lips rarely smiled, and when they did, they seemed to lie, for the dark eyes revealed the truth. If it were not for the cold evil that seemed to emanate from them, they might have been considered handsome. But Katrina saw the devil himself in the carriage, and from what she knew of Randolph she did not think much better of the devil's son.

Lawrence treated Randolph like a son, but Rina knew he was really his nephew. When Lawrence was three years old, his mother, who had lain with countless men since her brief affair with William Easton's father, gave birth to a second bastard child, a girl. Lawrence hated his mother for the mark of shame he and his half-sister, Anna, were doomed to bear for life. He had tried to protect his delicate little sister from the sneers and hatred, lavishing all his affections on her, the only person he had ever loved. At fifteen Anna had gotten pregnant, the secret of the father's identity dying

Duplicate Copy

Location

Class Number,
including date,
copy number,
volume number

Name _____ Date _____

M-179

9 perple

with her as she gave birth to a son. Her death nearly destroyed Lawrence. In his grief, he transferred the overpowering love he had had for his sister to the baby, and took him as his own to raise.

Lawrence held up a hand to shade his eyes from the blinding sun. God, it was warm. He began to wonder why he had decided to leave the coolness inside of Camray to inspect his fields. The heavy coat of black velvet and its dashingly handsome matching waistcoat were extremely hot, and Lawrence regretted the choice he had so carefully made when dressing. He removed a delicate handkerchief and wiped the sweat from his brow as he glanced around at the scattered workers, noticing for the first time that they were not working.

"Why are these people lazing about?" Langsford snapped in irritation at his foreman, a look of sheer disgust crossing his features at the workers' shabby appearance.

"They are having their midday break to eat and rest, my lord," replied the man riding next to the carriage.

"They seem to be finished eating. Get them back to work, now! They are wasting precious daylight." Dabbing at the perspiration on his upper lip, Langsford grabbed his whip and viciously cracked it over the horses' rumps, steering them back toward Camray. Impatient to reach the cool interior of the house, he drove them still faster, anxious for something to quench his thirst.

The foreman watched as the Langsford carriage disappeared over the hill, then ordered the people back to work. Slowly, everyone got to their feet, grumbling that their time had been cut short. Rina and John exchanged angry looks and they, too, silently went back to the field. They worked until darkness shrouded them, then, exhausted, trudged back to their homes, seeking the small comfort they provided.

Rina was silent and moody as she walked with John down the dry, dusty road. As they wound through the narrow, cobbled street he left her to her thoughts, sensing the cause of her dark mood. When they reached Rina's cottage she turned and walked into the shack next to the small, whitewashed hut. The smell of hay and manure drifted toward her, bringing a smile to her face as she quickly crossed to

the stall. She was greeted with a whinny as a warm, soft
nose nuzzled her neck. Stroking the muzzle, Rina whispered
lovingly into his ear, causing the horse to paw the floor in
delight at seeing his mistress. He was a magnificent animal,
as black as coal. Grabbing a handful of straw, Rina gently
began to rub him down. John automatically picked up some
hay and oats to feed Blackstar, then started cleaning out the
stall.

"How I hate that bastard!" she suddenly declared.

John paused in his work to look at the fury glaring in
her eyes, the pain on her face.

"I don't know how much longer I can sit by and do
nothing. I want to kill him for what he did to me and my
parents, but what he does to these good people is also a
crime! He's slowly killing them, too."

Rina stopped her stroking as she felt the uncontrollable
anger creeping over her once more. Sensing her tension,
Blackstar hesitated in his munching and turned to nibble
tenderly on her ear.

"He sits in his mansion . . . my mansion . . . surrounded
by wealth, not giving a damn that he is starving and working
these people to death. Every year he takes more and more,
leaving them less to live on. John, some of them will not
make it through another winter. The children . . . there have
been so many births this last year. So many to care for.
They won't survive without proper food, warmer clothing,
and more fuel for heat. Too many died of sickness last winter
. . . so unnecessarily!"

Rina's eyes clouded as she remembered each death. She
had fought for their lives with all the knowledge she possessed, but it was not enough. Over the years she had lost
too many friends to the diseases that winter's cold brings.
It was a losing battle and that terrified her.

"We can't hunt for our food in the forests on Camray's
land, since it takes game from Langsford's table. We are
alloted pitiful amounts of wood, to make sure he doesn't
get cold in that huge mansion. He wastes enough food in
one meal to feed this whole village. What he spends on one
suit of clothing would provide warm clothes for everyone.
Did you know that most of these women have little more

than a shawl to ward off the cold? And the children...
some don't even have shoes! Damn! Damn his murdering
soul to hell!"

Rina struggled to control her overwhelming rage. John
pulled her to him, holding her trembling body, trying to
calm her. Slowly, the fires inside her began to subside in
the security and comfort of John's arms. When she had
regained control of her emotions, Rina began to curry Blackstar's shining coat.

"John, we must find a way to feed everyone. I can't bear
to watch them suffer and die anymore. Not while those rich,
hypocritical bastards sit on their fat behinds and their fine
ladies do needlepoint, dripping in jewels worth a small
fortune."

"I know how you feel, Kat. But what can we do? You
can't be responsible for everyone in the whole village, not
now anyway. When you take Camray back, then you can
help these people. No one expects you to bear all their
problems." John knew the compassion and love that Rina
had for the people in Tattershall, but what could a girl of
nineteen years do? He also knew that as an Easton she felt
it her duty to care for them and provide for them as best
she could. Seeing that his words were falling on deaf ears,
he tried again.

"Langsford is cruel and ungiving, but we can't do anything to stop him. We can't just take what we need or we'd
be hung for stealing. There is nothing we can do, Kat."

"That's it!" she cried. "That's it, John! Perhaps we should
start taking what we need to survive! Like Robin Hood!"
Rina paused a moment, her eyes gleaming with excitement,
biting her lip as she contemplated what she had just said.

John knew from the look in her eyes that she was serious.
"Don't be crazy, Kat," he protested. "They would hang us
for sure."

"Not if they didn't know who we were. We could wear
hoods, concealing our faces, just like Langsford did when
he killed my parents. We could get a few more men from
the village, ones we could fully trust, to form a band of
highwaymen. All we steal can be given to families in need.

Wealthy people are always on the roads at night and they always have jewels and gold. They'd never expect it!"

"And what would you suggest we ride? You're the only one with a fast horse. We'd need good weapons and saddles. Just how do you figure we'd get them?" John questioned smugly.

Rina gave it some thought before she answered. "I have my sapphire-and-diamond jewelry. I could sell them for the funds we need to buy horses and weapons."

"No!" John yelled. "That's all you have left from your mother and father, Kat. You can't sell them. They mean so much to you and you could never replace them."

"I'm certain that my parents would understand my reasons for selling them. They're only jewels, John. I'll always have my memories, with or without them. I would have sold them long ago if Jake and Jenny hadn't insisted I keep them. But I will not take no for an answer this time. Don't you see, John? I have to try! I can no longer sit back and do nothing while innocent people die because of one man's insatiable greed. This is one way we can fight back. Will you help me?" Rina pleaded, looking desperately into John's eyes.

He shook his head slowly. When she looked at him like that, he could deny her nothing. "You know I will. Actually, it would be nice to see Langsford through the sight of my pistol, shaking in his boots." At that thought they both laughed until their sides ached. Finally, their laughter subsided and John got up. "Well . . . I'd better go."

They said their good-byes and left plan-making for another day.

Sunday was glorious, a bit warmer than usual, especially in the rough woolen dress Rina wore. Her Sunday best had to be worn winter and summer, and the light woolen garment was unbearably warm and scratchy during the summer months, but too light in the bitter-cold winter. Father Murray's sermon seemed terribly long, and the small, cramped parish was stifling. She found it difficult to concentrate on what he was saying as his voice droned on. Her thoughts wandered to her secret swimming hole and the cool, clear water she longed to be in. Finally, Father Murray concluded the sermon, realizing the congregation was getting restless. Outside the small church, he stopped to speak with Rina.

"Rina, my child. How are you today?" Father Murray's smile was warm as he enveloped her in a loving hug.

"Hot!" laughed Rina, returning his hug affectionately.

"Yes, it is a bit warmer than usual, but a truly lovely day. Have you heard any more about Lord Roberts? Has his health improved any?"

"I'm afraid I haven't heard anything recently, but I am planning to ride over to Windsong this afternoon to see him." Sadness clouded Rina's eyes as she whispered, "Father, I'm so afraid that he's going to die."

"We all must die sometime, Rina. It is God's will. I know Lord Roberts was extremely fond of you. You helped him many times by tending his horses." Seeing her concern, he guided Rina to the church garden, hoping to comfort her and ease her fears. Rina was special to him, and it distressed him terribly that someone so young bore so many responsibilities. She should be free to think of marriage and children.

As they walked through the small, perfect garden, Rina spoke her thoughts out loud. "He is a good and fair man. He treats everyone with kindness, no matter whose blood runs in their veins. Why do the good men have to die, while evil men are allowed to live? It's not right!" Rina's fist began clenching and unclenching as the fire began to build inside her once more.

Father Murray was taken back as he saw the sheer hatred glowing in her dark eyes. "Rina, I worry about the bitter feelings you carry in your heart. You mustn't be so angry."

"Father, I am sorry, but you, of all people, should know that I have good reason to hate that man who sits at Camray."

"There is no good reason to hate. You must learn to forget that night and forgive him for his deeds. He will pay for his sins. It is not for you to judge," Father Murray gently admonished Rina but knew his words had no effect.

"Forget?" she asked. "The nightmares don't let me forget. Eight years have passed and still I remember every detail of that night. I remember the gory, mangled bodies of innocent men, the pain and surprise forever etched on their faces in death. My own father's and mother's blood soaking my white dress until I could feel its warm stickiness, so dark against the pure whiteness. . . ." Rina paused as if seeing it all before her once again.

"I'll never forget! Forgive? Can I forgive him for the private hell we all live in? Can I forgive him for murdering my parents before my very eyes? Can I forgive him his greed? Last winter, he hanged Paul Lanbeth for poaching a rabbit on his private game reserve. One small, insignificant rabbit to help feed his hungry children. Can I forgive him for that? Can I forgive him for leaving a woman widowed, with five children to feed? Can I forgive him for all the children who die each year because his greed leaves us less and less to live on? Father, how many must I watch die because of this one man? No . . . I will not forget and I will not forgive!"

The anguish on Rina's face tore at Father Murray's heart. She was so good and kind, always giving and helping unselfishly. It saddened him to know that as long as Langsford lived, this grief would possess Rina, giving her no peace from the bitterness she nurtured within. With tears in his eyes, he cupped her face in strong hands, kissing her on both cheeks.

"I love you, my child. I have had the privilege of watching you grow into the woman you are today. I know you carry much love and goodness inside of you for all, except this one man. I will pray that soon you will be relieved of this dreadful burden you carry in your soul."

"Thank you, Father. I am sorry if I've distressed you. You've given me so much since I came here to live. Perhaps someday I'll be deserving of your love." Giving him a kiss on his weathered, aging cheek, she left the secluded garden and started down the road to her house.

As she thought of the ride to Windsong, her spirits lifted. Blackstar would be as anxious as she for the run. She passed through her gate and paused to pluck a rose from a nearby bush before entering the three-room cottage. The main room was the kitchen, with its large stone fireplace along one wall and the rough wooden table in the center. A worn, rough cupboard and the door to Jake and Jenny's room took up another wall. A ladder leading to Rina's attic bedroom, several old chairs, and a couple of sunny windows with shutters completed their cozy home. The smell of yeast drifted to Rina as she entered to see Jenny elbow deep in bread dough. Smiling, she crossed to the older woman, giving her a warm hug, tucking the red rosebud into her graying hair.

" 'Ello, luv. Ye shouldna' be wastin' those pretty flowers on an old woman like me. If yer still wantin' t' ride o'er 'n see Lord Roberts, ye'd best be gettin' so as t' be 'ome fer our Sunday meal." Jenny's wide grin split her wrinkled face, showing a missing tooth or two.

"Yes, I'll hurry. Make sure that scoundrel husband of yours doesn't eat all that bread before I get back."

"I 'eard Lord Roberts' oldest grandson, Blake, is cummin' 'ome. I also 'eard 'e's a devilishly good-lookin' man," cackled Jenny, nudging Rina in the side, with a broad wink. "Yer not gettin' any younger, girl. Ye'd best be thinkin' of gettin' yerself a man an' marryin' or yer goin' t' end up an old maid."

Rina raised a delicate eyebrow in amusement, her voice quite serious as she jested with Jenny. "Now, what would a nobleman like Blake Roberts want with a mere commoner like me?"

"Commoner! Lady Katrina Easton! Yer a lady o' fine breedin! An' dun't ye be fergettin' it! Yer every bit as good as 'e is," scolded the older woman, ruffled at the thought of her Rina not being good enough for any man.

"But he wouldn't know that, would he, Jenny? I would love to stay and argue with you, but I have to go or I'll be late getting back. So no more talk of marriage." Ending the conversation, Rina dashed up the ladder to change. Gladly, she shucked the hot brown dress and pulled on a pair of worn breeches, a soft cotton shirt, and scuffed, black boots. She pulled the pins from her hair, unwinding the long, golden braid from its neat coil, leaving it to hang loose down her back. Rina climbed down and started for the door; hearing Jenny's gasp of annoyance, she stopped.

"Lordy, ye aren't goin' t' visit Sir Roberts lookin' like

tha' are ye? I've told ye it isn't decent for a woman t' wear men's breeches. Wha' am I t' do with ye?" clucked Jenny, throwing her hands up in dismay.

"Jenny, he has seen me in breeches before. Besides, it's so much easier to ride in breeches. Would you have me hiking my dress up around my waist to sit astride Blackstar?" Rina's face was sober and innocent, only the sparkle of mischief in her eyes giving her away. Seeing the shocked look on Jenny's face, Rina could not stop the giggle that escaped.

"A lady does no' ride astride!" Indignant, Jenny started pounding the mound of dough in front of her. "But I s'ppose ye are old enough t' wear wha' ye wan'. I declare, no man will want ye as wild and unruly as ye are! Lord knows, I did me best t' raise ye right!"

Rina laughed and pecked Jenny on the cheek once more, wiping the flour off her nose. "Stop your fretting. You know I love you. Besides, I am only being practical. Dresses are so confining." Seeing Jenny's smile, she disappeared through the door, practically running to the shed where Blackstar was waiting.

He had heard Rina's voice and excitedly called to her, pawing the ground impatiently. He always seemed to know when Rina was going to ride him, and he trembled from anticipation. Grabbing the bridle, she quickly climbed onto his broad, muscular back and guided him from the shack and onto the cobbled road. Blackstar was anxious to stretch his muscles and skittishly pranced through town with Rina holding him back. When they reached the edge of the village, Rina gave the animal his freedom, and he bolted into a run. Down the road to Windsong they raced, rider and horse as one. The magnificent black stallion stretched his powerful legs, carrying them as fast as the wind, streaking past the countryside in a blur. It was at times like these, with the wind blowing in her face and Blackstar thundering down the road, that Katrina was truly happy. All the problems that haunted her vanished. No one existed but Rina and Blackstar. She allowed him to run until he tired, then slowed his pace to a gallop. Rina's hair had come loose from its braid and hung in a tangled disarray around her shoulders. Her cheeks were rosy and her blue eyes sparkled feverishly from the tantalizing ride.

As she approached Windsong, she ran her fingers through her hair, attempting to straighten the unruly mane, but found it hopeless and gave up. She rode on to the stables, where she was greeted fondly by Jenkins, the old stable master. Walking around to the servants' entrance, she entered the kitchen. She was warmly greeted and sat to chat while enjoying a cool glass of lemonade. After a servant went upstairs to announce Rina's presence, she was taken to Lord Roberts' chamber. Rina knocked quietly and entered.

"Come in, come in, Rina my girl. I'm so glad you took the time to come and see a dying old man." Feebly, Lord Roberts held up a hand as Rina crossed and clasp it with her own. It felt very cold.

"You mustn't talk that way, Lord Roberts. You will be well soon." Though she spoke confidently, her heart ached as she looked at the man lying in his sick bed. He was so pale and gaunt, and his skin had a grayish pallor.

"I'm afraid not, Rina. My time has come. But you needn't grieve. I've had a full life with many blessings. Now ... no more talk of death. I can see you have been riding. I suppose you rode that black beast over here. You look absolutely radiant." Lord Roberts smiled, his weakened gaze taking in every detail of her appearance. "You do love that horse, don't you?"

"Yes, he is one of my most prized possessions. I can never thank you enough for your gift."

"It is I who owe you thanks, my dear. You save his mother and him, for I most certainly would have lost them both had it not been for you. You were here for days, sleeping in the barn with her, tending to her hours on end." He sighed at the memory. "I still remember the first time my stable master sent for you. He was quite certain you could help when everyone else had failed. That was four years ago, wasn't it? You were just fifteen years old and quite scrawny. I saw you work magic with the beasts, and since then you have always come when we needed you, helping many of my prized horses. Blackstar was merely a token of my sincere appreciation and gratitude for your coming into my life. I know now that you two belong together. It was meant for you to have him, Rina."

Rina blushed, his sincere praise touching her heart. "You have been more than generous, Lord Roberts. I can never repay you for all the baskets of food and clothing you've sent to me over the years."

Seeing the surprised look cross over his features, Rina laughed, and the sound was warm and gentle to his ears. "Just because your servant always left them anonymously on my doorstep does not mean I did not know who sent them. I had always assumed you were the culprit, and my suspicions were confirmed when I saw your manservant sneaking away one night after depositing his bundle of gifts."

"So you knew it was me, did you? Well . . . I admit to my plot, but you have deceived me as well."

Seeing her face become grave and concerned, he quickly added, his voice admiring, rather than scolding, "You gave away most of the things I sent, things I had meant for you."

"There were people who needed them more than I," whispered Rina, afraid she had offended him.

"No need to fret. I understand . . . perhaps more than you think. You have a heart of gold, your kindness and compassion are quite refreshing to this old man. You're a good woman Rina, and always remember, if ever you need help, do not hesitate to come to this house. You will not be denied, no matter what your request. You will always have a home to come to. Do not forget."

Rina was overwhelmed, her eyes reflecting gratitude and love. Her voice shook slightly. "I don't know what to say. It's comforting to know I have such a friend by my side and forever in my heart. After my parents died, I thought I was alone in the world, and slowly, I've found myself surrounded by a new family. One as devoted and caring as the one I lost. I am grateful to you, my lord."

Tears glistened in the old man's eyes as they sat in silence, their hands clasped. Finally, sleep overtook the frail man, and gently Katrina kissed his cheek, whispering good-bye as she left. As she quietly closed the door, she knew they would never see each other again in this world, but his memory would be with her forever.

Chapter 4

Blake stopped on the crest of the hill and gazed over the surrounding countryside. In the distance lay Windsong, the stately mansion spread out in grand splendor, its many windows reflecting the bright sunshine. A warm happiness spread through him, the love for his lands shining in his golden eyes. He could smell the salt air, hear the sound of waves breaking against the rocky shoreline, as he envisioned the violent waters swirling around the gray stones, the mist spraying the air. It was a beautiful place, enchanting and mysterious. At night the fog would roll in like a silent giant to shroud the coast in its frosty cloak and the winds off the North Sea would sing the sad and lonely songs that gave Windsong her name. The forests in the distance provided a dark green background for the estate, making nature's artwork complete.

Each and every time Blake Roberts came home after a long absence he wondered at the perfection and beauty of his home. How he missed this place! He had long ago shucked his jacket and waistcoat, leaving his snowy white shirt open to his waist. Sitting atop his gray-dappled Arabian mare, he spotted a cloud of dust in the distance. Blake made no move, waiting as the rider approached from Windsong.

As Rina and Blackstar nearly reached the top of the hill, she spotted the horse and rider and slowed her breakneck pace. Blake continued to watch intently as the black horse drew nearer, surprise washing over him when he found that the rider was a woman. Rina's cheeks were flushed with a rosy hue, framed by the tangled golden hair whipping about her shoulders. Her blue eyes sparkled mischievously as she boldly returned his stare, her head coming up proudly. His eyes rudely raked over her, taking in every detail as she reined her mount to a slow walk.

Rina's own breath was taken away as she found herself staring into golden eyes that seemed to take fire as they roguishly roved over her body. He was certainly the most handsome man Rina had ever seen, with strong, rugged features and soft, curly brown hair. As a slow, devilish smile crossed his face, boyish dimples appeared. Heavy eyebrows, a strong aristocratic nose, and a neatly trimmed mustache enhanced his strikingly good looks. He had powerful, wide shoulders that tapered to a slender waist and strong legs, the muscles straining against the fabric of his breeches.

Blake felt a familiar warmth spreading in his loins as he watched the golden beauty ride by. His smile widened, revealing his even white teeth as his head moved in a slight nod of greeting. Rina's answering smile lit up her lovely face. Blake nudged his mount forward, intending to learn her name, but Rina saw the naked desire flicker in his eyes and sent Blackstar leaping ahead into a run. Blake considered going after her but decided against it. He would make sure they met again.

There was something about her, an untamed wildness that exhilarated Blake. The way she carelessly returned his stare, proud and unafraid, with a touch of arrogance. With his thoughts on the mysterious golden girl, he continued on to Windsong.

Anticipation flooded through Blake as he rode down the familiar oak-lined lane to the estate. The trees' giant arms spread their full, green foliage protectively over him, shielding him from the bright sun. The lush green lawns with their immaculately groomed flowerbeds delighted his senses as he rode up to the house. The three-story brick mansion, with wrought-iron balconies and large, sunny windows seemed to greet him as he gracefully jumped off his horse and ran up the stone steps two at a time. The front door flew open, and a man, six years younger than Blake, warmly grabbed his hand.

"Blake! It's about time you showed up!" Unable to contain his excitement any longer, Ryon grabbed his brother in a bear hug. "God, I've missed you."

Laughing, the two men entered the house, and Blake happily slapped the younger man on the back. "Ryon, it's good to be home."

They walked into the sitting room off the main hallway, and a woman crossed the room to greet them. She was small and pretty, with a slender figure and fine delicate features. Her beautiful auburn hair was neatly arranged around her oval face and cascaded in soft curls to her shoulders. Brown eyes that sparkled with happiness were set off by smooth ivory skin. Ryon proudly took her hand and introduced her to Blake.

"My dearest brother, I would like you to meet my wife, Rebecca."

"I am happy to meet you at last. You are certainly as beautiful as my brother boasted in his letters." Blake kissed her soft hand; then, noticing her slim figure, he added, "Am I to assume I am now an uncle as well as a brother-in-law?"

Rebecca blushed and smiled happily as she pointed to a cradle by the settee. "She was born two weeks ago."

Rebecca lifted the blanket so Blake could take a peek at the sleeping babe. Its tiny hand seemed so small as he took it in his own, caressing it softly. A strange feeling of awe overwhelmed him as the infant's eyes opened briefly, then closed in slumber once again.

"Blake, we named her Laura Ann."

Grinning, Blake exclaimed, "Laura? You named her after Mother! She would be so proud, Ryon. Thank you."

Suddenly growing solemn, Blake turned to Ryon. "How is he? Can I see him?"

Blake studied his brother carefully as Ryon sat down beside his wife. Ryon resembled Blake in build and height, but his hair was darker and his eyes were brown. There was still a youthful innocence in his features that had disappeared from Blake's own face long ago, but Blake could see the pain in Ryon's eyes and knew with a surge of guilt that it must have been difficult for him since their grandfather had become ill.

"Grandfather is dying. The doctor says he hasn't long to live, but what time he does have left will be happy and content, now that you are home." Ryon's voice broke and Blake turned to stare silently out the window. After taking a few moments to compose himself, Ryon whispered hoarsely, "He's asleep now, but you can see him when he awakens."

Blake turned his sad, golden gaze to his brother. "Ryon, I'm so sorry you two have had to bear this alone. I should have been here; instead I've been running about making business my number one concern. Now it's too late and I have so little time to be with him."

"No, Blake, you shouldn't feel that way. You've always handled everything. You carry all the responsibilities of this family on your shoulders so that we can live here in comfort. I know how much you love Grandfather, how hard you worked to make him proud of you. You have always protected and cared for me, and for the first time in our lives, I have been able to carry some responsibility, and hopefully save you some pain. You could have done nothing more than has already been done—you couldn't protect him from death. He's old, Blake, and ready to die. He is happy and well cared for, and now his older grandson can be with him for his last days."

As they grasped each other in an unusual display of tenderness, the love between the two brothers seemed to fill the room. A tear slipped down Rebecca's soft cheek as she witnessed their affection. She knew then that she liked her brother-in-law very much.

Wanting to bathe before seeing his grandfather, Blake went up to his room. Elegantly furnished in dark and light blue, his bedroom was warm and pleasing to the eye. A huge four-poster bed with dark blue coverlet and hangings, an elaborate closet, and a dresser with matching nightstands were arranged neatly about the room. A large stone fireplace with huge ceiling-to-floor windows on either side covered with heavy velvet occupied one entire wall. When the drapes were pulled aside, sun poured into the room and the view was breathtakingly beautiful. A pair of fine, winged leather chairs and ottomans sat comfortably in front of the hearth, and a large writing desk occupied one corner.

Blake pulled off his damp shirt, then pulled off his boots. As he crossed through to the adjoining room, he rid himself of his dusty breeches. The air was steamy from the tub of hot water waiting for him, and he smiled, pleased at his manservant's preparations. He had had the private bathing chambers added several years before, modeled after those he had seen in Constantinople, and found them to be the best improvement he'd made at Windsong. A huge marble tub was built into the floor with a rim wide enough to sit on, and piped-in hot and cold water made it easier to bathe often.

Sliding into the bath, Blake felt the warmth soak into his tired body, and a sigh of contentment came from his lips. He had ridden hard from London to get here early, but the exercise had felt good after six weeks on ship.

He relaxed, his eyes closing, allowing the heat to massage his sore muscles, bringing beads of perspiration to his forehead. His thoughts drifted from his grandfather, to his brother and sister-in-law and niece. Suddenly, a pair of seductive blue eyes floated into his mind, filling his head with visions of the girl on the black stallion. He remembered how her moist cotton shirt clung tightly, enhancing her enticing curves to perfection, and the way her soft breasts rose and fell as she rode by with her breeches molded to her slim hips and buttocks. He saw her sensuous full lips, the color of roses, soft and ready to be kissed. Desire spread through him like fire. If she could do that to him in his thoughts, imagine what she could do in the flesh! Smiling at the thought, he grabbed a sponge and began to soap his body vigorously, thinking of the delight such a woman could provide. He rinsed off and stepped from the tub to rub himself dry, then wrapped the towel about his waist and went back into the other room. His trunks had arrived and been brought up and unpacked. A fresh suit of clothing in dark gray silk with a crisp white shirt had been meticulously laid upon the bed. As Blake finished dressing, a knock sounded on the door and a small, thin man entered.

"It's good to have you home, sir," stated the servant, his usually grim face giving way to one of his rare smiles.

"How are you, Jacob?" Blake reached out a hand to take the one extended to him. Jacob had been with the family for Blake's entire life, and from the looks of his withered face, perhaps several more lifetimes.

"Fine, sir. Your grandfather is awake and quite anxious to see you."

Pulling on his jacket, Blake nodded and followed the old man out the door into the long hall. When they reached Lord Roberts' private chamber, Jacob knocked, then opened the door for Blake. The room was gloomy, the smell of illness thick in the stale air. His grandfather was sitting up in bed, his face pinched and drawn. His eyes were sunk back into his head, glazed with fever. His lips were thin and bloodless, his skin was a deathly shade that alarmed Blake. This man was so different from the man Blake had always known. Lord Roberts had always been healthy and strong, with only a touch of gray sprinkling his dark head, and eyes of gold that sparkled with intensity and life.

Suddenly aware of his grandson's presence, Lord Roberts' face lit up with joy as he held out his frail, shaking hands to embrace him. Blake felt like a boy again as he pulled his grandfather into his strong embrace.

"Blake! Oh, my boy! I'm so happy you have come home. Now I can die with my family all here."

Blake pulled a chair near the bed and grasped the older man's hand. "Grandpa, you shouldn't talk like that."

"And why not? I am dying and no one can stop that. It's best to face that now. I've never been one to avoid the truth and neither should you. Now sit awhile and let an old man rattle on a bit."

Pausing a moment, as if to collect his thoughts, Lord Roberts patted the hand holding his. "I've loved you two boys with all my heart. Blake, you have made me very proud. You have done well. You've taken care of us the best way you knew how, and I know you'll continue to do so in the future. Ryon has made me a happy and proud great-grandfather, just as I hoped he would. Perhaps someday you will also find someone to make you happy as Ryon is with Rebecca. I only wish I could live long enough to see it."

Lord Roberts gripped Blake's hand tightly, tears of joy coursing unheeded down his wrinkled face. "It will take an exceptional woman to suit you, son, and only one comes to mind. I pray to God you will not be blind when you find her. You are stubborn and have an evil temper that would try a saint. Now, I realize that you've had bad experiences in the past, but just heed an old man's advice. All women are not the same! Your mother and grandmother were wonderful ladies."

"Yes, they were. If you have someone special in mind, Grandpa, you'd best let me know who she is," Blake answered wryly, not really caring for the topic of conversation his grandfather had chosen.

"No! If you don't find her on your own, you certainly won't deserve her! You're on you own, Blake. If you're obstinate and willful, you will end up living your life alone and empty. You will never know the pleasure of love and the true happiness you would find in sharing your life with someone special. You will never know the joy of having a son, and then, God willing, a grandson as I have. The only thing I can tell you is that the woman for you will not bend to your will, and will allow no man to rule her. Do not try, or you will lose her. Respect her and, most of all, treat her as your equal, and she will love you to the end of time, giving you happiness no man has ever dreamed of."

Blake listened to his words but could not agree with them. Love was not something he gave easily, especially to women. All this talk of respect and equality seemed strange and almost laughable to him.

"Ah, I see from the look on your face you think that perhaps I am getting senile. Well, maybe someday my words will make sense to you, and it will not be too late for you. . . . I hear the dinner bell, so you had better go. Maggie runs a tight ship, my boy, and will wait dinner on no one, even you. Will you return and read to me before you retire?"

"I will be here." As he stood and crossed to the door Blake paused and turned back around to look at his grandfather once more. "I love you very much." The words came out in a hoarse whisper as his throat tightened and his eyes blurred from the dull ache in his heart. How could he bear to lose this old man who meant the world to him?

"I love you, too, Blake. You must remember that I am going to a much better place than this. I will be with your mother and father, and most of all, the one I loved more than life itself, your grandmother, my wife. I have been too long without her dear company, and I want to be with her again. I hope you can understand that, son. You are young and have your whole life ahead of you. Blake, dear boy, I am ready to die. My only sadness is that I must leave you and Ryon."

"I shall miss you terribly."

"Go now, we will have time to talk later."

The days rolled by languidly, Blake spending most of his time with his grandfather. Lord Roberts seemed to improve, and his heart was filled with the joy of Blake's homecoming. On the fourth day after his return, while enjoying a ride at sundown, Blake spotted the gypsy camp. As he rode Hera nearer he was cheerfully greeted by the small band of wanderers who invited him to share the warmth of their fire and gaiety of their music. For the last fifteen years they had camped on the Robertses' land as they passed through, traveling north with their stock. Blake was more than happy to accept.

As the sun set, he sat with the gypsies watching the orange and red flames of the campfire dance and leap into the air, hungrily consuming the dry, brittle wood. It cracked and popped, spewing hot embers onto the bare ground, casting its warm glow on the people surrounding it. Though the day had been warm, night brought with it a cool crispness that made the fire welcome.

The strong wine began to work its heady magic on Blake, and the bitterness of the cheap brew began to fade as he drained each cup, losing himself in the gay music and dance. A pretty young gypsy girl swayed seductively to the beat, her body twisting and turning, holding Blake's bold gaze. Absorbed by her dancing he did not even notice the approaching black horse, much less its rider.

Rina slid off Blackstar and greeted her friends joyfully. She was dressed, like the gypsy women, in a full skirt and peasant top, with her dainty feet bare and her hair carefully tucked into a colorful scarf. Proudly, she showed off her dress, a fine gift the camp had given her when they made her an honorary daughter. An older man, the king of their clan, grabbed Rina in a powerful bear hug. Laughing, he swung her high into the air as if she were a small child, delighted she had come to their gathering.

Sitting her back down on the ground, Jaco smiled fondly at her. It had been three years since Rina had first come to the camp of the roving gypsies. A fever had spread among them, and no one would help. Jaco stared down into Rina's laughing, gentle eyes and remembered. No one had come except for this amazing little girl. Her knowledge and dedication had surprised the older man and his people. Rina stayed for seven weeks, caring for the sick, living in the back of a wagon, unable to return to her village for fear of spreading what ailed them. Her work was exhausting, yet she'd never seemed to tire. A few had died and Rina faithfully buried them, her own words their only epitaph. Then, miraculously, the fever had come to an end, thanks to the Lord and this good woman. They owed her their very lives, and yet she asked for nothing in return. Jaco was proud to consider her one of their family.

"Rina, I am so glad you have come. Now we can celebrate!" Grabbing her small face in his large hands, he kissed her soundly on both cheeks, then pulled her into another mighty hug that left her breathless. The gaiety and joy surrounding her lightened her spirits and her laughter joined with theirs. As she sat sipping the wine, the problems clouding her mind began to disappear with the wisps of smoke rising from the fire.

Slowly, the music began weaving its spell, its beat coursing through Rina, causing her pulse to quicken. Watching

the dancers twirl around the fire, she began to feel a pair
of eyes on her. Looking up, Rina's heart skipped a beat,
her breath caught in her throat. Unprepared for her physical
response to the stranger she'd met on the hilltop, Rina hesitated in confusion, the dark, red drink she had consumed
garbling her thoughts further.

Golden eyes locked with deep blue ones. Blake saw her
bewilderment at his presence and was unable to comprehend
completely his own reaction to seeing her again. There was
an undeniable physical attraction to the woman, but deep
inside he felt there was something more. She was different
. . . she was special. How he knew this was a mystery. He
felt like a drowning man drawn deeper and deeper into a
dark pool, unable to save himself from whatever lay ahead.

Rina continued to sit, silent and still, hypnotized by the
blazing gold eyes that contained more heat than the fire that
was reflected in them. They consumed her, boldly and intimately, leaving her breathless and strangely excited. A
strong sensation she had never felt before stirred deep within
her, warming her blood. The wine, excitement, joy, and
desire all worked on Rina's normal defenses, weakening
them dangerously, making her feel wickedly wanton.

"Hey, little girl! Will you honor us by dancing for me!
It has been too long since I last saw you dance." Jaco's
hearty laughter filled the air as he pulled Rina from her
place on the ground. The others shouted their encouragement. The violins began their rhythmic wail, filling Rina's
head with music as she began to dance the romantic, passionate steps so familiar to the gypsies. She slowly swayed
to the music, the beat taking over her body, willing it to do
its biding.

Blake's hungry eyes followed her every move as she
sensuously twisted to the sound. Rina was aware of his eyes
on her body, and to her own surprise, she was pleased. Her
skirts swirled up daringly around her thighs, showing off
long, slender legs and delicate, trim ankles. Her blouse slid
off one shoulder, baring her creamy, white skin to Blake's
ardent gaze. Rina's scarf slipped off, her hair tumbling down
in a cascade of honey and gold, streaked with strands of
copper that glistened in the firelight, giving the curls a life

of their own. Rina found herself dancing for the stranger, seeing only him among the faces. No one else existed but the man with the fire in his eyes. Faster and faster she danced until the music finally reached a frenzied climax and ended.

Everyone stood mesmerized for a moment, entranced by the silence around them, then broke into applause and laughter as they showed their appreciation for her talent. One of the younger men who had also been bewitched by Rina's seductive moves reached out and pulled her into his arms. Before he was able to kiss her, he saw the flicker of steel and then felt the cold blade against his throat. The passion in his eyes fled.

Rina twisted from his grasp and spoke to him softly. "If you try that again, I'll slit your throat from ear to ear."

Cautiously, she removed the knife and tucked it back into its hiding place, then walked away. Shrugging his shoulders at her fickleness, the would-be seducer soon forgot Rina, replacing her with a willing young woman who seemed eager to please him.

Across the way, Jaco shook his head, knowing the young man should have had better sense than to take on the high-spirited Rina. She had grown into a very beautiful woman and certainly would not be so easy to tame. Jaco envied the man she allowed into her bed and supple arms.

Blake had also been watching Rina's encounter with the amorous gypsy. A smile crossed his face as he tried to work his way toward her. He found himself extremely attracted to this slip of a girl who could handle a knife so well. But just as he reached her side, Rina was swept away by the jubilant dancers and Blake found himself surrounded by the gypsy women, who were anxious to get his attention and keep him from seeking out his golden girl.

The evening flew by as the wine flowed generously and the gaiety filled the night. Blake sighted Rina as she said her good-nights to Jaco and the others. A bit light-headed from the wine, she started for Blackstar, anxious for home and sleep. It had been a long day, and she was weary. She would sleep well tonight, undisturbed by the haunting nightmares. Weaving slightly, Rina steadied herself against Blackstar, unaware of the man approaching her.

Blake silently reached out and slipped an arm around
Rina, carefully grabbing her wrists before she had time to
pull out her knife. He pulled her into his strong arms as
Rina gasped. Before she could speak, Blake flashed a
charming smile, disarming her by whispering in her ear, "I
don't believe we've been properly introduced."

A chill passed through Rina as she felt his warm breath
on her neck, the pleasant smell of him filling her senses.
Her mind was fuzzy from too much drink. His mere presence
excited her, clouded her reason. His voice was soft and
caressing as his lips brushed against her neck, leaving a
trail of fire in their wake. "I am Blake Roberts."

Rina's mind became a mass of jumbled thoughts as her
heart raced wildly in her chest. Yet, to her own amazement,
she calmly said, "I am Rina."

"Rina," he said softly, "you are so very beautiful. Do
you know that you have driven me wild since I saw you
four days ago. You have haunted my mind, totally bewitched
me. Are you a witch or a woman?"

Without waiting for an answer, Blake brought his lips to
hers in a passionate, demanding kiss. Desperately, she tried
to fight the feelings that were spreading slowly through her
body. Her heart beat wildly as she began to tremble from
the battle going on between her body and her mind. Blake
released her wrists, and without understanding why, she
wrapped them around his neck, her lips clinging tenderly
to his.

Blake drank deeply of Rina's yielding, red lips, feeling
her form mold itself to his, her silky curves soft against his
hard muscles. He felt the slight trembling of her body and
saw the uncertainty and fear in her eyes. In that one moment,
she looked so frail and alone, so unlike the spirited, knife-
wielding vixen he had seen earlier.

"I have to go," whispered Rina, unsure of what she truly
wanted.

Blake, on the other hand, knew what he wanted, and it
was not to let her go. He wanted this woman with a ferocity
and passion he had never felt before. Yet common sense
prevailed; he knew he could not take her here.

"You should not be out riding alone, little one," he answered, "I will take you home."

Gently, he rubbed a finger down her lovely cheek. A thrill ran over her. He mounted Hera and pulled Rina in front of him. Their bodies burned like fire where they touched. He grabbed Blackstar's reins and they started for the village.

Sounds of the night drifted to their ears as the horses lazily clomped down the road to Tattershall. Rina tried to think clearly, but the wine still dulled her thoughts while her body reacted to the closeness of Blake Roberts. Unwillingly, she found herself relaxing against his wide chest, his strong arms giving her the unusual feeling of safety as they wrapped tightly about her waist. Rina was surprised to realize how nice it felt to be with him, then immediately chided herself for being so trusting of a total stranger. She should not have allowed any of this to happen, and she wondered nervously what he would do when they reached Tattershall.

Her eyes widened in apprehension and she furtively glanced at Blake, thinking to herself, "Surely, he would not be so bold!" All too soon, Hera and her passengers reached the small village, Blackstar loyally following his mistress. Once they were inside the horse's small shelter, Blake gently kissed Rina's warm, tender lips once more.

"Another time, Rina," said Blake, sending her inside to bed. At that moment, she looked more like an innocent child than the wild, enticing dancer she had been. As he watched her disappear into her home, he immediately wished she was still in his arms. Sighing, Blake tended to the stallion and headed for his own empty bed, to dream of his dancing, golden girl.

The rest of the week went by, Blake enjoying the time he had left with his grandfather. Whenever he was alone, his thoughts would drift back to the beautiful Rina. That morning he had ridden to the fields, and concealed by the trees, he had watched Rina as she worked. He had no idea what had compelled him to do such a thing; he only knew he had to see her again. As he watched her, Blake noticed the big, blond man who never seemed to leave her side. He also observed the way she touched his arm and smiled tenderly at what he said. The longer Blake watched the two young people, the angrier he became, jealousy building inside him until he could no longer bear to watch them. Turning Hera back toward Windsong, he rode like a madman, trying to rid himself of the insane rage he felt toward a woman he barely knew, a woman who should mean nothing to him.

When he arrived at the estate, Ryon met his brother and told him that his grandfather was asking for him. Blake rushed upstairs to see him, entering the room quietly. Lord Roberts lay still as Blake pulled the chair next to the bed.

"How are you today? Didn't you sleep well?" Concern filled Blake as he watched his grandfather's irregular breathing.

"I am tired," said Lord Roberts. "Stay with me, son. It's the last time we will have to spend together."

Blake took his grandfather's hand, trying desperately to control the overwhelming emotions welling up inside of him.

"I don't want you to grieve for me, Blake," Lord Roberts said wearily, reading his grandson's thoughts. "I want no long mourning period in this home. There is no need for all of you to stop living because an old man has left you. Promise me that after I'm buried you will continue on as you always have. No black dresses for Rebecca. She is a new mother and should not be forced to wear such somber clothes and mourn for a year."

"I promise," said Blake.

Blake stayed by his grandfather's side, talking with him until the old man fell asleep. Ryon and Rebecca sat with them for a while, then quietly left. Sometime in the night, as Blake slept in the chair by his bed, Lord Roberts passed away. Blake awoke abruptly, alert to the sudden stillness in the room, and in the privacy of the night, he grieved.

The funeral was over and the people were gone. Blake stood alone saying his farewell to the man he loved and admired. He walked to the door of the church and paused, looking back at the grave now laden with flowers.

Rina reined Blackstar to a halt and slid off his back, grasping the single red rose in her hand. Seeing no one around, she entered the graveyard and walked over to the freshly dug grave where Lord Roberts now lay. Unaware that Blake stood just inside the church, Rina spoke.

"I will miss you dearly, Lord Roberts. You were a good friend and a kind man. Windsong will not be the same without your presence." Kneeling, Rina laid the dark rose on the mound and turned to leave but stopped as she felt someone watching her. Glancing around, she spotted Blake standing in the shadows. Rina blushed as she remembered the night at the gypsy camp.

Blake was also remembering. He had dreamed of her, had longed to possess her lovely, enchanting body. Blake started toward her but stopped as Ryon called to him from inside the church.

Rina turned and quickly left, mounting Blackstar just outside the gate. As Ryon came up beside Blake, Rina bolted past them, racing down the road for home and safety.

"She's very beautiful, isn't she, Blake?"

"Yes. Very. Did she know grandfather?"

"Rina knew him quite well. He gave her the stallion she is riding." Seeing the questioning look on Blake's face, Ryon continued with his story. "She's cared for all our sick horses for about three years now. Has quite a way with the beasts. A couple of years ago, one of our best mares was having a difficult time foaling, so we sent for her. Grandpa thought we'd lose both the mare and colt, but Rina saved them. Quite a job really, stayed three days. So he gave her the colt. Everyone around here says there isn't anyone who knows more about horses than she does. Grandfather was extremely fond of Rina."

"How fond was he of her?"

The question came out before Blake realized he had asked it. Taken off guard by the blunt question and the anger in his brother's golden eyes, Ryon answered, "Just friends, Blake. Nothing amorous, I'm sure. They used to play chess sometimes, or go riding. All quite aboveboard and innocent.

She was just a kid when she first came here!" Ryon gave
his brother an appraising look. "Why does it matter so much
to you?"

"It just does, that's all!" Blake turned and walked away,
leaving Ryon totally bewildered. Mounting Hera, Blake
started for Windsong, angry at his own reactions. He didn't
understand what kind of hold that woman had on him. He
hadn't even bedded her yet, and she was driving him mad!

Chapter 5

Rina rode from the graveyard as fast as Blackstar could carry her. Seeing Blake Roberts brought back the confused thoughts that had plagued her since he kissed her. She had blamed the feelings he had aroused in her the night of the gypsy camp on the wine. But now . . . she wasn't sure. The shock that had gone through her at the sight of him completely shattered her confidence. He stood so strong and tall, his broad shoulders filling the church doorway. As her eyes met his, the same feelings that had overwhelmed her the other night came over her. How could the sight of this one man do this to her? She was always in total control of her mind and emotions; why did this man so easily destroy her self-discipline?

Chiding herself for her silliness, Rina tried to shake off the disturbing thoughts of Blake Roberts. She was determined to keep him from her mind. It was a lovely afternoon, and the sun warmed her back as she rode across the countryside. Deciding to take advantage of the unusually warm day, Rina turned off the road and headed for her secluded swimming hole. She had discovered it many years ago, when she still lived at Camray. There was a waterfall and pond with lush vegetation and flowers surrounding it. It was a tiny bit of paradise completely hidden from the world.

Whenever Rina needed to be alone with her troubles and fears, she would visit her secret place, spending many hours swimming in the pond or just staring into its crystal-blue depths, looking for the answers to whatever troubled her in the water. Many things crowded her mind today, but her thoughts always seemed to wander back to Blake Roberts.

Carefully, Blackstar made his way through the thick trees, knowing the way as well as Rina. Soon they came to what seemed to be a dead end, a sheer rock wall rising in front of them, but Blackstar stepped behind some brush and through a concealed opening. On the other side, they passed under a waterfall and out into the sun to see the blue pool, its grassy banks sloping up into dense foliage, ending in the unbroken circle of rock. No matter how many times she came here, she always found it breathtakingly beautiful.

Sliding off of Blackstar, she allowed him to wander and nibble the tender grass. Her own thoughts were on the water. Colorful bouquets of wildflowers stood out among the deep green of the foliage surrounding her, delighting her senses. The sparkling water beckoned her, its cool, clear depths promising relief from the afternoon sun. Sitting down, Rina quickly shed her boots to soak her feet, stretching out on her back in the soft, cushiony moss, watching the puffs of clouds drift lazily across the sky. Rina began to relax as the peacefulness relieved the tension inside her. She thought of Lord Roberts, feeling a sadness in her heart. She would miss him terribly. Rina sighed drowsily and closed her eyes against the brightness, drifting off to sleep.

Unknown to Rina, one other person knew of the waterfall and pond, though it had been over fifteen years since he had seen them. As he came out from under the waterfall, he wound around to the other side of the pond, thinking it had changed little over the years. Unable to bear the confines of Windsong, Blake had quickly changed to his riding clothes and left, not really knowing where he wished to go. Somehow he had ended up here and it seemed a pleasing place to be. It wasn't until he dismounted that he saw Blackstar grazing in the grass. Surprised that he'd been so deep in thought that he hadn't noticed the girl asleep on the bank, he quietly hid himself among the trees, where he had a close, clear view of Rina. For the moment, he was content to lie back and watch her sleep.

Rina stirred, her slumber filled with dreams. She saw a pair of golden eyes wanting her, stirring the passions inside her . . . confusing her. But then the fiery eyes were replaced by cold, black ones . . . the eyes of Lawrence Langsford.

Blake noticed with concern the change in her delicate features as the nightmare began. Suddenly, Rina awakened screaming out in fear as she remembered that long-ago night. Blackstar, hearing her cry, nuzzled her gently on the neck, comforting his mistress in the only way he knew. Stroking his soft, black muzzle, Rina murmured to him, quietly, passionately.

"I'll kill him, Blackstar. Yes . . . someday, when the time is right, I'll kill the bastard!"

Once more Blackstar wandered off to graze, sensing Rina was all right again. Deciding that a swim would clear her head, she began to pull off her pants and shirt. After she had shed her clothes, she dove into the pool, surfacing a few feet from the bank.

Blake watched intently as Rina gracefully swam around the small pond, his heart racing wildly. God, she was even more beautiful than he had imagined. Her body was the color of honey, tanned from the sun, creamy and smooth. Her hair billowed out in a fan of dark gold as she floated about the calm water. Swimming over to the waterfall, she climbed onto the rocks and let the cool water shower over her in a misty veil, running over the delicate curves of her body. Blake felt an overwhelming desire to jump in and join her, taking her right there on the rocks where she now stood. He needed to satisfy the lust consuming him, but for some reason he knew he could not take her by force. He wanted her to come to him willingly, yielding all her passions to his expert touch. As he watched her, he wondered why such a beauty was not married. Perhaps she was free with her favors to all the young men of the village, like the big, blond fellow she seemed so fond of.

At that thought, Blake tensed in anger, then forced himself to relax. Why should it matter to him if she was a virgin or not? It would be much easier to bed her if she wasn't chaste. Rina seemed bolder than most woman. She probably had had many lovers. But everyone seemed to have such high regard for her, though she wore breeches and rode astride and handled a knife like a man. She was a peasant, living no better than the others of her village, but she had the air of a lady. Shaking his head in total confusion, Blake whispered to himself, "Damned if I can figure you out, little one."

Rina floated around, luxuriating in the soothing water as it glided over her body, massaging away her tension. She swam over to the mossy bank, where she stood, the drops of water reflecting the golden rays of the sun as they dripped between her breasts and ran off her body. Wringing the excess water from her thick hair, she flung the heavy tresses out of her face, stretching her arms high above her head. The sun gently kissed her wet body, bathing her luscious form in a golden haze as she raised her arms above her head, like a sun goddess paying tribute. Still unaware that she was not alone, Rina walked over to her pile of clothes and started to pull them on. The garments clung to her moist body, the shirt becoming nearly transparent. As she sat and began to pull on her boots something caught her eye. She glanced about quickly, and spotted Blake's horse moving in search of sweeter grass. Rina's eyes narrowed suspiciously as she recognized the mare. Carefully, she searched the green area for its owner and hurriedly pulled on the other boot. Anger washed over her and her cheeks flushed with embarrassment. She jumped up and swiftly ran to Blackstar. Grabbing a handful of his long, slick mane, she started to mount him, but strong, long arms reached out and caught her around the waist, lifting her from the ground.

"Where are you going, little one?" Blake's breath tickled Rina's ear and he twirled her around, crushing her to his chest.

"Let me go! You son-of-a-bitch! How dare you spy on me!" Rina spat out in her rage, her lips curling back into a snarl.

Blake grabbed her wrist, just in time to save his face

from her sharp claws. Rina's indrawn breath became a hiss
as her eyes turned as dark as the midnight sky. It seemed
as if he could lose himself in their depth, and Blake momentarily forgot his purpose. Rina sensed his hesitation and
brought her knee up, but Blake was more alert than she
thought. He turned slightly and she missed his groin, throwing them both off balance, tumbling them to the ground.
Rina nimbly twisted from his arms and turned to face her
enemy. Blake started toward her but stopped as he caught
the flash of the steel blade in her hands. Her hair was tangled
in a wet mass, cascading around her shoulders and down
her back. Her breathing was ragged as her heart pounded
wildly with rage. Rina's eyes were flashing angrily, spewing
blue sparks as she stood facing him, legs braced apart, ready
to fend off this arrogant lord.

Blake's gaze took in every detail as his eyes boldly raked
over her wet, tousled hair, admiring the way her shirt and
pants molded seductively to every curve of her body. His
gaze lingered on the gentle swell of her breasts straining
against the tight shirt, her nipples taunt and teasing. Her
lips were parted slightly; her face was flushed and showed
no fear. Blake shook his head and started to laugh, the sound
echoing off the walls. Rina's eyes became slits as she warily
watched Blake, not trusting him a bit.

"God! You're the most confusing woman I have ever
known!" Smiling, Blake relaxed and leaned against a tree,
seemingly unconcerned that Rina still held a knife in her
hand.

"You, sir, do not know me!" hissed Rina. "If you did,
you would not find me so confusing."

Blake's laughter stopped, his eyes becoming serious as
the fires of desire started to dance in them. "I want nothing
more than to get to know you, Rina. I want to get to know
every beautiful inch . . . very intimately."

Blake spoke softly, so softly that Rina had to listen carefully to hear his words. As they sank into her mind a blush
crept over her face.

"Your body's lovely, Rina, and you nearly drove me mad
when you came out of the water."

"You bastard! You *were* spying on me! You...you...
I..." sputtered Rina.

"What are you so damned angry about?" snapped Blake
irritably. "You certainly don't think twice about swimming
naked in a pond in the middle of the country. It wouldn't
surprise me if you knew all along that I was here. Perhaps
you are the type of whore who likes to tease, then back
away pretending to be virtuous." Suddenly Blake was furious with her. He seemed to lose all composure as she stood
before him, looking shocked and hurt. He thought he would
go mad from the lust she inspired. Why wasn't she willingly
spreading her long luscious legs so he could ease his agony?
Instead, the little vamp was standing there, gorgeously at-
tractive, dangerously wielding a knife, daring him to come
closer with those damnable eyes.

"A...a...whore!" As the shock of his words wore off,
a blinding rage shook Rina. The word reverberated in her
mind with a numbing force. She felt hurt that he *could* think
such a thing, and furious that he *would* think such a thing.
"I am no man's whore!"

The words came out even and calm, but the cold hatred
in her voice should have warned Blake to stop. Instead, he
continued to blunder on, careless of the pain he was inflict-
ing. "What about your big blond lover? I saw the way you
looked at him. Do you spread your legs for him at night?
How many others do you lie with, Rina? Do you play the
whore for money, or pleasure?"

The immense violence Rina barely held in check shattered at his brutally uttered words. Springing at Blake, she
flew through the air, knife flashing and teeth bared. A scream
of shock and rage escaped from deep within her, startling
Blake into action. His reactions were quick, and he blocked
her assault easily, but Rina was fast on her feet and continued
slashing at him furiously. Although Blake was twice Rina's
size, he had his hands full trying to keep her from shredding
him to ribbons. She was like a jungle cat, agile and strong,
her small size distracting. Her strength surprised Blake, just
as everything else about her had. Rina's blind fury caused
her to be careless, and he was able to grab her wrist, wrenching the knife from her hand.

Wrestling her to the ground, Blake laid his full weight on top of her, stilling her wriggling form. Rina's wrists were held firmly in his iron grip. The wench had actually tried to kill him! The teasing, lying bitch! The muscle in Blake's jaw twitched, his gaze full of fire as he stared into her cold blue eyes. Many men would have feared the look on Blake's face, but Rina did not look away or flinch. Her courage fed his anger.

"This is what you were made for, witch! To lie beneath a man and warm his bed!" Cruelly his mouth took Rina's in a kiss that was demanding and brutal. He seemed to suck the breath from her as he searched her mouth with his tongue. Blake's free hand slowly snaked through her long strands of hair, wrenching her head back painfully. Rina thought he was going to snap her neck like a twig, but she made no sound. He pulled away from her lips and looked deep into her eyes, wanting to find evidence of the agony he was causing. He found no pain and no fear in them, only icy fury. Damn her! Twisting even harder, he jerked her head back, and her eyes closed momentarily but no cry escaped her lips. Once again, his lips possessed hers, hungry for the soft sweetness of her mouth. Slowly, his savage grip eased. He kissed her neck, tenderly caressing it with his lips. A shiver ran through Rina as Blake's mouth traveled to her breasts. Unwillingly, a sigh escaped her, her rage betraying her as another, stronger emotion took over her body and mind. Blake nibbled gently on her earlobe, the small, gold earring she wore hard and smooth between his teeth, his breath warm and soft.

"Should you have succeeded in killing me, you would have been hung."

As he continued to kiss and caress, Rina tried desperately to retain control of her emotions. "I have no fear of death, Lord Roberts."

Her genuinely honest answer surprised Blake, and he stopped to look at her. Strangely, his anger was being replaced by curiosity. "Who are you, Rina? You must be a witch. You made me go mad, and I hurt you, when all I wanted was to make love to you. It would be worth your time, little one. You would have many things as my mistress.

And when I tired of your beautiful little body, I would make certain you are well cared for."

Rina's head snapped back as if she had been slapped. Gone were the feelings he had aroused in her sensuous body, leaving only a cold, empty ache.

"I told you before, I am no man's whore! I don't want your trinkets and baubles! I don't need you, Lord Roberts!"

The words came out in an icy sneer. Rina knew her statement had an effect on Blake as his muscles tensed, his grip becoming cruel and painful once again. Rina shuddered slightly as she felt the power and strength he had.

Blake's voice was deadly calm. "Bitch! I intend to show you exactly what your luscious body is for . . . to pleasure a man and relieve the ache in his loins." Blake held both her wrists in one hand and began to undress Rina with the other, delighted at her helpless look. She began to squirm, desperately trying to loosen the viselike grip.

"You might as well stop wriggling about. I will have you and you can't do anything to stop me." He smiled down on Rina, but the smile did not reach his eyes.

Rina saw the truth of his words, and for the second time in her life, she felt helpless. She ceased struggling and looked into the hard, golden eyes of her captor. Her voice was soft, but determined, as she stated her feelings.

"You can rape me and beat me. You may break my bones and even kill me. Because you are stronger, you can do any, or all of these things . . . but you, sir, will never defeat me. You will never be master over me and break my spirit. I am my own woman, and no man shall own me. I am no man's whore!"

"You will be mine!"

"No! Am I so much less than a man that I am to be used like a dog, and discarded when I am no longer wanted? Did God put me here to be subjected to rape and degradation? I have pride, just as you do, and can suffer humiliation as no man can ever know."

The emotional intensity of her words rang clear in Blake's mind, bringing him back to his senses. Gradually, his mind cleared as he realized with sickening clarity what his passions and rage had nearly driven him to. How could he have been so foolish? Blake rolled away from Rina, running a hand through his hair. Silently, he lay on his back looking up at the clouds, cursing his stupidity. How could one woman drive him so wild?

"You seem to bring out the worst in me, little one." Blake sighed as he lifted himself onto one elbow, looking at Rina, who lay silent and still. "I intend to make love to you, Rina. Not today, but I will make you mine. You needn't worry that I will rape you, you have my word. I will wait until you come willingly to my arms."

Rina gazed warily into his golden eyes. They were no longer cold and hard; instead, they were warm, catching the sunlight, sparkling like amber.

"You had best keep your word, Lord Roberts. I made a mistake today when I tried to kill you." Rina paused, noticing Blake's raised eyebrows and the amused look on his face. "Do not misunderstand me, my mistake was allowing my anger to take control. It caused me to be careless and give you the advantage. I was taught better than that. But I was also taught to learn from my mistakes. Break your promise and I shall kill you."

"Many men have tried what you threaten to do . . . and failed. Normally, if any man said to me what you have, I would pay no mind. If he tried, he would surely die. If a woman other than you had said it, I would merely laugh. But for some strange reason, I intend to make sure you never have a reason to come at me with a knife again. You must truly be a sorceress, for you are like no woman I have ever known."

"I suppose all the women you are acquainted with are spineless and empty-headed, thinking of nothing but marriage, children, and needlepoint. They have no opinions, except those of their husbands, and gossiping is the highlight of every long, boring day." Her voice grew strong and determined. "Women are left ignorant of all except the things men feel are women's work. We are born, live, and die in the shadows of men. But perhaps there are some of us who wish to cast our own shadows." Her words came tumbling out, but not in anger—it was gone, leaving her feeling drained of all emotion.

"You talk nonsense, Rina," said Blake as he stood, not certain why it made him so uncomfortable to listen to her unusual convictions.

"I am a woman. Though I am smaller of frame and more fragile of body, I am your equal. My mind is as capable of learning and comprehending as yours. Is that so difficult to understand?"

"Yes . . . yes, it is. You were meant to be made love to, and taken care of, to be protected against the evil in this world. You were meant to bear children and run a household. It's so simple, why must you make it sound so terrible?" This was ridiculous, he thought to himself. How strange . . . it was as if he had had this same conversation with someone else recently. But with whom?

"No. It is you who make it so difficult. For not seeing me as I really am." Sighing, Rina also stood, straightening her clothing.

"You are a confusing wench who fights like a wildcat and dreams impossible dreams."

"Perhaps. But dreams are all I have."

Without saying another word, Rina left in search of Blackstar. Their violent encounter was over. So why did she feel a twinge of disappointment? She found her horse grazing near Blake's Arabian mare, and she gently ran her hand over his horse's back, feeling her hard, sinewy muscles. Admiration for the magnificent animal showed clearly in her eyes. The horse moved nervously but quickly calmed down as Rina's soft, smooth voice soothed her.

Blake walked up behind her, an amazed look on his face. "What did you say to her? She usually allows no one near except me. Have you cast your spells on her, too?"

Rina ignored his remark and continued to pet the horse's soft muzzle. "What do you call her?"

"Hera," he replied.

"After the Greek queen of gods." Considering this, she smiled. "It suits her, for she is truly a queen." Rina did not notice the raised eyebrow at her knowledge of the Greek name. "Blackstar likes her too."

Rina laughed openly as her own horse nudged her jealously, wanting her attention as well. Again Blake was taken aback by her loveliness as her face lit up with a stunning smile that added sparkle to her sapphire eyes. Her laughter warmed his heart, and he foolishly wished he could always make Rina laugh.

"You should laugh more often, little one. It makes you even more beautiful."

She eyed him warily, but Rina could not keep a blush from staining her cheeks at his compliment.

"You are far too serious for someone so young." Absently, Blake ran his finger down her pinkened cheek, tracing her delicate jaw line.

Rina pulled away, feeling as if his light touch had left a trail of fire. Even though her voice was even and controlled, Rina felt as if a battle was going on inside of her. "I have so little to laugh about," she said, hoping that conversation would calm her. Even anger was safer than the feelings he aroused.

"Now, what could possibly cause you so much worry and strife?"

"Many things. I worry how the people of my village will make it through the coming winter. How many children will get sick, perhaps die. Will we have sufficient wood to heat our homes? Will the small amount of food we have be enough? How will we fight starvation, freezing cold, and disease? We break our backs planting and harvesting, but most of it goes to Lord Langsford. Each year I see the suffering, each year I see people die. They die because of the greed of one man!"

For a moment Blake saw the pain on Rina's face and it tore at his heart. "Those are problems that the master of Camray should see to. This land should provide for everyone."

Rina tensed as she thought of her enemy, and Blake saw the change in her mood. He was taken back by the sheer cold hatred he saw.

"Langsford is a fool!" Rina hissed between clenched teeth. Closing her eyes, she fought to control her feelings. She should be careful of what she said in front of Blake Roberts. She really didn't know this man at all.

Blake wrapped his arms protectively around her and

whispered, "Rina, I did not mean to upset you with my careless words." Tenderly, he kissed the top of her head.

Cradled in his strong arms, Rina felt confused by his sudden gentleness and the feeling of security it gave her. Bewildered by her own thoughts, Rina pulled away from his warm embrace and turned back to Hera. "May I ride her, Lord Roberts?"

It took Blake a few seconds to adjust to the emptiness of his arms. "Please call me Blake, little one."

Rina hesitated at his request but complied with a shrug of indifference. "May I ride her . . . Blake?"

"I'm afraid she allows no one to ride her except me. We could ride together," he offered, hoping she would accept, anxious to have her in his arms again.

"Perhaps no one else has asked her properly. She's such a noble and grand lady, but she is also fickle. Only those who truly respect her may sit on her back. It would be an honor to ride her, and the rider must know that." Rina spoke gently and lovingly to Hera, as if she knew the horse understood her words. Surprising Blake, she mounted Hera, her eyes meeting his astonished gaze.

"Is that what you want, Rina? A man who will understand and respect you? A man who will know what an honor it is to make love to you?"

It was an honest question, with no sarcasm or cruelty intended. Rina did not turn away but instead held his eyes steadily. Blake read the hesitation in them, her answer barely above a whipser. "Perhaps . . . I truly don't know."

"What of love and marriage? Most women want . . . no, need them," asked Blake, eager to understand her.

"I don't believe I will ever have them." A touch of sadness in her words reached Blake, tugging at his heart, as Rina prompted Hera into a gallop. His eyes never left her. Never had he been so intrigued and bewildered at the same time. One moment he wanted to thrash her, the next he wanted to hold and protect her. His desire for her was maddening! He felt the need to take her and tame her wild nature. Yet he wanted her willing, full of passion and fire. He was certain she was just a clever whore, but she had an air of innocence he could not explain. Was she trying to play him for a fool? Why had he made that silly promise to wait for her to come to him?

Rina was totally unaware of Blake's thoughts as she rode Hera around the pool. Returning to where he stood, she started to climb off the horse when his arms wrapped around her waist, pulling her close as she slowly slid down the length of his body. They seemed frozen, their eyes locked as they were unable to move. Gently, he kissed her, slowly, sweetly. Rina felt her knees grow weak, as if he had physically drained her. Blake supported her in his arms, his lips roaming to her eyes and the lovely curve of her neck. Burying his face in her soft, golden hair, he moaned into her ear, more to himself than to Rina.

"God, you will drive me mad!" As if he could no longer stand to touch her, Blake quickly released her and turned away.

Rina blinked, startled by his sudden action, and she stared forlornly at his back. She started to reach out and touch him, but hesitated. Instead, she went to Blackstar and mounted; she should go home.

It was getting late and it would soon be dark. She silently made her way from her . . . no, their, secret place. She was so immersed in her thoughts that she did not notice Blake following closely behind her. When she did, she turned and spoke. "I know my way home. You need not go out of your way on my account."

Once again, Blake was composed, his self-assured air once again intact. "A gentleman would never allow a lady to ride about unescorted." All the passion was gone from his voice, his eyes were shadowed and unreadable. This was the Blake Roberts most people saw.

It was dark when they arrived in the village, and Blake helped Rina rub down Blackstar and feed him. The uncomfortable silence was broken as Blake prepared to leave. Rina was staring at the ground when Blake gently lifted her chin so he could look into her eyes.

"Good night, little one. I shall see you soon."

Gracefully, Blake climbed into the saddle and rode away. Rina stood watching the lone figure disappear into the darkness, feeling very, very alone.

Chapter 6

Hera and Blake quickly left Windsong behind, the endless piles of paperwork forgotten, as were the last weeks he had spent confined in his office. Without realizing his direction, Blake ended up looking down on the village of Tattershall. It had been almost five weeks since he had seen Rina at the pool. His nights were filled with visions of the tawny-haired vixen. She had haunted him, like a ghost who would not rest. Even in his dreams she aroused him to the point of madness.

Why was he so interested in this little spitfire? There were plenty of women to warm his bed, and they were quite a bit more willing than Rina. So why on earth must he have her? She seemed to bring out the worst in him. Why did he want to see this woman so badly? Blake continued to ask himself all of these questions, and more, as he went through the small village to Rina's cottage. Would he ever know what he felt for her?

Knocking loudly on the door, he waited until a plump, jolly-looking woman answered. Her pale blue eyes looked at Blake curiously as she addressed him in a thick accent. "Good day, me lord. Wha' is it I can do fer ye?" she asked.

Giving her one of his most charming smiles, Blake bowed

low, in a graceful, fluid motion. "Please allow me to introduce myself. I am Blake Roberts."

A bit flustered to have the master of Windsong at her door, Jenny giggled like a young lass. "I be Jenny Tidwell. T' wha' do I owe this 'onor, me lord?"

"I believe the young lady Rina lives here?"

"Aye, she does." A twinkle came to Jenny's eyes as she smiled widely at the gentleman. "But she's no' 'ere at the moment. Would ye care t' come in an' wait fer 'er?" Seeing his nod, she let him enter. "Would ye sit an' share a cup o' ale, Lord Roberts?"

"I most surely would, kind lady."

Another giggle escaped as she blushed under his warm, golden gaze. "Well, come righ' in an' make yerself comfortable. It's no' fancy, but it's 'ome an' the ale is good." Jenny grabbed two cups and poured them full as Blake sat at the table.

He gladly accepted the cup and motioned for Jenny to join him. "Please, don't fret, for I find it quite relaxing here. Charming in fact. Much more so than most stuffy mansions I find myself obligated to visit."

Jenny beamed proudly at his compliment, deciding quickly that she did indeed like this young man. "If ye don't mind an old woman's nosiness, jus' wha' did ye come t' see Rina about? Do ye 'ave a 'orse she needs t' tend?"

"No. I have no horses she needs to see. I met Rina several weeks ago and I wished to see her again."

Blake noted the amused smile on the older woman's face as she took in his casual appearance.

Jenny was noticing everything about the young lord, especially his broad shoulders that tapered down to a slim waist. His linen shirt was opened carelessly, showing a mass of curly brown hair on his wide chest. Jenny pursed her lips as she studied his handsome face. "An' wha' would a 'andsome, rich gentleman like yerself be wantin' wi' Rina?" She paused a minute as if expecting an answer, but came to a conclusion on her own. "Ah . . . I suppose the answer be clear, bu' I'm no' sure I be liken' wha' yer thinkin'."

Wary of the direction the woman had taken, Blake feigned

a look of hurt. "Would you deny a gentleman the pleasure that a few minutes of her company would bring?"

Jenny was not fooled. "I'm no' daft, young man! It's the other pleasures ye'll be wantin' tha's no' t' me likin'."

Blake considered lying, to ease her fears for her niece, but that was not his way. Quickly, he decided to tell her the truth. "Your niece is very beautiful and I'll not deny that I desire her. Whatever happens between us will be Rina's decision."

As Blake drained his mug, Jenny let out a cackle and stood to refill it. "Yer 'onest! I like tha' in a man! Well . . . I suppose if ye can tame the girl enough t' bed 'er, ye certainly 'ave earned it. Ye don't seem t' be the type t' 'arm 'er none, but I'll be warnin' ye now, if ye did, it would no' be good fer yer 'ealth. So, I won't be stickin' me nose where it doesna' belong. It wouldna' do no good . . . 'as a mind of 'er own, she does!"

Jenny knew Rina too well. The girl would do as she pleased, no matter what Jenny said. Rina never allowed what others thought to interfere with her private life. This was, after all, between Blake and Rina. Jenny only wanted her to be happy; she deserved that much out of life. Perhaps this would even lead to love.

Blake misunderstood Jenny's casual acceptance of the situation, thinking Rina must have had many lovers before. Certainly if she had been a virgin, Jenny would have objected to his intentions.

"I'm glad you understand," replied Blake.

"Well, young man, ye 'avena' go' 'er yet. Me Rina is no mousy lady. Ye'll 'ave yer 'ands full sweet-talkin' 'er."

Taking another drink, Blake drawled, "I'm sure I will."

Just at that moment Rina rode up to the cottage and dismounted in front. She stopped to stroke Hera, giving herself time to calm her racing heart. Why on earth should she react in such a way? Just because Blake Roberts was obviously inside was no reason for her to feel so strange. As serenely as possible, Rina entered the house.

Blake rose to his feet, realizing at that moment how much he had missed not seeing her in the last few weeks. Her hair was loose, falling about her in a mass of golden curls that he ached to touch. Her color was high from the ride, and her eyes sparkled brilliantly as she glanced quickly from Blake to Jenny.

"Good afternoon, Lord Roberts." Rina extended a slender hand and Blake took it gently, pressing it intimately to his lips. They both felt the sensation the small, innocent gesture had created, and their eyes locked.

"Good afternoon, Rina. I was beginning to think that I would miss you. I'm glad you are here." Blake's words were like a gentle caress to Rina's ears, bringing a blush to her cheeks.

Jenny watched the two young people closely, a smile coming to her face. Yes . . . maybe it would lead to love. "Rina, dear, since ye are back early, I should 'ave time t' take this bread t' Mrs. McNally. I promised she would 'ave it by dinner." Jenny wrapped the bread carefully and placed it in a basket as she talked. "Lord Roberts, it was so nice o' ye t' come. I'm sure tha' ye will forgive me leavin'. After all, ye did come t' see Rina an' no' an old woman like me."

Before either of them could say a word, Jenny disappeared through the door, her distinctive crackle drifting behind her retreating form.

"Why are you here?" Rina's question cut through the awkward silence, Blake's stare unnerving her already frayed emotions.

"I came to see you. I told you I would. I'd have come sooner, but business kept me away."

"Why couldn't you just leave me alone?" Rina's question came out almost as a plea as she recalled the many nights she had dreamed of the man now standing before her.

"Oh, little one. You could not expect me to stay away. Not when you haunt my dreams at night. I could no longer bear such torture."

Rina jumped nervously as she heard her thoughts echoed in his words. "Please, you must go." Rina's words were barely above a whisper, and Blake had to strain to hear what she had said.

"I have not seen you for weeks; surely you would not deny me a few minutes." Blake moved, grasping Rina's hand in his own, feeling her warmth meld with his. "You are too beautiful. How can I forget the loveliness of your body. How can I exorcise you from my mind?" He kissed her hand, palm up, his tongue lightly running to her fingertips. Turning her delicately formed hand over, his lips tenderly caressed a small scar just below her smallest finger, frowning at the hurt the injury must have caused her.

Rina pulled her hand from his as waves of pleasure ran over her, muddling her mind even further. She was so weak! How could her body continue to betray her in such a way?

"Don't you see? We were meant for one another." Blake pulled her into his arms, crushing her to him in his aching need as his lips possessed hers. He held her tightly so Rina could feel his rising desire hard against her. Her composure fled, leaving only her own immense passions. They clung to each other, and Rina ignored the warnings her mind was screaming, feeling only the sensuality of his touch. Blake pulled away from her, his eyes dark and smoldering. His voice was husky and full of feeling.

"You are a witch! One kiss and I'm your slave! You cast your spells and work your black magic, how am I to fight against your mystic charms?"

Could it be that he was as enslaved as she, Rina wondered dazedly. Could he be feeling as lost, as confused as she was by what was between them? Suddenly, she remembered the last time he'd spoken of his need for her that day at the pool. When he'd asked her to be his mistress . . . and called her his whore. That was all he wanted her to be! She stiffened, and Blake felt the sudden change as Rina whispered, her voice broken and strained, "I have no hold on you, Lord Roberts. You are free to go, and I think it would be best for you to do just that!"

Blake's laughter grated on her raw nerves, but it held no humor. His eyes turned hard and cold as he muttered in a low voice, "If you are toying with me, Rina, let me warn you, I am not in the mood."

"I'm certain you find all this very amusing, but I do not! Now, if you would be kind enough to leave . . . I am expecting someone." She turned her back to him, not wanting him to see her turmoil.

"One of your lovers?"

Rina spun about, her eyes narrowed. Her voice dripped with hatred and shook slightly with fury. "I believe it is none of your business whom I am expecting. Since you seem so adept at jumping to conclusions on your own, whether they be true or not, I'll not bother dignifying your question with a denial!" She spoke the words through gritted teeth. Why couldn't he leave her be?

"You needn't act so insulted. When I made it clear to your aunt that I wanted you, she laughed and all but wished me luck! She must be accustomed to your lovers. How many have you had, Rina?" The last question came out as an accusation, making Rina's anger peak like an explosion.

"Get out! I don't ever want to see you again!"

Blake's own temper was beginning to rise dangerously as he continued to barrage her with hurtful remarks. "Is it your big blond lover, Rina? Are you planning to wriggle and twist with passion beneath his body tonight? Do you hunger for his touch?"

His questions were like arrows piercing her heart, leaving her speechless. Out of control, Blake grabbed her shoulders harshly and began to shake her, whipping her head back and forth painfully. "Do you love him, Rina?"

The words slipped out before Blake had time to think. He could have kicked himself, for he didn't care if she did. Or did he? He suddenly let go, sending Rina reeling backward into the table. Once again Rina should have been warned by the evil glow in his eyes, but she had been pushed too far. Rina had never been able to lie, but she was not adverse to not telling the whole truth.

"Yes, I love him!" she all but screamed at Blake. Rina knew he would not know her love was like that of a sister for a brother. She wanted more than anything to hurt Blake Roberts as he had hurt her, and her anger spurred her on. "I would give my life for him! I would kill for him!"

Her words accomplished what she had intended, and she knew it, glorying in his pain. Blake went numb for a moment, unable to understand why it would matter so damn much that she loved the man. But it did! And that made him even angrier than Rina had.

"Then why hasn't he married you?" Blake no longer

cared what he said as he carelessly went on. "But then, why would he want to marry a whore like you? He can use you until he tires of you, and then marry a pretty little virgin. You must remember, Rina, men marry virgins . . . not whores!"

Rina could not take any more of his venomous words. Putting her hands over her ears to shut out his ugly words, she shook her head back and forth. Dashing past Blake to the door, she ran outside. Blinded by her rage, Rina ran into John as he walked toward the cottage door. Relief flooded through her as she looked into John's soft brown eyes. Seeing her distress, he wrapped his arms about her protectively. She felt his muscles tense as Blake appeared in the doorway, his eyes smoldering, his anger barely in check.

Quickly, Blake took in the touching scene before him. A strange feeling tugged at his heart as he noticed John's arms wrapped about Rina. Casually, he leaned against the door frame, an evil grin on his face as he drawled, "Well, we meet at last."

John ignored the sarcastic words and turned to Rina. "Are you all right? Is he bothering you?"

"I'm fine, Johnny. Really," she assured him, wanting to avoid a fight between the two men. Nervously, she glanced at Blake and said, "Lord Roberts was leaving. *Weren't you?*"

The last was more a demand than a question, and Blake's eyebrow shot up in amusement as he considered her request. "Yes . . . I was just leaving. Another time, little one."

Without another word, Blake walked past them and mounted Hera. Nodding to Rina and John, he rode off, leaving one confused and the other angry.

Nudging Hera into a gallop, Blake allowed her to run freely. As he pounded down the road toward Windsong, he felt the tension inside him ease slightly. He couldn't understand why Rina could cause him to lose his temper so easily. It would be better if he just forgot this willful female! She was trouble and he knew it. He would certainly be better off without her. Yes, he decided firmly, I'll just put her from my mind. There are plenty of women to occupy my time. What do I need with a wildcat like her?

All the way home, Blake scolded himself for letting the wench get under his skin. By the time he had cleaned up for dinner, he was determined to forget Rina and her damned beautiful eyes.

"Are you going to tell me what that was all about?" John asked Rina as they watched Blake Roberts ride away. He could sense her anger and recognized the look in her eyes. Silence followed his question as Rina fought to control her emotions. John was patient, knowing she needed time to collect her thoughts. They walked over to Blackstar and led him to his stall. Rina could feel the tension leaving her as she combed his silky black coat.

"If he's hurt you, Kat, I'll kill him. I don't care who he is!" John's heated words broke through the wall of silence surrounding Rina. She saw the confusion and anger in his eyes and reached up to touch his cheek. The touch was tender and loving; Rina knew she could have no better friend in all the world.

"No, John, he did not hurt me. He makes me so angry, though, I think I could kill him myself! I do not understand why he can make me explode so easily. I should have better control, but when he's near me I lose all reason. I think I hate him and then when he kisses me, I want only to love him. I'm so confused." Rina's face flushed with embarrassment.

A surprised look registered on John's face and concern edged his voice. "Kat, you are a grown woman now, and for the first time you're experiencing the desires of a woman. I'm not so sure I like it. I know you're capable of making your own decisions concerning men, but it's hard for me because I feel so protective of you. I could not stand it if someone hurt you."

Together they lay down on the pile of hay, just as they had done since they were children. John chewed thoughtfully on a small straw as Rina leaned on one elbow facing him.

"He wants me to be his mistress." Rina watched John for a reaction but saw none. Disappointed, she glanced away.

"And you told him to go to hell." John smiled.

Rina sat up, her eyes widened in surprise. "How did you know?"

"You would never allow yourself to be tied to a man in such a way. I believe you could give your love freely, with no inhibitions or obligations, but never as a kept woman." John was a bit amazed at his own thoughts as he spoke them out loud. He knew Rina was a virgin and the kiss she spoke of was her first, but Rina never spoke of marriage. Her future was tied to a promise and Camray, a promise he knew she would not forget. If she was to give her love to a man, it would not matter if it was in marriage or not, and he believed that once she had given her love, it would be for life. Yes, his Kat would die before betraying a promise of the heart.

"You seem to know me better than I do, but it is something I must work out myself. So . . . enough of my problem, we have more to discuss."

"Yes, if you're still set on this harebrained scheme, we had better plan to go to London soon and sell your jewelry. I already have two men willing to ride with us. Now, shall we go inside and tell Jake and Jenny your crazy plan? I heard them return just a few moments ago."

John rose to his feet and pulled Rina to hers. Rina squared her shoulders, preparing herself for the confrontation. Jake and Jenny were like family, and she knew they would object for fear of her safety, but she must convince them.

Their reaction was just as she'd feared it would be.

"Are ye crazy, girl? Ye could be 'ung if yer caught. 'Ave ye thought o' tha'?" Jake yelled, shaking his head in frustration. He could see by the tilt of her chin and that damned determined look in her eyes she would not be swayed, but he had to try to talk some sense into her thick, foolish head.

"Yes, I've thought of that. It's a chance I am willing to take. Anyone who rides with me must realize the risks he takes, too." Rina sighed as she looked at Jake, then turned to Jenny. "My mind is set. I'll do it with or without your help. It will be two more years before I can try to claim my inheritance. I cannot sit by any longer and watch people suffer because of Langsford. This is one way we can survive! We can take from those who have plenty to give. It's the only way!"

"We canna' let ye take the chance," sobbed Jenny, dabbing at her eyes with her giant apron. "Ye could be killed!"

Rina took a deep breath, gathering her strength for what she knew she must do. "I love you both dearly. I believe you both know that, but you cannot protect me any longer. Jake, you have spent eight years teaching and training me as my father wished. Did you teach me to think for myself and to be independent and strong just so I'd sit idly by and do nothing? My future will be determined by the promises I made to my father. I will fulfill them or die. Will you stop me from doing what you know I have sworn to do? Would you willingly destroy me in such a way?"

Jake and Jenny exchanged glances. Would they deliberately stop Katrina Easton, knowing she could not live with a broken promise? They both knew the answer. Her destiny was inevitable, and no one could stop her.

"All right, me girl. Ye can count me in," Jake conceded.

"Oh, Rina, 'tis all ye 'ave left, ye canna' sell them," protested Jenny, having kept the jewelry safe for all these years. Many times Rina had wanted to sell them, but Jenny had stubbornly kept them hidden.

Lovingly, Rina took Jenny's withered hand in hers and looked into her saddened eyes. "We must have them. I think mother and father would understand, Jenny. It will be to help many people and perhaps save some lives that would otherwise be lost this winter."

Without speaking, Jenny stood and went to her bedroom. She came back with the small leather pouch containing the jewelry and handed it to Rina, her voice full of emotion. "I'm sure yer mother an' father would be very proud o' ye, Katrina Easton. The Lord 'as watched o'er ye so far, so I believe 'e will continue t' do so."

She gathered Rina in a warm hug, tears running down her old cheeks. Rina knew how difficult it was for these two people she loved so dearly to give in to her, for they only wanted to keep her out of harm's way. But this was something she had to do. She had stood by too long, and now was the time to begin fighting back.

"Thank you, Jenny. I'll be careful, I promise, for I do not desire to hang at the end of a noose. John and I will go to London to sell the jewelry, so we should leave in a few days. The sooner the better."

John agreed with Rina and they continued to arrange their trip. In two days they would take the public coach from Sleaford to London, stopping for two nights along the way. The trip would take about a week, but they would get a much better price for the necklace and earrings in London.

The sun was peeking over the hills, turning the horizon pink and orange. Rina sat on the hard bench, deep in thought, a frown creasing her forehead. She had on her worn, brown dress and her hair was pulled back into a bun. She pulled her cape about her snugly to ward off the early-morning chill. A small tapestry bag lay in her lap; her fingers fidgeted absently with the frayed handle as her mind roamed over what had happened. Rina knew that Jake and Jenny would be angry with her, but John . . . he would be furious! Perhaps she should not go alone. She glanced up at the cloudy sky and knew it would rain again. The roads were already muddy from yesterday's downpour, and if she waited too much longer, the roads could be impassable for weeks, or months. No, she had to go now. Rina pulled the cape more securely around her, wishing the coach from Lincoln would hurry up and get there.

Yes, John would be furious with her for sneaking off without waiting for him. Why did he have to slip and sprain his ankle now? He wouldn't be able to walk for a few days yet, or travel for a week, so their trip would have been delayed. It was important that Rina sell her jewelry as soon as possible; so, without telling anyone, she'd risen early and left. After finding a ride to Sleaford, she sat waiting for the coach, just as they had planned. Rina frowned slightly, for she knew when Jenny found her note all hell would break loose. But she would be on her way to London by then.

It began to drizzle, so Rina pulled her hood up and sighed with relief as she saw the coach lumbering down the road. It pulled up, coming to a halt in front of her. She paid her fare and climbed in, sitting in the corner by the window. All eyes watched her as she made herself as comfortable as possible on the hard bench. The rig jerked into motion, reminding everyone of the unpleasant ride ahead of them. Looking out the window, Rina ignored the curious stares and watched the passing countryside.

Chapter 7

Blake pulled his collar up, cursing the rain as he looked at the black clouds gathering in the morning sky. Again, he wondered why he was even out on a day such as this, much less on his way to London! That little fool! What was she doing going to London alone? Blake's mood was blacker than the clouds that loomed above him.

He grimly remembered his argument with Rina the last time he saw her, and also the promise he had made to himself to forget her. Damn her anyway! His anger was barely in check as his mind raced over all that had happened that morning. He'd ridden over to see Rina and found, instead, mass confusion. He eventually made sense of it all, then his own anger took over. Blake all but ordered Jake to stay behind and let him find Rina. He'd spoken harshly to the elderly couple, demanding to know how they could allow Rina such freedom. He noticed the look exchanged between Jake and Jenny before she answered him. "Lord Roberts, if ye knew Rina well enough, ye would know tha' she does wha' she feels she must do. This trip was important t' 'er, and knowin' 'er, she though' nothin' o' goin' alone. But yer right, she shouldna' be alone, so please, go, an' make sure she comes t' no 'arm."

Would he ever understand what went on in that pretty little head of hers? He didn't even understand himself anymore! What on earth could possibly be so important that she would risk traveling alone? Questions continued to plague Blake as he made his way through the drenching rain to London. The roads were quickly becoming muddy bogs, slowing his progress. He knew the rain would impede the coach's progress even more. If he was lucky, he would arrive in London before she did.

The rain continued to fall throughout the day, dampening Rina's spirits as well as those of the others in the coach. Rina listened to all their complaints and ailments, only nodding when a reply was required. By the time they had finally pulled into the inn where they would stay the night, Rina's patience was nearly gone. She declined to dine with the small group. The men were overzealous in their pleading, but the headache she had used as an excuse was indeed causing her pain.

After asking for a tray to be taken to her room, Rina slowly climbed the steep stairs, thinking only of the bed that awaited her. She paid no attention to the tall man who entered the taproom, shaking the rain from his hair. He watched her until she disappeared down the hall, noticing angrily that he was not the only one in the room who watched Rina. All the men, even the oldest of them, had noticed the beautiful, golden-haired girl, and *that* seemed to trouble him immensely.

Sitting down, Blake ordered food and drink, his mood becoming even darker as he heard the whispered comments about Rina. The bloody fool! Didn't she realize the trouble she was causing?

The next morning Rina woke early and went down to the kitchen where they were busy cooking the morning meal. No one else was up and about yet, so Rina had time to enjoy her tea. It wasn't long until the guests began to appear, and soon they were on their way.

The rain persisted, making their progress slow and uncomfortable. Rina had thoroughly enjoyed the unusual spell of sunshine they had had, but now fall was here and with it the

continuous rain. Tattershall would soon feel the icy winds from
the cold North Sea, and before long, snow and ice would cover
the ground. As Rina thought of what was ahead, she steeled
herself against the discomfort she felt, for she was in the process of starting something that, perhaps, would bring a better
life to many people. If not, she would at least be comforted
with the knowledge that she had tried.

The day was long and tiring, and the night was uncomfortable as nightmares disturbed her sleep, leaving her exhausted by the time morning arrived. It was as if time had
not passed, for the new day offered the same monotonous
events as the day before. Then, finally, the coach pulled
into London. The streets were deserted and dark as they
bumped over the wet cobblestones, the noise loud in the
still night. The rain had caused the gutters to overflow and
the putrid smell made Rina feel ill. Fog mixed with smoke
and stagnant air. Tall gray buildings lined the gloomy, over-
crowded streets. Rina knew she would always prefer to live
in the country.

Blake stood in the window of his room watching as the
coach lumbered into the empty yard. So his little she-fox
had finally made it to London. He watched jealously as all
the men fell over each other trying to be the one to help
her from the coach. His eyes grew dark and dangerous.

Rina smiled tiredly at the young man who helped her
from the coach. She felt an uneasiness inside of her, as if
someone were watching her. Glancing up, she saw a man
standing at a window of the inn, his face shadowed and
unrecognizable. Quickly, she disappeared inside to the
warmth and dryness the building provided.

Rina slept later than she had intended; she'd tossed and
turned most of the night until exhaustion had finally taken
over. After eating, Rina felt a bit refreshed and started for
the place Jake had told her about, where an old friend of
his would give her a good price for her jewelry. The rain
continued to fall, but Rina pulled her hood over her head
and set out. It would be quite a walk, but she looked forward
to the exercise after three days on the road.

Despite the rain, the streets had come alive with people.
Coaches, wagons, and horses rumbled past Rina, splashing

her dress with muddy water. Smoke continued to hang low in the sky, burning her eyes as she stepped carefully among the people in the crowded lanes. Rina walked past many shops filled with bright and tempting wares. Tantalizing smells drifted in the air—breads, tarts, custards, biscuits, scones, and sweets of all sorts, mixing with the tangy smell of bitter ale, brewing tea and coffees, even some hot chocolate for those with a sweeter taste. People as varied as the products they bought lined the streets, crowding into the shops to escape the rain as others tried to ignore the dampness and cold.

Every once in a while, Rina stopped to look at something that had caught her eye in a shop window, and she became acutely aware of a tall, darkly clad gentleman in the distance. As she continued on her way, she caught sight of him several times; he was always too far away to be seen clearly, but seemed strangely familiar. Rina soon forgot him when she arrived at her destination. As she entered the small shop, a bell rang overhead. Very promptly a tiny, elderly man appeared, smiling at Rina pleasantly.

"What may I help you with, young lady?"

"Would you be Elmer Jackson, sir?"

"Yes, I am," he said.

"My name is Rina, Jake Tidwell's niece. He told me you are an old and dear friend of his." Rina saw the old man's face light up and he took her hand in his.

"Yes, yes. Jake and I go back a long way. Why, I never realized that he even had a niece. And one so beautiful! I am so happy you came by. How is Jake?"

"As cantankerous as ever," laughed Rina.

"That's Jake all right. Now what brings you all the way to London, my dear?"

"I have some jewelry I need to sell and Jake assured me you were the man to see." Rina's smile made Elmer wish he was twenty years younger.

"Yes, indeed, I am more than happy to help you. Do you have the jewelry with you?"

Rina pulled the leather bag from her cape and removed the necklace and earrings. Elmer's eyes widened as he noticed the fine quality of the expensive pieces. As he examined them, he muttered to Rina. "It is truly a fine set. I must admit I am a bit surprised at the quality." He glanced up into Rina's eyes that were the same deep blue as the sapphires he held. Yes, they would bring them out to perfection. It was a shame she had to sell them.

Rina read the questioning look in his eyes.

"They were a gift, from someone very special." A sadness flickered across her face, and her voice quivered slightly. She drew a deep breath and looked away for a moment. "Would it matter if I had stolen them?"

The question caught Elmer off guard as he watched the young woman who seemed quite calm under his scrutiny. "No, it doesn't matter where you got them. If Jake sent you, I would ask no questions."

"Thank you. I will take whatever you think is fair."

Rina felt empty and depressed as she left the shop, knowing she had just sold part of her past. She stared blankly down the street, totally unaware of the man watching her. After a moment, Rina did become aware of other stares she was receiving and quickly pulled the hood of her cloak up and started down the street. She walked only a short distance, deciding to stop in a small cafe for tea. Deep in thought, Rina didn't notice her pursuer go into Elmer Jackson's shop.

Melancholy settled heavily on Rina, an emotion she rarely allowed to control her. But the sleepless nights and tiring trip had taken their toll. She wandered listlessly from street to street. Time slipped by unnoticed. Finally, the misty fog began to swirl about, thicker and heavier, bringing her out of her dazed reverie. There were no longer many people about, and Rina began to realize that she did not know where she was. She started to look about for a cab, drifting down the different streets hoping to run into one. But, instead, she ran into trouble.

Two men stumbled down the street toward Rina, stopping only a few feet in front of her. Wanting to avoid a confrontation, she tried to go around them, but one stepped directly in front of her. He reeked of alcohol and his clothing was stained and dirty. His face was coarse and ugly, his body short and thick. The man who stood at his side was a giant. He towered over them both, a grin showing his missing teeth.

"Wha' 'ave we 'ere, Ralph? She looks lost, don' she?" The short man's lascivious stare made Rina's stomach churn as he literally drooled over her.

"Yeah, maybe we'd better 'elp 'er, 'uh, Mack?" Ralph walked up behind her. Then he yanked off her hood. "'Ey! She's a fine one, too!"

"Yer right. A real beauty, mate. 'Ow 'bout ye let us buy ye a drink."

Rina stared straight into Mack's beady black eyes. Her voice was steady and unwavering. "Get out of my way."

"Aw, com' on darlin'. Yer no' bein' very friendly, is she, Ralph?"

"Uh, uh." Ralph saw the gold ribbon shimmering in her hair and reached up a filthy hand to loosen it.

At his touch, Rina whirled around and brought her knee up, swiftly and accurately, into the big man's groin. He doubled over in pain, and in the next second Rina pulled her knife, turning viciously on Mack. His face lost all color as he stared into her cold, hard eyes and she muttered in a low, steely voice, "Make one move, you bastard, and you'll never be fit to have a woman again. Do we understand each other?"

The pressure of her knife on his crotch brought sweat to Mack's upper lip as he sobered immediately. He nodded in mute agreement, knowing from the look in her eyes that she would do as she threatened. At that same moment a cab rumbled by and Rina quickly hailed it, immediately jumping inside. As the cab pulled away, Rina closed her eyes in relief. Mack's curses filled the air, the vulgar words sending a shiver through her.

Blake stopped short when he saw Rina jump into the carriage. He had been following her and always stayed a good distance away. When he saw the two men stop her, he had started to run to help her, but before he could reach Rina, she was climbing safely into a cab. He looked at the groaning giant and the man cursing the disappearing coach, wondering how she had managed to escape them. He longed to stay and teach the bastards a very permanent lesson, but

caution intervened, and wanting to see Rina make it safely
back to the inn, Blake left, following her.

Once he had been assured that Rina was safely in her
room, Blake went to his own. He stretched out before the
fire, a snifter of brandy in his hand. On the table near him
lay her necklace and earrings, the ones she had sold that
day. He glanced once more at the jewels, wondering where
Rina had gotten them. Perhaps they'd been a lover's gift?
Blake leaned his head back against the chair, remembering
the feeling he had experienced when he saw those two
drunks approach her. Had it been fear? God, he was being
silly again, but he would certainly be relieved to see her
safely back at Tattershall. Yes, it would be good to get
home.

Rina lay in bed and stared at the ceiling, sleep evading
her. How could she have allowed herself to be so tied up
with her emotions as to actually lose her way? Rina squeezed
her eyes shut to block out the image of Mack's evil, dark
eyes. Without realizing it, her hands clamped over her ears
to quiet the curses he had shouted as she had pulled away
in the coach. An involuntary shiver swept through her as
she heard his shouts echoing in her dulled mind.

"Ye whorin' bitch! Ye'll regret wha' ye 'ave done! I'll
fin' ye and enjoy plantin' myself between yer sweet li'tle
legs yet! I'll fin' ye, slut!"

Jumping from the bed, Rina moved across the room to
stand in front of the fire and added a piece of wood to warm
the chilled room. Staring into the flames, she could not
shake the feeling that she had not seen the last of those two.
They would meet again. . . . Rina was certain of that.

"Is my life to be filled with violence and death? Shall I
ever have happiness and love?" The words were barely
above a whisper, the flames offering no answer. The dark
room was silent, except for the crackling of the fire, its
light casting shadows on the wall. Rina could feel its warmth
on her face as a pair of golden eyes filled her thoughts.

"And how do you fit into my life, Blake Roberts? I want
desperately not to love you. My future belongs to a promise,
it cannot belong to a man. So why have you come into my

life—to torment and torture me? You make me want you with every fiber of my being! I yearn for your touch and my lips burn for your kiss. You call me witch, and yet it is you who has cast a spell on me. For the first time in my life, I want to know what it is to be a woman and have a man make love to me. Damn you! Damn you for interfering in my life!"

Rina turned and slid back into the large bed, only to toss and turn some more. What exhausted sleep she managed to get was filled with troublesome dreams. When she finally crawled out and prepared to leave, dark circles showed under her tired eyes.

The rain was worse, pouring down in solid sheets of cold water, making the roads muddy and dangerous. The coach made its way slowly out of London and down the road headed north, the strong horses struggling through the thick mire. The day droned on, and by late afternoon exhaustion finally overtook Rina as she leaned against the jolting carriage, her eyes closed. The coach stopped once, allowing another person to board, his horse to be tied to the back. The rain was battering down in drenching torrents, making it impossible for a man to travel on horseback. Rina did not even bother to open her eyes. If she had, she would have been shocked to find Blake Roberts staring angrily at her.

Rina did not move for the rest of the day's trip, choosing to remain in her own private world. Once in a while, she drifted into a restless, uncomfortable sleep. After the coach had stopped, she continued to feign sleep until the coach had been completely emptied, then she went into the inn. She went straight to her room. Even though her stomach was empty, food held no temptation. Only the bed she crawled into made her smile, and sleep instantly overtook her.

Blake had noticed the dark smudges beneath her eyes, her pale face. After acquiring the room next to hers, he asked if a bath could be set up after he had eaten. The taproom was crowded and noisy as Blake stretched out by the fire. He had ridden most of the day in the cold, pouring rain and looked forward to a hot bath. Plates of steaming food were set before him as he sipped the wine he had ordered. The inn wasn't fancy, but the food was hearty and

good. After he had eaten his fill, he leaned back to smoke
a cheroot and finish his bottle of wine. The burgundy liquid
warmed him, taking the chill from his bones. The guests
began to disappear, each seeking his own room. Blake decided that was where he should be; his bath was probably
ready by now.

Rina slept deeply, soundly, her hair spread out in a halo
of gold. The moonlight from the window picked up the
streaks of copper, making it shimmer like a fine fabric. The
rain spattered against the windowpane as four silent shadows
moved into the room. She looked so peaceful, her exhaustion having sent her into a heavy, dreamless slumber.

Suddenly, a hand clamped over Rina's mouth, while another jerked her from her sleep, twisting an arm painfully
behind her back. To her horror, she saw a familiar ugly face
with evil black eyes glaring at her, only inches away. A
wicked grin spread across Mack's face as he saw the anger
in her cobalt eyes. Behind him, Ralph stood waiting. A
third man was holding her from behind, and a fourth stood
near Ralph, guarding the door.

"I told ye I would fin' ye, bitch! I foun' the cab driver
an' 'e told me where ye went t'. Then, I followed ye 'ere!
Now we're goin' t' show ye wha' ye missed out on yesterday
when ye made th' mistake o' pullin' a blade on me. No
one, 'spec'ly no whorin' lit'le bitch, is goin' t' make a fool
o' me! By th' time we be done wi' ye, ye'll be wishin' ye
were dead!"

His mouth twisted gruesomely as he spit the words at
Rina, a murderous gleam in his eyes. The man she couldn't
see wrenched her arm terribly, sending streaks of pain through
her arm and shoulder. Mack's hands began to roam over
Rina's supple curves, stopping to squeeze and pinch her
breast painfully, as his tongue licked his dry lips. She struggled and kicked, managing to loosen the grip of the man
behind her. She bit down on his hand with all her strength,
and he let out a bellow of pain, letting her go. As Mack
reached for Rina she shoved him back with her foot, grabbing under her pillow for the knife she had placed there
earlier. Just as Mack lunged at her, she brought up the blade,

slashing it across his face, then twisted about in the same fluid motion, to plunge the knife into the other's exposed throat. Blood spurted everywhere as he fell forward, his throat making a sickening, gurgling sound as his severed windpipe drew in air and blood. He slumped over Rina, and Mack gave a piercing cry.

The giant, Ralph, crossed the room and cruelly grabbed a handful of the hair he had admired so much. Completely lifting Rina's small body from the bed, he brutally slammed her into the wall, knocking the breath from her. He came at her as she slowly slid to the floor, dazed, the back of her head bleeding from the blow. Ralph's eyes were glazed with fury as he seized Rina, his massive hand easily encircling her slender, delicate neck; the other crushing her tiny wrist to prevent her from using the bloody dagger again. Her hand grew numb, the blade finally fell to the floor. The hand on her throat tightened in a deadly grip as he lifted her into the air. Holding her against the wall, he continued to wrench the life from her, the room twirling about as Rina desperately kicked and clawed. The giant was unmoved.

Just then, the door came crashing in and Blake grabbed the fourth man as he lunged at him. Rina saw them scuffle across the floor through blurry eyes, then Blake locked his forearm around the man's neck and quickly twisted it. She heard the awful cracking as the bones in his neck snapped under Blake's unyielding pressure and he crumpled to the floor, dead. In the next second, Blake was flying through the air as he crashed into the huge giant, breaking his hold on Rina. Falling to the floor, she choked and gasped for air, each breath burning and painful. As her vision began to clear, she saw Blake's fist smash into Ralph's face, the loud snap leaving no doubt that his nose was broken. The blow sent him staggering backwards, his clumsy weight making him lose his balance. Ralph went reeling through the window, his scream rending the air as he fell to the ground with a dull thud.

Immediately, Rina heard another piercing scream as people rushed into the room to see what had happened. The scene about her was gruesome. Two men lay dead, one in a pool of blood, the other with his neck twisted at a horrible angle. Mack was gone, a trail of blood leading out of the room. As if in a trance, Rina walked over to the window, her knees shaking weakly as she looked out beyond the shattered glass. Expecting to see Ralph's mutilated body, she was shocked to see that he was gone. A chill passed over her once again.

Strong arms pulled Rina away from the cold window as rain dampened her face and gown. People were crowded into the room and down the hall, staring in horror and curiosity, their voices a loud hum in Rina's ears. Blake gathered her into his arms, carrying her out of the room and away from prying eyes. Barking orders to everyone, he made his way to his own room and slammed the door, giving them privacy. Carefully, he put her down, and Rina stood unmoving, staring at her reflection in the mirror. Blood covered her white linen nightgown, the torn shoulder revealing black-and-red bruises on her neck and wrist. She could feel the sticky warmth of blood in her hair from the cut on the back of her head. Her eyes were glassy and stood out from her pale, bloodless face. As she looked into the mirror, horrified, she remembered another time . . . another place. Her dress had been stained with blood then, too. Her father's blood.

The innkeeper knocked and entered the room, the sheriff right behind him. Their eyes were immediately drawn to Rina. Blake crossed the room angrily, impatient to tend to her. He had noticed the unnatural look in her eyes and the extreme paleness of her skin. She didn't move, she just stood there, staring into the mirror as if unsure of the reflection she saw. Briefly, Blake explained what had happened to the sheriff, assuring the innkeeper he would pay for all the damages.

"Do you know the young lady?" the sheriff questioned.

"Yes, I do."

"Lucky for her you were here to help. She probably would have been killed if you hadn't heard that fellow's scream." The man noticed Blake's look of aggravation and cleared his throat nervously. "So, the two men in the other room, you killed them?"

Blake held a tight reign on his anger, knowing the sheriff

was only doing his job. "No, I killed the one with the broken neck. The other was killed by Rina. The large man went through the window but seems to have walked away, and the fourth man was maimed severely by her. I doubt you will find either of them."

Amazement entered the man's voice. "It seems the woman can hold her own. Looks a bit pale, though. Is she going to be all right?"

The innkeeper finally found his tongue. "I'll send a girl up to tend to her."

"No, I'll see to her myself." Blake's voice was firm, brooking no argument from the two men. Seeing their hesitation, he added more gently, "I assure you gentlemen, I have no intention of harming her. She's in shock and I intend to see that she is cleaned up and put to bed, but most of all, I intend to see that no one else tries to harm her."

"Whatever you say, Lord Roberts," agreed the innkeeper readily.

"Are you certain she doesn't need a doctor? She is so quiet . . . most women would be hysterical. She doesn't even weep." The sheriff watched Rina closely, his words drawing the other's attention back to her.

"If she needs a doctor, I'll send for one. That's a nasty bump on her head, but it's not serious. I'll take good care of her, you needn't worry."

Satisfied, they left. Rina did not stir. Gently, Blake pulled the bloodied nightgown over her head. Rina seemed not to care that she was nude beneath it. She winced as her arm was moved. Bruises were showing all over her battered body now.

Blake lifted her carefully and placed her into the hot tub of water, tenderly washing the blood from her body. He knew she was in shock, for she never objected to his personal ministrations. He washed her hair, heedful of the injury on her head. Then wrapping her in a warm, soft towel, he sat her down before the crackling fire. Pouring her a brandy, Blake made Rina drink it, hoping it would revive her from her stupor. Then with care, he combed out her tangled, wet hair.

While he sat brushing the long, soft strands of gold,

Blake was amazed how the ends seemed to curl about his fingers, as if they were alive. For the first time, he allowed himself to think of how close he had come to losing this woman. Blake could not bear the thought. He pulled her silent form into his strong arms. A strange warmth filled him as he held her, and like a child, she curled against his chest, comforted by the security surrounding her. Speaking tender, loving words to Rina, he felt the need to take away her pain and make her better again. She never spoke and the brandy soon made her drift off to sleep. After tucking her into his bed, Blake stripped down and washed himself, keeping an eye on her all the while.

He silently slid into bed, careful not to disturb her sleep. For a long time he gazed at her, noticing how delicate she looked, wondering at the strength and determination that made her capable of facing four men alone, in a fight for her life.

Sleep finally overtook Blake, but he was awakened a few hours later by Rina's thrashing. He tried to hold her down, but she fought him. Just as she awoke, Blake clamped his hand over her mouth in time to muffle the terrified scream that erupted.

"It's all right, Rina. It's all right."

Pulling her to him, Blake cradled her in his arms, soothing and comforting her. It seemed so strange to see Rina vulnerable, and somehow he knew it did not happen often. It pleased him tremendously to know that she needed him, if only for tonight. They both fell asleep, wrapped securely in each other's arms, Rina's head resting against Blake's chest.

Rina woke the next morning, still lying in his arms. A gasp of surprise escaped as she realized where she was and with whom. She shyly peeked at Blake, finding his golden eyes looking down at her. For a few seconds, Rina was paralyzed, unable to look away. Suddenly, she pulled away from his arms, color flooding her face at her nudity. She stuttered in embarrassment and wrapped the sheet around her body.

"There is no need to be shy, little one. Please come back.

You seem to fit so perfectly in my arms." His words were a soft whisper, his eyes full of the desire he felt.

Rina finally found her voice, though it came out hoarse and barely above a whisper. "It was you who was following me?"

"Yes, I was asked to make sure you came to no harm. If I had known how difficult a request it was, I would have declined."

Her temper flared immediately and she retorted, "I had no way of knowing I would be attacked! I'm sorry to have inconvenienced you." As soon as the words were out, Rina realized he had been teasing. "I'm sorry. I owe you my sincere gratitude, and instead, I snap out in anger. I owe you my life. How does one repay such a debt?"

"You were a fool to come alone, little one. I thank God I was here to help."

"I'm afraid I have no way to repay you." Rina drew a deep breath, steadying her nerves as she looked straight into Blake's heated gaze. "I have only myself to give."

"Oh, Rina, it's such a tempting offer, but you owe me nothing. Don't look so surprised. I want you, little one . . . I want you very much. But I don't wish for you to come to me because you owe me a debt. No, I want you to come to my bed only when your desire is as great as my own."

Rina stared in confusion at her hands, grateful yet disappointed. "Thank you," she whispered, uncertain if she was truly thankful or not.

Chapter 8

The countryside had turned into a colorful mélange of fall colors as bouquets of golds, oranges, rusts, browns, and reds burst forth. Morning fog still clung low, swirling eerily, making Blake feel isolated from the rest of the world. The air was chilly and damp, but the rain had stopped for the moment. Blake inhaled deeply of the crisp, fresh air; a hint of smoke clung to it from the fireplaces in the homes he saw in the distance. His thoughts began to drift back to the two days he had spent with Rina in London.

A smile crossed his face as he thought of what Ryon's reaction would have been if he had known Blake had spent two days and two nights with a beautiful woman and had not made love to her. Instead, they had spent their time talking and learning more about each other. It had amazed Blake how well educated and intelligent Rina was. Nothing she did reflected the coarseness of the people she lived among. Yet all the people she dealt with felt at ease with her. Blake sensed that Rina could sit at court with a room full of high-society ladies and no one would know she was a poor country girl. But put one of those high-society ladies in a room with poor working women ... well, it just wouldn't be done. Most aristocratic ladies wouldn't lower themselves even to talk to the poorer class of people.

Blake knew she was extremely sore from the battering she had received and noticed she put some herbs in her tea for the painful headaches that plagued her, but she never once complained. She laughed and talked, though her voice was crackly and hoarse, acting as though nothing had happened. Every once in a while a shadow would pass over her face and she would pale slightly, and Blake would know Rina had thought of the violence of that night. Neither one talked about it, but her nights were once again filled with nightmares. Somehow, he sensed that something other than the attack was disturbing her. Perhaps it was from a past that she never talked about, a secret Rina chose not to share with him.

His memories brought a strange feeling of contentment as he remembered holding and comforting her as she trembled in her half sleep. It seemed the only time that he saw the vulnerable side of Rina, and that he was the one to hold her in his arms pleased him considerably. He wished he could be the only one ever to hold her when she was frightened; the thought of another man doing so angered him immensely.

The jealousy that stabbed at Blake was strange to him, and he cursed himself for being a fool. Rina was strong and independent; she would never admit to needing him. The most disturbing thing about her was the quiet calmness she possessed. After all she had been through, Blake never saw her cry. She would awaken from a nightmare, terrified, shaken from horrors he could only try to imagine, haunted by ghosts he could not see. Her eyes would be filled with fear and pain, but no tears would come. Blake found it quite unusual, for all women he had known cried easily. When he had mentioned it to Rina, she merely shrugged her shoulders.

"The last time I cried was over eight years ago, when my mother and father were taken from me. I have no more tears to shed."

The words sounded hollow to Blake's ears, and he could see the pain she felt. He found himself wanting to share the anguish she was experiencing, and he asked, "How did they die, little one?"

Rina stared silently for a moment at Blake and he thought he saw a flash of anger in her blank eyes. "They were murdered. I saw them slaughtered before they could even defend themselves."

Her voice was cold and unfeeling, her eyes devoid of any expression. Unknowingly, she grasped the ring hanging about her neck, as if it could give her comfort. Blake did not have to see or hear her pain, for he sensed it and said no more. When she wanted him to know more, she would tell him. He remembered the death of his own parents, only a year apart, and the hurt he had felt at the age of six. But to see them murdered would be terrifying to a young child. Perhaps this was the source of the nightmares and terror she reexperienced each night. Blake put his arms around Rina; her body was rigid and tense.

"Is that why you learned to use a knife and to defend yourself so well? You didn't want to be helpless and unable to fight if you needed to?"

"It was one reason . . . but not the main one. You see, I know who murdered my parents . . . and I intend to kill him."

The statement was calm and matter-of-fact, as emotion-less and empty as she felt inside. The hatred and anger was there, as it had been for eight long years, but Rina was too tired at that moment to feel anything. Her head ached and her whole body was sore. Leaning her head against Blake's shoulder, she closed her eyes wearily.

Lifting her into his arms, Blake carried her to the bed and laid her on it. Instantly, Rina was asleep. Blake continued to stare at her as all the tension left her face in slumber. He could still hear her last remark, spoken so softly, and yet so surely. In her sleep she looked so innocent and young, too young to have lived with the knowledge of her family's murderer for all of these years. If only he could help, but he knew she would not accept his aid.

Blake was brought back to the present as Hera moved impatiently beneath him, anxious to get going again. He had been so immersed in his thoughts he had completely forgotten about his destination.

As he rode up to the small cottage, Blake began to wonder if perhaps he had lost his mind. It had been only one day since he had brought Rina home, and already he missed her company. All day he found himself thinking about her. His night had been filled with dreams of Rina, and when he awoke that morning, he knew he had to see her. The door opened suddenly as he reached it and he found himself looking into her big, beautiful eyes. It was as if he had no voice.

Rina broke the silence, her smile lighting up her whole face, a blush staining her cheeks. "Good morning, Blake. What brings you all the way out here?"

Blake smiled in return. "I came to see how you were doing, little one. Do you feel like riding?"

"I was just on my way out to visit a friend. I delivered her baby a few weeks ago, and I thought I would see that they are doing all right. I also made a few things for the babe. I would enjoy the company if you would like to ride along."

For the first time, Blake noticed her cape and the bundle in her arms. "Here you are bruised and battered and you're concerned for someone else's health."

"I'm fine, Blake. Really I am. You needn't be worried about me. I'll get Blackstar, then we can go." Rina turned to go to the shack, but Blake put out his arm, stopping her.

"You shouldn't try riding that black beast with your sore arm."

Suddenly, Blake swooped her into his arms and walked over to his horse, setting Rina on Hera. When she started to protest, Blake swung up behind her and said, "I'll have no argument from you, little one. I'll not be denied the chance to hold you close."

His breath was warm and tingly against her neck, sending chills down her spine as he pulled her close. After she pointed the direction she wished to go, they started off down the road. Blake's arm was wrapped tightly around Rina's waist, his palm against her flat stomach. He could smell the scent of roses in her hair as he marveled at the array of colors the sun brought out in the soft curls. Rina found it difficult to think with his body molded against her back.

She could feel the muscles in his thigh ripple as the horse moved beneath them. A stirring deep inside began to arouse her senses, warming her blood and causing her pulse to quicken. It seemed that every movement he made sent tremors through her. Rina could feel the hardness in Blake's loins, and she felt a strange tightening in her own. His lips were moist and hot on her neck as he gently kissed the bruises; the tip of his tongue traced the delicate curve of her neck. Rina's head fell back against Blake's shoulder as his hand moved to her breast.

They entered a thickly wooded area and Hera stopped when Blake dropped the reins. Lifting Rina, he turned her to him, his lips hungrily seeking her own soft ones. She could no longer hear what cautions her mind was screaming, she knew only the immense desire building inside of her, demanding release. She remembered his long, lean body as he lay next to her at the inn, his strong arms comforting and protecting her; his gentleness as he bathed the blood from her body and hair; his understanding and friendship when she had needed it most. Rina's mind reeled as it all came back to her, suddenly realizing that she wanted him! She desired him, just as he desired her! A moan escaped her, for he had won. Rina no longer had control over her own mind and body, but at that very moment, it didn't matter. Nothing mattered. Only the feel of his lips on hers, and the passion that coursed through her body.

Blake was burning with desire as Rina returned his kisses and caresses with equal passion. He sensed her defeat and knew at that moment she was his. "Oh, God, little one! You do something to me no other woman has. Come with me to Windsong, now! You'll be my woman, and you'll lack for nothing as long as you continue to bewitch me as you have."

As the words he spoke drifted through Rina's muddled mind, her senses slowly returned. When the full impact of what he intended hit her, she stiffened.

"Rina, what's wrong? Did I hurt you?" Blake could see the change in her face as anger and disbelief washed through her, quickly ridding her of the desire that had so easily consumed her.

"No . . . No, you still don't understand! You bastard!"
Rina lost all control, screaming out in her anger and hurt,
bringing her fists up to strike. Confused, Blake grabbed her
wrists before she could hit him as she continued to yell
abuses at him.

"What the hell's the matter with you? What are you
talking about?" Shaking her roughly until she quieted down,
he once again asked her what was wrong.

Rina stared into his angry, golden eyes; her own were
filled with pain. How could she have been so stupid as to
think he finally understood her? The tender days at the inn
were only a ruse to get her into his bed.

"You want me to be your mistress?"

"Of course I do. I've told you that before." Blake just
could not figure out what the problem was.

"And I told you that I cannot be bought! I don't want
the future you have offered me. I don't need your fine
clothes, fancy houses, and expensive jewels. I won't be
your chattel. . . . I'll not be owned!"

"Rina, I cannot offer you any other kind of future."

Rina's head came up proudly, her chin stubbornly tilted.
"I have asked for none."

"I don't understand you, Rina! I have offered you a way
out of your poor existence. You wouldn't have to break your
back in the field or freeze in the winter. I would take care
of you."

"Blake, I don't need anyone to take care of me, and I
don't want an easy escape from the life I live. I have my
pride, just as you do. If I were to become your mistress,
bought and paid for, you would strip me of my pride and
shame me, leaving me with nothing! Not all the material
things in this world could replace my honor and pride."

"Whore, mistress, lover! What the hell is the difference?
You cannot deny the desire in your eyes, the passion in your
kiss! You danced for me, little one; I'll not be denied what
you have promised."

Touching his angry face with the palm of her hand, Rina
once again felt the power he had over her. "To deny the
feelings you arouse in me would be futile, for they are there.
You wound me with your words, Blake, for to me there is

a vast difference between whore, mistress, and lover. A whore accepts payment to spread her legs for any man who has the price. A mistress, though a bit more selective, is still little more than a kept woman. But a lover gives freely of herself because of the feelings she carries in her heart, because she cannot bear to be without his love. Blake Roberts, it will be my choice to lie with you or even to love you, but if I do so, it will be given freely, without obligation and promises. It will be without shame or dishonor. Do not try to buy those things, for I'll not sell myself to you or anyone!"

"God! You are a complicated woman! Why couldn't I desire a simpleminded wench who was eager to please?" Grabbing the reins, Blake nudged Hera into a gallop, and the remainder of the trip was made in silence.

Blake strode into the house, an angry scowl on his handsome face. It had been almost two weeks since he had seen Rina. Today was the third time he had stopped to see her, and each time she was off somewhere helping someone. No one knew where she had gone today, and it aggravated him that she ran about alone and unescorted. Why the hell did it seem to matter so much where she was? And with whom?

His mood black, Blake filled a brandy glass and drained it, then promptly poured another one. The little fool! No . . . perhaps he was the fool! Yes, a fool to care and a bigger fool to let her obsess him this way. He had learned his lesson once and he wouldn't allow himself to be tricked again. Never again! He would have her and enjoy her luscious body until he tired of it . . . then, he would find another. She was just like the others! Rina wanted something from him that he couldn't give her. Damn her anyway!

Just as he drained the second glassful, Blake heard the front door slam shut, and Ryon entered the room.

"Well, here you are, Blake! You missed all the excitement!" Ryon frowned as he noticed his brother's angry glare. "Did you get up on the wrong side of the bed this morning?"

Ignoring the younger man's sarcasm, Blake asked, "What are you talking about?"

"Well, that new stallion you brought from America, the wild one that no one can get close to?"

Testily, Blake interrupted. "Yes, did he get loose again?"

"No, but he tried and cut his leg pretty damn bad. Old Jenkins and one of the stable hands tried to tend it. Jenkins got his shoulder pulled out of place trying to hold that devil down and the boy was kicked in the head. Cut him badly, knocked him out, too."

Blake slammed his glass down and started for the door. "Are they all right? Did someone stop the horse's bleeding?" He was hollering these questions as he ran down the steps with Ryon close behind.

"We sent for someone right away, and Jenkins and the boy are fine. She's tending to the stallion now."

Ryon almost ran into Blake as he stopped dead in his tracks. The look Ryon saw in his brother's eyes made him back up instinctively. He had seen that look before, but never had it been directed at him. Blake's voice was low as he tried to control the anger inside of him.

"Whom did you send for?"

Ryon couldn't understand Blake's anger, his own beginning to rise. "Rina, of course. Jenkins wouldn't allow anyone else to tend his horses but her."

Before the last words were out of Ryon's mouth, Blake was gone, running directly for the stables. Ryon followed close behind, stopping beside his older brother, uncertain of what to do. Blake's face became hard as stone, his gaze taking in the scene before him. His face paled slightly and neither man moved.

Rina was kneeling on the hay, unaware of Blake's presence. Blood stained everything, including her own clothes, as she worked on the stallion's leg. She never stopped talking to the animal, her voice soft and soothing. The horse moved nervously, his whole body quivering from fear. Suddenly, he pulled back and Rina grabbed for the rope around his neck. The stallion reared up and jerked her sore arm, causing her to wince from pain.

Blake took a step forward, but Ryon stopped him. "You'll frighten the horse and do more damage than good. She can handle him, Blake. I saw her go right up to him when no one else could even get near the stall. You have to leave her be."

Blake shot Ryon an angry glare but knew he was right. Once again, Rina was working on the cut leg, applying a salve, then wrapping it carefully. For the first time, Blake noticed Jenkins standing off to the side, a sling on his arm and shoulder. He had a proud smile on his face as he watched the girl. Finally, Rina was finished and stood to stroke the horse, calming it with the gentle words she whispered in his ear. Soon, he was nuzzling her and eating from her hand. When she left the stall, Jenkins came up to her, a wide grin splitting his face.

"Rina, girl! Ye certainly 'ave God's gift o' understandin' the animals. Ye were wonderful, child! Ye 'ad 'im as tame as a kitten."

It was then that Blake came alive. "You old fool! She could have been killed! And you, Ryon, how could you send for a little girl to do what all you men couldn't? And you"—his finger pointed at Rina—"I should turn you over my knee and spank you. Just what do you think you are doing? He could have trampled you!"

The two men stood, unable to speak, as Rina slowly walked over to Blake. Her eyes were narrowed and her fists were clenched by her side. She stopped directly in front of him. With hands planted firmly on her hips, she looked up to Blake, unflinching and as angry as he was.

"I'll tell you what I was doing, you bastard! I was saving your damn horse! How dare you blame Jenkins or Ryon. It was my decision to treat the stallion. Furthermore, I am *not* a little girl, and as any fool can see, the horse did not injure me! If you think you can spank me, you go right ahead and try!"

Jenkins' face paled and Ryon's mouth dropped open in surprise. They looked from one to the other in confusion.

"I should have let that giant son-of-a-bitch strangle your scrawny little neck! He would have done me a tremendous favor by getting you out of my mind, and out of my life!"

Blake's angry words hit Rina like a slap, the color draining from her face. Satisfied that he had hurt her, Blake turned and stormed out, leaving her standing alone. Silence filled the stable for several minutes before Ryon awkwardly found his voice.

"Rina, I don't know what to say. I've never seen him this way. He was angry when he came home. I'm so sorry." Ryon rambled on, embarrassed by his brother's actions.

"You needn't apologize for his rudeness, Ryon. He was angry with me and I'm sorry you both received the brunt of it. There is more involved than what has just happened today. I hope you'll understand if I don't explain further." Rina took a deep breath, letting it out slowly. "Jenkins, I'll be by in a few days to check on the stallion. If you need me, just send for me and I'll come right away. I've tended your horses for years, and nothing Blake Roberts can do will stop me from doing so again!"

As Rina rode from the stable, Blake watched from his bedroom window. He lifted his glass in salute and mumbled, "Here's to you, my little witch!" Half the bottle of brandy was already gone, and Blake was determined to empty it. By the time Ryon got to his rooms, he was well on his way to being drunk. Seeing he would get no explanation from him, Ryon went to his own rooms, leaving his brother to his madness.

The days passed and Blake never offered any reason for what had happened, and Ryon did not ask. Rina returned to treat the horse several times, but she and Blake went out of their way to avoid one another.

The sun was sinking and Blake impatiently looked at his pocket watch once more. "Ryon, what the hell is taking her so long? If she doesn't come down soon, we'll be late." Blake continued his pacing in front of the fireplace, reminding his brother of a caged animal.

"Rebecca will be down in a moment. She wants to look her best tonight. It's the first time we've gone out since the baby was born."

Once again Blake stopped to gaze at the flames as they danced, consuming the dry wood. His mind drifted off to a night about three weeks ago. He could almost feel the softness of her hair, gently curling around his finger as he brushed the long, silky strands.

Ryon watched Blake and could see the change in his face as it went from impatience to tenderness. "You're thinking of Rina again. You seem to spend a lot of time thinking about the girl. Have you bedded her yet?"

The question took Blake completely by surprise, and he flashed his brother an angry look. "What do you think?" His lazy drawl held a note of boredom, but Ryon could see his annoyance.

"No, I don't think so. Is that why you are so angry with her?"

"It's none of your business, Ryon. You might as well forget about her. I have. I've no intention of ever seeing her again." Blake turned his back to Ryon, pretending to be interested in the fire, hoping he would drop the subject that was so sensitive right now.

But Ryon was not to be swayed. "Forget her! You haven't forgotten Rina, Blake! You think of her constantly! I'm beginning to think you're in love with her!"

"In love! Only fools fall in love!" Blake felt anger rising inside him. In love, indeed!

"No, big brother. A fool is a man who thinks he is immune to the feeling and too damned stubborn to see it."

At that moment, Rebecca entered the room, cutting off Blake's sarcastic rejoinder. He was not looking forward to the dinner party given by Lawrence Langsford at Camray, having disliked the man immensely the few times he had seen him, but Rebecca insisted it would be bad manners to decline the invitation. So Blake found himself on his way to Camray for a long, boring evening.

Camray was a beautiful estate, smaller than Windsong, but equally magnificent. Sir Lawrence Langsford greeted his guests as his son, Randolph, stood in his shadow, his eyes rudely devouring all the women present. They were promptly led into an elegant drawing room to meet the other guests. It had been years since Blake had seen many of these people, and he found himself the center of attention. The last of those invited finally arrived, having timed her grand entrance perfectly. Catherine Ramsey was dressed in dark green silk, cut low to reveal the top of her creamy white breasts to perfection. Her hair was fiery red, elegantly arranged with diamond pins that held each curl perfectly in place. Her sharp, green eyes glanced around the room, stopping when they reached Blake.

Boldly, Blake watched her as she greeted everyone, making her way directly to him. She hadn't changed any since he last saw her, excepting that she was now a wealthy widow. She was like a bitch in heat, and Blake could see from the look in her emerald eyes that she hadn't changed at all over the years.

"Lord Roberts. It's so *very* nice to see you again. You have been away *much* too long." Catherine smiled sweetly at Blake as he gracefully bowed and kissed her extended hand.

"The pleasure is all mine, Lady Ramsey," he lied. Although his manner was polite, Catherine could see the bored look on his face. Grinding her teeth in irritation, she gave him her most charming smile. Blake Roberts was one of the richest men in England, the world for that matter, and Catherine Ramsey was determined to have him for herself. The fact that she had refused his proposal of marriage over twelve years ago was a minor drawback, but one that could be quickly remedied. If he had fallen in love with her once, he would do so again. After all, she knew how beautiful she was and had learned to use it to her fullest advantage early in life. It was only a matter of time before she would be Lady Roberts.

But Blake had other plans, for he knew Catherine for what she really was. For the moment, it amused him to let her try to seduce him as if he were a foolish schoolboy. As she chattered endlessly, his mind wandered, and had Catherine known for whom he smiled warmly, she would have been furious.

Dinner was a long-drawn-out affair, and to Blake's dismay, he was seated by Lady Ramsey. Elaborate courses were served, one after the other, making him wish fervently that he were somewhere else. Unwillingly, he thought again of Rina, wondering what she was doing at that moment. He wanted to forget the wench, but his brother was right, he did nothing but dream of her. His memory was etched with her picture, his senses filled with her delightful scent,

and her silky touch. Blake could not forget her, any more
than he could deny his own existence.

Dinner finally came to an end, and entertainment was
provided by the ladies as they sang and played the piano.
As Catherine was coaxed to play, Blake found himself thinking of Rina as she had worked on the stallion. Her skills
were much more important than playing a damned piano
and singing. And yet, he had wished her to be more like
these ladies. He even understood Catherine better than he
did Rina. Yes, Blake could understand Catherine's hollow
selfishness and lying ways. Is that what he wanted from
Rina?

Blake couldn't stand the stifling atmosphere and didn't
know if he could take any more of Lady Ramsey's cloying
attention. As she started an encore, Blake slipped from the
room. Finding the door to the library open, he wandered in
to see a fire burning cheerfully. He looked about the room;
the shelves were well stocked with a variety of reading
material. Several portraits hung on the walls, and Blake's
eyes were drawn to one particular painting. He recognized
William and Virginia Easton, and sitting between them,
their daughter. He couldn't remember her name, for she
must have been five or six the last time he saw her. She
looked to be about ten or eleven in the portrait. Blake recalled hearing of their murder by highwaymen and shook
his head in regret at the tragedy of it. As he stared at the
woman, something seemed vaguely familiar about her. Blake
decided he was imagining things . . . they had been dead for
over eight years. He heard a noise behind him and whirled
around. Lawrence Langsford stood in the doorway.

"She was quite a beautiful woman, wasn't she?"

Blake watched Langsford warily and nodded in agreement.

"It was such a tragedy that they were all killed. Even the
little girl. What a shame." As Langsford spoke, Blake noticed his voice held the appropriate note of sadness but his
eyes remained cold and hard. At that moment Blake knew
his instincts had been right; this man was never to be trusted.

Lawrence saw a brief flicker in the unreadable gold eyes

and suddenly felt ill at ease. "Shall we return before the ladies miss us?"

Once again, Blake merely nodded, and the two men returned to the drawing room. Immediately, Catherine was by his side.

Chapter 9

Nestled among a grove of trees a short distance from the village stood the old stone building that used to be Camray's winery. It had not been used in over a hundred years. The walls had crumbled with age and were covered with ivy and moss. The doors hung loosely on broken hinges, and all the windows were long since gone. The moon cast eerie shadows as Rina walked along the wall that surrounded the ancient buildings. The front gate creaked in the still night as the wind whistled through the iron grille, but Rina did not slip inside to the inner courtyard. Instead, she continued on around the high wall until she was in the back, where trees and shrubs grew wild everywhere, making the path difficult to follow. Suddenly, she disappeared, ducking behind a large bush and into a hidden door. As Rina carefully made her way down the steep stairs and dark corridor, she remembered her explorations as a child among the supposedly haunted walls of the winery. When she had discovered the secret entrance and passage she now walked down, Rina had been delighted, if slightly frightened, by the dark caverns she wound up in. Even her father had not known of their existence, and she doubted if anyone else did.

After several moments, she could see a light in the distance, and she soon emerged into a well-lit room. It was to be used as their stables and was large enough for five horses, with another smaller area that they could be exercised in. Hay was stacked in one corner with barrels of oats and water near by.

It was perfect, Rina thought with satisfaction, walking into another adjoining room. This was quite a bit smaller, with a table and chairs, and a few other comforts of home scattered about. Four men looked up and greeted Rina warmly as she entered. Jake and John smiled, excitement lighting their faces. They had thought her plans foolish at first, but now that the first night had come, they couldn't contain the exhilaration coursing through them. Rina looked at the two other men who had thrown in with them. For two weeks they had made preparations, buying what they would need. They all knew the countryside within a hundred miles like the backs of their hands. All five horses were solid black with no distinguishing markings, and they would all dress in black clothing. The men had already changed, their black hoods on the table before them. As Rina went behind the blanket they had hung for her privacy, they checked their pistols, knives, and swords hanging from their waist.

Donning her own outfit, Rina also felt a strange feeling stir deep inside her body. Her hair was covered completely by a black scarf. Her pants fit tightly, outlining her slender thighs; the shirt clung to her enticingly. The sleeves were full with cuffs buttoning at her wrists. The collar was high but Rina noticed for the first time that it cut daringly low in front, revealing the gentle swell of her breasts. She decided to leave it that way, hoping the men she robbed would pay more attention to her cleavage and less to her face. The belt fastened snuggly about her tiny waist, with places for her sword and pistols on it. The soft kid boots slid onto her feet up to her knees, a pair of gloves lay by her cape. A plumed hat and mask completed the outfit, and Rina smiled, knowing the people she robbed would not soon forget her.

As she came out from behind the blanket, all eyes turned to her shapely form. To cover her immediate embarrassment, Rina joked, "Well, what do you think? Shall we be striking terror in the hearts of the aristocrats?"

A grin spread across John's face, his eyes twinked mischievously. "You certainly will strike something, but it won't be terror, Rina."

A blush colored Rina's cheeks as she playfully threw a glove at him. Her expression turned serious as she sat down with the men.

"Tom, Charlie, this is the last chance you'll have to back out. I'll understand if you change your minds. There is always a chance we could be caught and the danger will always be there. If so, we could hang for our crimes. All of us will be depending on each other for our very lives, so you must be certain of your commitment. We cannot afford any mistakes." She paused to give her words the emphasis they merited. "Tom, you have a family; and Charlie, a new bride. Are you positive you want to ride with me?"

Tom looked at Rina, admiration in his voice as he spoke, "I 'ave known ye since ye first came t' us, Rina, nothin' but a small child. I could name the endless times ye 'ave given, an' never do ye ask for anythin' in return. Ye need not ask me again, for I would ride with ye into hell itself, if ye asked me t'."

Rina felt a tightening in her throat as she turned to Charlie. "And you? Do you wish to ride with me?"

Charlie glanced shyly at Rina, embarrassment causing him to struggle for the right words. He swallowed hard and said what was in his heart. "When I broke me leg three years ago durin' tha' snowstorm, I knew I was goin' t' die. Darkness fell and no one came for me. If I didna' freeze t' death first, the wolves would 'ave killed me. I 'ad no 'ope. Then ye appeared out of nowhere, an' I wasna' even sure ye were real. I 'ad 'eard the whispered tales tha' ye were a witch or sorceress, with yer strange understandin' of the beasts. I wondered meself when the wolves became gentle at yer appearance, but I 'ave decided ye are an angel, and I would gladly die fer ye."

A single tear slid down his cheek and Rina could hear Jake sniffing loudly. Rina looked tenderly at her friends, touched by their words. "I don't know what to say, except that no one can be as fortunate as I, to have such friends."

Breaking the somber mood, John picked up Rina and tossed her like a feather into the air. Her squeal brought cascades of laughter from the men. "If you ask me, she's a funny-looking angel! Who ever saw an angel dressed totally in black?"

Tom picked up his mug, lifting it into the air in a salute. " 'Ere's t' an Angel in Black."

The others picked up their cups in salute to Rina. Then, pouring herself some ale, she looked at her men proudly. "Here's to all of us!"

Silently they led their horses down the tunnels until they came out a hidden entrance in the woods. The men put their hoods on, concealing their faces. Rina's mask covered hers. Without any words they headed for Camray.

There weren't any social functions that Rina couldn't find out about from the many loyal people she knew. The dinner party at Camray was the perfect place to begin their new career. Rina's spirits soared. For the first time in many years she felt as if she could help the people she loved. The rich would consider them highwaymen, villains and thieves, worthy only of hanging, but if it meant making the lives of the poor any easier, to Rina it would be worth it.

As they neared the estate, they could see the lights glowing from the many elegant rooms. Rina's heart beat faster as they sat near the house, for it had been so long since she had been inside those beloved walls. Carefully, they made their way to the side entrance, and Rina, Tom, and Charlie quietly entered the house. John and Jake continued on to position themselves outside the patio entrance to the drawing room where the people were all gathered. Rina knew the servants would be in the kitchen, waiting for the bell to ring when they were needed, one or two servants working inside the drawing room. Silently, Rina cut the cord to the bell and checked the other rooms, finding them empty.

Laughter and music drifted to them as they stood outside the doors. Rina took a deep breath, winked confidently at Tom and Charlie as she swung the double doors open. With their guns ready, the trio stepped into the room, drawing the attention of the host and his guests. Rina stood in the center with Tom and Charlie on either side. As the music stopped and the crowd became silent, Rina took another step forward.

"Ladies and gentlemen, I am so sorry to disturb you at this time, but I would like a moment, if you please." Her French accent was thick and her smile charming. Someone in the crowd asked Langsford if it was some sort of joke, and Rina answered him. "No, monsieur, this is no joke. We are most definitely robbing you. Now, if you would be so kind as to raise your hands where my men and I can see them? As you can see, I have two more capable pistols over by the patio doors, so I would suggest you cooperate."

A woman fainted, her scream fading into a moan as she slumped into a nearby chair. "There is no need to be frightened, ladies. I assure you, if no one reacts in a most stupid manner, no one will be harmed."

With a quick motion of her gun, Rina lined them up and in a pleasant voice asked for their money. "I am certain the money will be appreciated, and please, if you ladies would be so kind and donate one item of jewelry. No, no, madame, I would not think of taking all your fabulous jewels, one will be sufficient. Just anything you will not miss overly much will be fine."

Tom collected the money and jewelry as Rina walked over to Langsford. Quickly, her expression hardened and her eyes glowed with anger and hatred. "Since you are the host of this fine party, perhaps you would care to donate everything." Her voice was no longer pleasant as she pointed the pistol at him dangerously. Their eyes locked and a chill swept over Lawrence, as if a ghost had just touched him. His hand trembled slightly from anger as she removed all the jewelry he wore. His fury was immense, but caution prevailed.

Randolph watched his father's humiliation. Slowly, he eased over a step and reached for the cord to alert the servants waiting in the kitchen. Before his hand was able to grasp the cord a dagger was hurled through the air, the blade sinking into the wall, the cord firmly skewered by its point.

"Tsk, tsk," scolded Rina as she crossed to stand in front of the startled man. "You really shouldn't have done that, monsieur. It was not very polite; besides, it would have done you no good, I took the time to silence the bell so we would not be disturbed."

With deliberate boldness, Rina stretched out her arm and pulled the knife from the wall, Randolph's face only an inch from its deadly edge. Then, smiling sweetly, she put it back into its sheath on her belt.

"Well . . . aren't any of you man enough to stop them? After all, it is only a woman and you outnumber the men!"

Rina whirled around to see who had been the one to speak and found herself looking into Blake's golden eyes. He actually seemed amused, and next to him was the woman who had spoken. Rina's eyes narrowed as she walked over to stand before the red-haired woman.

Catherine clung to Blake's arm as if he would protect her, but he didn't seem interested. Boldly, he stared at the charming thief. Something seemed familiar to him, but he knew no Frenchwoman around here.

Rina smiled coldly at Catherine. "Perhaps you, too, would care to donate *all* of your jewelry. They will feed many people."

Catherine was appalled but complied with the demand, shaking with anger and fear. Unaffected by the smoldering looks she received, Rina glanced at Blake and actually found him smiling. "And you, monsieur, do you find this all amusing?"

"Not at all, I find your company utterly enchanting, and you have certainly brightened up a somewhat dull evening."

Blake had said it low enough so only Rina and Catherine had heard his words. The look on the haughty redhead's face made Rina burst out laughing. As the light hit her face, Blake noticed the fading marks of bruises on her neck, and his whole body stiffened.

"I hope we shall meet again, monsieur, you are certainly a most delightful man."

Before Rina could turn and leave, Blake leaned over and whispered into her ear. "I'm sure we will, little one." The words were in French and his voice was strained as he fought to control the rage inside of him. Rina quickly glanced up to see the look in his eyes and knew he had found her out.

She desperately fought back the panic she felt and casually strolled away. Signaling to John and Jake, they locked the inside doors and then they all prepared to take their leave from the patio.

"I must say, you have all been terribly generous, and I thank you sincerely for your cooperation tonight. Perhaps we shall meet again. *Adieu,* mesdames, messieurs!"

Quickly they disappeared in the dark, blocking the doors behind them. In minutes, they were on their horses, leaving Camray far behind. The thieves were well into the darkened forests by the time Lawrence and Randolph had broken the doors down.

The horses flew along the road, their hooves echoing in the still, dark night. Rina felt the cool air against her face, its refreshing dampness bringing color to her cheeks. They veered off the road, plunged into the foliage, and disappeared into its blackness. Rina dropped behind and stopped, allowing the others to continue. As the noise of the others' horses faded into the distance, she sat still and listened for anyone who might follow. The night was silent, only the hooting of an owl disturbed the quietness. Satisfied that they were safe, Rina continued to their hideout. She could hear laughter as she came within distance to see the lighted room. When she entered, the men had already dismounted and removed their hoods. John ran to Rina and swung her into the air with joy.

"There's more money than I've ever seen in my life, Rina! It was so easy, and you were magnificent! Your French accent was perfect!" He hugged Rina and carried her to the table, setting her down effortlessly. The others gathered around her, everyone speaking in their excitement. They had been lucky indeed, for everyone had been carrying quite a bit of money, and the jewels were worth a small fortune.

"Rina, when will we go out again?" asked Tom anxiously.

"I don't know right now. I'll let you know. It's getting late, so we had best be tending to our horses and getting home. I want you to know how proud I am of all of you. This money will feed and clothe many people."

They all agreed and went about preparing to leave. As the men finished, they said their good-nights and made their way home. Jake figured John and Rina would like to talk alone and left without waiting for her. John waited patiently as Rina changed her clothes.

"What did Lord Roberts say to you, Kat?"

He had noticed the slight change in her expression and knew he had seen anger in Blake's eyes. Rina walked out from behind the blanket, surprised by his remark.

"You don't miss much, do you?" John nodded and waited for her to continue. "I'm afraid my French accent didn't fool him. He knew it was me."

John's expression did not change, for he had suspected as much. "I thought so. Will he be dangerous to us?"

Rina shook her head. "I just don't know what gave me away, John. I suppose I will find out tomorrow. He'll be furious, I'm sure."

Grinning at Rina, he replied, "Well, I'm not sure I'd blame him for being mad. I know myself, at times you are too headstrong for your own good. What you need is a man to keep you under control. Maybe a good beating would help."

Rina sprang at John, seeing the teasing glint in his eyes. They fell together, laughing, in a pile on the floor, John gathering her into his arms. Rina sighed as she looked seriously into the warm, brown eyes, feeling a great love for this man who had been like a brother to her.

"Are you still angry with me for going to London alone?"

"Oh, God! I was tempted to beat you myself! I've never felt so helpless and frustrated. Kat, you don't realize that a young, beautiful woman does not go about alone. You would have been killed if Lord Roberts hadn't followed you! You still have the bruises on your neck."

Touching her neck gently, John once again felt the heartbreaking pain he had felt when Blake had brought her home. How could he ever bear to lose her? He closed his eyes as he remembered how angry he'd been, both at the men who attacked her, and at Kat for being so damned independent. He hadn't questioned her about the two days she had spent with Blake Roberts but sensed it had been a special time for them. John remembered the hurt in her eyes when she talked to him of the argument they had had at Windsong.

He knew that both Rina and Blake were too stubborn to admit to themselves, or each other, what was happening between them.

Rina sat silently, curled comfortably in his arms, and watched the many expressions cross over his face. She left him to his thoughts, knowing he would talk to her in his own time.

"Lord Roberts will be angry as hell, Kat. He won't understand your reasons, and he definitely will not like the idea of a woman leading a gang of thieves. He doesn't know, yet, that you don't take orders and can't be swayed from your purpose once you've set your mind to it."

"Well, let him be angry! It doesn't matter to me." Rina knew her statement wasn't true and John was not fooled at all.

"Ah, it does matter to you and you know it as well as I do. Doesn't it?"

Anger flashed through Rina's mind that it was so obvious, and she felt foolish to be so confused. It was true, it did matter. In defeat, Rina whispered to John, "Oh, God, it matters a lot, but it doesn't change anything between us. I'll not change to suit Blake Roberts and his silly notions of what a woman should be like. I'll change for no man!"

Lifting her chin so that Rina looked directly into his eyes, John saw the confusion and uncertainty. "Do you love him, Kat?"

The question took Katrina totally by surprise, and she was tempted to turn away, but John held her chin firmly and repeated the question. Knowing it would be useless to lie to him, Rina sighed. She had been unable to ask herself that very question, fearing the answer she would find. Suddenly, she knew it was true.

"Yes, I love him. I don't want to, but I do. Whenever we are together, we fight and hurt each other. I love him and yet I hate him, too. Oh, Johnny, I'm so confused. There can be no future for us. To love him is hopeless . . . but I do!"

"I'm afraid I have no easy answers for you. I wish I did." After several moments of silence, John stood up, lifting Rina with him, then placed her on the floor. "Let's go home, Kat."

Moaning, Rina pulled the covers over her head. She sleepily tried to blot out the early-morning sun as it streamed through the paned window in a fan of prismed light, painting its pattern onto the rough wooden floor. No, it couldn't be morning already; she had gone to bed only minutes before! Drifting off into an exhausted sleep once more, Rina began to dream. In her half sleep, she began to wonder why her dreams were so noisy, and why did she have to hear Blake's voice? He was angry. Yes, he was always angry . . . except at the inn.

Thoughts floated through her mind and she turned over, hoping the noise would go away, but instead it got louder.

"Go away, *please*. I'm so tired. Let me sleep."

"It's no wonder you're exhausted, little one, riding around playing thief in the middle of the night!"

Rina's eyes flew open. Blake stood across the room. Sitting up, she pulled the covers up to her chin and hissed at him, "How dare you burst in here like this! Get out! Get out this minute!"

Unconcerned by her orders, Blake leaned casually against the wall, looking around the sparsely furnished room. He could feel the drafts of cold air seeping around the window and through the cracks. "Just what do you intend to do if I choose not to leave?" He watched Rina in her disheveled state with a mocking smirk on his face. Even in his furious haze of emotion, he could feel the stirring of desire. How gold her hair looked as the morning sun glinted off of its tangled tresses that fell below her tiny waist. He could see the outlines of her firm young breasts through that transparently thin gown she wore. His hands longed to slide down the curve of her hips and the slender length of her legs. Rina's face was flushed as she absently licked her lips, drawing Blake's attention to their rosy softness. He could see the confusion in her eyes as sleep still muddled her mind, and his bold stare unnerved her.

Rina became uneasily aware that there were no sounds downstairs and snapped, "Where are Jake and Jenny?"

A smile of satisfaction played on Blake's lips as he drawled, "I asked them to leave. This is between you and me."

"How dare you! How dare you force your way into *their* home and demand they leave! Of all the nerve!" The burst of anger fled as quickly as it came, and Rina became acutely aware that they were all alone.

"Please, Blake, go. We have nothing to say to each other." Rina looked away, unable to bear his gaze any longer. Desperately, she fought to maintain control over her fleeting emotions. The mere sight of him caused her pulse to quicken. She closed her eyes, trying to clear her mind, and jumped nervously as Blake spoke directly in front of her.

"We have plenty to talk about. Why, Rina? Did you hope to make a fool of me?"

Looking up into his furious face, Rina noticed how his eyes seemed to spew fire, copper flaring out like flames from the dark pupils. "I don't know what you mean?"

Blake grabbed Rina roughly, pulling her from the bed until she was only inches from his face. "Don't play games with me. I'm in no mood for them. I recognized you last night. You were very convincing with the French accent, but you forgot one thing. You still have slight bruises on your neck! Now, how many women have nearly been strangled to death lately who are your height and weight, with haunting, dark blue eyes? Did you really think to fool me?"

Rina's own anger surfaced, exploding in her mind. "I don't really give a damn whether I fooled you or not. What I do is none of your business!"

"It is my business when you break the law. It is my business when you steal from me!"

"You can afford it, you bastard! You all can! So do not cry to me about stealing from you! And if you are so concerned about the laws that I am breaking, then turn me in to the sheriff! I'm sure you would get a tremendous pleasure in seeing me hang. Didn't you say you wanted me out of your mind and out of your life? Well, here's your chance, Blake Roberts, for I'll not stop because of you!"

Blake let Rina go, unable to think clearly anymore. He

could see the marks on her arms where he had grabbed her. It seemed she always made him hurt her.

"Oh, God, Rina. I don't want you to hang, but that's what all this foolishness will accomplish. Is it worth dying for?" Blake ran his hand through his curly, tangled hair and for the first time, Rina noticed his appearance. He looked as if he had been up all night, his face unshaven and clothes rumpled.

How could she make him understand? "Yes, it is worth dying for! Blake, don't you see? Dying is easy. For the poor . . . it's the living that is difficult."

Blake stared blankly at Rina, as if he didn't really see her. It all sounded so simple, but he couldn't accept it. Not when it meant the possibility of losing her.

"I don't want to lose you, Rina."

Unsure she had heard him right, Rina whispered, "Why?"

But no answer came. Turning his back to her, Blake walked to the stairs and left. He didn't know the answer either.

Rina watched Blake disappear and went to her window with a sad, lonely feeling weighing her down. As he mounted his horse he glanced one last time at her, his face shadowed and unreadable. A strong urge to run after him filled Rina. She needed to feel his arms around her, loving and tender. She closed her eyes and leaned wearily against the window frame, for she knew it would never be. When she finally opened her eyes, Blake was gone.

Chapter 10

The sun streaked weakly through the mist. Blake watched the dark gray clouds as they threatened to swallow up the sun once again and perhaps rain on the small group out for a ride. In a way, Blake hoped it would; then perhaps they would be forced to turn back, ending this outing and satisfying his social obligation. Glancing to the right of him, Catherine Ramsey continued her conversation with Rebecca, trying to ignore Blake's foul mood.

Biting her lip in aggravation, Catherine watched him from under her lowered lashes. Why did he always have to be so moody? She fought to keep control of her irritation, trying to be patient and understanding, but she found it extremely trying. Catherine had taken extra time with her hair and she knew the riding habit fit her to perfection. So why did he continue to avoid her? She squared her shoulders, determined in her goal. She smiled becomingly at Blake Roberts. Well, even if it took a little longer than she had expected, it would be worth it. Hadn't she married that fat, old man, even put up with his withered lovemaking to be a viscountess? As Lady Roberts, she would be a contessa, and the thought of Blake's lovemaking caused her pulse to quicken.

Blake watched Catherine, recognizing the look in her eyes, and began to wonder what plans she was conniving at that moment. He ached to let Hera go and ride hard, hopefully easing the foul mood inside of him. But he knew the ladies could not mess up their hair. Suddenly, the image of Rina filled his mind, her hair loose and tangled as she raced Blackstar across the fields. She wore breeches and sat astride like a man, her eyes flashing angrily as she dared fortune to take her, the pair racing like the wind, all precautions and danger ignored.

"A penny for your thoughts, Lord Roberts."

Catherine leaned over toward Blake, intent on getting his full attention, her sly green eyes batting shyly. Blake smothered his laughter, thinking how coy flirtation didn't suit her. Smiling in spite of himself, Blake casually answered, "I don't believe you would like to know my thoughts, Lady Ramsey."

Her curiosity piqued, Catherine would not give up. "Surely, a gentleman such as you would not be thinking something so indecent that you cannot speak of it to a lady."

"My thoughts were not indecent, and you would be amazed how ungentlemanly I can be." Shrugging his shoulders indifferently, Blake tried to be patient with her.

"You have only intrigued me more." With an unbecoming whine, she pleaded, "Do tell me, Blake."

Seeing her determination, he gave in. "Actually, I was thinking of a wild, golden-haired beauty who can ride like the devil. She has eyes like sapphires and skin the color of honey, touched by the sun." His words were soft and sweet, a note of gentleness in them Catherine had not heard from Blake in a long time.

Catherine seethed with anger. Never had she dreamed he would be thinking of another woman! How humiliating! Quickly, she glanced around to see if anyone had overheard their conversation. Relief flooded through her as she saw the others were busy. Nudging her mount forward, she glared at Blake and made no other attempt to talk to him during the rest of the ride. By the time they reached Windsong, she had worked herself into a tantrum.

Using her whip frequently, Catherine took her anger out

on the gentle mare, making her nervous and frenzied. She clattered into the stable yard, fighting to control her mount, and suddenly found her way blocked by a beautiful, golden-haired girl with eyes of sapphire, just as Blake had so eloquently described. Sharp green eyes clashed with icy-cold blue ones as the rest of the riding party followed Catherine into the yard. Rina did not move but watched Lady Ramsey cruelly whip the mare as she tried to keep her still.

"Out of my way, girl, or I'll run you down!" The last of Catherine's control left her, for she knew that this was the woman Blake had been thinking of. Her words came out a hiss as she glared at Rina's defiant stance. The mare reared, almost unseating her passenger, making matters worse. "You old nag, I should have you shot!" The whip came down hard on the poor horse's already welted rump, and Rina grabbed at the reins.

"Perhaps she does not care for the bitch who is riding her!" The words slipped out as Rina attempted to calm the frightened mare, her own anger growing.

Catherine gasped at her arrogance; no one had ever dared to speak to her in such a manner. She lifted the whip into the air and lashed out at Rina. It caught her off guard, slapping her directly across the face, cutting her cheek and throwing her off balance. At the same time the horse reared, knocking her to the ground. Unable to control the mount anymore, Catherine hung on, trying to keep her seat.

Blake reacted quickly. He jumped from Hera and dove for Rina, snatching her from under the horse's flying hooves just before they came crashing down. They rolled away from the frantic mare as Ryon took the reins from Catherine.

Furious, Blake grabbed the whip from Lady Ramsey. His voice was low and deadly. "I don't ever want to see you mistreating a horse again, do you hear? And if you ever so much as touch Rina again, I'll be forced to beat you within an inch of your life! Now leave, before I use this whip on you." He snapped it in two, sending a chill through Catherine. He turned and in two long strides knelt beside Rina, who had not moved. Before she could say a word, Blake swooped her up into his arms and started for the house. Catherine stared after them, jealousy lighting her green eyes.

Sweeping into the house, Blake gently sat Rina on a sofa in the sitting room. He hollered for some water and a cloth, sending the servants scattering. Rina finally found her voice.

"I . . . I'm fine, Blake. There's no need to fuss over me." Standing, Rina tried to leave but Blake firmly pushed her back onto the couch. She could see in his eyes he would brook no argument, and Rina did not feel like giving any. Quietly, she sat while he tended to the cut on her cheek, gently cleaning the blood from it.

"It's swelling a bit and slightly bruised, but it's not deep enough to scar. I hate to see your beautiful face so marked, little one." His voice was soft and whispery, his words soothing and calm.

"She had no right to treat that mare so terribly." Rina's own voice came out a hushed whisper, more to herself than to Blake. "I'm sorry if I spoiled your ride."

"No, Rina, I'm the one who's sorry." He saw her confusion and continued, "Lady Ramsey was angry with me, and I'm afraid you got the brunt of it. Why are you here?"

"I came to see the stallion. His leg has healed very nicely. Would you like to see him?" Rina sensed the temporary truce they once again seemed to have and found it to be a pleasant change from their constant battling.

Blake had hoped for a second that she had come to see him and tried not to show the disappointment that went through him momentarily. Nodding, he silently walked with her to the stables. As Rina approached the stall, the huge stallion neighed his greeting. She stroked his soft muzzle as Blake watched in amazement, unable to believe the horse's tameness.

"He is really a wonderful animal, Blake. I'm sure he'll allow you to ride him now. He was merely afraid and confused by the unfamiliar surroundings."

Walking over to them, Blake gently rubbed the horse's neck. "I suppose you had a long talk with him and explained everything." Rina's indrawn breath and flash of anger in her eyes warned Blake. "I'm not making sport of you, Rina . . . honest. It wouldn't surprise me a bit if you could talk to the horse. I guess, in a way, you do, but not with words.

You talk with your gentleness and love. I only wish you
would talk to me in such a way."

"If I did, could you accept it as I give it? Or would you
want to twist and form the meaning to suit your own needs?"
She turned to look into his eyes. "I cannot and will not live
my life as your mistress! I make my own decisions, my
own mistakes! I'll be my own person!"

"And does being your own person and making your own
mistakes include robbing people? Don't you think that hanging is one mistake too many? In the last three weeks you've
been riding about terrorizing the aristocrats. Did you know
that the King has sent in troops to stop you? You've got a
price on your head, little one. I don't want to see you
hanging from the end of a rope. *Please*, let the Angel in
Black ride no more." His face reflected the genuine concern
he felt as he pleaded with her.

Rina's heart skipped a beat, and she felt extremely pleased
that he did not wish to see any harm come to her. But her
commitment to herself and to her people was far stronger
than these new and strange feelings she felt for Blake Roberts. Sadly, she replied, "I can't do as you ask. So, please,
do not ask again."

Turning away from his scowl, Rina walked out into the
filtered sunlight, noticing for the first time the commotion
at the house. A small garrison of soldiers had gathered there
and Rina knew they must be the troops Blake had spoken
of. Blake silently came up behind her, watching closely for
some reaction from her. He saw none. Without another
word, he left Rina and went to greet the Lieutenant that
rode in the lead.

As Rina rode out on Blackstar, she felt Blake's eyes on
her. When she turned to look at him, her eyes, instead, met
the intent gaze of the young officer standing near him. She
calmly looked from one to the other, her stare unwavering,
and to Blake's chagrin, unafraid. She gently nudged Blackstar into a run. Blake continued to watch her until Rina was
completely out of sight, then turned his attention back to
Lieutenant Greerson. A frown of disapproval darkened his
features as he noticed the admiring twinkle in the other
man's eyes.

"Beautiful!" murmured the man, more to himself than to Lord Roberts. When he caught the smoldering look Blake shot at him, he cautiously added, "The horse! A magnificent animal!"

An amused look quickly replaced Blake's scalding one as he watched the man's apparent discomfort. "Yes," he drawled, "a magnificent animal. Now, Lieutenant Greerson, what can I do for you?"

"As I'm sure you know, I have been sent by the King to apprehend the band of highwaymen that has plagued this area. I've already spoken with Sir Langsford of Camray. He was the one who petitioned the King for military reinforcement to help solve this problem. Sir Langsford seems to feel that the lives of all the gentry are in danger. I was wondering if I might question you and your brother. I was told you were among those who have been robbed."

"I'd be pleased to answer any questions you may have. Shall we go inside?"

After they were seated comfortably and Ryon had joined them, the Lieutenant began.

"Sir Langsford informed me that the band consists of four men and, apparently, one Frenchwoman, who seems to be the leader."

"Yes! A very charming woman, indeed!" laughed Ryon.

"What makes you say that, sir?" inquired the man, his curiosity aroused.

"Well, for one thing, she was very courteous. She asked the ladies to contribute only one item, the choice was left to them. She could have taken everything, but she didn't. The Angel in Black made you think you were making a donation to charity, rather than being robbed."

"The Angel in Black?"

"Yes, Lieutenant Greerson, the people here have named her the Angel in Black. It seems that she is coming to the aid of the poor with what she steals from the aristocrats. She has become their heroine. You could say she is a female Robin Hood."

Blake sat quietly, carefully watching the officer's reactions. It was extremely difficult to sit calmly when he knew the threat this man was to Rina.

"That's very interesting. It seems that Sir Langsford felt that this so-called Angel in Black is very dangerous. Do you agree, Lord Roberts?"

The question was directed at Blake, who had said nothing so far. Hard golden eyes met the Lieutenant's sharp green ones. "No, I don't believe they are dangerous to us. They aren't murderers, at least I didn't get that impression. As long as no one acts foolishly, there should be no violence."

"You mentioned that most of the people think of this woman as a heroine of some sorts. I suppose it will be futile to expect any help from them."

"No doubt," agreed Ryon.

The other man was silent a moment. "I am anxious to meet my opponent. I would like to get to know the band's movements and ways before I consider setting any kind of trap for them."

"Well, I'm certain if you frequent any dinner parties or social affairs given, you will get your chance, Lieutenant Greerson," Blake stated, rising when the young man did.

"I hope I can count on you, should the need arise, Lord Roberts." Extending his hand to Blake, then Ryon, he moved to leave. "I appreciate your time and I'm sure we will see each other again."

"Until then." Blake watched grimly as the Lieutenant left with his men. Ryon stood by his brother, knowing he was troubled by something. "I don't think he will catch her, Blake. What about you?"

"I pray he doesn't, Ryon."

Blake's answer was filled with an anguish that shocked the younger man. Why would this matter so much to him? Then Ryon understood and he said, "You know who she is, don't you?"

The question took Blake by surprise. "No, of course not," he lied unconvincingly.

"I don't believe you, brother, but I'll leave it be for now. I'm going upstairs to change."

After Ryon had left the room, Blake poured himself a brandy, his thoughts far away. The rustling of skirts brought Blake back to reality, and he turned to see his sister-in-law enter the room. Her smile always seemed to bring sunshine to a room, and he could smell the delicate fragrance of lilacs that Rebecca seemed to prefer.

"Oh, Blake! How is Rina? I hope Lady Ramsey didn't hurt her badly." Concern filled Rebecca's eyes as she sat on the sofa near where Blake stood.

"She'll be fine, Rebecca. It would take more than a whip to hurt Rina."

"Thank goodness. You know, sometimes Lady Ramsey can make me so angry! She has no consideration for anyone or anything. I'm beginning to wish I hadn't accepted the invitation to her dinner party tomorrow night."

"We don't have to go, you know. I'm not sure I could take her overbearing presence again so soon."

A dismayed expression crossed Rebecca's features as she considered the idea. "No, we couldn't do that. We accepted and we must go."

"You're always one for doing what's proper and expected. All right, we shall not be rude and cause any undue gossip." Blake smiled warmly at Rebecca as he saw the relief flood her features.

"Thank you, Blake." Suddenly, a thought occurred to her. "Do you think we will be robbed again?"

"Perhaps," he replied honestly. "Are you afraid?"

"No, I don't think so. As a matter of fact, it is rather exciting! I just don't want anyone to get hurt."

Blake understood her meaning. "I assure you, I have no intention of trying any heroics."

"I'm so glad." Patting his hand affectionately, Rebecca started to leave, then paused. "Ryon and I have been discussing having a dance, and we thought it would be nice to have it Christmas Eve. What do you think?"

"If it is a Christmas ball you want, then we shall have it! It has been too long since we've had a dance at Windsong. So, whatever you want, it's fine with me." Blake laughed as Rebecca's eyes lit up at the prospect of a ball. She hugged him and flew up the stairs to find her husband and tell him her news. There would be so much to do.

Blake watched Rebecca in her excitement and decided it was nice having a woman at Windsong once again. He looked at his dusty riding clothes and decided he, too, needed to change and bathe.

Blake sat across the table from Lieutenant Greerson, watching as he nervously glanced around once again. The officer's men were positioned about the estate in the hope that the Angel in Black would show up. The evening seemed endless. It didn't help that he had to put up with Catherine Ramsey's incessant small talk. She had been extra-sweet tonight, trying to make Blake forget the little incident at Windsong the day before.

The dinner was over and Blake quickly sought refuge from the crowded, noisy room. He walked out onto the veranda, the fresh air clearing his mind.

The night was dark, a new moon casting no light from the meager sliver it presented. Staring into the darkness, Blake's mind filled with thoughts of Rina . . . always thoughts of Rina. She was so damn stubborn! But God, she was spirited and beautiful! Only in her dreams did she fear anyone or anything. She possessed a strength he had never seen in a woman before, not only of body, but of mind as well, and he had witnessed the justice her tiny hands could mete out. Now she rode through the countryside, stealing from the rich so that she could give to the poor. What had she said? "Dying is easy. For the poor, it's the living that is difficult." What had happened to Rina? What caused her to treat death so casually, without fear or caution.

"Blake, darling! What are you doing out here?"

Catherine's voice broke through Blake's thoughts. He winced in aggravation before turning to face her. "I just stepped out for some fresh air, Lady Ramsey."

Stepping close to Blake, she leaned enticingly toward him, revealing the low décolletage of her gown. Her breasts brushed against him, her eyes dark with anticipation. Blake found it all quite amusing, for the moment, and made no attempt to stop her.

"I'm glad you decided to come to my dinner party. I would have been terribly disappointed if you had not come. You really shouldn't tease me so, Blake. I'm afraid my temper is hard to control."

"I noticed." Blake's voice was hard and his eyes unfeeling.

Grinding her teeth, Lady Ramsey smiled, determined not to lose her temper again. "You're teasing, aren't you? You know I'm attracted to you, Blake. I think we could be wonderful together." Reaching up, she entwined her arms around Blake's neck and stood on her toes to pull his lips to her own. She kissed him deeply while Blake firmly grasped her arms and pulled them from him. This game was suddenly becoming very distasteful.

"You could stay with me tonight, darling."

Stepping back from her smothering affections, Blake's cold eyes showed none of the emotions that Catherine's did. "No . . . Lady Ramsey. I have other plans tonight."

"Why, you bastard! I suppose you will be occupied with that little whore I ran into yesterday! Really, Blake! Do you enjoy sleeping with peasant trash so much?"

As soon as the words slipped out in her anger and jealousy, Catherine knew she had gone too far. The angry amber eyes sent a shiver down her spine, and the hard set of his jaw made her tremble in fear.

"I really hate to disturb your little spat, madame, but your presence is required inside."

Both turned to face the Angel in Black. Catherine's eyes widened with fear as she saw the pistol aimed directly at them.

"Please, I do not have all night." Rina's voice was hard, and Blake heard a note of pain in it.

Catherine's feet turned to lead and Blake had to guide her into the drawing room like a child. Everyone else was already gathered inside with the Angel's four men standing guard.

Rina looked at Blake, her eyes angry and hurt. "Now that we are all present, shall we begin with our donations tonight? Madame Ramsey, since this is your party, shall we begin with you?"

Biting her lip, Catherine pulled off a ring and reluctantly dropped it into the bag. An amusing glint lit up Rina's eyes and she could not resist taunting the woman. "Ah, madame!

I see that you have learned to curb your tongue, *n'est-ce pas? Très bien!*"

Rina turned to Blake, all amusement gone. He put his money into the bag and his pocket watch went after it. His lips were a thin line, his eyes stating what he could not say.

"So, we meet again, monsieur! You do seem to frequent these boring affairs quite often!"

"I was hoping you might decide to come. I was most anxious to see you again." His words were amusing and light, but his eyes remained cold with fury.

"What a charmer you are!" Rina retreated from his chilling look and casually walked over to the handsome Lieutenant. "I don't believe *we* have had the pleasure, monsieur."

Lieutenant Greerson stood straight, stiffly watching Rina. Bowing to the Angel, he smiled warmly and said, "Lieutenant Greerson, mademoiselle. The pleasure is all mine."

"So . . . you are the soldier sent to stop me and my men. I'm flattered, but I hope you will not be too disappointed if you fail." Rina's smile dazzled him as she glanced about to see her men finish their job. "And please, Lieutenant, do not be too harsh on your men. We came in *very* quietly. Now, what do you wish to donate to a very worthy cause?"

"I'm afraid I didn't bring any coin with me and I wear no jewelry."

The Angel grinned in amusement and said, "You are very wise not to carry money, one never knows when one may be robbed . . . does one?"

Her humor was not lost on the young man and he could not help but smile at her candor. Then the Angel's eyes turned serious as she reached out a gloved finger and flicked at the watch chain showing on his vest. "Ah, but you do have a handsome watch, monsieur, and I think it would do fine."

His smile disappeared as he pulled the expensive gold piece from his pocket, and Rina noticed the sadness that mingled with anger in his eyes.

"Now, I'm sure you will forgive me if I leave before the party is over, but I really must be going. Till we meet again, Lieutenant."

"It may be sooner than you think, Angel," he challenged.

"I shall count the minutes. *Adieu,* monsieur!"

Quickly and silently, they slipped from the room, Rina the last to go. She met Blake's furious look, then disappeared. No one moved for a brief second, then the Lieutenant moved swiftly to the door, Blake right behind him. Shouting for his men, he ran for his horse and mounted. Blake moved to where he had Hera tied and turned to Greerson.

"I'm going with you!"

The group hurriedly rode out after the Angel and her gang. Rina and her men rode hard until they reached the outskirts of the forest, then split up. With no moon and the misting fog, the way was dark and dangerous. The Lieutenant and his soldiers did not know the area; they would find the Angel very difficult to follow.

Rina flew over the rough terrain, the way familiar to her, with Blake and the Lieutenant in pursuit. The trees whipped past her as her horse tore through the thick forest. Her heart pounded in her chest, excitement and exhilaration coursing through her veins. She felt warm, even in the cold night air.

Rina continued on, pushing her mount to his limits, the noise of his racing hooves making it impossible to hear if others were following, though instinct told her they were not far behind. Time seemed to fly by as swiftly as the surrounding scenery, and soon Rina came to the secret entrance to the hidden pond and waterfall. If someone was chasing her, she could easily slip though the rock wall and hide within.

Stopping, she walked her mount into the dark shadows of the trees and turned to watch, finally hearing two riders as they approached. In the distance she saw the flash of gray and knew Blake was one of them, assuming the other to be the Lieutenant. Just as she turned to disappear behind the brush, Rina heard a horse stumble, throwing its rider to the ground. The animal's cry of pain echoed in the still night air, and Rina stood frozen, the blood draining from her as fear gripped her with its steely hand. Her knees grew weak and shaky as she turned on her horse to look into the darkness, fearfully searching for the two men and their horses.

Holding her breath, Rina finally spotted Hera as Blake slid from her back onto the ground. She heard him call to Lieutenant Greerson, "Are you all right?"

"Yes, I'm fine, Lord Roberts. My horse tripped and threw me. I think his leg is hurt."

Quietly, Rina watched the two men as they examined the horse. "It looks like a bad sprain, I'm afraid I must go back. We've lost her anyway."

Rina could hear the twinge of disappointment in his voice as relief flooded into her trembling body. Then she heard Blake's reply, his voice sending shivers down her spine. "You go ahead. I want to look around a bit, then I'll catch up with you."

Dismayed, the Lieutenant started back to see if his men had had any luck. Rina silently entered the hidden refuge and dismounted. Her hands still shook slightly from the shock she had felt when she feared Blake had been hurt.

"Rina, are you all right?"

Startled, she spun around and found herself facing Blake's angry form. Grabbing her shoulders roughly, he shook her. "I asked you a question!" His voice was frenzied and violent.

"Yes!" spat Rina. "I'd be better if you would unhand me!"

Blake dropped his hands as if she had burned him; then suddenly, he reached up and pulled the mask and scarf from her head. Her hair tumbled down around her shoulders, the paleness shimmering even in the dark night as he grabbed a handful of soft, golden tresses. Twisting it around his hand, Blake pulled her head back cruelly.

Angrily, she glared into his eyes and held his gaze. "Let me go, Blake Roberts," Rina hissed through clenched teeth.

"Do you enjoy putting me through hell, little one?"

"I don't know what you're talking about!"

"Yes you do. Every time you decide to ride out as this Angel in Black, you make me suffer. God damn you, woman! I can't bear the thought of you being in constant danger." His hold on her hair tightened as he remembered the fear that had jolted through him only moments before.

"What I do is none of your affair!"

"Until I get you out of my blood it will be." Blake's lips

came down hard on Rina's, demanding and brutal. Not caring if he hurt her, he pulled harder on her hair, leaving her no room to pull away. His tongue invaded her mouth, searching and plundering its sweetness, his lips bruising her. He seemed to draw her will from her body. Rina felt her pulse quicken and her blood race through her. Her arms went about his neck, pulling his body closer, molding herself against his strong, lean frame. Finally, his hand let go of her hair and slid to her softly rounded bottom. Grasping her, Blake lifted her hips until she was off the ground and pressed Rina against the hardness of his desire, sending spasms of pleasure through her.

Rina lost all control of reality. She knew only the tremendous desire and passion she felt.

"Oh, God, wench! You were made for me to love! Why must you torture me?"

"I do not wish to torture you, Blake."

"I should take you now!"

Rina pulled away, trying to regain control of her rioting emotions. "No, Blake! I must go . . . please, I must go."

"Yes, so must I, but mark my words, Rina. You will be mine, and soon!"

"You promised to wait until I came to you," whispered Rina.

"And that will be soon."

Whether it was a question or a statement, Rina didn't know. Turning before he changed his mind, Blake leaped on Hera and, without another word, left.

Chapter 11

Rina made her way carefully through the dark night. Silently, she slipped into the hidden tunnel that led to the inner rooms. The others had already arrived and were quietly waiting for her return. John found this waiting for Rina to be the worst time. Now that the military had been called in, the danger was much more extreme for all of them.

When he heard the sound of horse's hooves, he rushed to the dark corridor. Without a word, he pulled Rina from her horse into his arms and held her in a breathless, powerful hug.

"John, really! I'm just fine. You can put me down now."

Gently, he put her on the ground and together they walked inside the well-lit room. After congratulating her on her safe return, the others left, giving them privacy to talk.

"Did anyone give you any trouble?" inquired Rina as she sat down at the table.

"Now, we each lost the soldiers easily. They don't know the terrain, and with no moon to light the way, they didn't stand a chance." John threw his long legs over the bench and sat down across from Rina. "Did you have any trouble, Kat? You took so long getting here."

"Lieutenant Greerson and Blake came after me. The

Lieutenant's horse slipped and sprained his leg, so he turned back. We did very well tonight," Rina said as she started rummaging through the bag, examining its contents. Pulling the watch she had taken from the officer out of the sack, Rina opened it and read the inscription so neatly engraved inside: "To my dear son, with love, from a proud father." Now she understood the sadness she had seen in his eyes when she had taken it.

"Are you all right, Kat?" John touched Rina's arm and brought her back from the melancholy thoughts in her mind.

"Yes . . . John, we can't keep this." Handing it to him, he read it and quickly agreed.

"How do you intend to give it back?"

"Simple. I'll just give it to him the next chance I get."

Shaking his head, John laughed. "Sometimes I wonder if you are crazy, Kat. We have the military after us, ready to hang us, and you want to give a watch back to the man who is leading them. You don't risk your life for money . . . no . . . you give it all away. You know, you could live longer if you would stop thinking of everyone over yourself. Kat . . . you can't take care of everybody."

"No, John, not everyone, but I will do what I can as long as I can. I could not live with my conscience if I did nothing to help these people. They need me! Why is it that you and Blake insist on protecting me? I'm not a helpless little girl! I'm not going to stay at home and do needlepoint and raise a dozen children!"

Frustration overwhelmed Rina as she fought to control her anger at the men in her life. "You of all people should know how I feel! If the money we share saves one child from sickness or death, I'll rob a thousand rich bastards! And don't you concern yourself with me hanging, because I have no intention of being caught. If I were you, I would concentrate on my own safety, instead of worrying about me!"

"Calm down, Kat. What are you so riled about? Please . . . I didn't mean to make you mad." John grabbed Rina's hand and caressed it tenderly.

Rina smiled warmly at John, her anger fleeing as fast as it had come. "Oh, John, I'm sorry. I guess I'm tired."

"You haven't been sleeping well, have you? Are the nightmares bothering you a lot?"

"Yes, I'm afraid so. John, will I ever sleep without reliving the horrors of that night?" Rina's voice came out in a desperate whisper. John had noticed the dark smudges under her eyes, and she had lost some weight. But Rina had always been one to push herself, not giving in to anything or anyone.

"Kat, if you don't get some rest, you could put us all in danger. Have you tried some of those special herbs you have for sleeping?" Lovingly, John pushed a strand of stray hair from her face as she shook her head in reply. "Then I suggest you do so, and perhaps slow down a bit. You do too much."

"All right, I'll try the herbs tonight. We'd better go home." Patting John, she got up and together they left.

Rina slept soundly; the herbs gave her the deep, peace she needed desperately. Awakening later than usual, she climbed out of bed, the cold air encouraging her to dress quickly. As she climbed down the ladder to the kitchen Jenny was bustling around. A kettle of water boiled over the fire and a wooden tub sat filled with steaming hot water.

"Good mornin', Rina, darlin'. I thought ye might like a nice 'ot bath."

"That's just what I need! Thank you, Jenny."

Rina tested the water, then quickly undressed. Sliding into the small tub, she could feel the warmth soak into her body, relaxing her muscles. She grabbed the cake of soap and started to lather her body, then stopped, a pleased smile on her face. The smell of roses drifted to her nose as she stared at the small scented bar.

"Jenny, where did you get this soap? It smells wonderful!"

"I bought it from a travelin' salesman. I thought ye might like it." A wide grin split Jenny's old face, seeing the sparkle of pleasure in Rina's eyes.

"Like it! Oh, Jenny, you think of everything."

Delighted by the surprise, Rina washed her hair and lingered in the bath until the water became cold. After wrapping herself in the soft towel Jenny had warmed by the fire, she brushed her hair until it dried. After a hearty meal, Rina felt better than she had in weeks.

Pulling her cloak tighter to prevent the cold wind from chilling her, Rina quickly walked down the street to the church. She entered and heard the laughter of children as they played games with Father Murray. Joining the group, she was welcomed with their cheers and smiles. It was about an hour later that Blake and Lieutenant Greerson found Rina surrounded by delighted children playing around her. They watched several minutes before she saw them.

"Lord Roberts, what can I do for you?" asked Rina as she excused herself from the group, her surprise well hidden.

"Rina, I would like you to meet Lieutenant Greerson." Then, turning to him, Blake continued, "This is Rina."

"Miss Rina, I was told you were the person to see about my horse."

"What seems to be the problem, Lieutenant?" she asked innocently.

"I think it's a sprain. Would you mind riding out and looking at it?"

"Not at all." Rina left and spoke a few words with Father Murray and said her good-byes to the disappointed children. Each had to have a kiss and a hug before she could leave.

Turning to Blake, Lieutenant Greerson replied, "She seems to have a way with children. I was told told she also has a remarkable way with animals."

"Yes, Rina is very special." Blake watched Rina tenderly as she finally hugged the last one, ruffling his hair good-naturedly. As they left, the children hollered good-bye and waved until they were out of sight.

"I'll go get my horse." She started down the street to do just that, when Blake pulled her back.

"You can ride with me, then I'll bring you home." The tone of his voice warned Rina not to argue, and not wanting to ruin her day, she relented.

An amused look filled the other man's green eyes as he quickly averted his face to hide the smile he could not suppress. Somehow he knew Rina's easy acceptance was a rare occurrence.

Blake pulled Rina onto Hera, settling her comfortably in

front of him. Her hair spread out over her shoulders like a finely woven fabric of gold, and was sweet with the scent of roses. Instinctively, he buried his head in her hair, feeling the softness against his face. His arm tightened protectively around her small waist. Rina gasped and blushed profusely.

"Blake, please . . ." whispered Rina, trying to pry loose from his strong grip. The more she wiggled, the more aroused Blake became.

"If you don't stop moving about, you will be even more embarrassed when I stop and take you on the road." Blake's breath tickled Rina's ear as he softly spoke to her, sending chills through her. Immediately, she stopped twisting about, her eyes wide from surprise. She could feel his desire pressing against her hips and knew he could be bold enough to do as he threatened.

Risking a glance at Lieutenant Greerson, Rina colored even more when she met his twinkling gaze. Biting her lip to keep back the angry words, she tried to occupy herself with the scenery surrounding her. She found it difficult with Blake molded against her back, his muscles hard and strong. Neither said anything, both concentrating on keeping their desire in check. Finally, they arrived at the inn in Bardney where the Lieutenant and his men were staying. Blake helped Rina dismount and walked with her to the stable.

As she tended to the lame horse, the two men watched silently. Blake had been uneasy about getting Rina to tend to the horse, but Lieutenant Greerson had been told by the innkeeper that she was the one to see. Blake worried that he might recognize the Angel in Black.

"That's a nasty bruise on her cheek, Lord Roberts. Now, you don't seem to be the type to hit a woman, especially one so beautiful. Would I be intruding if I ask how she got it?"

Blake didn't seem to mind the man's question and casually answered. "Lady Ramsey struck her with a whip. Just before you came to Windsong the first time. It seems the lady did not like seeing Rina at the stables."

"Ah, yes. I seem to remember the young lady riding off on a black stallion. A fine horse indeed. Excellent breeding, if I am correct." Carefully, Lieutenant Greerson watched Blake.

"Yes. It's a magnificent animal," said Blake wryly, repeating the Lieutenant's previous observation.

"Must be worth quite a lot. I find it puzzling that she would own such an expensive horse."

"It was a gift... from my grandfather." Blake showed no expression on his face, carefully guarding his emotions from the young man.

"She certainly has a way with animals."

Nodding agreement, Blake turned his attention back to Rina. She finished wrapping the leg and walked over to the men, who stood patiently waiting for her.

"I've treated the sprain and wrapped it. I'll stop by again tomorrow. It will take only a few treatments to get the swelling down, but you must not ride the horse for a few weeks."

"Thank you very much for your trouble. How much is the charge?" Lieutenant Greerson asked.

"There is no charge, Lieutenant." Rina's dark eyes turned to Blake. "Shall we go? I have to check on a sick child this afternoon."

"Then I'll not detain you any further. Until we meet again." David Greerson nodded to Rina and Blake, then left.

Crossing the yard to Hera, Blake gracefully mounted her and helped Rina up. "Do you really have a sick child to see, little one?"

"Yes, I do." Rina turned so she could see Blake, and from the look in his eyes, she knew why he had asked.

"That's too bad. I would very much like to kidnap you for the afternoon and make passionate love to you... but if there is a sick child, I'll wait for another day." Lightly, he brushed his lips over hers and nudged Hera into a trot.

Lieutenant Greerson stood in the doorway of the inn, watching the couple on the horse. He saw the intimate way Blake held Rina and the tender kiss he had given her before they left. Smiling, he turned and went inside.

* * *

The fire crackled and spit red embers out in a spray as the wood popped under the consuming blaze. Enjoying the warmth against her face, Rina stared into the orange flames, her brush forgotten by her side. Her just-washed hair curled softly about her shoulders, the glow of the fire bringing out the streaks of copper and gold. The smell of roses still lingered in the air from the bath Rina had luxuriated in only moments before. A light snow had begun to fall, covering the ground with a soft, white blanket. It was Christmas Eve and Rina wondered how the ball at Windsong was going. Visions of Blake in the arms of other women caused her much anxiety and depression. Everyone of importance was to be there tonight. Rina's thoughts changed and she forgot the other women, her mind focusing on the trap that had been carefully set for the Angel and her men.

Lieutenant Greerson had convinced Blake to allow him to set up an ambush. Convinced that they would strike at the ball, the Lieutenant had called in more men and planned to position them at all possible escape routes. His plan was perfect!

Or so he thought. Rina smiled to herself. Even before she learned of the trap, she had decided to pass up the ball. Too many people would be there, and she did not wish to take any chances with the lives of her men or those attending the dance. Greerson's mistake was in thinking greed ruled them, but no amount of money was worth dying for. No, tonight the Angel would not steal from anyone! Tonight, she wanted only to give.

It was late, Jake and Jenny had gone to bed. John had left earlier, unaware of Rina's plans. Slowly, she got to her feet and pulled on her pants and shirt. They were not her worn riding pants but her black ones, and silently she donned the rest of the Angel in Black's outfit. In a small bag she placed her ragged clothes; then, taking only one pistol and her knife, she left. The cape she wore was her own and tonight she rode Blackstar.

The snow muffled the hoofbeats as Blackstar and his mistress pounded down the road to Windsong. As she neared the estate, she slowed her pace and looked warily around her. When she came into view of the house, she silently slid off Blackstar's broad back and made her way to the stables. She managed to get inside undetected, breathed a sigh of relief, and guided the horse to an empty stall. Hearing a noise behind her, she whirled about, pulling her pistol from her belt.

Jenkins stood there, the surprise on his face quickly replaced by concern. "Lord! What are ye doin' 'ere? Ye were warned tha' they are waitin' fer ye, Rina, girl! 'Ave ye lost yer mind?" He glanced about nervously.

Then it was Rina's turn to be shocked. "How did you know it was me, Jenkins?"

"Ah, come now, girl. There are some of us who know ye better than ye do yerself! Ol' Jacob an' me figured it out right off. Now, tell me, Rina, why are ye 'ere?" Jenkins' brows wrinkled in worry as he thought of the danger she was in.

"I'm alone tonight. No need to fret. I'm not here to rob anyone. I just hate to disappoint the Lieutenant after he went to so much trouble." Rina's eyes lit up teasingly as she smiled at Jenkins.

"An' tell me, ye foolish girl, just 'ow do ye intend on gettin' out o' 'ere after ye pay yer visit t' the man?"

He could see the hesitation in Rina's expression before she finally answered. "I don't plan to leave tonight, I'm staying." As she looked at Jenkins her face flushed, and he understood her meaning. "If you will see that these clothes get to Jacob, I'll leave early in the morning as Rina." Handing him the bag and her cape, Jenkins gently took her hand in his own, gnarled one.

"Ye love 'im, don't ye, lass?"

"Yes, Jenkins, I do. And I want to be with him tonight."

As the two stood silently, Jenkins understood, and prayed Lord Roberts would return the love he saw in Rina's blue eyes.

"I'll take care o' everythin', includin' this beast o' yours. Now go, but be careful." He kissed her affectionately on the cheek and sent her on her way.

Rina didn't know when she had decided to go to Blake. Perhaps it was the day she had treated the Lieutenant's horse . . . it didn't really matter. She knew only the tremendous desire to be with him, to feed the love that was growing inside her. Katrina had argued with herself for hours, but her heart was stronger than her mind. She wanted to share tonight with the man she loved . . . tomorrow, well . . . she would face it when it came.

Knowing her way around Wingsong from her many visits over the years, Rina easily found the library. Impatiently, she waited until all the guests had gone. Ryon and Rebecca said good night to the Lieutenant and Blake, leaving them alone. Guessing that the Lieutenant would be the last and most reluctant to leave, Rina hoped Blake would offer him a brandy before leaving. Her hunch was correct.

Disappointed that the Angel had not shown up, the young man gladly accepted Blake's offer. The fire was burning brightly as the two men entered the library, shutting the door behind them.

"Lieutenant Greerson, I tried to warn you that the ball would be too large a gathering for the Angel to chance a robbery." Blake poured two snifters of brandy and handed one to Greerson.

"That's just what I thought would attract her. There would be much to gain in jewels and coin tonight. So why didn't she come?"

"You thought greed would bring her here tonight?" At the Lieutenant's nod Blake shook his head. "No, the Angel isn't a thief because of greed. She does it for other reasons, for humanity, love, and compassion, but never greed."

"Lord Roberts, just how is it you seem to understand so much about this woman?"

"You would too if you saw and heard what I do. I see the love these people have for the Angel and what she does. After all, she does it for them. I see the way their lives have improved since she started thieving. I know that it's your duty to capture this woman, but I cannot help feel a bitter sadness at the thought." Blake took a deep swallow of his drink, thinking he would actually die a bit inside if she was caught.

"I only know that she has committed crimes against the Crown, and it is my sworn duty to see that she is captured and punished. I cannot allow my heart to rule my actions. She must be stopped! No matter what her reasons may be."

"I admire your dedication, Lieutenant Greerson. But I must disagree."

Stepping out from behind the heavy drapes, Rina pointed her pistol at the two surprised men. "Perhaps what I do is against the law, but I assure you, my reward is much more gratifying than yours, monsieur. You may gain the favor of the King himself, but mine comes from the people. You see, my heart *does* rule my actions, and I hope never to change."

Finding his tongue, the officer asked, "Even if it means forfeiting your life?"

"*Oui*, I'd gladly do so. It is not so difficult to die, Lieutenant Greerson. It is the living that provides the challenge!"

Silence filled the room as the young man looked at the Angel in Black, confused by her presence. "Why are you here? The guests have all gone. You have little to gain by robbing us."

"I knew of the trouble you went to to set a perfect snare for me and my men. I hated to disappoint you, monsieur. Tonight is Christmas Eve, a time for giving, not taking." Walking over to the man she directed her words to, she could see the questions in his eyes. "Merry Christmas, Lieutenant Greerson."

Handing him a small box, Rina watched as he opened it to find his watch neatly tucked among the paper. "I read the inscription inside and knew it must have great sentimental value. Since I do allow my heart to rule my actions, I could not keep it."

David stared at the watch and read the familiar words, grateful to see them and feel the precious object once more. He had thought he would never see this treasure again.

When he looked up to say something, the Angel was gone and the door stood open. Alarmed, he ran over to it and looked out into the empty hall. He turned to Blake, knowing Blake had seen her go, but had said nothing.

"I must go after her." Hesitating a moment, the Lieutenant turned and left. Once outside he gathered his men, but found that no one had seen any sign of her. Insisting she couldn't just disappear into thin air, he rode off to search for her.

The night became still once again and Blake poured himself another drink. He lifted the glass in a salute and murmured, "To the Angel in Black." After draining the glass, he walked slowly up the stairs to his bedchamber. There was nothing he could do for Rina now.

Once inside, he pulled off his jacket and vest and threw them carelessly over a chair. Blake stood before the fire, his mind wandering to another night, the night he sat before a fire gently brushing Rina's long, velvety hair, holding her trembling body. Suddenly, he could even smell the delicate scent of roses in the air. Twirling about, he came face to face with Rina.

"Am I dreaming, little one? Or are you real?" He whispered the words, afraid any noise would cause her to disappear into the mist of dreams, leaving him painfully alone again.

Reaching up, Rina caressed his cheek, her hand tingling from the touch. "I am real, Blake. You're not dreaming."

"Why have you come?" Without realizing it, Blake held his breath, fearing the answer would not be the one he wished to hear.

"I want you, Blake. I need you tonight." Rina spoke so softly that Blake wasn't sure he had heard her.

"Oh, God! I've wanted you forever, and now that you are here, I am almost afraid to believe it." His voice trembled slightly from the desire he had kept in check for so long.

"I am here and I shall not go." As she put her arms around his neck Rina's own voice was husky with passion. "Blake, we will have tonight, but I can promise you no more. Love me, if only for this one night, and I shall love you."

All the love Rina felt shone in her gaze as she searched Blake's face for his answer. The warm tenderness in his eyes was his reply, and he slowly bent his head to taste her lips. The kiss began softly, tenderly, each savoring the moment as the rest of the world melted away. Neither thought of the past or the future, only of each other. As the kiss grew more passionate, Rina felt the stirring deep within her as her pulse began to quicken. Blake's lips, hungry and warm, moved to her neck. He sent shivers through her, his hands expertly caressing her back and hips. Standing back, Rina shyly began to remove Blake's shirt, kissing his chest and running her nimble fingers teasingly through the hair that covered it. Each touch made Blake delirious, but he fought to control himself, wanting to prolong the magic.

Gently, he removed Rina's clothing and quickly shucked the rest of his. The flames cast shadows over their bodies as Blake looked at his golden girl. She was even more beautiful than he remembered. He tenderly lifted her into his arms and carried her to the bed. With her arms still wrapped tightly about Blake's neck, Rina pulled his lips to hers and hungrily possessed them. She felt his hands touching her intimately, leaving a trembling wherever they trailed. Her own small hands boldly took on a life of their own, exploring with delight his lean, muscular body. She could feel his desire for her as she instinctively hugged him to her with her long, slender legs.

Blake's lips moved to one perfectly rounded breast, and he suckled the already hard nipple, his tongue teasing and wet. Rina could feel the throb in her loins as he moved from one rosy-tipped breast to the other. Her senses reeled as her hips began to move against his and a low moan escaped Blake as he fought to maintain control. His warm lips traced the slender curve of her neck, then he kissed the base of her throat, where her pulse was beating wildly. His tongue licked out to feel her cheek and ran along her closed lids, where he tasted her soft, fluttery lashes. Wandering further, Blake nipped at her earlobe and quickly kissed it afterward, his hands continuing their exploration of her silken body.

Once again, he claimed her sensuous lips, his tongue plundering the sweetness they offered, only to wander back to her delicious breasts. He left a trail of fire as he made his way down to her soft, flat stomach, playing with her tiny belly button. Rina thought she would go mad with desire, with her wanting of this man. Her hips arched in the ancient rhythms of love, seductive and sensuous.

A small gasp escaped Rina as Blake went even lower, his warm lips and tongue touching the center of her passions.

A new and startling sensation began to build inside of Rina
as Blake expertly sent her higher and higher, and a strange
and wonderful warmth spread through her like fire. The
intensity of desire climbed until Rina felt a tremulous explosion within her. Yelling his name, she dug her nails into
his back as the tremendous pleasure shattered through her.
Slowly, she drifted down, feeling wonderfully and totally
drained. She pulled Blake to her. His lips tasted of herself.

Gently, Blake started the fires in Rina again, making her
pleasure his own. His leg parted hers and his manhood found
her softness, moist and ready. Wrapping her slender, muscular legs around his hips, he slowly entered her, the silky
warmth sending waves of pleasure through him. He paused
momentarily as he felt the resistance of her virginity, his
eyes questioning her. Smiling in answer, Rina urged him
on with her hips, and as she arched against him, she sent
his hardened shaft deeper within her. Rina felt the sharp
pain as he destroyed her maidenhead, but it only added to
her passion. Blake began a slow rhythm with his hips as
Rina felt the wonderful sensation building inside her again.
Her passionate response was wild and unguarded, giving
Blake pleasure he had never dreamed existed. Their desires
peaked together, leaving them spent and trembling in each
other's arms. As Rina lay curled in Blake's arms, she felt
truly happy, knowing the love she had given was total and
complete. Then they slept.

Chapter 12

The sun was barely peeking over the horizon, casting its first rays of light on the snow-covered land as the streaked fans of pale yellow plunged through the misty fog. Rina stretched lazily, a content smile on her lovely face. Blake looked so peaceful and Rina lovingly caressed his face, the slight roughness of a morning beard scratchy against her soft palm. Unwillingly, she slipped from under the warm covers and out of Blake's arms. She dressed silently, her mind still clouded from his lovemaking.

"Where do you think you're going?"

Turning back to look at the bed, Rina found golden eyes watching her as Blake leaned casually on one arm. As she looked at him all the feelings they had shared that night flooded through her, making her knees weak.

"Where are you going, little one?"

Rina longed to go to him but knew it could not be. "I must go, Blake; it will be full light soon." She picked up her bag and walked over to the bed.

Sitting up, Blake grabbed her arm, a frown creasing his forehead. "There is no need for you to go, Rina. You will stay here now."

Rina stared at him in confusion. "I have no intention of staying here." ·

"Now, don't be stubborn, Rina. After last night I have no intention of letting you go."

Rina's eyes widened, her anger beginning to surface. "You've got to be joking!"

His hold on her arm tightened possessively. "No... You're mine now!"

"Yours! You egotistical bastard! I belong to no one!" Rage blinded Rina as she twisted free of his hurting grip. "I promised you last night, no more! I've made myself very clear! I will not be your whore!"

"You are already my whore!" His voice was low, barely suppressing the choking fury he felt at her stubbornness.

The words stabbed at Rina's heart, and instinctively she slapped Blake hard across the face. "You bastard!" hissed Rina as she turned to leave. Before she could make it to the door, Blake blocked it with his bulk.

"What does it take to buy you, Rina? I know you can be bought!" Reaching over to the table, Blake pulled the drawer open and picked up a leather pouch. Throwing it at her, he sneered, his words ugly and cruel, "Is that what it takes? Jewels? Who gave you those pretty trinkets? Did you promise him yourself... only not to deliver! What is it you expect from me? What tricks are you planning in that devious little mind of yours?"

Rina stood frozen, unable to move as she stared mutely at the leather pouch. She didn't need to look inside to know what it held, she knew the worn item well. Inside were the diamond and sapphire pendant and earrings her father and mother had given her. He must have followed her to the pawnshop and assumed they were a lover's gift. Where else was he to think she had gotten such expensive jewelry.

"Tell me, bitch! What made you come to me?" Seizing her shoulders painfully, he shook her, yelling uncontrollably. "You were a virgin! I want to know what price you have put on your virtue!"

Unable to stand any more, Rina swung at Blake, her hurt turning to rage as she struck him with her fist, splitting his lip. She clawed and kicked, wanting only to hurt him as he had hurt her. Finally, Blake managed to grab both her wrists in his steely hands and pull her to him, his face only inches from hers.

"Who gave you the jewelry? How many others have tried to lay you on your back, witch?" Each word tore at Rina, draining her of her will. He could not have been crueler if he had taken a whip to her.

Evil jealousy wound its way firmly into Blake's heated mind, his temper totally out of control. "Perhaps one of them was my own grandfather! Why else would he have been so fond of you? Or my brother? Tell me what you are about, I'll not be made a fool of! If you're considering blackmail, bitch, it won't work! You'll not draw me into your conniving trap! God damn it! Tell me, you little whore!"

Something snapped in Rina as he yelled the horrendous insults at her. Never had she felt such pain. From deep within her erupted all her anguish and fury as she screamed, "No!"

It echoed in the large room, and she brought her knee up into Blake's naked groin. Loosing his tight hold on her, he doubled over, gasping for breath as he fell to the floor. Desperately, Rina fumbled with the knob and finally opened the heavy door blocking her way. As she ran from the room she passed a confused Jacob and nearly ran into Ryon as he stumbled into the hall, a robe carelessly thrown on in his haste. She pushed past him and flew down the stairs and out of the house.

Blake grimaced in pain, grabbed his breeches and shouted for everyone to mind their own damn business. Making his way to his bed, he sat on the edge to pull on his pants. "Damn it! Damn her and her stubbornness! What did the deceitful chit want!"

To give herself to him made no sense. She refused to be his mistress and she knew he would not marry her, so why? The question went unanswered as Blake quickly pulled on the rest of his clothes and ran out.

When he reached the stables, Jenkins had already saddled Hera and had her waiting. At the questioning look, Jenkins stated, "I saw 'er storm out o' 'ere madder than 'ell, and I figured ye would no' be far behind."

Storming out of the yard, Blake raced after Rina. He must have the answers, even if he had to beat them out of her!

Rina felt numb, unable to think as her throat constricted, with tears that failed to come and ease her pain. She loved him, but he cared nothing for her. He thought her a whore, to use until he tired of her body, then carelessly throw away. Never had she felt so empty and alone.

When she rounded a curve, she almost ran straight into Lieutenant Greerson. Blackstar reared in surprise as their mounts nearly collided, and Rina tried desperately to hold on. She fell to the ground in a heap. Instantly, the Lieutenant was by her side.

"Are you hurt?" he asked urgently.

Rina quickly gathered her wits and started to stand, the young man helping her up. "I'm fine, thank you," mumbled Rina.

"You could have been killed! Why on earth were you riding so carelessly fast?"

Pulling from his grasp, Rina took out her anger on him. "I ride fast because I *like* to!"

David took a step back, the anger in her eyes warning him to be wary.

At that moment Blake thundered up and jumped from Hera before she had completely stopped.

"Rina, are you all right?" He grabbed her and looked her over to see if she was injured, then felt foolish to have shown such concern over her welfare.

She pushed him away, yelling, "Leave me alone, Blake Roberts! I never want to see you again!" She started to leave but Blake stopped her.

"We have a few things to discuss, Rina." Blake's voice was hard as he tried to control himself in front of the other man.

"I believe you made everything *perfectly* clear only minutes ago. Now let me make something *perfectly* clear for you. I don't *ever* want to see you again! Not ever!" Rina was nearly hysterical.

"Rina! I must talk to you. I *will* know why!"

Rina stopped and looked at Blake, a blank expression in

her eyes. "It's too late, Blake, leave me alone." She walked over to her horse and Blake came up behind her. When he touched her, she turned, her eyes flashing dangerously as she hissed, "I hate you! Don't ever touch me again, or I'll stick my knife into your cold, unfeeling heart!"

Rina mounted the black stallion and left without another word. This time Blake made no move to stop her. His pride would not allow him to go after her. He would not make a fool of himself! He did not need her, and he would easily forget her!

"Good God, man! What did you do to make her so furious?" Lieutenant Greerson exclaimed, bringing Blake's attention back to him.

"It's not important. No woman's worth going through hell for." He turned, mounted Hera, and left.

The young officer watched Blake as he rode off, amused by what he had seen. "Ah, Lord Roberts, I believe you are wrong. For this woman you will go through hell . . . but you just don't realize it yet."

The weeks passed slowly, agonizingly, as Blake desperately tried to forget Rina. He buried himself in his work, hoping it would occupy his mind and exorcise the tormenting memories. But it seemed that no matter how hard he worked, thoughts of her luscious body or enchanting eyes would creep in and shatter his willpower. Several times he caught himself riding to Tattershall. He always stopped himself before he arrived. His pride would not allow him to seek her out.

Slamming his fist down on the desk, Blake shoved back his chair angrily. What power did she have over him? Even the comely servant girls no longer tempted him. It seemed he wanted Rina more now than he had before. Their one night of lovemaking had only increased Blake's insane desire for her. Never before had he experienced such fulfillment with a woman. Rina was as passionate in love as she was in everything else she did. How could one woman be so intriguing? So beautiful? And so stubborn! He walked over to the brandy, poured himself a generous portion, and drained it.

"I don't think that will help solve your problem, Blake."

Ryon entered the room and casually took a seat. Blake's scowl would have warned any other man off, but Ryon was used to his brother's surly moods. In fact, it seemed Blake was in a black mood all of the time lately.

"What do you want, Ryon?" snapped Blake impatiently.

"Why don't you go to her? I am sure she is as miserable as you are."

Blake sloshed some more of the amber liquid into his empty glass. "You always were too nosy for your own good. As for Rina, she is out of my life for good. She was more trouble than she was worth."

"You're lying again. Really, Blake, I'm not blind but I am beginning to think that perhaps you are. For the first time in my life, I believe you're being quite foolish. Maybe stupid is a better word. God, man! You're in love with her and just too damned stubborn and proud to admit it."

Blake smashed his glass into the fireplace and in two long strides had reached his brother. He grabbed him roughly by the shirt and pulled Ryon to his feet, drawing his fist back to strike.

"Go ahead! Hit me if it will make you feel better!" Ryon made no move to free himself.

Confusion quickly took over as Blake realized what he had been about to do. It sickened him to think he'd been about to strike his very own brother. And for what? Releasing Ryon, Blake walked from the room, leaving his brother staring sadly at his retreating back.

Once in his rooms Blake sat before the fire trying to make sense of his thoughts and feelings. His brother's words kept echoing in his mind. Did he love her? Even if he did, Rina had made it clear how much she hated him. At one time, she may have loved him, but he had changed that love to hate. He deserved his own misery. Visions of the love shining in her eyes when she had finally come to him floated before him. Then suddenly, he saw them filled with hate, as they had been when she had told him to leave her be.

Rina had not stopped her thieving and had made no attempt to see Blake. Perhaps it was best that he leave for a while. He did have some business to attend to in London.

He would leave in the morning. Maybe then he could get Rina from his mind and from his heart.

Blake awoke feeling the pain in his head from too much drink, just as he had done too many times in the last two months. His mind was immediately filled with thoughts of Rina. It seemed no matter how hard he tried to rid himself of the memories, they were still there, haunting and arousing him.

The room filled with the first pink rays of morning that filtered through the fog that wrapped itself around the gray stone buildings of London. Blake swung his long legs over the side of the bed and paused when a dull throb pounded in his head. The fire had long ago burned out and left the room chilled, but Blake did not seem to notice as he moved to the window. He pulled the heavy drapes aside to watch the sun make its daily pilgrimage into the gray sky.

Blue eyes danced before him. He could see the sparkle of her laughter lighting them, and her luscious lips curving delightfully, showing even white teeth. He could almost feel Rina's satiny smooth skin, the color of honey, and the firmness of her small breasts and roundness of her hips. He felt the long, well-muscled legs that wrapped around his own, slender arms pulling him closer so that her lips could taste his own.

Was she vixen or angel? What was this torturous spell she had cast on him, leaving him to endure this private hell? He was like a schoolboy, left with no will of his own. She possessed him, seduced him, and haunted his every moment. What must he do to rid himself of her forever? Or was it even possible? Any more than it was possible to rid himself of his own soul?

Question after question barraged him, leaving him confused and tormented, for there were no answers. If he saw her, would it really change anything? Would he continue to say things to hurt her, and would she continue to fight him every step of the way? Would they always battle, instead of making love? Blake had no answers.

Chapter 13

The bitter cold wind whistled through the bare trees, making the thick fog swirl about eerily. Rina pulled her blanket closer about her shoulders as she felt the chill in the room. Awakened by a nightmare, she sat curled up in bed, her mind reeling from the memories that had once again assaulted her slumber. Rina had had the immense pleasure of robbing Lawrence and Randolph Langsford that night, but as usual it brought back the horrors of the past.

There had been a dinner party at one of the country estates; and the Angel and her men had planned to rob it. When they arrived, Rina checked out the security Lieutenant Greerson had set up. Smiling to herself, she thought about how much more careful the young Lieutenant had become, for he made it much too dangerous for them tonight. Silently, they left. But the night was not to be a total loss, for Rina decided to wait for the guests as they started home. The Lieutenant could not be everywhere. The Angel hit three different carriages bound for their estates, catching them totally off guard. She had saved Langsford until last, picking the same spot where he had attacked her and her parents years before. Rina could not help but smile now at the irony, even if Langsford had not been aware of it. He and his son were livid with anger as the bandits waylaid the carriage.

Rina had slid gracefully off her horse and aimed a pistol directly at the two men as they stood shaking with wrath. She could see in their eyes how badly they wanted to react to her challenge.

"Good evening, messieurs! I trust your dinner was pleasant." Even though her words were honeyed, they held a note of hatred that Lawrence and Randolph could not ignore. "Now, if you would be so kind, it's time for your donations. Tonight, I want everything you have."

Having known there would be strict security at the party, Lawrence had never dreamed of being robbed and had worn a lot of expensive jewelry. Almost choking on his anger, he answered, "You will hang for this, you bitch!"

She stepped daringly close, her eyes flashing, and smiled wickedly. "If I am to hang for thievery, I would just as soon hang for murder, Monsieur Langsford! It would give me much pleasure to see you die!"

Lawrence's face drained of all color as he stared into the hardest blue eyes he had ever seen. He felt a sudden chill run through him, as if death had touched him. Standing in the same spot where he had murdered his half-brother and his family, Lawrence knew fear. He had a dreadful, strange feeling that this woman knew.

Turning her attention to Randolph, Katrina noticed the angry twitch in the chiseled line of his jaw and smiled in amusement, undaunted by the mute rage in his dark eyes.

"And now, it is the son of the jackal's turn," she taunted carelessly.

Unable to endure his humiliation any longer, Randolph suddenly moved. Bringing his hand across Rina's face, he knocked her off her feet. Leaping for his pistol on the ground, he rolled and brought it up to fire. But Rina was quicker, and as Randolph's eyes met hers, her own pistol blazed, shooting the weapon from his hand. Lawrence had no time to move, the four other bandits having leveled their own weapons on him.

"You are a foolish man and a lucky one, too. I am in a most generous mood tonight, but let this be a reminder that to be so foolish again would result in your immediate death. As you can see, monsieur, I know how to use this weapon." Rina felt quite amused by Randolph's futile attempt. It provoked him even further when she laughed outright to see him sprawled on his backside.

She walked over to her mount and cried, "Beware, gentleman! I hear that ghosts haunt this road! And late at night you can hear the screams of terror from those who died here!"

Deliberately, she sent the carriage careening precariously down the road, minus its two distinguished inhabitants. Smiling contentedly, Rina tipped her hat to the men. "We will meet again. That, I guarantee, monsieurs. *Adieu!*"

As Rina brought her attention back to the present she was still smiling. Then, suddenly sober, she knew that the time would soon come when she'd fulfill her promise to her father.

A sigh escaped Rina, and stretching out her legs, she climbed from her narrow cot. Looking from the small attic window, she watched the first rays of dawn touch the sky. Sadness overwhelmed her as thoughts of Blake haunted her. He was in London now, far away from her touch. Rina remembered the tenderness of his lips as they claimed hers, leaving her breathless and weak. When he laughed, his eyes crinkled up and boyish dimples creased his cheeks. His hands were strong yet gentle as they aroused her body. His whole body was muscled and hard. Rina's breath quickened as she envisioned it.

Blake had made Rina a woman, bringing out her passions to their full potential. Now he was gone, leaving her empty and alone. As she stood staring into the quiet countryside, Rina's words came back to torment her: I hate you! . . . I hate you! . . . I hate you! Closing her eyes, she tried to block the vision of Blake as she screamed those untrue words at him. He deserved her anger, for his hateful accusations had wounded Rina deeply, but she did not hate him. No . . . she loved him. Regardless of what her mind told her and no matter how lonely she might be, no other man could ever fill the emptiness that Blake had created.

Did he think of her? Was Blake Roberts' life as miserable

as her own? Finding no answers in the early-morning sky, Rina began to pull on her clothes. Winter had just about run itself out; soon spring would be here. She was tired of the bitter cold, endless winds, and damp fog that shrouded the country. It would be nice to feel the sun warm against her skin.

Still feeling the depressing loneliness inside her, Rina found the cottage too confining. Riding out of the small shed on Blackstar, Rina gave him his head. The cold slapped her in the face and brought color to her cheeks. They sped down the empty streets. All thoughts left Rina, leaving only the exhilaration of the ride. Out of town they swept, Blackstar and his lady, neither caring where they were going.

They were a sight, streaking across the countryside, the magnificent black stallion and his beautiful rider with long golden hair streaming behind her. They quickly left the village far behind and rode into the darkness of the forest. Coming to a stream, Rina pulled Blackstar to a halt and slid breathlessly from his back, allowing him to drink. Standing silently among the many trees, she closed her eyes, allowing nothing to penetrate her thoughts except the sounds around her. Suddenly, the sound of another horse approaching reached her sensitive ears. Quickly she stepped behind some large trees to wait for the rider to appear.

Lieutenant Greerson emerged from the trees, and searching the area, spotted Blackstar by the stream. Quickly looking around, the young man rode over to the horse and dismounted. Puzzled, he glanced around once again for Rina.

"Miss Rina. Are you here?"

She stepped from her hiding place and walked over to him.

"Good God, woman! I've been trying to catch up to you and that beast you ride and was beginning to think you had lost control. Are you all right?" A concerned look crossed over his handsome features, bringing a smile to Rina's flushed face.

"Of course I'm all right. It's just that we both enjoy a fast ride, and sometimes we do lose all thought of the world around us. I must admit, I never even saw you, Lieutenant Greerson."

Rina's eyes sparkled from the stimulating ride, and her smile warmed the Lieutenant's heart. Shyly, he said, "Please, call me David."

"All right, David. Now, what was it you wished to see me about?"

David read the cautious look in her eyes and decided to be blunt. "You're out early today, Rina. I would think you would still be sleeping, considering how late you were out last night."

If he had meant to surprise Rina, Lieutenant Greerson failed, for she never blinked an eye. "Why, I don't know what you are talking about, David. I was in bed quite early last night, though I certainly don't feel it's any of your business."

"But it is my business if you happen to be the Angel in Black."

David was taken aback by Rina's sudden outburst of laughter. "I hate to disappoint you, Lieutenant, but you have the wrong woman." Rina knew he was playing a guessing game with her, and feeling no alarm for the moment, she played along.

David watched Rina closely, hoping to force some sign of panic or confession from her. He continued, "I think I have the right woman. I've been watching you for months, and there is something strangely similar about you and the Angel. Perhaps I am just guessing, but I'd bet on it. You both ride as well as any person I've seen, and both ride astride like a man. Your eyes are the same deep blue, though the Angel has a very realistic French accent. The people I have talked to love you deeply, and I can see you love them in return, enough to risk your life for them. You are careful and I have no evidence against you, but I know. For God's sake, Rina, heed my warning. Let the Angel die, and ride no more. I admire you more than any woman I've ever known, but I have my duty to the King and my country to perform. You must stop! Now!"

Rina stood quietly, feeling the sincerity of David's words

as she contemplated her next step. "If you are so convinced I am this Angel, why risk coming to tell me so?"

A sad sigh escaped David as he looked deep into Rina's eyes. "I came to beg you to stop this madness, for if you do not . . . I shall be forced to do something I have no heart for."

Reaching up, Rina gently touched his cheek. "I'm sorry, David, I cannot help you."

As she pulled her hand away, David grabbed it, anger flashing in his green eyes. "You cannot, or will not?"

Rina did not answer, and freeing her hand, she turned to leave.

"Are you the Angel in Black?"

She looked back at David as she started to mount Blackstar and answered, "It doesn't matter whether I say yes or no. You will believe what you want."

"Yes," David muttered, aggravated by her calmness, "I suppose I will."

As Rina rode past him, she paused a moment and looked down at him. "Take care, David." Then, urging Blackstar on, Rina rode away and left him standing alone among the giant trees as they swayed gently in the wind.

When Rina neared home, she decided it would be best if no one knew of her encounter with Lieutenant Greerson.

During the next month the Angel in Black continued to raid dinner parties and coaches. Evading the Lieutenant and his men was becoming more and more difficult with each passing day. Finally, Rina came to the decision that it was too dangerous for her men and she must no longer ride as the Angel. Sitting at the table with her men, she waited for their reaction.

"Well, I agree wit' the child." Jake nodded. "We've 'ad luck on our side so far, but 'tis best no' t' push a good thin' too far. I ain't gettin' younger, ye know, and I need a break from all this excitement." Laughing, Jake patted Rina fondly on the hand, knowing she had been worried over something. Perhaps this was it.

John also nodded his agreement. "You know best, Rina. Whatever you want is fine with me. We all knew it couldn't last forever, but while it did, we helped many people. The

Angel in Black will always be remembered and loved by everyone."

Tom and Charlie smiled, willing to do whatever she asked.

"Shall we make tonight our last night?" asked Tom.

"Yes, I think it fittin' tha' we ride together fer one last time. What do ye say, Rina?" Jake's eyes glittered with excitement as he winked at her.

Rina laughed in agreement. No matter how Jake talked of being too old for their line of work, he had loved the last months of derring-do. It showed in his face, in his walk, just as it did in all of them. Rina poured five cups of wine, then raised her own cup to propose a toast. "To the men who risked much for me. Friends that I shall never forget."

The four men drank deeply and watched their leader as she emptied her cup in salute to them.

Then John spoke to Rina, "To a remarkable woman, who is truly an angel. A woman for whom we would ride into the very pits of hell."

Rina flushed proudly as her men drank to her, leaving her speechless. Charlie finally broke the awkward silence with his question, "Wha' are we goin' t' hit tonight?"

"Let's make it somethin' special!" suggested Tom.

"Well, there is a fancy dinner party at one o' the estates tonight."

"And it's crawling with Lieutenant Greerson's men, Jake, just waiting for us to take the bait," warned Rina. Suddenly, an idea struck her. "Lawrence Langsford is at that dinner party and Camray is empty. We started this because of his greed, so I think it only fitting to dedicate our final effort to robbing his precious Camray." Her eyes lit up mischievously as she thought of the delight it would give her.

They all agreed and rode out to Camray. The house stood silent; the servants had sought out their own beds. Carefully, Rina led the way to the back entrance and into the interior of the familiar house. Without speaking, each went to carry out his assignment. Rina headed for the library. After closing the doors, she turned to look about, old memories flooding through her. The full moon lit the room well; its faded yellow glow even illuminated the portrait above the fireplace. Rina felt as if her father were actually smiling down at her. Yes, she knew William Easton would see the humor in her actions. She moved over to the bookshelves, quickly finding what she sought. A safe, hidden by several books, opened easily under her swift fingers as they remembered the combination from her childhood. Her father had been more farsighted than he could have imagined when he taught Katrina this secret. She grinned as she pulled several bundles of money and boxes of jewels from it and carefully placed the booty in a bag. She then closed the safe, replaced the books, and turned to glance once again at the portrait. Her life at Camray seemed so long ago.

"Soon, Papa . . . very soon, I shall claim what is mine."

The others were already waiting outside. She handed the bag to John, then mounted her horse. Quietly, they rode away. After they were safely away from the estate, the five horsemen urged their mounts into a run. After a bit, they plunged into the woods, each ready to take a separate route back to the winery.

Rina paused a moment to watch each of her men ride on. Something caught her eye as she searched the woods. A rider appeared out of nowhere and, having spotted Tom, disappeared into the foliage after him. It was Lieutenant Greerson. Rina moved forward, scanning the area for other soldiers. There were none. Rina rode hard to cut off the Lieutenant before he caught up to Tom.

The trees slapped at her as she surged toward Greerson, running out directly in his path. The Lieutenant's horse reared nervously from surprise, catching the young man off guard. Tom was still far enough ahead not to see or hear anything, and he rode out of danger. Rina turned to look at David as he fought to keep his seat and yelled to him, "It's me you want, monsieur! Leave the man be!"

Then, as quickly as she had appeared, the Angel darted off into the dense forest, determined to draw his attention from her men. The Lieutenant gave chase close behind her, and the two horses thundered through the woods.

Rina crouched as low as she could, urging her horse forward, hearing the Lieutenant close behind. Then her horse stumbled slightly, and David Greerson was beside her

in seconds. In one swift motion, he lunged at her, pulling
her from her horse, sending them both tumbling to the
ground. Nimbly, Rina pulled herself free, and dashed to the
safety of the shadows. She stopped searching for her mount
when a loud moan escaped Lieutenant Greerson, who lay
motionless where he had fallen.

Rina froze as indecision flooded her. Her horse was only
a few feet away from them. Another groan reached her ears
as she started forward, ready to flee. David did not move.
Carefully, Rina moved back to him, unable to leave him
injured. He did not open his eyes as she stood over him.
She leaned down, trying to locate the origin of his pain. In
that moment, David's hands grasped her own in a steely
grip.

Rina gasped in surprise, her eyes wide with anger. "You
bastard! You tricked me!"

As David pulled himself up to his feet, she brought her
knee up, catching him in the stomach. Freeing her wrists,
Rina twisted away and pulled her sword to defend herself.
Anger at his trickery surged through her as she turned to
face him.

Instinctively, David pulled his own sword, seeing the
fury in his opponent's icy blue eyes.

"I'll not be so easy to take, monsieur." Rina's words
came out in a hiss and they dripped with sarcasm and fury.

"I had no doubt about that," he replied calmly.

The Angel's strength surprised the Lieutenant as he fended
off her agile attack. Again and again she struck, her prowess
with a sword shocking her enemy. David's own expertise
proved a good match, but Rina's steely determination and
temper gave her an advantage. He could not believe his
eyes as she continually outmaneuvered him and put him at
a disadvantage. Rarely had he fought anyone so talented
with a blade. Where did the woman get her power and
stamina?

There was no time for answers, for at that moment Rina
deftly disarmed David, and brought her sword swiftly to
his throat. She stood there, unable to move, as he watched
her confusion play in her eyes.

"It is your move, Angel. Kill me now and you can be

rid of your enemy." David waited, his eyes locked with hers.

Slowly, Rina lowered her blade. "I am not a murderer, but a thief. If I could not ride off earlier and leave you injured, I certainly cannot kill you now."

David sighed, relieved. "Yes, I know. You deliberately cut me off from your man and led me away. It was a brave thing to do, but foolish."

"Perhaps." She shrugged, seemingly unconcerned. "Now what do you plan to do?"

Rina stood waiting for an answer, but none came. David reached up and pulled the scarf and mask from her face, and she made no attempt to stop him. It was time for truth. He showed no surprise as he looked into the Angel's deep blue eyes.

"I would have given anything for it not to be you." David's voice was strained, and Rina felt touched. "You have put me in a difficult situation, and I know not what to do. God, Rina, why couldn't you have done as I asked? Why?"

"I was," she whispered, a sad smile touching her lips.

"What?" asked David.

"Tonight was our last raid. There will be no more Angel in Black. It was decided tonight."

Doubt filled David's mind. "How can I believe a thief? You have lied to me before."

"I have no reason to lie, not now. I will not risk the lives of my men any longer, or yours. We all knew it would end, eventually. Either I would stop on my own, or you would end it. It is unfortunate for me both alternatives happened at the same time. But even if I hang, it was worth my life."

"You are the most confusing of women. How is it that you can be so unselfish and good?" David's face shone with admiration as he watched Rina closely.

She shook her head sadly, her voice strained and soft. "No . . . no, David. You are so wrong. At times I'm so filled with ugliness and hate, I don't know any other emotions. That evil provides my strength and determination. My life, my very future, belongs to this hatred. I have no control over it, it burns in me like an eternal fire." Rina's eyes became as dark as the night sky, as her words shook with intensity. "Sometimes I believe it's this very hate that leads me to do good. In order to keep my sanity, I must balance this overbearing violence within me. I must counter hate with love. The love I have for the people around me keeps me in balance. So you see, I could kill for this hate I feel and would gladly die for this love."

Rina paused and took Lieutenant Greerson's hand in her own smaller one. "David, I am no different from anyone else. Perhaps I am a bit more passionate ... whether it be passionate in hate ... or passionate in love. You have only seen what I do for love. Should you witness my all-consuming hatred, you would not find me unselfish and good. So dispel your saintly visions of me, for I don't deserve them. . . . I am a thief, no matter what my reasons, but I can live with that. Can you?"

He leaned down and gently kissed Rina. "Yes, I can. I expect you to keep your word, Rina, no more Angel in Black."

"No more Angel in Black," she agreed. She turned to leave and David watched her, knowing if she did not love another man, he could easily fall in love with her. But even though it was not to be, he knew he would not regret letting the Angel go.

Pushing her hood back from her head, Rina lifted her face to feel the sunshine on it. There was still a chill in the air, but the sun had decided to make an appearance that day. Rina had gone for a long walk and ended up in the forest nearest the village. As she walked, the sun filtered through the trees and cast shadows over the soft earth. She listened to the sounds around her and felt at peace, something she had felt little of lately. Several weeks had passed since Rina had last ridden as the Angel. Nightmares haunted her nights, just as Blake haunted her every waking moment.

Finding a soft pile of leaves, Rina sat down and leaned against a giant tree. Pulling a cloth from her cape she carefully unfolded it and began to nibble on some cheese and bread she had brought along. After eating her fill, she leaned her head against the trunk and closed her eyes. Exhaustion took its toll and soon Rina was fast asleep.

Startled, Rina awakened, quickly coming to her feet. The sound of horses riding hard filtered to her ears, followed by the baying of fox hounds. They were coming toward her. Only seconds later, a small red fox darted from the underbrush. Unaware of her presence, the little fox paused to catch his breath, searching for a way to escape the dogs, which were not far behind. Another round of baying sent the creature scurrying past Rina, actually brushing underneath her skirts. She watched the tiny animal disappear, and concern for his safety made her forget her own danger. In only a moment she found herself facing the hounds as they came crashing noisily through the trees, the scent of the fox still strong. Confusion filled them as her own scent mingled with the animal they had chased, and they quickly surrounded her, cutting off any attempt Rina may have made to flee.

Unconcerned that the dogs might harm her, she decided to wait until the riders appeared, then go about her own business. But to her disgust it was Lawrence and Randolph Langsford who rode up, and following not far behind was Catherine Ramsey.

"What the hell is going on here?" Lawrence Langsford yelled, his anger apparent at having lost the fox. "Who are you, girl?"

Catherine Ramsey's green eyes narrowed dangerously as she watched Rina. "She is from Tattershall, Lawrence. I believe her name is Rina. One of the peasants who works your fields."

Langsford took another look at her, licking his lips as his eyes roamed boldly over her body. "You have spoiled our fun, girl. I don't like that."

"I don't really care what you like or don't like." Rina's eyes were filled with hate, her own temper barely under control. She was in a difficult spot, her chance of escaping on foot miniscule; but no matter what, she would not grovel to Langsford.

"It sounds like the wench has a sharp tongue." Randolph nudged his horse forward, scattering the dogs as he neared

Rina. "You could be a bit more friendly, you know," he said, reaching down to run his finger along her cheek, causing Rina to flinch in disgust.

"Well, I think since she helped our fox to escape, she should become our prey. It might be great sport, Randolph." Catherine's suggestion pleased the men, as he imagined the pleasure Rina would provide, after the capture.

Lawrence looked to the lady. "And after we have caught her?"

Shrugging her shoulders, Catherine laughed, "She's yours, of course!"

Rina could not believe her ears. Reacting swiftly, she darted past Randolph's horse, startling it and its rider. Running as fast as she could, she disappeared into the trees, knowing her only chance would be to reach the road. On and on she went, aware of the horses behind her. God, she could not allow them to catch her! The three riders had split up, in order to circle around her and close in. Rina knew she could be trapped and slipped quietly behind a large rock to wait for a rider to come by.

As Catherine Ramsey rode by, Rina jumped out, startling her mount and unseating the surprised woman. Before Catherine could get to her feet, Rina had vanished.

"Over here! She is over here!" Randolph yelled as he spotted Rina trying to make it to the road. Instantly, Lawrence and his son were after her.

Rina ran as fast as her legs would carry her, but the horses closed in. They would be on her soon. Reaching down, Randolph grabbed the fleeing girl and pulled her onto his horse as she kicked and screamed her fury.

Unable to hold on to her, he dropped Rina hard on the ground, sliding off almost on top of her. Lawrence reined his own horse and flew off, landing in front of his son and the struggling girl. He grabbed a handful of her hair, twisting it as he yanked her head back painfully. Rina kicked with all her might, knocking him to the ground. Nimbly, she wrenched free of Randolph's brutal grasp and brought her fist up hard, clipping his jaw painfully. Whether it was the actual force of the blow or the fact that a woman had hit him with her fists, he stood dazed for a brief second. In that moment Rina ran with all the strength she had left, the men at her heels in a flash. Finally, she emerged from the trees and slid to a halt. A drop of about twenty feet blocked her escape to the road below. She could climb down but there was no time. She turned and pulled her knife to face the two men only a few feet away.

Two riders suddenly appeared on the road. They had heard the noise and rode to see what it was. Their yell sent Lawrence and Randolph back into the cover of the forest. Surprised, Rina put her knife away and turned to see who it was. She was closer to the edge than she thought and slipped on the loose dirt beneath her feet, losing her balance. Tumbling down the bank, Rina landed with a dull thud just as Lieutenant Greerson and Ryon Roberts rode up.

David was quickly by her side and gently pulled the unconscious girl into his arms. Rina had hit her head on a rock and it was bleeding badly from a large gash.

"God! It's Rina!" David lifted her into his arms and handed her to Ryon. "She's badly hurt!"

"We'll take her to Windsong." Holding her firmly, Ryon urged his horse into a run with David following close behind.

Chapter 14

Ryon heard the door slam, jumped from his chair, and practically ran to the entryway. "Blake! I'm glad you're home!"

A look of surprise lit Blake's face as he happily grabbed his brother in an affectionate hug. "Ryon, you didn't let me know you were coming to London! Well, I suppose it's the time when everyone starts drifting into town from their country estates."

Ryon's look was serious. "Actually, we hadn't planned to come for a while yet, but we found it necessary to come now. Let's go into the library and talk."

Blake followed his brother, noticing the concern that lined his face. "Is Rebecca or the baby ill? Are they all right?"

"Yes, Blake, they're just fine. Here, let me get you a drink."

Ryon poured his older brother a brandy and handed it to him. Blake tried to be patient with Ryon but found it difficult. "Are you going to tell me why you're being so mysterious?"

Ryon took a drink and decided it best to say his news outright. "Rina was hurt a few days ago."

Blake's face drained of all color but he made no move; he only sat staring at Ryon, waiting for his next words.

Ryon was somewhat amazed by Blake's apparent control and calm, unable to see the haunting visions that intruded into Blake's stricken mind. He saw all the horrible fears he had conjured in the tension-filled months since Rina had begun her dangerous life as a thief. One after another flickered across his thoughts, leaving him numb, unable to move. He held his breath as Ryon continued with the story.

"She fell down a hill, about twenty feet or so, cutting her head quite badly. Lieutenant Greerson and I just happened to be riding down the road when we heard a scream and some men yelling. We rode toward the noise and spotted a girl running away from two men. She came to the embankment and stopped, then turned to face them. I saw a flash, I believe the sun reflected off a knife she held in her hand; there was one on her. When the two men saw us coming, they disappeared into the forest. Rina turned and slipped, tumbling down to the road, where she hit her head on a large rock. We took her to Windsong and sent for a doctor. She was unconscious for three days."

Ryon paused and Blake could stand no more. "She's awake now, isn't she?"

"Oh, yes." The younger man nodded.

"Who were the men, Ryon?"

The question took Ryon by surprise, for he had been so preoccupied with everything else he had not thought about it. "I don't know. We were too far away to see their faces. We actually didn't know the woman we saw was Rina until she had tumbled down to the road."

"But she's all right?" Blake tried to calm the fear and apprehension inside him.

"She's here, Blake."

Immediately, Blake jumped up and headed for the door, only to be intercepted by Ryon. "Please, Blake. You can't go upstairs now, she's sleeping." He drew a deep breath and motioned toward the chairs. "There's something else, so let's sit down."

"She is all right? You said she was!" Blake couldn't

understand his brother's hesitation. "What the hell is going on, Ryon?"

"Rina is going to be fine," he assured Blake. "We sent for a doctor as soon as we arrived here this afternoon. She was extremely tired from the long trip, so he gave her a sleeping draught, that's all. He said she would probably sleep till morning. It's best if we let her rest. She's still experiencing some fainting spells and dizziness from the blow to her head. Rina hasn't complained any, but I know she's been plagued with severe headaches, too. She just needs a lot of rest, then she'll be as good as new."

Blake sat as his brother suggested. "If she is going to be fine, what's the 'something else'?"

"Perhaps it would be best to just explain everything that happened once we arrived at Windsong."

"Please do," urged Blake impatiently.

Nodding, Ryon complied. "As I said, we sent for a doctor and he examined Rina, confirming that she had a severe concussion. She had not stirred at all, but he said there was nothing we could do except wait for her to awaken. The next day Rina became delirious, drifting in and out of consciousness. She seemed to be experiencing terrible nightmares and awakened several times screaming hysterically. It was during her delirium that she spoke to us, Blake, and I still can't believe what has been discovered. We called her Rina and she informed us her name was not Rina, but Katrina... Katrina Easton. It seems that Rina is actually Katrina Easton, the daughter of William and Virginia Easton of Camray."

"Don't be absurd! She was killed over nine years ago!" blurted out Blake.

"No one knows for sure what happened to the child, Blake. Her body was never recovered. We questioned Jake and Jenny Tidwell, but they insisted she was their niece. But I could see they were nervous and afraid, so I left them be. Rina continued to insist she was Katrina Easton. When she finally awoke from her fevered delirium, Rebecca and I questioned her. Rina was confused and distraught, her head paining her terribly, so we sent for the doctor again. It's hard to believe, Blake, but Rina *is* Katrina Easton."

"What makes you believe that?" questioned Blake, unable—perhaps unwilling—to see any truth in what Ryon was saying.

"Why on earth would she claim to be Katrina Easton if she wasn't! She was feverish and raving, Blake, floating back and forth between a dazed reality and unconsciousness. And what's even more incredible is that, until she fell and hit her head, she didn't *remember* who she was. Rina spoke privately with Jake and Jenny. She must have assured them it was all right to tell us what really happened. According to them, they found her half-dead, wandering about lost. She could not remember who she was or how she had gotten there. She called herself Rina. Rina must have wandered for days, for they found her miles away from Camray. So Jake and Jenny took her in and merely told everyone she was their niece. The girl thought so, too, and was raised by them."

Ryon shook his head in amazement and continued. "The doctor seems to think that Rina witnessed the murder of her parents and escaped into the forest. After such a traumatic experience, the child forced that night from her mind by forgetting everything, even who she was. He says it is not uncommon for children to deal with frightening moments in such a way. The blow to her head brought it all back. Just think, Blake, she could have gone her entire life not knowing she was Katrina Easton."

Blake's mind was racing as he tried to put all the pieces together. Rina was actually Katrina Easton! Then the portrait in the library at Camray floated into his mind and he realized why it seemed familiar. If someone knew what to look for, there *was* a family resemblance. Not enough to have made the connection earlier, but obvious to him now. And the ring! It was the one Rina wore around her neck on a chain. She was Katrina!

"My God!" exclaimed Blake aloud. "But why have you brought her here?"

Ryon explained further. "As Katrina Easton, she is the rightful heir to Camray. She told us she was going to petition the King for her inheritance. We insisted she stay here with us. Rina argued, but Rebecca wouldn't take no for an answer. I hope it isn't going to be difficult for you, I mean . . . you two . . ."

Blake smiled wryly at his brother's discomfort. "I promise to behave, Ryon. Rina, or should I say Katrina, is welcome to stay as long as she wishes. I'll do my best to keep the peace between us."

"Good!" sighed Ryon, obviously relieved. "Rebecca will be pleased to hear that!"

As Blake made his way to his rooms later that evening he could not resist pausing in front of Rina's door. Simply knowing she was in the room, just beyond, made his heart beat faster. Images floated before his eyes, entrancing him . . . enchanting him. Before he realized what he was doing, Blake had opened the barrier that stood between them and walked inside the darkened room. After his eyes had made the adjustment to the dimness, Blake saw Katrina sleeping soundly. He did not expect the rush of emotions that grabbed him; their intensity took him off guard. His breathing became ragged and his hand trembled slightly as it captured a stray curl on her forehead and gently caressed the soft, silken strand. Blake closed his eyes a moment, the scent of roses as arousing as the vision of her loveliness.

"Oh, little one. I have missed you, more than I can ever admit."

Reaching out, Blake ran the tip of his finger over her soft, full lips, wishing fervently that he could possess them with his own. With a tortured moan, he turned and left, the overwhelming temptation leaving him visibly shaken.

It was late morning before Katrina opened her eyes again to find the room empty and dark. Rising from the bed, she crossed over to the large window and pulled the heavy velvet curtains aside, allowing the bright sunshine to penetrate the darkness.

She stood by the window and gazed thoughtfully out but saw nothing as she sorted out the events of the past few days. Everyone knew now that she was really Katrina Easton, and she had a believable story as to why she had not come forward with the truth long ago. Smiling to herself, Katrina thought it all fit together well.

Turning, Rina walked to the dressing table mirror and picked up a brush. Hard, cold eyes stared back at her. A cruel smile curved her soft mouth as the irony flitted across her mind. How fitting that Langsford's own stupidity and lust had caused her fall, thus giving her the chance to come forward as an Easton. Once Camray was hers, she would be able to plan his death. For years she had yearned for revenge but never knew exactly how to accomplish all she had promised. Now it all seemed to be falling into place and fate made the plans for her.

A knock sounded at her door and Katrina grabbed her robe and pulled it on. Blake casually entered the room. When Katrina shot him an angry look, Blake knew she was feeling better.

Raising an amused eyebrow, he stated, "I heard a noise and thought you would be up. You look to be your old self again, little one."

Quickly, Katrina brought her emotions under control and smiled warmly at her host. "Yes, I seem to be remembering everything quite clearly now. I'm sorry to be so much trouble. I'll try not to impose very long."

A frown creased his handsome face as he noted the uneasy formality in her voice. "There is much I wish to talk to you about, Rina. I guess it is really Katrina, isn't it? I must say, it was quite a shock to find out that after all these years you are not dead. It must have been difficult having amnesia and forgetting everything."

He walked over to where Katrina stood, stiff and uncomfortable, and gently touched her cheek. The shock that went through her did nothing to soothe the turmoil she was feeling inside.

"Why didn't you tell me you were Katrina Easton?" Blake's question brought Rina out of her daze. He tried hard not to lose his temper, wanting to know the truth, yet afraid of driving her further away from him. It hurt him deeply to think of the lies she had lived. Now he was going to give her the chance to tell the truth and save what was left of the bond they shared.

"I . . . I don't know what you mean. I didn't know myself who I really was."

Blake's gaze darkened and Katrina wanted to look away, finding it difficult to lie to him. His temper flared uncontrollably. Did she think him a fool? "Don't lie to me! I've been with you when you had your nightmares. You remembered that night your parents were killed as if it were yesterday! You've never forgotten for one moment that you were Katrina Easton. Now tell me! Why the amnesia story? Why have you hidden your identity all of these years?"

Pulling away from his angry face, Katrina sought the right words. "Believe me, Blake," she stated, turning back to face him, "I had my reasons!"

"What? What are those reasons?" he shouted, his anger at her deception finally surfacing.

"I can't tell you," whispered Rina, feeling helpless and sad. "Please, I beg you, no one must know anything but what has been told. Don't you see? I can't explain my real reasons for what I have done. It would put me in danger."

Blake saw the urgency in her eyes, and her voice shook slightly with emotion.

"What kind of danger?" asked Blake. Then, before Katrina could answer, the words she had spoken to him at the inn came back and the reason grew clear.

"You told me once that you knew your mother and father's murderer, and you intended to kill him for what he had done. Is this the danger you speak of? This man who kills innocent women and defenseless men is still alive, and you have hidden from him all of these years as Rina?"

Katrina nodded her head in agreement as she tried to explain. "Yes, but if I pretend to have suffered amnesia all this time, it would explain my disappearance. I will say I remember what happened now, but I do not know who killed them. Now is my chance to get Camray back!"

"Damn it, Katrina! Is it so important that you would risk your life to be Katrina Easton again?"

"Yes," she screamed. "Yes, it is so very important! Langsford is cruel and greedy. You've seen what it has been like for my people since he inherited Camray. If it were mine again, I could right all the wrongs he has created."

Blake was silent for a moment as he contemplated all

she had told him. There were still so many unanswered questions. "Who killed your parents, Rina?"

"I cannot tell you."

"What games do you play, little one?" Blake's voice was hard, holding a note of warning, but she would not heed the danger.

"I do not play games, Blake. What I do is deadly serious. But it does not concern you."

Angrily, he grabbed Katrina's shoulders and shook her. "You fool, tell me! Tell me so that I can help you!"

"No!" She pulled away, her own anger flaring again. "It is none of your affair, Blake Roberts, so don't ask again!"

Blake clinched his fists helplessly and shouted, "You are determined to get yourself killed, aren't you? What about the Angel in Black? What of her?"

"She no longer exists," she snapped.

Blake threw up his hands in exasperation and exclaimed sarcastically, "Well, at least you have sense enough to give up that foolishness."

Hurt by his snideness, Katrina muttered, "I had no choice!"

Suddenly, Blake's immense anger left as concern filled him. "Why? What happened?"

Rina turned away, angry that she had said anything, but Blake gripped her shoulders firmly and pulled her around to face him again. "What happened?"

Blake's voice was firm and she knew she must tell him. "Lieutenant Greerson knows that I am the Angel in Black."

Katrina's statement sent a shock through Blake and his face paled slightly. Seeing his reaction, she quickly continued. "He agreed to say nothing if I stopped, so about a month ago we retired from our night riding." Rina deliberately left out the details. "Then I fell and hit my head. When I awoke, I discovered that I had exposed my true identity. So I made up the story for Jake and Jenny to tell. Now I have the opportunity to be who I really am. Please, give me this chance, Blake."

"I'll say nothing." Blake sadly conceded this one thing to her. A strained silence seemed to fill the air with tension. "Who was chasing you before you fell?" Blake asked abruptly.

The sudden change of subject caught Katrina off guard as she saw the deadly glint in Blake's eyes. "I . . . don't know who it was," she lied, wincing at his stare.

Blake saw her discomfort and did not press her any further. It hurt him, but he knew she would continue to keep things from him. "Once you have Camray back, then what?"

There was no answer from her, but he saw it in her eyes as he thought of her cold, deadly words spoken at the inn. Yes, he knew exactly what she would do next. Sadly, Blake said, "Forget the hate that's inside you, Katrina. It will only destroy you."

Katrina drew a long, ragged breath as his words hit a sensitive nerve. When her eyes met his again, Blake could see the venom in them.

"Forget? You make it sound so easy, but it's not! You cannot expect me to forget something that has burned in me for all of these long years."

Her words sounded sad and tired, carrying none of the fire he saw in her eyes. "Blake, you can never truly understand this hatred I carry. Can you understand the feelings of a child who watched her parents being cut down in cold blood? Could you forget the fear and loneliness? But most of all, could you forget the face of the man who laughed at the brutal carnage he'd created? No, I think you would not forget! Just as I cannot forget this hate that burns within me, for it consumes my very soul. It has given me my very reason for living. Hatred helped me to endure each back-breaking day and to live with hunger and cold. It gives me the strength I need to face death without fear and live each day, no matter what."

Rina paused, drawing on the silence to ease her anguish. "That bastard took everything from me that I loved! Can I simply forget that? No . . . don't ask me to rid myself of this hatred! Vengeance is mine! I'll not share it with anyone!"

Katrina paced back and forth in front of Blake, her anguish and anger exploding in her mind. Reaching out, Blake pulled her into his arms to stop her frenzied pacing, wanting only to assuage the torment she was experiencing. She looked into his warm eyes and stated firmly, "I must kill him, Blake. I *must* keep my promises. Not only will I kill the murderer of my mother and father, but I will also kill the evil hatred that I carry in my heart. Then my future will be my own, free of all promises."

As Katrina whispered the last words to Blake they struck a chord in his heart. "And what about us, little one? Is it so easy to forget what has happened between us?"

Pain-filled eyes looked into his. "What about us, Blake? It seems whatever was between us was destroyed at Windsong."

"Perhaps," he ventured, "we could start anew?"

"I . . . I don't know," Rina whispered, her head aching terribly once again. "Oh, Blake, there is never a tomorrow for us. Can't you see that? I cannot forget and I cannot forgive! I warn you now, do not stand in my path, for I'll stop at nothing to fulfill my promises! Even you cannot stop me. The need for vengeance is firmly planted in me, and if forced to choose between it and my feelings for you, I would choose the hatred. I cannot deny it!"

Blake pulled Katrina to him and buried his face in the masses of golden curls. Finding her slender neck, Blake kissed the scented flesh tenderly. Katrina's senses came alive as his hands roamed over her back, caressing her rounded hips as he pulled her closer.

"And you be warned, little one, I'll not give up so easily! Oh, God, I hate your stubbornness and independence! You confuse the hell out of me, and still, I would be disappointed if you didn't."

Pulling back so she could look into Blake's eyes, Katrina saw the tenderness and passion. "I need some time to sort out my feelings, Blake. Let's not think of what tomorrow may bring, but only of the moment at hand. We must not speak of the future or make demands we cannot keep. Today is all that matters."

Katrina stood on her toes and pulled Blake down to her as her lips pressed gently against his own, as if sealing the words she had spoken.

Blake sat quietly as he waited with Ryon and Rebecca for Katrina to come down for dinner. Blake had been tempted many times to rush up the stairs and burst into the rooms

Katrina now occupied. His desire to make love to her was overwhelming. But he knew he must exercise caution. After all, she was still suffering from a concussion, and he had promised to give her time to sort out her feelings.

Blake's heart stopped as he heard the rustle of satin in the hall. Rebecca immediately went to the door and greeted Katrina. Blake found himself unable to move, his golden eyes fixed on the beautiful woman coming toward him.

She was dressed in a lovely blue silk gown, the exact shade of her eyes. Her hair had been painstakingly curled and pinned into a becoming style, with matching blue ribbons entwined among the gold strands. The gold chain hung about her neck, the heavy gold signet ring lying between the gentle swells of her breasts as they rose enticingly from the fashionably low-cut bodice. When Katrina neared Blake, the soft scent of roses drifted to him and caused him to nearly lose control and pull her into his longing arms. The need to feel those soft lips against his own was overpowering.

Rina offered her hand to Blake. He brushed his lips over its softness and a shiver of immense pleasure swept over her, causing a slight blush to stain her cheeks.

"Good evening, Blake," she acknowledged with a nod of her head, pulling her hand from his warm grasp.

Blake guided her to a chair and helped her to be seated, then, leaning over, whispered into her ear, "Ah, little one, you are truly a vision of beauty. How am I to fight against such charms?"

The warmth of his breath was like a shock, bolting through Rina, leaving her breathless. He was so dashingly handsome and virile, his nearness shattering all the defenses she had stubbornly put up. How could he destroy her will so easily? Why was there a tremendous knot in the pit of her stomach? Good Lord! She was trembling!

No words formed in Katrina's dazed mind, and an uncomfortable silence filled the room, which was finally broken by a loud cough from Ryon. The noise freed Rina from the spell of Blake's heated look, and she shyly glanced down at her hands as they nervously twisted in her lap.

During dinner, Blake continued to play the charming host to his beautiful guest, which brought a smile to her lips that warmed his heart. After the meal was finished, they all sat in the drawing room, the women enjoying a cup of tea while the men savored a glass of port. Laura slept soundly in a nearby cradle, her mother rocking it gently back and forth.

"Rina," started Rebecca hesitantly, "I was wondering about something. I hope you don't think I'm intruding, but there is something I cannot get from my mind."

"What is it Rebecca?" asked Katrina, concerned by her frown.

"During the time you were ill, you called to your father many times. In your delirium you must have thought Ryon was him. Once you asked him to forgive you for selling some jewelry and you begged him to understand your reasons. Rina, you were nearly hysterical! I can't forget how important the necklace and earrings you spoke of seemed to you and how distraught you were about selling them. Were they very special?"

Katrina sat silent for a moment, then glanced down at her hands to hide the pain she was feeling. "Yes . . . they were *very* special, Rebecca. The sapphire-and-diamond jewelry was a birthday gift from my mother and father, given to me the day they were killed. After I was found, I couldn't remember what made them so special, I just knew they were. Jenny kept them safe for me, but I had to sell them recently. It saddened me to do so, but I couldn't say why. Now I know."

Blake sat stock-still, his eyes locking with hers as Rina glanced up. They had been a gift from her parents, not a would-be lover!

"Oh, dear!" cried Rebecca. "Is there no way to get them back?"

"No, Rebecca." Rina smiled warmly, trying to lighten the somber mood. "What's done is done."

The smile was forced, for she had grown tired and her head was beginning to ache again. Blake noticed the fatigue in her eyes and suggested she retire. Neither spoke as he escorted her to her rooms. Katrina felt shivers of delight run through her as she rested her hand on his arm and felt the muscle beneath the coat's fine fabric. Blake fought to maintain control over his desire, not wishing to strain their uneasy peace. He longed to hold her in his arms, to ask forgiveness for his blunder, but he could not. She had asked for time and he would give it. He owed her that much.

They halted in front of her door, and Blake took the delicate hand that lay on his arm, bringing it to his lips. After kissing the back of it lightly, he turned it over and touched the palm. Katrina gasped and he raised his eyes to her. Her face was flushed as her breathing became rapid, matching the beat of her heart. Her eyes shone brightly, and Blake could see how his small gesture had aroused her. A small groan escaped him.

"God, little one! You shall drive me crazy!" He gently pulled her nearer. Lightly he brushed her lips with his own, then suddenly he turned and left. He knew if he stayed a second longer, he would lose all control. It was still fairly early and Blake did not think he could bear being in the same house with Rina, so he left for the sanctuary of his favorite club.

It was late when he finally made his way back to the townhouse, and everyone had long since retired. The house was dark and still as Blake walked up the staircase, his coat casually tossed over his shoulder. His vest was unbuttoned, and the snowy white shirt was open to the waist. He walked past Katrina's door and paused, greatly tempted to go in. As he stood there, indecisive, soft sounds from within drifted to his ears. He carefully eased the door open. Katrina lay tossing and turning. Blake watched as she faced the horrors of her dreams. Concerned, he silently entered the room and crossed to her bed.

Her golden hair lay tangled across the pillow; her blankets were kicked to the floor, revealing her thin nightgown, twisted in her sleep about her hips. Blake's pulse quickened as he gently stroked her forehead and felt the moisture that dampened the small tendrils of hair around her face.

"Katrina, little one . . . wake up! It's only a dream. Wake up, Katrina!"

Grasping her shoulders firmly, Blake tried to awaken her. She began to struggle, still deep in sleep. Finally, she awakened; her eyes opened wide in fright as she sat up and screamed. Blake immediately covered her mouth with his hand, smothering the sound. Pulling her trembling body to him, he cradled her, smoothing her hair from her face.

"Shh . . . it's all right . . . there's nothing to be frightened of."

His words were soft, lulling Katrina back to reality. Blake kissed her head tenderly, his voice kind and reassuring. "Shh . . . it's all right."

Slowly, she became aware of what had happened and who held her in his arms. Embarrassed, she quickly pulled away, trying to cover her exposed legs. The strap of her gown came loose, and slid off one shoulder, and Rina pulled it up, fumbling with the ribbon in an attempt to retie it.

Blake put his hand on hers, stopping her futile attempts at making a bow. "Never mind that." He lifted Katrina's delicate face with a finger so that he could look into her dark eyes. Unable to resist, he pulled her to him and kissed her as he'd yearned to all day. A shiver went through her as his kiss became more and more demanding, bringing alive her own senses. She could feel the soft curly hair on his broad chest as he brought her even closer to him. Blake's hand slid up her leg and caressed her hip, and Rina moaned in delight. Leaning back on the bed, he pulled her beneath him, feeling the soft curves of her body molded against him. His senses began to reel as he buried his head in her hair, the scent of roses driving his passions to the brink.

Katrina slowly felt her own desires overwhelming her, consuming the last fragments of reality. Desperately, she fought for control, her plea coming in a slight whisper. "No . . . Blake."

Reluctantly, he rolled away from her. "Oh, God, I fear I cannot control my need for you, little one. Please forgive me." Blake's voice shook slightly as he fought to master his desire.

"I'm sorry." Katrina had never felt so confused, so shaken and weak. Gently, she touched Blake's cheek, and when he looked at her, he could see all in her face. It tore at his heart, knowing she desired him but could not forget the pain he had inflicted.

Smiling tenderly, he kissed the palm of her hand once again. "Good night, Katrina."

The door clicked shut and Katrina stared into the darkness, an overwhelming loneliness filling her heart. Her lips still tingled from his kiss, and she had to hold back an impulse to call him back to her.

The next day was sunny, bringing warmth to the streets of London. At breakfast Blake was very courteous and asked if Katrina would like to go for a ride. Anxious for a day in the sun, she accepted and Blake escorted her to the waiting carriage. Rina's eyes were wide with excitement and wonder as they toured the busy city. On her pervious trips, she had seen relatively little of the beauty London had to offer. Blake was an excellent tour guide. Never before had Rina seen so much in one day. They stopped for a light lunch at a most charming cafe, and she could not remember when she'd had a happier, more delightful day.

Katrina was dressed in a caraco jacket of rose-colored silk damask with floral design, trimmed with delicate Chantilly lace that spilled charmingly from her throat and the sleeves. A matching skirt and a becoming broad-brimmed hat trimmed in fresh flowers completed her outfit. Blake wore a silk jacket of dark gold that brought out the intense color of his eyes. Breeches of the same rich color clung snugly to his muscled legs, and brown leather boots gave him a trim, elegant look. Never one to wear a hat long, Blake let his hair be tousled by the wind. Everywhere they went, people could not help but stare at the handsome couple.

By the time Blake and Katrina returned to the townhouse, she was feeling quite tired. She had slept little that night and went upstairs for a nap before dinner. Slipping from her dress, she crossed the room to the dressing table and picked up the silver brush lying on it. After pulling all the pins from her hair, she began to brush the long tresses, her mind wandering to the day spent with Blake. With a long sigh, she stood, stretched like a cat, then walked to the large, canopied bed and crawled beneath the warm comforter. Within minutes exhaustion conquered her.

Katrina slept soundly, feeling greatly refreshed when she finally awakened. It was dark outside and she knew it must be near dinnertime. She jumped from the bed and quickly ran a brush through her hair. The clock in the hall chimed the hour. Why hadn't someone woke her? She selected a simple, light woolen gown from among those she'd been given by Rebecca and hurriedly put it on. The pale gold of the dress seemed to blend with the flaxen strands of her hair. There was no time to do anything with her hair, so she decided to leave it free.

Closing the door softly behind her, Katrina hurried down the hall. As she descended the stairs, Blake's deep voice drifted to her, and she flushed at the sound. When she entered the room, Blake stopped in midsentence, his concentration totally lost as he boldly stared at her. In a few long strides, he was at her side, his eyes devouring his golden girl as Ryon watched in amusement and pleasure.

The dinner was a pleasant interlude, but Blake excused himself soon after it was over, saying he had a previous appointment he was unable to break. Katrina felt an emptiness after he left, even though Ryon, Rebecca, and the babe were pleasant company. When she went to her room, Mary, one of the servants, was waiting for her. A hot bath was ready, and the young girl explained her reason for not helping her dress for dinner.

"Lady Rebecca though' tha' ye might want t' sleep through dinner, so I didna' come earlier. I though' ye might like yer bath now, mum."

Rina smiled gratefully at the girl, still feeling awkward to have servants seeing to her needs. "Oh, thank you, Mary. Perhaps it will relax me. I seem to be a bit nervous. I think I slept too long this afternoon. I'm afraid I won't be able to sleep tonight."

"Well, miss, Lord Roberts 'as lots of books in 'is library. I'm sure ye could find one tha' ye would enjoy readin'. I'll see a fire is set so ye can go down after yer bath, if ye wish."

"Yes, I think I'll need something to help me sleep. Thank you, Mary."

After removing her gown and undergarments, Katrina

piled her hair on her head and pinned it in place. She sank into the fragrant water and felt the tension leaving her body. Leaning her head back, she closed her eyes, allowing her mind to drift recklessly. Immediately, visions of Blake teased her. His eyes were filled with desire as a roguish smile played on his lips. Wide shoulders with strong arms and a bare chest, covered with soft curly brown hair, bronzed by the sun, took shape in her thoughts. The massive shoulders tapered down to a small, flat waist and long, well-muscled legs that seemed to ripple as he moved. His whole body emanated the carefully controlled power of a jungle cat. Yet Katrina saw a gentleness in the man she envisioned. He was a gentle lover. A skilled lover, who could make her feel like a whole woman. A man who could fill the emptiness in her.

Her eyes flew open as she realized where her thoughts had taken her. She blushed furiously. "Damn!" she muttered. "Why can't I keep him from my mind!"

Grabbing the scented bar of soap, Rina began to lather her body, determined to blot out the image of Blake that seemed to be branded on her mind. After rinsing, she dried herself with the soft towel Mary had left and slipped into her silken nightgown. She found she wasn't any sleepier, so she picked up a candle and made her way downstairs to the library.

A cozy fire was burning as Katrina entered. The house was quiet. Everyone had retired to their rooms. Holding the candle up, she began to examine the many fine volumes lining the shelves. There were so many, she found it difficult to choose. Finally she settled on a book and started to leave.

"Don't go." A low voice startled her as she quickly looked about. Blake stepped from the shadows into the light of the fire. "Don't go, Rina."

"Blake! I didn't see you when I came in. I couldn't sleep, so I came to find something to read. I didn't mean to disturb you."

"On the contrary, little one, you are always a delight to see and I don't think it's possible for you to disturb me. Unless . . . it is in a different sort of way." His voice was low and sensuous, and when Katrina saw the gleam in his eyes, she understood what he was saying. She stood mesmerized by his golden gaze.

"I'm sorry you cannot sleep, Katrina." Blake continued to watch her.

Rina glanced about nervously, unsure of what to do. "I didn't mean to sleep so long this afternoon; now I find sleep evading me."

Silence filled the room and Blake slowly walked over to her. Standing before her, he lifted her chin to look up at him. "You are so beautiful. Do you know what torture it is to have you so close . . . and yet so far?"

Katrina licked her lips uneasily in an innocent gesture that caused a tightening in Blake's gut. He suddenly turned away, as if he could not stand to see her any longer, but the scent of her filled the air, whirling his passions further.

A frown etched Rina's face as she looked at his broad back. Misunderstanding his reaction as anger, she gently laid a hand on his arm and turned him to face her once again. "Don't be angry with me, Blake."

Closing his eyes a second, he opened them to watch the emotions flickering in her eyes. "I'm not angry, little one, but I must know one thing. Does the desire still burn in you as it does in me?"

"Yes," whispered Rina honestly.

She saw the relief and joy on his face as he rushed on, "God! I've been a fool! Can you ever forgive my—"

Katrina put her hand up and lightly touched Blake's lips, stopping whatever he had been about to say. "Please . . . say no more; it doesn't matter now. I could not sleep last night after you left me. I felt an emptiness that I cannot understand, and desire that only you can quench. Blake, in my heart, there is love . . . in my body, there is an aching need . . . in my mind, there is still pain and bitterness . . . but tonight, it does not matter."

Blake's hand slipped behind Katrina's neck as he bent down to kiss her, devouring the sweetness she offered, starting the fires of passion between them. His lips moved from hers, down her slender neck to her smooth white shoulder, then back to the softness of her mouth. Katrina clung to him as the last of her doubts fled, leaving only the tremendous desire that burned in her. Blake's hands caressed the delightful contour of her back, then slid lower to the softness of her hips. Gently, he pulled Rina against him, lifting her until she could feel his manhood hard against her. A soft moan of pleasure escaped her as she felt the delightful madness shooting through her. Blake lifted her into his arms and carried her up the stairs.

Once in her room, he gently laid her on the bed and began to undress. Katrina's eyes were dark with desire as she watched him, unembarrassed at the sight of his naked body. Slowly, he lifted her gown over her head, kissing each inch of her sweet flesh as he exposed it to his eyes and lips. His tongue tormented her, sending wave after wave of sensation sweeping through her. His lips were like brands, burning a trail of fire everywhere they touched. Tenderly, Blake took Katrina to the dizzying heights where she knew only the tremendous desire to have him fill her with himself, to drive deep within her moist center, and bring her to that ultimate ecstasy. Katrina's hips arched to the rhythm of lovers and together they spiraled and shattered in splendid rapture. Then they lay entwined in each other's arms and slept.

When Rina woke the next morning, she found the place where Blake had been empty. Briefly, she wondered if it all had been a dream, but the imprint of his head still creased the pillow next to her own. Then, as she moved, her body reminded her with a slight soreness that she had been ardently loved. Stretching, she flung her legs over the edge of the bed, the plush rug soft beneath her feet. The heavy drapes prevented any light from flooding the room. Crossing to the large windows, Katrina pushed them aside to allow the bright morning sun to enter. Turning, she froze in mid-motion, surprise etching her face. The entire room was filled with red roses.

She smiled in delight. How had they gotten there? Had she really slept so soundly that she did not hear anything? Walking from one bouquet to another, Rina examined each one, amazed at the perfection of the delicate blossoms. Reaching her dressing table, she saw that nestled among the many flowers was the familiar, worn leather pouch. With shaky fingers, she picked it up, treasuring the feel of it. Dumping the contents into her open palm, Katrina felt her throat tighten as she gazed at the sapphire-and-diamond jewelry. A small note fell out, and she unfolded the paper carefully, uncertain of the feelings inside of her. It read simply "Forgive me?"

Chapter 15

Katrina held her breath in awe as their landau rambled up the lane toward Windsor Castle. The great stone blocks formed endless walls dominated by the great round tower, an unbelievable eighty feet high, with four other smaller towers rising from the walls to flank it. The mighty Thames reflected the structure's magnificence in the ever-flowing waters that gave life to the large city. West of the central tower, in the lower ward, was St. George's Chapel, its belled steeples and spirals standing guard over the worshipers who entered its haven. Stained-glass windows, arching into domed ceilings, stood out brightly against the weathered gray stone.

Blake helped Katrina from the carriage, and they were escorted inside past huge, double doors of hand-carved oak. As they walked through the spacious rooms with tall graceful windows, finely ornamented doors, painted ceilings, and delicate plasterwork, Katrina felt as if she were in a kaleidoscope of color and texture.

Once in the great hall, Katrina was questioned thoroughly, by the King's advisers, and now they awaited word from the King himself. Blake watched her as she stood by the large window, her attention focused on the trimmed parterres and terraces of the palace gardens. She studied in wonder the sunken gardens with their immaculate flowerbeds and hedges, winding walkways, and sparkling ponds and fountains. Pavilions and gazebos with statues of gleaming marble pleased her eyes, and a smile touched her lips as she watched the many ducks, geese, and swans wandering freely about.

Dressed in a gown of smoky, blue-gray velvet, Katrina was stunning, and Blake could not help but stare. Feeling his eyes on her, Katrina turned to meet the warm amber gaze, a smile touching her lips as she gracefully came to sit beside him. How calm she seems, thought Blake as he reached out and laid his hand on hers in a loving, possessive manner. Even an audience with the King doesn't frighten her.

Blake knew how crucial this meeting was for Katrina. The King and his advisers were to decide if she was truly the daughter of William and Virginia Easton of Camray. Soon Blake was asked to enter the adjoining room, leaving Katrina sitting alone.

"Ah, Lord Roberts, it is good to see you again."

Blake crossed the room and bowed elegantly to his King, who impatiently waved away his advisers who hovered nearby.

King George III was not a handsome man, but fifty-two years had lined his face with character, and he commanded attention. Of medium height, he had a rounded chin, with full lips, and eyebrows that formed a half circle above hooded eyes. His face was completed regally by a long, straight nose with nostrils that flared out slightly.

"Yes, yes, dear boy! My court needs a handsome rogue like you to keep all the women swooning. It's been far too long since you attended a season here. Always off somewhere, I hear!"

"I must admit it is good to be home, Your Majesty." Blake smiled.

"Good, good. Now, tell me, what of Katrina Easton? I've been told that your family has known her as Rina for several years. Is she who she claims to be?"

Nodding, Blake answered, "Yes, she is Katrina Easton."

The King was thoughtful for a moment, then stated firmly, "Well, my advisers are convinced she is the daughter of

William Easton, a man several of them knew quite well. And you, sir, do not strike me as a man to easily be fooled. So, before I meet Lady Easton, I have just one more question."

A twinkle sparkled in King George's eyes and a smile spread across his face. "Is she as beautiful as I remember Virginia Easton to have been?"

Blake's laughter filled the room. "Yes, Your Majesty. Even more so!"

"Then I should like to see the lady . . . alone." The older man winked conspiratorially.

Clearing his throat, Blake became serious as he considered his next words. "My Lord, may I be honest with you?"

The seriousness in Blake's voice gave the King a moment's concern as he nodded his consent.

"Katrina Easton is an independent, willful person. I hope you will give consideration to what life has been like for her the last nine years."

The King drew his eyebrows together in a frown, and his lips pursed thoughtfully. "Has a sharp tongue, does she? Well . . . I've been warned and I'll take my chances, young man." Then with a smile and another wink, he waved Blake away.

Katrina entered the large room and crossed to where the King stood, seemingly interested in an object that lay on the table nearby. Falling gracefully into a low curtsy, Katrina bowed her head humbly. Under lowered lids, King George had watched her entrance and now looked openly at the delicate head before him.

"Rise, my child, and sit. We have much to talk about." His hand indicated a chair for Katrina to take, then he, too, sat down.

Though she presented an outwardly calm exterior, she felt flushed with excitement, her heart racing inside her breast. This man had the power to grant her everything she desired. The right to be called Katrina Easton, to take her inheritance. Would she finally fulfill one of her promises? Would Camray be hers? Or would King George deny her?

As her worries continued to vex her, Katrina determinedly brought her mind to the matter at hand. She met her King's eyes, feeling encouraged by the gentleness she saw in their depths.

King George found himself looking across at one of the most beautiful women he had ever seen. Magnificent eyes, he thought, then expressed another thought out loud. "When your mother, Virginia, was your age, I thought no one could surpass her beauty, but I must say, her daughter has done so."

"Thank you, Your Majesty," whispered Katrina, taken aback by his blunt praise.

The King smiled to see the red stain in her cheeks and her downcast eyes. How unaware she was of her own beauty and grace. Delighted by her honest reaction, he continued. "I arranged for this private meeting to find out if you were truly Katrina Eastwood. Now that I know that you are who you claim to be, you can now go on with your life that was so horribly torn apart. I assume you will want to return to Camray."

"Yes, that is my wish," answered Katrina.

"Well, word has been sent to your uncle and he should be arriving soon. I'm sure he will gladly welcome you in his home and act as your guardian."

Katrina stiffened at his words and her eyes became cold and hard. "No, I am the heir of Camray. It is my birthright and I claim it as mine."

The King stood and put his hands behind his back and walked about the room, deep in thought. "What you say is true, Katrina, but when it was thought you were dead, Camray was passed on to your only other relative. For nine years Lawrence Langsford has run the estate and increased its profits tremendously. He has proved to be a valued and loyal member of my court. Do you suggest I strip him of his lands and wealth?"

Katrina fought to keep her anger under control. She jumped from her chair, then paused in an attempt to maintain some composure, biting her lip in vexation. The King scrutinized her carefully, watching with amazement as she brought her emotions in check. Only her eyes refused to cooperate as they clearly showed her fury.

"May it please Your Majesty, I mean no disrespect, but

I must speak what is in my heart. This tremendous profit you speak of, so brilliantly brought about by Langsford, has surely proven most valuable to both my uncle and the Crown's treasury, but those funds were bled from the poor. My uncle is a greedy, evil man who knows no compassion. I have nothing but contempt and disdain for the man!"

"Your tongue is indeed sharp," mused the King, surprising Katrina. "But your accusations are very serious. You have put me in a difficult position, young lady, and now I must decide on a solution. In the meantime, since you have no other relative, I will make you my ward."

Astonished, Katrina bowed her head in acceptance. "I am honored, Your Majesty."

"If you wish to stay in the care of Ryon and Rebecca Roberts, I have no objections. You will, of course, attend all functions given at court; it will be an excellent opportunity to introduce you to society. There is a ball tomorrow night, and I'm certain Lord Roberts will have no objection to escorting such a beautiful lady."

"If it is what you wish, Your Majesty," Rina conceded.

"I find you truly refreshing, Katrina, but it will in no way influence my decision on Camray. I will have to do what I feel is the best for everyone, and that includes Lawrence Langsford. Do not mistake my leniency in allowing you to express your feelings and opinions as a weakness. I'll brook no disobedience from you! That would be treason. I want it to be clear that your future has been laid in my hands. Do you wish it to be this way?"

Katrina's mind whirled as she considered all he had said. There was no other way. She must trust her King. Her father would have wanted it so. So far, fate had led her here. She must continue, or give up forever. "Yes, Your Majesty. I will abide by your decision."

Now she could do naught but wait.

Katrina stared in awe at her own reflection in the long mirror, finding it hard to believe what she saw. The burgundy gown she wore was of the finest silk, clinging softly to her body as the design followed her womanly curves, the fabric reflecting the candlelight in its shimmering folds.

Golden embroidery decorated the hem and low bodice. Her delicate shoulders were bared with sleeves of sheer gold silk, fully gathered at her wrists. The same silk spilled out from under the top skirt as it split up both sides. At Katrina's insistence, Mary had done her hair in a strikingly simple style. The heavy blonde mane had been combed and secured on the top of her head with a decorative clasp. A long single braid fell down her back, with strands of shimmering thread entwined through it. A few wisps escaped and curled becomingly about her face, framing the striking eyes and soft red lips. The blush of her cheeks was natural, as Rina felt the nervousness that went with attending her first grand ball. She wore small gold loops in her ears, and on her right index finger was her father's ring.

"Oh, Miss Katrina! You're truly lovely! I've ne'er seen anyone more beautiful then ye," exclaimed Mary as she admired her lady.

"Thank you, Mary, you are always so sweet, but how could I not feel beautiful in this gown?"

"Oh, miss, ye'd best be goin'. Lord Roberts don' like t' be kept waitin'," reminded the girl as she handed Katrina her cloak of the same fine silk.

Just as she was about to leave, a knock sounded on the door and Blake entered. His eyes sparkled appreciatively at Katrina's beauty. Quietly, Mary slipped from the room, leaving the handsome couple alone.

"I'm not sure I wish to take you to the ball," teased Blake.

Katrina's eyes widened with worry. "I don't understand," she cried. "Don't you like the gown?"

Blake pulled her close and looked deep into her eyes. "I love the dress. But you are so beautiful, little one, I'm afraid my jealousy cannot abide all the admiration and attention you shall get tonight. You will have every man, married or not, falling in love with you. You are mine and I'll not share you!"

"Tonight I am yours and I do not wish to be shared. Promise me you won't leave me alone to fend for myself among so many boring strangers. I want only to be with you, Blake, no other. Promise me?"

Touching her cheek tenderly, Blake whispered, "I promise." Then he brushed his lips over hers. "I have something
for you, Katrina."

Blake pulled something from his pocket and handed it
to her. Katrina looked down at a black velvet box lying in
her hands and raised questioning eyes to him. "It was my
mother's. I would be pleased if you would wear it tonight.
For me."

A shiver ran over Rina as she opened the box and found
nestled among the velvet a magnificent gold necklace stud-
ded with dark rubies. Katrina was at a loss for words, but
Blake knew her answer.

"We really must go, so let me put it on." Grasping the
necklace, Blake clasped it firmly about Katrina's slender
neck.

It felt cold and heavy around her neck, but when she
looked into the mirror, she saw how well it complemented
her gown. "Oh, Blake, I've never seen anything so beautiful," sighed Katrina in awe.

"Neither have I, little one."

When Katrina met his eyes, she knew he had not meant
the necklace, and she blushed with pleasure.

"Shall we go?" asked Blake, holding out his arm to
Katrina. Together they left the room to join Ryon and
Rebecca, who waited downstairs.

Katrina did not hear the announcement of their arrival,
nor did she notice the room become silent as she and Blake
descended the grand staircase into the ballroom. She observed none of the stares, heard none of the hushed whis-
pers. All Katrina's attention was drawn to the magnificent
gilded cage they seemed to have walked into. Everywhere
she looked, gold glittered and white marble shone as thou-
sands of candles lit the enormous room, bathing everything
in their warm glow. Fresh flowers of every imaginable kind
filled the room with their fragrant perfume, and delighted
her eyes with their vibrant color.

Only moments after their arrival, trumpets blared as the
King and his Queen were announced. As the royal couple
passed by, Katrina and Blake bowed in respect.

After several minutes of introductions the dancing started, and much to Katrina's relief, Blake whirled her onto the dance floor. It felt so wonderful to be held in his strong arms as he led her effortlessly about the floor. Blake held her close, too close for propriety, but neither cared about the raised eyebrows and speculation they caused. This was their night and nothing and no one could do or say anything to ruin it.

They continued right on to the next dance and no man dared to break in. The few who tried were blatantly ignored. It became obvious that Blake Roberts had no intention of sharing the beautiful newcomer.

Later, as they stood sipping champagne, Katrina felt as if she were in a magical dream. Blake was so handsome. Dressed in dark gray, he looked quite somber compared to the colorful peacocks strutting around the room, with their powdered wigs and gold snuff boxes. He seemed to emit a sense of power and control. He made no effort to disguise his feelings for her and Katrina did not care. No, it did not matter to her if these strangers gossiped about them. It did not matter at all.

Turning to his brother, Ryon smiled devilishly, looking so very much like his older sibling. "Well, Blake, do you trust my honor enough to allow me the privilege of a dance with your lady? I assure you, your black looks will not send me away as they have everyone else."

Blake and Katrina burst out laughing and exchanged tender glances. "I'll make an exception only for you."

Katrina took Ryon's extended arm and allowed him to lead her onto the dance floor. This time Katrina was aware of the eyes that watched them and smiled as she remarked, "It seems we are being watched, Ryon."

"There is nothing you can do tonight that would not be noticed. I fear your reputation is being ripped apart by all the wicked women that are green with envy and jealousy. Blake's apparent possessiveness has not helped matters any."

Katrina's laughter mixed with the music, her eyes sparkling with delight.

"You don't care?" asked Ryon, seeing her lightheartedness.

Shaking her head, Katrina grinned. "Not in the least."

"They will assume that you and Blake are having an affair!"

Katrina met Ryon's brown eyes and stated simply, "But we *are* having an affair. I do not know these people, they are not my friends, so why should I care what they think or say? Those whom I do care about, know me and care for who I am, not what I do."

Ryon remained silent for a moment, then bluntly asked Rina a question. "Do you love Blake?"

"It does not matter if I do or not. You should know that Blake is incapable of truly loving a woman. To love someone, you must trust them. Blake does not know how to trust. I accept that. At this moment, he needs me and I need him. It is enough."

Ryon could see in her eyes that Katrina did love Blake, and for some reason, he felt sad. "Tell me, Katrina. Will it always be enough?"

"I don't know," she answered. "I try not to think of things to come. It does no good to dwell on the future, for it will be the same, no matter what."

At that moment the dance ended and they started back to Blake, who stood waiting. As they neared him, Katrina saw the bored look on his face, then spotted the cause. Catherine Ramsey was leaning close to him to whisper something in his ear, allowing him a clear view of her ample bosom. Katrina felt the old fury stir within her. Ryon glanced at Rina and saw the coldness and grim set of her mouth. He smiled. He wouldn't miss this encounter for the world!

As Katrina and Ryon weaved their way toward Blake, Catherine's shrill laughter reached her ears, grating on her nerves. Coming up behind Lady Ramsey, she heard her last remark to Blake.

"I'm certain you are not expected to dance with your little charge all night long, darling. I'm sure she would understand if you were to dance with others; after all, she is."

Katrina smiled at Blake as he lifted an eyebrow in amusement. Catherine noticed and spun around and found herself face to face with Katrina.

"Lady Ramsey, I assure you, Blake is free to dance with whomever he likes." Katrina spoke politely. None of the feelings that were so apparent in her eyes were heard in her smooth voice.

"That's very generous of you, Lady Easton." Catherine's voice dripped with sarcasm as her green eyes flashed. "After all, it was only out of courtesy to the King that he has escorted you. At least that is what I heard. You know how quickly gossip spreads at court."

Katrina moved to Blake's side and wrapped her hand around his arm, knowing that Catherine was grinding her teeth in jealousy. She parried with the older woman, her voice sweet and innocent. "Yes, Lady Ramsey, I am most fortunate to have this most handsome man as my escort. And to think that I also have the privilege of his company during the day"—she paused a second—"and night. I'm overwhelmed with gratitude."

Catherine gasped in surprise. Her eyes narrowed dangerously as she contemplated raking her nails across the younger woman's beautiful face.

"Oh, by the way"—Rina smiled—"I wouldn't bother saving a dance for Blake, he has promised them all to me. So sorry, dear, but tonight he is all mine."

Quickly, Blake pulled Katrina away before Lady Ramsey completely exploded, but most of all, before he broke out laughing. Ryon trailed behind them. Whispering into her ear, Blake chuckled softly, "You are vicious, little one."

Once the threesome reached a private alcove, Katrina turned to Blake. "She deserved it, Blake. I'll not allow anyone to walk all over me!"

"You would have disappointed me if you had." He smiled in return.

"And I, too, would have been dreadfully disillusioned had she bested you."

Everyone turned in surprise to see Lieutenant Greerson standing nearby as he stepped closer. Katrina's face lit up as she greeted him warmly. "David, I'm so glad to see you!"

"And I to see you. The last time I saw your beautiful face was after you had tumbled down an embankment and had a nasty cut on your head. I trust you are well?" David's eyes sparkled warmly as he took in every detail of Katrina's appearance. How was it that she could be even more lovely than before?

Blake was silent as he observed Lieutenant Greerson, seeing the obvious tenderness in his eyes. Katrina's warm reception did nothing to ease his sudden burst of jealousy, let alone his uneasiness with the fact that this man knew her secret.

Rina smiled and said, "I'm very well, David. Thanks to you."

"Yes," stated Blake, trying to cover the hostility he'd felt at hearing Rina call Greerson by his first name. Offering his hand to the man, he managed to keep his voice neutral. "It was fortunate that you and Ryon were nearby to help. I'm very grateful."

At that moment Katrina was approached by a servant and told that the King wished to have the next dance with his ward, so she quickly rushed off. Ryon excused himself to find Rebecca, leaving the two men standing alone. The next few minutes were awkward as they stood and watched Katrina dance with the King of England.

"She is quite a woman, Lord Roberts. You are a very lucky man," said David wistfully. "Very lucky indeed."

Blake's face clouded as the now familiar jealousy began to twist at his common sense. He could see the admiration plastered on the young man's face as the Lieutenant watched Rina's every movement. Blake's voice turned as cold and unfeeling as his eyes. "Tell me, Lieutenant, what did Katrina do to convince you to let her go? She told me you knew she was the Angel, and yet you allowed her to go free. Why?"

Shock registered on the Lieutenant's face as he glanced nervously about him. "No need to worry, Lieutenant Greerson," assured Blake. "It seems we both share Rina's secret. Now tell me, what changed your mind? It seems you not only risk your career, but your life as well, by allowing the Angel her freedom."

David looked at Blake frankly, calm under his fiery scrutiny and dark suspicions. "It surprises me, Lord Roberts, that you trust Katrina so little. Katrina Easton is truly a most remarkable woman. I don't know that I've ever admired a woman more. She has her beliefs and convictions, and she stands by them even in the face of death. As to why I actually let her go, it's hard to explain. Let's say I followed my heart, as she does. How could I condemn a woman with so much love in her heart? And no matter what, I shall always stand by her . . . as her friend."

Blake stopped a servant and relieved him of a couple of glasses of champagne and handed a glass to David, his anger gone. "Sometimes I act the fool, especially when it concerns Katrina. It seems she chooses her friends well, so please forgive my rudeness. Shall we start again, David?"

David smiled and lifted his glass in salute: "To Katrina."

"To what do I owe such a tribute?" interrupted Katrina as she walked into the private corner to join them.

Blake looked at Katrina tenderly, his voice as soft as a caress. "Just for giving us the privilege of knowing you, little one."

Katrina's eyes glowed with love as she looked at each man. "No, I am the fortunate one to have such men in my life." She lifted her own glass and drank to them. "To three very special men!"

Blake's face became hard and unreadable as he stared at Katrina, her own look unflinching. "Three?" he questioned quietly.

"David," she said turning her gaze to him, "dear friend, I have broken your laws and lied to you. I have drawn my sword against you, and yet, you have proven to be a good and loyal friend. How could I ever repay such a debt?"

David took Katrina's hand and kissed it gently, his eyes filled with tenderness. "I ask only for your friendship and I shall always be near."

Smiling, Katrina turned to Blake. His eyes were still cold and hard. "Blake, my love, you have saved my life, you even killed to protect me. What have I given you, except worry and pain?"

Blake looked deep into her eyes. Could it be true? Was it love he saw there, or something else? Did he even deserve to be loved by such a woman?

"Oh, little one," whispered Blake, "you have given of yourself. You, Katrina, have given me everything."

Blake kissed the inside of her palm, sending shivers of delight through her. David coughed to get their attention. "You spoke of another man, Katrina," reminded David, his curiosity getting the best of him.

"Yes, I did. The third special man is not here, but back at Tattershall." Katrina spoke, her eyes filling with a tender look of devotion. "John, my dear John. I miss him so."

Blake fought hard to control the jealousy, but his voice came out strained. "The big blond fellow?"

Katrina nodded. "Yes, to him I owe such devotion and love." Seeing the hurt and anger in Blake's eyes, she quickly continued. "Blake, in truth he is no kin, but in my heart, John is my brother and I am his sister. The bond of our love is as strong as the bond of blood and nothing can break it or destroy it. Please understand, John will always be special to me, for he is the brother I never had."

"To John then," said David.

Katrina was about to speak further when she heard her name called. She turned and froze as she saw who had called her. Coming nearer were her uncle, Lawrence Langsford, and his son, Randolph, an ever-present shadow. For a brief instant, Rina was reminded of the devil's disciple.

"Katrina! Is it really you?" cried Lawrence in mock surprise, hugging her to him.

Stiffening, Katrina pulled away, unable to bear his touch. Langsford was taken back by the hatred in her eyes but continued to speak. "It is so amazing that you have been alive all these years."

Langsford's voice simply gushed with sympathy for his niece, but Katrina saw the evil flicker deep in his dark eyes. "I trust you have recovered from the terrible fall you took?"

"Yes," stated Rina flatly. "Isn't it ironic that those two bastards who meant to rape me actually did me a favor?"

Katrina watched him carefully as he replied, "In what way, Katrina?"

"Had they not been chasing me, I wouldn't have fallen and hit my head and recovered my memory. It seems I owe them a great deal, and they don't even know it."

She casually glanced from one man to the other, her eyes showing clearly that she knew it had been they, but for now, that would be between them.

Wary of her reasons for keeping silent, Lawrence cleared his throat nervously and smiled at her. "Katrina, there is much we must discuss. I was hoping to stop by soon and visit. It will give us the chance to make up for lost time and perhaps clear up a few minor details. When would be best for you, dear?"

Katrina's expression never changed and her voice was even and clear. "We have nothing at all to discuss, Langsford, and I do *not* wish to see you again. Furthermore, I am not your *dear,* and you would be wise not to call me that again!"

Katrina then turned away rudely, ignoring the gasp of surprise and the flicker of anger in the shocked man's eyes. Smiling sweetly, she said to Blake, "I believe this dance is yours."

Chapter 16

The streets were dark and empty, for most people had sought
the safety and warmth of their homes as the storm continued
to release its fury. A downpour battered the lone rider, and
the wind tore about him, whipping the rain into his face.
Slowly, he made his way to the inn just ahead, stopping in
front of its sign, which swung precariously on its hinges.
Stiffly, Blake slid from his weary horse and opened the door
to step inside. As the cold gust of wind and rain blew into
the room, everyone turned to see who had dared to so disturb
them, but words of anger froze in their throats as they took
in the stranger's large, muscular frame. Blake ignored them
all, speaking only to the innkeeper who hurried to do Blake's
bidding. After he had been led to his small but comfortable
room, Blake stretched out on the bed, wishing he was in
London and not stuck on the coast of France waiting for a
storm to pass.

God, he was tired. Closing his eyes, Blake once again
began to wonder why Ryon had sent him that message telling
him to return home as quickly as possible. Was something
wrong with Katrina? No, it couldn't be. Beautiful Katrina!
He missed her more than he cared to admit. He hadn't
wanted to take this trip at all, and he'd been away for a

whole damn month. But when he received word that his chief manager in Constantinople had died, he had no choice but to go. The man had managed all of Blake's business in the city—shipping and trade companies, warehouses filled with merchandise, land and properties and other smaller enterprises in the largest trading center between Europe and Asia. The Roberts empire had many interests in Turkey, and it was extremely important a new manager be selected as quickly as possible.

Blake had made certain the man's widow and family were well provided for and it took some time to find someone to fill his position, but Blake felt confident he had done well in choosing a replacement. He was about to return home when he received his brother's brief message. He'd left immediately, but just off the coast of Spain a spring storm had forced his ship to seek a safe harbor. Hoping that he could cover at least some distance by land, Blake had bought a horse and traveled north, but the weather grew worse. So here he waited in a small village in France, his mind filled with worry as he tried to figure out what could possibly be wrong. Why hadn't Ryon explained in the message? What could possibly be so urgent? Once again he thought of Katrina and his tension eased.

They had shared a wonderful two weeks following the ball. He'd sent for Jake, Jenny, and John, surprising Katrina. He had never seen her so happy. He had devoted the whole two weeks to her and had taken time to get to know John better. Though Blake grew to like the young man very much, he still envied the love and devotion between Kat and John.

In the privacy of Blake's rooms, Katrina and Blake made love as often as they could. Never had Blake experienced such hunger as he felt with Katrina. The more he had her, the more he wanted her. He was beginning to doubt he would ever tire of her, and with this thought Blake fell asleep, his dreams gentle and arousing as Katrina filled his unconscious mind.

One day crept into two, and two into three as Blake waited impatiently for the storm to pass. His mood became black as worry ate at him, leaving him exhausted and worn.

Finally, he was on his way home. Home to Katrina. As he neared London dread at what he would discover there began to build. He felt near panic when he reached his townhouse and held his breath as he waited for Ryon to explain why he had sent for him.

"Good God, Blake! I was beginning to think you weren't going to get here in time." Ryon paced nervously in front of his brother.

"In time for what? Where is Katrina? I want to see her," demanded Blake, his fears mounting as he watched Ryon's unease.

Ryon stopped his pacing and faced Blake, sympathy apparent on his face. "She is not here, Blake. She will not be back."

Anger filled him, his voice grew hoarse and strained, "What do you mean, she won't be back? Where is she?"

"Katrina is at the palace. She is to be married this afternoon." Ryon watched Blake, alarmed by the pinched, drawn look on his face and dark circles under his eyes. "Blake, it was the King's decision. She is to marry Randolph Langsford. I sent for you as soon as he told her."

"That's absurd!" cried Blake. "Randolph is Katrina's first cousin!"

Ryon shook his head sadly. "No, he isn't, Blake. Randolph is really Lawrence's nephew, not his son. There is no blood relation whatsoever between Katrina and Randolph."

"How? How could this happen?" asked Blake wearily, slumping into a nearby chair. "Tell me everything, Ryon."

"The King sent for Katrina only a few days after you left. He had come to a decision about Camray. I went with her. I thought she might need the support. You and I both realized how much influence Langsford has gained over the years with those at court and with the King himself. King George couldn't take lands for Katrina without alarming many others. They would wonder at the King's stripping a man of his title and lands only to give them to a woman, even if she was a legitimate heir. But I never thought he would marry her to Randolph; certainly Katrina didn't. But it solves his problem—Langsford remains at Camray, but Katrina is also Camray's mistress."

"Katrina," mumbled Blake. "How did she take the news?"

Ryon cleared his throat and saw the torment in Blake's face. "When he told her his decision she became as pale as a ghost. She only stared, unable to speak, and she started to tremble violently. I thought she was going to pass out, but instead she stood and walked out of the room. She said nothing as we rode home, then went straight to her room. When she finally came downstairs, Katrina told us she did not wish to speak of the matter. What must be done, would be done."

Blake stood, a determined look on his face. "I must see her! I cannot let this happen!"

Ryon reached out to stop Blake as he headed for the door. "No, there's nothing you can do. It's too late. The ceremony is in a few hours. Stop and think, Blake! Don't allow your anger to rule you."

Blake pulled his brother's hands from his arm, a hard gleam deep in the gold. "I *will* see her, Ryon. No one can stop me!"

Katrina heard the chime of the small clock sitting on her dressing table and frowned at being reminded of the hour. Soon . . . too soon, she would be married. The thought made her skin crawl. Closing her eyes, she tried to think of other things, something more pleasant . . . something less dreadful than being wed to Randolph Langsford.

"Oh, Blake. Where are you?" whispered Katrina sadly.

"I am here, little one."

Rina whirled about to see Blake standing in her room, and briefly she wondered if he were merely a vision of her longings. Her doubt disappeared as he gathered her into his arms, crushing her to him in desperation, driven by despair and the long weeks apart.

"Oh, God! What trouble have you gotten into while I was gone?"

Katrina pulled away from him. "I had no say in the matter, Blake. It was the King's decision, not mine!"

Blake ran his hand through his tousled hair in frustration. "You can't marry that bastard, Katrina!"

"I have no choice."

"Yes you do!" shouted Blake, pain showing on his weary face. "Come with me, little one. We shall go away . . . we can be together, just you and I."

Touching his cheek, Katrina tried to suppress her joy at his show of devotion, but she knew it was impossible. "I cannot, Blake. I gave my word to the King that I would abide by his decision . . . and no matter how it displeases me, I must stand by my promise. I will not defy my King!"

Anger slipped easily into Blake's numbed mind, overpowering all reason or caution. "Don't argue with me, woman! I'll not let you marry Randolph! You are mine! Even the King will not take what I have claimed as my own!"

"Damn you!" Katrina cried, losing control. "Damn you, you egotistical bastard! I belong to no one! Do you understand! I *belong* to *no one!*"

"Do you *wish* to marry him?" Blake asked quietly, the fury in his eyes frightening.

"I wish to do the honorable thing. I wish to keep my word." Her words were tired and strained.

Blake's mind snapped. "To hell with your promises! God damn it, Rina! I'll not give in to your righteous principles! Not this time!"

"Damn you!" Katrina exclaimed in exasperation. How could she convince him? She remembered the hours of heated argument with John. The fools! Did they think it so damned easy to defy their King! Jake's curses and Jenny's endless tears . . . Rina felt like screaming! She felt her own fear; how was she to deal with everyone else's, too? Drawing a deep, calming breath, she set her mind to the task at hand.

"Blake, you must listen to reason!" she begged, trying to get through the hostility and anger she read in his eyes.

"Reason!" he bellowed. "I'll not stand by and let you marry that swaggering fop! Run away with me! I'll take care of you."

"You are a fool!" Katrina spat angrily. "Do not expect me to be one, too!"

Her cruel words brought a hardened stare from Blake, his jaw tensing at the look in her eyes. "What do you mean, a fool?"

Rina flinched slightly at the cold tone of his words but knew what she must do. She could not allow Blake to endanger himself by defying the King. "Yes, a fool, Blake Roberts! You expect me to go away with you and mark myself a traitor! You, sir, are not worth such dishonor! You ask me to leave my home and friends forever! I would never see my Camray, it means *everything* to me! I could not leave Jake and Jenny, and what of my dearest John? Then there are all the people of Tattershall; if I was willing to hang to help them, I certainly can marry for them! What do you offer that is worth giving up everything in my life for?"

Hurt registered clearly in Blake's eyes, "We would be together, Rina. As it should be."

"What? Are you offering marriage, Blake?" Her blunt question caught him off guard, the surprise leaving him speechless. "Just as I thought! You will *never* offer me marriage, but Randolph *has!* You really are a fool! Do not ask me to go away with you, I've no taste for fools!"

Katrina felt her heart breaking. Her own torture was greater than that she inflicted. She wanted more than anything to beg his forgiveness, but she could not. Her word had been given, and no matter how distasteful this marriage was to her, she would be wed to Randolph. She would deal with Lawrence and Randolph on her own.

"You lie! I can see the lies you tell me, your eyes betray you, Rina!"

"No, Blake," she replied evenly, "it is the truth!"

"No! You're lying!" insisted Blake stubbornly, the hurt overwhelming. "The lies come so easily . . . don't they, Rina? As long as they achieve whatever it is you are after."

Blake *could not* believe her ugly words, not after the weeks of loving and gentleness they had shared. To believe her would break his heart . . . she *was* lying! "Well . . . the lies falling so quickly from your lovely lips have accomplished one thing, I hope it is what you had meant to achieve, little one. You will have it as you wish, I'll not play the fool and interfere with the marriage."

Turning in frustration and anger, Blake walked away from Katrina, missing the look of relief on her face... missing the look of pain in her eyes. It was one of the hardest things she had ever done, to stand by and let him leave her life for good.

Blake stood next to Ryon and Rebecca, waiting for the ceremony to begin, unaware of anything but his own pain. He heard none of the gossip and saw none of the curious glances; he only waited. When at last Randolph Langsford appeared, his father close behind, Blake stood perfectly still; only his eyes betrayed the hot anger. As Randolph stood looking over the crowd, he met the hostile amber eyes that locked with his in silent combat.

Randolph stirred uneasily, the hair on the back of his neck prickling with a fear he seldom felt. He had heard of Lord Roberts' expertise with pistol and sword. He prayed he would never have to fight this menacing man, for Randolph was not so naive as to believe he would stand a chance against such power and skill. Lawrence Langsford also saw Blake's fiery stare but smiled calmly, unconcerned. After tomorrow Katrina Easton would no longer be a threat to either of them, and Camray would continue to be his and his only.

Suddenly, the music changed and everyone turned to see the bride enter. Blake's heart jumped when he saw Katrina walking down the long aisle on the King's arm. Never had she been more beautiful. As she came closer, Blake could see that her lovely face was blank; her sapphire eyes held no emotion or sparkle. Blake's mind screamed at him and strained his already taunt nerves to the point of breaking. Katrina deserved better than this! Why hadn't he married her long ago!

As Katrina walked numbly to the altar, she willed her mind to emptiness, forcing the overwhelming sense of loneliness to recede into a dark corner. She looked at no one, but when she neared the front where Blake stood, Rina could feel his presence and stiffly turned to meet his gaze. Her breath caught in her throat when she saw the agony he felt etched so clearly on his face. She turned pale and stumbled slightly. If it had not been for the King's strong arm, she would have fallen.

Blake started to reach out for her, thinking she was going to faint, but Ryon held him back. For a brief moment he saw the fear in Katrina's eyes, and her lower lip trembled slightly. He remembered seeing the same terror and vulnerability only during the times he had comforted her after one of her terrifying nightmares. Then it was gone as Katrina defiantly held up her head, determination overtaking her fears.

Dear God, thought Katrina as she made the last few steps, what am I to do? The man I truly love can only stand by and do nothing. Because I am a woman, I am unable to determine my own destiny. The King may use me as a pawn to satisfy the men surrounding him.

Katrina stepped up to the altar and stood beside Randolph, her spirit returning. No! she decided to herself. I will not be beaten by these bastards! I *will* find a way out. Even the King cannot control my mind; it is mine and mine alone! I have chosen to give my love to Blake Roberts, and no other man can claim it, no matter whom I find myself married to!

Unflinchingly, she met Randolph's eyes, her gaze steady and calm. Suddenly her fears vanished, and she felt a surge of the inner strength she had survived on for so long.

The ceremony seemed to drag on forever but Blake's eyes never left Katrina. She was dressed in an extravagant gown of creamy satin and lace, a long train trailing behind her in folds of shimmering fabric. Hundreds of tiny pearls adorned the gown, with strands carefully styled into her golden hair, and a delicate necklace of the same pearls lay gently around her neck. Katrina was truly the most beautiful bride Blake had ever seen.

He suddenly became aware of the uneasy silence in the chapel. Everyone waited for Katrina's "I do," but none came. The Bishop repeated the question nervously but Katrina stood in silence. Blake could see Randolph's lips tighten in anger, but she steadfastly refused to answer. Blake knew she would not. Everyone began to fidget nervously and finally the King himself answered for her. When Randolph went to place the gold band on her hand, he had to reach for it, and when he bent to kiss her, Katrina turned her head away, allowing only a peck on the cheek. As the couple left the chapel, Randolph was red-faced with humiliation and fury.

Once out of sight, Randolph jerked Katrina around and grabbed her shoulders painfully. "You little bitch! I should beat you for that little scene you caused!"

Katrina ignored the painful grasp and narrowed her eyes at him. "Lay one hand on me and you will never see tomorrow."

The words came out in a vicious hiss that took Randolph by surprise. Katrina wrenched free and stormed off, leaving her new husband standing alone. Blake emerged from the church just in time to see her disappear. He could tell by her walk that she was angry and by the expression on Randolph's face that he was shocked to find his bride such a hot-tempered vixen. Blake could not help but smile.

Katrina ran into the powder room, startling the young girls waiting to attend the needs of the ladies. They stared in surprise as the beautiful bride slammed the door angrily and then kicked it with a vengeance. Katrina noticed their frightened expressions and knew they feared her anger would be vented on them. Her own personal maid stood and crossed to her. Becky's face showed no fear, for over the last few weeks she had gotten to know Katrina well.

"Becky, I have this terrible need to break something!" fumed Katrina.

Picking up an empty pitcher, Becky handed it to her. "Here, try this, mum."

Grabbing it, Katrina hurled it against the wall, letting out an angry yell. All the girls' eyes became wider as they watched the object hit the wall and shatter into hundreds of pieces. The sound of it breaking seemed to soothe Katrina somewhat, and when she turned back around, laughter began to take over.

"Oh, dear," giggled Rina, "I feel so silly, but it felt so wonderful! I imagined it to be Langsford's head!"

Laughter erupted contagiously among all the women in the room until they finally managed to control themselves.

Katrina wet a cloth and soothed her warm brow, knowing she would have to go back to the reception and dinner. Smiling at Becky, Katrina removed the heavy gold band that Randolph had placed on her finger only moments before.

"Here, Becky, this should make up for the extra work I have caused you. Split whatever you get with all the girls here. Buy yourselves something frivolous for a change."

Becky stood, staring down at the gold band, knowing it would bring more money than any of them would ever see at one time. Shaking her head, Becky stammered, "Oh, mum! No! 'Tis yer weddin' band. Ye cannot give it away!"

Shrugging her shoulders nonchalantly, Katrina answered the girl, "I don't want it. If you don't take it, I'll just throw it away! I will never wear it."

With tears in her eyes, Becky nodded, slipping it into her pocket, and promised to share with the others. Katrina hugged her happily, then said, "I think we had better clean up my mess, before someone else comes in."

"Oh, no! We can do tha'! Ye sit down an' I'll make sure yer hair is in place.

Obeying her, Katrina sat in front of a large mirror and let Becky work on her hair. Just then, the door flew open and Catherine Ramsey flounced in, a wicked smile on her face.

"So, there you are! You naughty girl. You certainly know how to cause trouble." She crossed the room to Katrina and noticed the shattered pitcher. "Really, Katrina! You must learn to control that temper of yours. You may buffalo Randolph, but I assure you, Lawrence will not put up with it."

Stiffly, Katrina stood, her anger returning. Biting back the snide remarks that came to mind, she ignored Catherine's taunts.

Raising an eyebrow at the controlled silence of her foe, Catherine continued, determined to put Katrina in her place. "Well, I'm sure Randolph will keep you with child all the time. Blake will not want you, fat with another man's brat! Then he will be mine!"

Katrina became incensed at the mention of having

Randolph's children. The woman had no decency at all. "You had best watch your tongue, Catherine, my patience is worn quite thin and I don't think you would like me angry."

Catherine did not heed her warning, her own fury showing. "You have no right to Blake! He should be my lover! Not yours! It is really too bad that Lawrence and Randolph did not catch you that day, they would have torn you apart, but now you're at their mercy once again and I doubt that you last very long. It is a husband's right to beat his wife, and today you have given him sufficient reason. I've been told that Randolph enjoys using a whip!"

Katrina's endurance snapped, and had she had the knife she usually carried, she would have used it. Instead, she grabbed a pitcher full of water and threw it into Lady Ramsey's face, soaking her thoroughly. Screaming, Catherine turned to the mirror—her gown was ruined and her hair drenched.

Calm once again, Katrina returned the water pitcher and said, "Blake Roberts will never be yours. He would never lower himself to sleep with a bitch like you."

Catherine sputtered her rage, and Katrina left the room smiling. Just outside the door, Rebecca came running up to her. "What was that scream? Is everything all right?"

"Everything is fine, Rebecca. I am afraid I accidentally spilled water all over Lady Ramsey's new gown and totally ruined her lovely hair. It is a pity that she won't be able to attend the reception and dinner." Katrina's eyes sparkled mischievously as she tried to suppress a giggle. Rebecca looked at her friend and back to the closed door, where Catherine's tantrum could still be heard.

Smiling too, Rebecca put her arm through Katrina's and said, "Yes, what a pity."

Together they burst out laughing and, in a happy mood, returned to the dull, strained reception and dinner.

Randolph glowered menacingly at his wife when she came to stand by his side. Blake watched them, curious at the amused look on her face. Even as Randolph whispered hotly in her ear, Katrina smiled, ignoring him. Rebecca returned to Ryon and Blake; and after much probing, the men learned the reason for their mirth. David and John joined Blake to wait in the reception line slowly filing by the newly married couple.

David noticed that everyone was smiling and asked curiously, "What is so funny, Blake? I didn't think I would find you smiling today."

"It seems our little wildcat is up to mischief. I do believe she will succeed in making Randolph, and the King himself, regret making her marry." Blake smiled but his friends could see the flicker of anger deep in his eyes. It was hard for them all to stand by and do nothing.

John also smiled but it did not relieve the agony he felt inside. "Yes, Kat does not like to have her life controlled, even by King George. Nothing will stop her from making life miserable for Randolph and Lawrence. Her behavior during the ceremony was only the beginning."

Ryon nodded in agreement as did all the others. "She just dumped a pitcher of water on Catherine Ramsey's head. I would have given anything to see that!"

The group's laughter brought strange stares from the other guests and drew Katrina's attention to her friends. Just as Ryon and Rebecca reached her, Randolph snatched her hand roughly and demanded, "Where is your wedding ring, Katrina?"

Calmly, she smiled at her husband, but Katrina's eyes remained hard. "I threw it away."

The words struck Randolph like a blow, and for a brief moment everyone tensed, thinking he would hit her. Katrina stood her ground, daring him to strike her in front of her friends. Even Lawrence paled at her audacity and nerve. Randolph wanted to beat the smile from her face, but common sense stopped him, as he feared the wrath of the men surrounding him.

Turning to Blake, Rina smiled devilishly. "Perhaps this gentleman would like to kiss the bride?"

Blake knew she was going too far but could not resist her tempting lips. He was willing to die for one last kiss. Katrina boldly put her arms around Blake's neck as he pulled her to him. Randolph moved to stop her, but John quickly blocked his way.

Blake finally released Katrina, who stood on her toes and whispered into his ear, "Wait for me tonight."

Blake paused, then nodded and, without a word to Randolph, walked on. Randolph's fury did not lessen, but every time he glanced around, Blake and the others were not too far off. During dinner, Randolph drank excessively of the fine wine, undoubtedly trying to drown his problems. Finally, the huge clock reminded everyone of the lateness of the hour, and Randolph leaned toward his bride. His breath reeked of wine and his voice was slurred as he spoke.

"You had best go upstairs and prepare for your wedding night, and remember, you bitch, it is I who will come to your bed, not Blake Roberts! You shall regret the trouble you have caused today." Randolph drained his goblet once more, swaying slightly in his chair. His eyes drooped and he yawned rudely.

A satisfied smile crossed Katrina's face as she whispered, "Never!"

Just as Randolph was about to make her explain herself, Katrina stood and left the great hall, and Rebecca quietly followed. Randolph filled and drained the wine goblet again, brooding over her curious smile. She had looked like a cat who had just caught the mouse. Damn that bitch! He would make her pay tonight! Another great yawn overtook him.

When it was time for Randolph to go to his young bride, many of the men gaily followed. By the time he had reached his bedchamber only four were left. When he glanced about him, laughing, his eyes grew big and he nearly choked as he found himself staring at Blake Roberts. The three others were Ryon, David, and John.

"W-what's going on?" inquired Randolph drunkenly.

"Why, nothing," explained Blake smoothly. "We've come to deliver you to your lovely bride, nothing else."

Randolph swayed precariously and Blake had to slip an arm around him to keep him from falling. They opened the door and all but carried him inside the room. Katrina stood dressed in a gown and robe, obviously in control and surprisingly calm. Randolph looked at her nervously through heavy-lidded, bloodshot eyes.

"Wh-why aren't you in...bed?" Shaking, Randolph grabbed the post at the end of the bed. He felt so tired. The wine...he had drunk too much wine. Perhaps if he just lay down for a moment. He dragged himself to the side of the bed, sprawled onto it and passed out, forgetting about the men in his room, forgetting his bride, who stood watching him with disgust.

"Good Lord!" exclaimed David. "He's out cold."

Blake looked at Katrina and saw the satisfied smile curling her lips. "What did you give him?"

"Just some powder to make sure he sleeps through the night."

"What about tomorrow night, and the next?" asked Blake, concern edging his voice.

Katrina answered him honestly. "I don't know. I am not sure of anything any longer. Oh, Blake, I can think only of the day at hand...leave the visions of tomorrow be. Let us think only of today...of this very moment. I want tonight to be ours."

When the couple turned to leave Randolph's chamber, they saw they were alone. Silently, they walked to Blake's room. Once inside, with the door bolted, Blake pulled her into his arms. "God, Katrina! I don't know if I can bear the thought of losing you! It seems we have just found something precious between us. I just cannot stand by and let it slip so easily from my fingers. Come with me, we will go away!"

Pulling away, Katrina shook her head. "No! I have told you, no! Do you forget so easily! My word is my honor, to break my word would bring dishonor! I could not bear such grief. Do not ask me to do such a thing!"

"I have not forgotten, Katrina! I remember the lies you told me earlier. I'll not believe you mean what you say! I will take you away, willing or not!" Blake scooped her into his arms, intending to do just that.

"No!" screamed Katrina, twisting about frantically, hitting him as hard as she could. "No! I cannot go with you! I cannot break my word!"

"God damn it, Rina! Your word is not so damned important!" Blake yelled unwisely, dropping her angrily onto the floor.

Katrina's eyes widened in anger, then narrowed. "Why?... Because I am a woman! Does that mean my promises do not matter! If I were a man, then could you respect my wishes?" There was no answer. "Bah! You insult me! You insult my honor and pride! Do you respect me so little, that you cannot consider my own feelings? For once, Blake Roberts, can't you think of someone else's needs besides your own pitiful ones! Do not insult me further by asking me to go with you again! I gave my word to the King, I will abide by his decision."

Blake saw the hurt in her eyes as he asked, "What are your needs, Rina? What is it you really want? Do not tell me lies of wanting to be married to Randolph, not in a million years will I believe that!"

"I will tell you the truth only if you promise to leave things be...let me work out my problems on my own, without interference from you."

He considered her request. He wanted desperately to force her to go with him. But she would never forgive him. Blake could see the grim determination in her eyes. "You have my promise not to interfere."

Rina saw how difficult it was for him to agree to her demand, but there was no other way. Not one she could consider, anyway.

"Oh, Katrina, what can you hope to achieve by this marriage?" asked Blake sadly.

"I will have my Camray back, it *will* be mine, just as it was my father's and great-grandfather's. I will not allow a bastard son to be her master. She *will* be mine!"

"Is it so very important?"

"Yes!" cried Katrina, her eyes pleading with Blake to understand. "It is more important than life itself!" Reaching up, she placed her palm against his cheek. "It is even more important than the love I have for you. My love is a new and tender feeling, whereas my need for Camray is old and established, woven into my heart and soul. Camray *must* be mine, as it should be, Blake."

Blake stood unable to speak. Had he heard her right?

Katrina loved him! Never before had he felt such elation. He cupped her face with trembling hands so that he could clearly see into her cobalt eyes. He saw the truth in them and his own closed momentarily as if to spare him of the pain that was to come.

"What of Randolph? He is your husband!"

"He is nothing! I have done as the King commanded, I will do no more. I give you my love, and only you will be my lover!"

"But tomorrow . . ." started Blake.

Katrina smiled warmly. "Again, you worry of things that have yet to come. Blake, we have only a few hours together. Let us not waste time on things we cannot change!"

He hugged her tightly to his body and whispered hoarsely, "If I were to lose you now, it would be more than I could bear."

"You can never lose me, Blake. I am forever yours, even in death. My soul is yours, so guard it carefully and lovingly." She reached down and pulled off her father's ring and slipped it onto Blake's little finger. "It is the most precious thing I have. As long as you wear this ring it will be a constant reminder of my love, even when we are apart."

Lifting Katrina into his arms, he kissed her tenderly. When he gazed into her eyes, he saw all the love she spoke of. Effortlessly, Blake carried her to the bed and gently laid her on it, removing her gown and robe.

Once he had removed his own clothes, he joined her, and together they shared the pleasure they could give one another. In Katrina's mind, Blake was her husband, and she his wife, their love binding them together in a way no mere ceremony could. As the sun crept into the heavens, Blake and Katrina slept, peacefully, with no worries of what that new day would bring.

Chapter 17

The morning dawned to reveal gray clouds hanging menacingly over the city. But nothing seemed to affect Katrina's happiness, not even the news that they would leave for Camray that same day. Perhaps once she was at Camray, she would find an answer to her current situation. And Blake would be nearby at Windsong.

Lawrence and Randolph were waiting impatiently for Katrina by the carriage. All the other wagons loaded with their trunks had been sent ahead. Katrina started to step inside the plush conveyance but paused to look up into a window. Blake stood watching her, his face only a shadow to her eyes, but she did not need to see his face to feel the sadness etched upon it. Raising her hand to her lips, she blew her love a kiss good-bye, caring not the gesture angered the two men standing next to her. Randolph shoved her roughly inside and crawled in beside her, his fury apparent on his scowling face. After Lawrence was settled comfortably inside the coach, they started home to Camray.

Katrina chose to ignore her companions and remained silent but Randolph did not. "You are a stupid bitch. You will pay for last night!"

She raised amused blue eyes to him, her smile incensing him further. "I trust you slept well?"

Lawrence's eyebrows shot up in surprise. So the gossip he had heard was true! Randolph's face flushed angrily at her casualness, and raising a hand, he slapped Katrina hard across the face, snapping her head back, leaving a stinging imprint of his hand. Expecting her to crumple into tears from such a blow, Randolph was stunned when she looked calmly at him with dry eyes filled with hate and anger. Suddenly, he recalled her earlier threat, as her eyes told him that he had made a mistake he would regret.

"My, my . . . we are such a spitfire, but a foolish one. You risk much with your sharp-tongued arrogance. The consequences could be very severe. It would be a shame to see such a lovely face marred. Even worse things could happen, Katrina." Lawrence's threats seemed to have no effect on her, which left him somewhat confused.

Instead, Katrina became mocking and even more daring. "Is this where I am suppose to swoon or faint dead away at your frightening insinuations? You're a pompous ass, Langsford, and I find it extremely amusing to toy with you and your *son*. Ah, I see I have hit a nerve, Langsford . . . are you getting furious with me?"

Katrina could see his self-control slipping but didn't care anymore. The nine years of hate inside her erupted like a dormant volcano.

"You are a murdering bastard, greedy and lecherous, living on the fear of others. But you will find no fear in me; you killed it over nine years ago when you slaughtered my parents!"

Lawrence choked and Randolph paled, his mouth dropping open in shock. Katrina waited, ready for their reactions. Suddenly, the coach swerved precariously and she heard a shout from the driver; then they came to an abrupt halt. Grasping her knife, which had been hidden among the folds of her skirt, firmly, Rina glanced out to see the driver fall to the ground dead, his throat slit from ear to ear.

Lawrence straightened his coat, unconcerned, his voice smooth. "I couldn't take the chance that you knew I murdered your parents, so I have made arrangements for you."

The door swung open and Katrina found herself looking at the scarred face of the man who tried to rape her at the inn.

"I believe you two know each other." Lawrence's cruel, wicked laughter filled the air, just as it had done the night he had killed his half-brother. "You are a dead woman, Katrina Easton."

Instead of panic, Katrina was filled with a strange calmness, her smile sending shivers through them all. "You thought me dead long ago, you son-of-a-bitch, but you made one mistake. You sent someone else to do your dirty work instead of doing it yourself. I see you have made that same mistake once again."

Suddenly, Katrina bolted, kicking Randolph back with her foot. In the same quick motion she lunged for the door, and when Lawrence reached for her, she slashed at him, cutting a long gash in his arm. Nimbly, she jumped from the carriage and ran for her life, her skirts lifted high to allow her freedom to move. She dashed around the corner of a nearby building and ran straight into scarface's partner, the giant. Before Katrina could make a move he grabbed her about the waist and covered her mouth with a cloth. Struggling, she inhaled the drug generously applied to the cloth and slowly sank into unconsciousness.

The giant carried Katrina back to the coach where Langsford was waiting. Dropping a heavy bag of gold coins into scarface's open hand, Langsford grinned in satisfaction. "Remember, when her body turns up you will receive the rest."

Looking at Katrina's inert body, hanging limply from the giant man's arms, he chuckled. "Unless she has nine lives, Katrina's a dead girl! It's really too bad you missed your chance to have her, Randolph. She really is quite lovely."

Slowly Katrina opened her eyes but closed them quickly when the room began to swim vertiginously about her. Her head felt so heavy she let it fall back onto whatever it was she lying on. She could hear mumbling not too far from her, but she couldn't make out what was being said. After several moments her eyes fluttered open again, this time adjusting to the light and her surroundings. Her head pounded noisily inside her skull as she tried to clear her muddled thoughts.

Dear God, Katrina thought in alarm, it wasn't just a horrible nightmare!

She stared in dismay at the two men across the room as she realized the trouble she was in. This time she knew Blake would not rescue her.

She glanced over to her captors and noticed with satisfaction the gruesome scar she had given the smaller one. It ran from his chin up to the corner of his mouth, across his cheek, and through his left eye, cutting his grizzled brow in two. The eye itself was useless. It rolled up, disappearing under the disfigured lid, leaving only the red-veined yellowed white showing.

Katrina's attention turned to the giant as he stood and moved about the room. The blow Blake had given his nose had left it permanently smashed. He walked with a definite limp, dragging his right foot behind him, and one shoulder seemed to hang quite a bit lower than the other. It was amazing that he had survived such a fall. Yes, these two bastards had reason enough to hate her.

Katrina closed her eyes once more to sleep. She wanted to be well rested before confronting her captors. She awoke abruptly as a foot prodded and kicked at her.

"Come on, bitch! It's time ye were up!" Mack delivered another swift kick, bruising Katrina's ribs and causing her to moan and roll away from him.

Peeking through her closed lids, she looked around her and found it had turned dark. A lamp glowed dimly on the table, where the giant seemed to be occupied with a deck of cards, uninterested in his partner's attempts to awaken her.

Leaning over Rina, Mack tried once again to awaken what he thought was a sluggish and drugged girl. "Up with ye! Me patience is gone!"

Suddenly, Katrina brought her elbow around with all her strength and caught him right in the gut. He doubled over in pain, unable to breathe. She shoved him backward, sending him sprawling on the dirty floor, then as nimbly as a cat, dashed for the door. Before the clumsy giant could reach her, she was gone.

Not knowing where she was, Katrina just ran. The streets were dark and empty, since not many people dared to wander about late at night. As she made her way through the trash and slimy sewage littering the alleys, Katrina prayed she would not meet anyone or anything.

Stopping to catch her breath and decide where to go, Katrina froze at the sight of the bright, beady red eyes of the huge dock rats. They continued to stare at each other, each waiting for the other to make a move. Katrina swallowed hard, facing the terrifying rodents, her fear mounting as the shadows, changed by a passing cloud, revealed their tremendous size. Since childhood, she had abhorred the disease-ridden creatures, and for the first time in many years, she felt genuine terror choking her. The rats seemed to sense her fear and started to move closer. Rina backed away slowly, picking up a large stick to defend herself. Looking behind her, she realized the alley was a dead end. To escape, she had to go past the rats in front of her.

All the horrible things she had heard about the creatures flew through her mind, stories of dock rats actually killing humans for food. In her panic, she believed she would die here, slashed to death by the filthy rats. Abruptly, the rats stopped, distracted by the sound of drunken men passing on the street. One of the men stumbled into the same alley where she stood. The rats suddenly scurried in all directions, one running over Katrina's feet, brushing against her legs. A scream escaped before she even realized she had made a sound. Hearing her, the other men started into the alley.

" 'Ey! 'At sounded like a lassy, it did. W'at would she be doin' in this 'ere alley, mates?"

Another added, "C'mon out, darlin'! Ain't nothin' t' be scared of. 'Ow 'bout a li'tle drink wi' me an' me frien's 'ere!"

Oh, God! screamed Katrina's mind in despair. What next? Preparing herself with the stick as her only weapon, she faced them, feeling more confident against a human foe than she'd felt facing the rodents.

"She don' look t' be too frien'ly, mates. A bit 'igh 'n mighty, methinks."

"Aye! Now c'mon, doxy, ye would no' wan' t' 'urt our feelin's, now would ye?"

Slowly, they crept forward, three against one.

"Com' now lassy. Put th' stick down. We jus' wan' a bit o' fun, we do."

"Yeah, ye'll be thankin' me later, wench, fer givn' ye the best lovin' ye ever 'ad!"

They all began to laugh, licking their lips in anticipation, like dogs about to eat a juicy bone. Katrina's stomach churned violently as she looked at the scum before her. One drooled down his chin as he babbled incessantly about what he was going to do to her. Finally, another man moved, grabbing her, but Katrina reacted quickly by smashing his head fiercely with her stick, sending him reeling backward as blood gushed from his forehead. The others paused in surprise, giving her the chance to dash past them. A pair of grimy hands snaked out and seized her arm, but she twisted, kicking their owner directly in the groin. His howls of pain echoed down the streets, adding to the ranting and raving of the one holding his bleeding head. Katrina ran from the darkened alley, glancing both ways as she emerged. To her right she saw scarface and the giant appear, alerted by the tremendous noise the drunks were making. Behind her came the third bum, the others not far behind him, so she quickly darted to her left. She ran as fast as she could with the five noisy bastards at her heels.

Unexpectedly, she heard the clatter of horse's hooves pounding down the cobbled street. Glancing behind her, she saw a horse and rider streak past her pursuers as he bore down on her. He caught up with her easily and, leaning down, swept her into his strong arms, lifting her onto the horse beside him, her only weapon slipping from her hand and clattering to the ground noisily. Katrina struggled against him, but he had a viselike grip on her. To quiet her yells, he nearly smothered her against his chest. Pulling his horse to a halt, he turned to wait for the others to catch up to him.

"What is going on here?"

All the men quickly recognized Captain Grant Walker,

well known around the docks as a smuggler and slave trader. Carefully, Walker surveyed them all, noticing the bleeding and stooped-over victims of the wildcat he now held.

Mack stepped forward and spoke. "The li'tle bitch got away from Ralph 'n me. We were lookin' fer 'er when these blokes started after 'er. She belongs t' me, Cap'n."

"She didna' belong t' no one when we 'appened on 'er. She damn near split me skull wi' tha' stick o' 'ers! An' blame near busted Sid's balls, she did! I say we share th' bitch!"

Captain Walker's laughter filled the still night air, echoing down the empty streets. "You mean to tell me that five of you could not keep this girl under control?"

His laughter mocked them, but none were foolish enough to say anything. Most of them depended on him for the few coins they made each year. Deciding Katrina wasn't worth the trouble, the three drunks drifted off in search of some more ale and, perhaps, a more willing wench.

"Maybe you and Ralph should explain why you have your hands on such an expensive piece of baggage. I'll deliver her to your shack. Meet me there!"

He looked down at the woman he held as he nudged his horse into a gallop. Pulling her head back with a handful of hair, he met sparkling blue eyes filled with indignant anger.

"Good God!" he exclaimed. "No wonder they were lusting after you, woman! You are a beauty!"

Katrina would have turned away from his bold gaze but he held her head firmly. In minutes they were back to where she had managed her escape, and he slid gracefully from his mount, Rina firmly in tow. Once inside, he locked and bolted the door, whirling about just in time to miss her swinging fist. He merely grinned at her, catching both wrists in one hand as he shoved her hard against the wall to keep her feet from landing against his shins. Pressed against her squirming body, the Captain felt the flare of his own passions.

"Keep struggling and I'll take you myself." His words brooked no disobedience, and Katrina immediately stopped fighting, deciding submissiveness would serve her best for the moment.

"Now, if I let you go, do you promise to behave?"

Katrina made no attempt to answer but turned stubbornly away from his glare.

"If you don't promise, I'll leave you to Mack and Ralph. I guarantee they will do things to you that you have never even imagined, and use you in ways a decent lady wouldn't even think of. You could be worth a lot of money to me, and no matter what Mack's reasons for having you are, I can buy you. Once you are mine, I'll see that no one touches you."

Turning back to look at him, Rina asked skeptically, "And who will protect me from you?"

Captain Walker grinned wickedly. "I never use my merchandise, even when they're as pretty as you. Should the need arise, there are always plenty of women in port willing to please me. Besides, I am not crazy about raping women. Selling them for profit, yes. In Mexico, you would bring me a fortune."

Katrina balked at being sold as a slave, but among the choices she presently had, going with the Captain was best. So much could happen between here and Mexico. It would give her time she did not have with Mack and Ralph. Making her decision, she gave her promise and Captain Walker released her.

Watching her carefully, Grant Walker sat down, stretching his long legs out before him. He was a tall, middle-aged man, with a long lean body, fit from many years at sea. He had light blue eyes and silvery gray hair that stood out in contrast to his sun-bronzed face. His rugged features and full lips might be considered appealing by most women, but Katrina saw only a man who traded in human lives.

"Take your hair down."

The command took Katrina by surprise as she turned to stare at the man. "Go to hell!" she hissed, her anger showing.

"I want to see what I am buying, wench!" His own patience was wearing thin and he snapped at her, "Do it, or I will do it myself!"

Quite abruptly, Rina recalled Mack's grizzled face, and she obeyed hesitantly, removing the few pins left in her hair. It fell to her waist in a shower of gold, the lamplight glistening off the lustrous curls. A pleased smile appeared on Captain Walker's face.

Standing, he walked to her, slowly making a circle around her. Lifting a handful of her hair, he could still smell the faint hint of roses. From the cut of her dress and her speech, she was a fine lady, but there was something different about her. Perhaps it was the defiant tilt of her chin, or maybe it was the way she looked so calm and unafraid. When he came back in front of her, Katrina met his gaze and did not look away.

"What is your name?"

"Katrina Easton."

"Why are you here?" Grant asked bluntly.

Katrina pondered what to tell him, the truth or a lie. Deciding on the truth, she answered, "I was married yesterday to the son of a man who murdered my family over nine years ago to steal our estate. He had me kidnapped this morning and has paid them to kill me."

Captain Walker raised an eyebrow in amusement at her uncaring attitude. "Then it should be simple enough to get Mack to sell you to me."

"I doubt that," she stated matter-of-factly.

Confused, Grant asked, "Why not? I know Mack as a greedy son-of-a-bitch. For gold he would do anything."

Katrina shrugged her shoulders, feigning disinterest. "Maybe so, but by killing me, Mack and Ralph will also achieve personal satisfaction and vengeance."

"You talk of being killed so casually, Katrina. Don't you fear what they would do to you?" The Captain continued to watch her face for some signs of emotion.

"No, I don't fear them," she said quite honestly.

A banging on the door interrupted Grant Walker, and he turned and yelled angrily, "Wait out there!"

The pounding stopped and Katrina could hear Mack's grumbling, but he waited outside as he was told.

"Now, why would that ugly bastard want to seek revenge on someone as lovely as you?" he asked quizzically.

"I ran into Mack and Ralph on a visit here. They tried to accost me, but I managed to get away." It was not a pleasant memory and Rina paused a moment, unwilling to go on.

The Captain, curious, prodded her. "Go on! That certainly isn't any reason to kidnap and murder you. Tell me!"

She was silent for a moment. Then, seeing that it made no difference one way or the other, Katrina decided to tell him. "They followed me with two others and that night at an inn, they broke into my room. They caught me asleep and were going to rape me. Mack's scar and Ralph's limp are the result of that night. But they're luckier than their two friends. They're dead."

"God! You're a little spitfire, aren't you?! If I hadn't seen some of your handiwork on those drunks out there, I'd find it hard to believe what you have just told me. You've got more meanness and guts than most of the men on my ship!" He threw back his head and laughed heartily. His luck was certainly with him tonight. What a gem!

His humor only further irritated Katrina. "Now what?" she snapped.

"Patience, little girl. Losing your temper won't help you any," the Captain chided, lighting a cigar.

Katrina's head whipped around angrily, her eyes spewing fire as she stood before him, hands on her hips. "I am not a little girl! And I am not your property! You're no better than Mack and Ralph, and I will do whatever I can to be free of all of you. You sell women for profit, and to me, you are the lowest of bastards!"

Reaching out, Walker seized Katrina roughly, his own temper flaring at her sharp tongue. Throwing her down onto the mat, he fell on top of her, pinning her body beneath him. He captured her wrists in one hand and jerked them above her head, while his other pulled out his knife. Furious, he held it against her long, slender neck, the blade cold against her flushed skin.

"So, I am a bastard, huh? You still think so?" whispered the man, his face only inches from hers.

"Yes," Katrina spat, feeling the blade dig into her tender skin. "You are a filthy bastard!"

A wicked grin spread across his face as he began to laugh. "Yes, I suppose you're right, and since I am such a bastard, I should take you myself, right now. Then leave you to the dogs outside."

"Yes, I suppose you could," Katrina agreed evenly.

"You are a hell of a woman, Katrina Easton, but it would be a shame to waste such beauty and spirit on Mack and Ralph. You may just be more trouble than you're worth, but I'm willing to take the risk. I may even have to change my rules about mixing business with pleasure." Laying his knife carelessly across her throat, he bent his head and kissed the soft flesh along the curve of her neck.

"But now I have business to take care of."

Chapter 18

"What do you mean she was kidnapped?" Blake angrily grabbed Lawrence Langsford, out of control with fear and fury. Ryon pulled his brother off Lawrence, knowing Blake could easily have killed him.

Holding his wounded arm, Langsford attempted to explain further, the black scowl on Blake's face making him fidget nervously. "The carriage was stopped at the edge of London; our driver was killed. One of the two men that accosted us threw open the door, and Katrina jumped out the other side and ran, but another giant of a man was waiting for her. He put something over her mouth and she blacked out. I thought they meant to rob us, but the big man carried her off, leaving us be. It was then I attempted to stop the man nearest the carriage, but he cut my arm with his knife. In a few seconds, they had both disappeared. I assume they intend to hold Katrina for ransom."

Blake's voice was hard and steely, his eyes liquid fire. "You had no weapons to protect yourselves and Katrina?"

"Of course not," snapped Lawrence defensively. "We would have caught up with the other wagons in no time at all. I never dreamed we'd be attacked!"

"What did these men look like?" Ryon asked quietly.

219

Lawrence cleared his throat before he began. "The man who caught Katrina was extremely large and stocky. The most noticeable thing about him was that he seemed to be somewhat crippled. His nose looked to have been broken quite badly and one shoulder slumped lower than the other, but most of all, he walked with a terrible limp, one leg dragging as he walked. The other was quite a bit smaller, but fearsome-looking. He had the most monstrous-looking scar from his chin up through his eyebrow. One eye was blind and gruesomely disfigured."

The room became grimly silent, and suddenly all their attention was drawn to Blake as the glass he held in his hand snapped, breaking into fragments as it fell to the floor.

"Those bastards! I'll kill them! I will hunt them down and kill them!" Blake started for the door but Ryon immediately blocked his exit.

"What is it, Blake?" he demanded. "What do you know about Katrina's kidnappers?"

Blake stopped dead in his tracks, as fear and sorrow mixed with his immediate fury. "Kidnappers, hell!" Suddenly, he felt so helpless and he finally voiced the horrendous truth out loud. "They are going to kill her."

Everyone was shocked; even Lawrence and Randolph managed to act alarmed. "What do you mean, Blake? Explain yourself!" Ryon cried.

"I mean those two sons-of-bitches will kill her! I cannot make it any clearer!"

Ryon looked down at his brother's bleeding hand and pulled a handkerchief from his pocket, then wrapped it to stop the flow of blood. "How can you be so sure? Did Katrina know them?"

Emotionally drained, Blake sank into a chair, and Ryon handed him another drink. After draining it, Blake carefully explained about the night at the inn. After he had finished, no one could speak. Silently, Blake stood and strode from the room, braced to begin his desperate search.

By the end of the third day, Blake was nearly insane from worry and frustration. The nights proved to be worse torture than the days, dreams of his golden-haired Rina and her enchanting beauty haunting him. So Blake slept little, which only added to his foul, ugly mood. He ate only to satisfy Rebecca's nagging; he had not shaved in several days, his clothes were dirty and rumpled from all the hours spent searching London for word of Katrina. His face was hard and grim, his golden eyes showing the barely controlled violence he held inside him.

After another futile day of searching with John and Ryon, they returned to Lord Roberts' townhouse, exhausted. Blake sank into his chair in the quiet library, a brandy in his hand. He felt totally numb as fatigue began to overcome him, leaving only the haunting memories of Katrina to drift wildly through his thoughts. Then all at once he saw the man with the scarred face and the giant, as his fears took over even his memories. Blake remembered how easily the giant's grip had encased Katrina's slender throat, crushing the life from her as he lifted her frail form off the floor. Mack's face began to torture him as he pictured Katrina being raped and beaten brutally. Her screams filled him with terror and fear, his body going cold and clammy as he sat frozen, unable to move. Blake could feel her degradation as an agonizing pain such as he had never experienced before ripped through him. He could hear her crying, see the tears streaming down her cheeks.

"Oh, God, no . . . !" cried Blake as his own tears started, releasing the unbearable despair building inside of him. "No!" He could hear Katrina's cries of pain, and despaired as he heard her calling his name.

"Katrina!" screamed Blake.

"Blake," said Ryon. "Are you all right?"

Blake's senses cleared and he knew it was Ryon who had been calling him and not Rina. But the screaming and crying . . . it had all seemed so real. Blake suddenly tensed as the sound of someone weeping did reach his ears. He jumped from his chair and turned to face his brother, all the blood draining from his face as a cold chill swept over him, leaving him weak-kneed. The look on Ryon's face was more than he could bear.

"I heard a scream?" whispered Blake faintly.

"It was Jenny," croaked Ryon. "A messenger just came,

Blake. They found Katrina." His voice broke as he searched for the right words, but none would come.

Blake bolted for the door. "I must go to her!"

"No! Blake!" yelled Ryon, clinging to him. "It's too late. Katrina's dead!"

Blake looked at his younger brother in disbelief, the words echoing in his crazed mind. Katrina's dead! Katrina's dead!

"Nooooo . . . !" The cry erupted from deep within him, like the howl of an injured animal. Blake lost all control as the tensions of the past week boiled to the surface in a violent storm. He knew only immense rage and pain at the two words he could not bear to hear.

Shoving Ryon aside, Blake bellowed like a madman, heading for the door. As he flew past his brother, David and John met him. Seeing the violence on his face, both tried to grab him. He threw them off as if they were nothing.

"Nooooo . . . !" He continued to scream, his yells echoing through the townhouse. "She's not dead! Not my Katrina!"

Soon they were all on him as he fought blindly, fiercely, not really knowing why he wanted to hurt them. He only knew he must go to Katrina. She would need him to ease her pain. No, no! His mind reeled. Maybe he was wrong . . . he needed her to ease his pain!

Yes! he thought. Katrina would ease his pain. Oh, God! Nooooo . . . ! They were lying!

They pulled Blake to the ground, but he continued to struggle to free himself. His mind began to blur as it fought with reality. Then, as suddenly as the rage had come, it went, leaving Blake lifeless as his brother watched him with deep concern. They finally let him go, but he made no move and his eyes stared blankly.

"Blake," whispered Ryon fearfully, "are you all right?" He helped Blake up, but still, Blake made no reply. Silently, they all followed Blake back into the library, no one certain of what to say or do.

Blake stared into the flames of the fire as sanity flooded back, leaving him spent and worn. When he finally spoke, it was in a hoarse whisper, barely audible to the men in the room. "Where is she?"

Ryon glanced about nervously, uncertain his brother was up to seeing Katrina. "At the palace chapel. The King ordered her body taken there. It was found only an hour ago."

"I must see her," stated Blake simply.

Ryon shook his head as he looked sadly at his older brother. If only he could spare him this agony. "No, Blake. I think it best you do not go. Not now. You have had quite a shock, you could not take another."

"Another?" questioned Blake, turning a puzzled look on him. "Tell me, Ryon, what could I not take?"

David stepped forward, sensing Ryon's despair and explained, "She has been beaten very badly, to the point of being unrecognizable, Blake."

"Then how the hell can they be certain it is Katrina?" Blake queried hopefully.

"It's Kat, Blake. She has on the dress and things she wore the day she left," replied John, his own grief showing on his strained face.

Determined, Blake turned to them. "I *am* going to see her."

A moan escaped Blake as the cloth covering Katrina's inert body was removed. Her body was battered and broken, beaten beyond recognition, telling Blake of the horrors she must have gone through before death finally released her from the pain. Her neck had been broken, and Blake could see the bruises and red marks where the giant's hand must have been. But his eyes were drawn to her cheeks, covered in blood and grime, a trail of tears streaking down the bruised and marred flesh. There was no longer any evidence of the beauty she had once possessed.

Blake's own tears ran down his bristled cheeks, unheeded. He did not care if the whole world witnessed his grief and sorrow. Nothing and no one existed but the defiled body lying before him. Pain ripped through him as he relived the agony Katrina must have experienced.

"I will kill the bastards!" Hatred began to burn inside Blake, giving him the will to go on. "I will kill them!"

Blake left Katrina, knowing that what he had just seen would haunt him forever.

                              * * *

Hera tore across the countryside as Blake leaned low over her neck, feeling the wind on his face. It seemed to clear his mind somewhat. The funeral of his beloved Katrina had left him empty and tremendously lonely. Unable to bear it any longer, Blake had started back for London, the scene he had left behind forever printed on his memory.

The small graveyard at Camray had been filled with grieving people; more had waited outside. Katrina had been loved by many and her violent death had come as a tremendous shock to them all. The love and devotion Blake saw touched him deeply as he watched the people file by the freshly dug grave. Now, after nine years, Katrina was finally laid to rest beside her mother and father.

Blake rode straight to London, stopping only to feed and rest Hera. Pushing himself to the point of exhaustion made it easier for Blake to sleep. Memories during his waking hours were enough to endure without the realistic dreams that came in his sleep. Once in London, he found it difficult to live with the constant memory of Katrina, and brandy became medicine to numb his pain. Nights were torturous, so Blake spent them gambling and drinking in a desperate attempt to forget, but nothing worked, for Katrina's spirit was indeed with him, her soul forever destined to remain in his heart.

Weeks passed in a blur as Blake drowned himself in sorrow and self-pity. David watched his friend in concern one night as Blake worked on sending himself to oblivion. "Don't you think it is time we headed for home? You look like you have had enough."

Blake stared at David through red, bloodshot eyes. "No!" he mumbled, his speech slurred. "Nooo! I have not had enough! Not until I pass out. Then she won't come."

He took another deep drink and slammed the glass down angrily. "Damn her! Damn that witch for haunting me!"

"Come on, Blake," coaxed David, standing, holding a hand out to help his drunken friend to stand.

"Leave me be!" Blake shoved David's hand away. "She was a witch, you know. From the first time I saw her, she bewitched me, weaving her spells on me! Just like she did those damn animals! Katrina was a witch, I say!"

David frowned at what Blake was muttering, glad no one was around to hear his words. "You don't know what you're saying. You're drunk!"

"Hell, I do know what I am saying! I can't get her out of my mind! How do you break the spell of a dead woman? Am I to live with the torture for the rest of my life? The pain only grows in intensity. She is with me every moment. Oh, God! Sometimes I can see her as clearly as I can see you, but when I reach out to touch her, she's gone. She disappears, leaving me alone, like an empty shell. Katrina said her soul was mine, to guard it carefully, but instead, she has taken mine."

"And you think this brandy will make you forget her?" asked David angrily, pushing the bottle away. "It's a good thing she can't see you now. You would disgust her. You're wallowing in self-pity, Blake, something I never thought I would ever see you do. Personally, I find it nauseating."

Blake jumped up and roughly grabbed his friend by the collar, slamming him against the wall. "I should break your head!" Blake muttered, then quickly released him, turning away. "Leave me alone!"

David straightened his clothes, picked up his hat and redingote, and stated, "With pleasure."

Blake sat alone, staring blankly at the floor. "Dear God, how can I learn to live with the pain I feel? How can I live without Katrina?" No answer came from the silence around him, no comfort and no peace. Slowly, Blake stood, tossed a handful of coins onto the table, and left. The air was cool and crisp. He took a deep breath and felt his head clear a bit, then he hailed a cab.

He climbed inside and ordered the man to drive about, anywhere, not really wishing to go home to an empty bed, but most of all, not wishing to return home and face the memories that waited for him. Leaning back, Blake watched out the carriage window as it made its way down the narrow, cobbled streets of London. It was not really so late, for Blake had started his drinking quite early. He knew there were plenty of places he could go, but he was not in the

mood to be around people. The brandy began to loosen its
hold on him, clearing his head of the numbness he had felt
earlier. Time passed as the coach wound through the dark
streets, its passenger silent and melancholy.

Suddenly, the carriage jolted to a stop, careening precariously from side to side. "What the hell!" Blake scowled,
looking out the window. Two drunken men jumped from
the deadly path of the horses, bellowing angry obscenities
to the driver.

Unconcerned, Blake started to lean back into the seat
when the street lantern illuminated the faces of the two men.
Feeling a chill pass over him, Blake froze, unable to believe
what he had just seen. The coach started up again, turning
the next corner it came to.

"Stop!" called Blake, practically jumping from the moving vehicle. Quickly, he paid the man and started back
around the corner. Carefully, Blake followed the men, the
hair on the back of his neck standing on end.

After several blocks, he was close enough to recognize
them clearly, and he began to stalk them boldly, allowing
them the chance to see they were being pursued. Mack and
Ralph soon became aware of the stranger following and
deliberately led him toward the empty, dangerous docks.

Blake's outward appearance was extremely calm as he
blatantly trailed them, knowing where they were leading
him. Like a jungle cat, Blake moved through the mass of
buildings, all his senses alert. He was after his game and
no one and nothing could stand in his way.

Darting down an alley, Mack and Ralph waited, ready
to spring on their pursuer, but no one came. Nervously,
Mack shrugged and looked at Ralph.

"Where the 'ell did 'e go?" mumbled Mack. Slowly, he
peeked out of the alley and down the street where the man
had been. It was empty.

"'E's gone!"

"Not quite." Blake smiled evilly from behind them in
the darkness.

Surprised, Ralph and Mack turned to see Blake leaning
casually against the building, his arms folded across his
chest.

"W'at ye want?" yelled Mack, his hand wrapping around the knife in his belt.

"I want you two," stated Blake evenly, calmly.

Confused, Mack did not recognize him. "W'at for?"

A flicker of light fell across his face and Blake saw the gruesome scar Katrina had given him. As they were taking a couple of steps forward, so that they could see Blake better, he answered, "I'm going to kill you bastards; so say your prayers, for your time has come!"

Mack moved forward, recognition finally lighting his eyes. "Ralph, 'tis the gent from the inn. 'E's the one who sent ye crashin' through the window."

Mack laughed nervously, the cackle echoing in the still, silent alley. "Ye may 'ave saved tha' li'tle bitch tha' night, but we got 'er anyway! Didn't we, Ralph? She was good at pleasurin' a man gent, but I'm sure ye know tha' already! Ain't no one goin' t' lay 'er again, though. Me 'n me mate 'ere, made sure o' tha'! Aye, we done 'er up fine, we did. Tha' whore's face looked worse than me own when we got done wi' 'er!"

Mack's words were like a sharp knife that twisted in Blake's gut. Blake moved forward, his eyes ablaze with hatred. "I'll kill you, you sons-of-bitches!" yelled Blake as he flew through the air with a powerful leap, throwing Mack to the ground. Blake's fist smashed into Mack's face before he could even react and jolted his head back painfully. Blake gracefully dodged Ralph's clumsy charge and brought his knee up sharply into his stomach. When the giant bent over in pain, Lord Roberts clobbered him between the shoulder blades with both hands clasped together, sending the giant sprawling onto the filthy alley floor.

Mack leaped at Blake's back, his knife flashing dangerously. Blake twisted as the blade missed its mark and slashed his arm instead. Grabbing Mack's extended wrist, Blake snapped it like a twig, the knife falling to the ground as Mack screamed in pain. Ralph seized Blake from behind in a tremendous bear hug, the giant's massive arms squeezing the life from his victim. As Mack turned, he saw Blake encased by Ralph's deadly hold, and slammed his good fist into his unprotected stomach. He started to strike a second blow when Blake brought his legs up and kicked out, landing both feet squarely on Mack's chest. Then, grabbing Ralph's head, his fingers wrapped around tufts of hair, Blake threw the big man over his head, smashing him into the stone wall. Unsheathing his own knife, he once again faced Mack as he charged madly at Blake, sending them both sprawling among the trash and debris. Together they tumbled about as Ralph slowly picked himself up. Just as the giant reached out his massive hands and lifted Blake from the ground, Blake stuck his knife deeply into Mack's thigh. Mack screeched in terror and pain, limping away from the two fighting men, blood spurting from the open wound and running down his leg like water from a spout. Horrified, the scarfaced man ran from the alley, fearing he would bleed to death within minutes.

Ralph slammed Blake into the wall, knocking the breath from him. His huge hands encircled Blake's neck in a deathly grip. Visions of the giant choking Katrina flashed in Blake's mind, giving him unbelievable strength as he began to pry the fingers from his throat. Finally breaking the giant's hold, Blake brought up his knee right into his groin, disabling him. Blake quickly seized the man from behind in a choke hold, his arm across his throat, crushing it, preventing him from breathing. Blake determinedly tightened his grip, draining the life from the groaning giant.

"This is for Katrina! You bastard!"

Blake hoarsely whispered the words into Ralph's ear as he gurgled and struggled to free himself. Finally, his movements ceased and his body went limp, but Blake continued to hang on, like a pit bull in the ring, showing no mercy for its victim. It wasn't until he heard the sound of bones snapping that he released him, the body slipping lifelessly to the cold, garbage-strewn ground. Looking about him, Blake saw that Mack had fled.

Breathing hard, Blake walked away from the alley, staggering slightly. Glancing down, he saw the blood soaking his coat. The wound in his arm was bleeding badly. He pulled a handkerchief from his pocket and wrapped it tightly about his arm, tying it securely. When he stepped out into the street, something caught his eye, and he bent down to pick it up. It was his knife, bloody from Mack's wound.

A trail of scarlet lead him down the street to his next victim. Within minutes he found his prey, weak from the loss of blood. Blake saw Katrina as she lay still and cold, her beauty forever destroyed by this bastard's brutality. He did not hear Mack's pleas for mercy, and like an enraged animal, Blake gave a guttural cry as pain, anger, hate, sorrow, and pure terror coursed through him, making him insane with cold, deadly fury.

Blake's large hand grasped Mack's head, his steely fingers digging painfully into his skull. With another blood-curdling cry, filled with unbearable emotions, Blake lifted the smaller man and slammed his head against the wall. As Blake released his hold, Mack fell dead to the ground, his one good eye open, mirroring the fear and pain of his last seconds in life, his mouth gaping open grotesquely in a silent scream.

Chapter 19

Grant Walker's cool, blue eyes watched in satisfaction as the seaman hauled the rolled-up carpet aboard. Roughly, the roll was dumped onto the ship's deck, and a muffled moan reached the Captain's ears. Grabbing the edge, the seaman unrolled it with a jerk, sending the woman tucked inside tumbling.

Captain Walker looked down as Katrina landed at his feet in a tangle, her petticoat riding up to her hips, exposing long, shapely legs. Unfortunately, every man on board also turned his attention to the beautiful woman who had been brought aboard. Turning to the man who had carried her, Walker ordered him to cut Katrina free of the gag and restraining ropes.

The seaman did as he was told, and Katrina lay passively on the deck until the last rope was removed from her feet. Instantly, she came alive, ignoring the pains of her body. Bringing her feet up, she shoved the seaman back, sending him sprawling on the ship's deck. Nimbly, Katrina sprang to her feet and darted across the ship but found herself quickly surrounded by the crew. Looking about her, she picked up the only thing within reach, a boarding pike.

Captain Walker made no move to step in but casually

leaned back against the ship's rail, his arms crossed on his chest. Katrina Easton looked damn good to him, standing there like a wildcat, unafraid of the men encircling her. Grant's curiosity as to what she would and could do kept him from interfering.

Carefully, Katrina watched the men as their grinning faces inched closer and closer. Their taunts and jeers went unheeded as she concentrated on their movements. Suddenly she lunged forward, taking one man by surprise, bringing the blunt end of the pike up, catching him under the chin. As he stumbled backward, she shoved past him, breaking out of the confining circle of men, and ran down the deck. Two of the younger men reacted quickly, catching up to her in a few easy strides. As one reached out to grab her, Rina whirled, slamming the pike into his stomach, knocking the breath from him. The other warily faced her, his eyes boldly roving over her body, taking in every detail and curve. Never before had he seen such a vision, and at that very moment, he vowed to have this woman, no matter the cost.

"Give me the pike, girl. Ye 'ave no place t' go." Willy's voice was deep and smooth as he coaxed her, but she made no move to give in, her eyes flashing angrily in answer to his request.

"Do no' be a fool, give ol' Willy the pike."

Katrina faced him squarely, unflinchingly, as her eyes dared him to make a move. "Go to hell, Willy."

Suddenly, he jumped for her, but she reacted quickly, moving from his charging path. In the same fluid motion, she expertly brought the pike across his arm, grazing it enough to draw blood, then nimbly she sliced across the other.

Willy was surprised but only smiled, appreciative of her skill with the clumsy pike. Again, he sprang for her, this time anticipating her move. Dodging the pike that had been dangerously thrust at his heart, Willy tackled Katrina, bringing her down hard onto the deck. He landed on top of her, his weight knocking the breath from her. Grabbing both hands as they clawed at him, Willy grinned down at her as she struggled beneath him. She could see the passion in his eyes as he stared at her, could feel his desire rubbing hard against her stomach and legs. Leaning down, he whispered into her ear, sending waves of repulsion through her.

"Ye were made fer a man t' ride between your legs, she-cat."

At that moment, Grant Walker crossed over to them and roughly pulled Willy off Katrina. "That's enough! All of you, get back to work!"

Then he turned to Willy and growled menacingly, "Keep it in your pants, mate, or I'll kill you. I'll not abide anyone using my merchandise, especially this one. Do I make myself clear?"

Grumbling, Willy nodded and walked away, his anger written on his face. When everyone's attention was turned away from her, Katrina ran for the side of the ship. She had climbed onto the rail and was about to leap into the water below when Grant's strong arm snaked out and pulled her back onto the deck.

"You don't ever give up, do you?" laughed Walker.

Katrina lifted her chin proudly and looked him straight in the eye. "No, never!"

"Put her in the hold," Captain Walker ordered a man standing nearby. "You had best be a good girl, Katrina. My men are mean and ugly. Give me too much trouble and I will let them have you. I don't think even you could survive that."

A shiver passed over Katrina as she was shoved to the hold. Suddenly, she felt sore and bruised as a numbing tiredness began to seep through her. Pushed down a ladder into a gloomy, dark hole, Katrina watched as the ladder was pulled up behind her, leaving no means for escape from the pit she found herself in. She continued to stand and stare as a heavy grating was lowered over the hole and the deck came alive as they made ready to sail. In moments they began to move, and she finally turned away to look about her, willing the feelings of hopelessness to disappear.

"It is a lonely feeling, don't you think?"

Katrina turned toward the voice, looking into the dark shadows. A young Chinese woman stepped out, her head shyly bowed. Her long shining hair, black as coal, hung thick and straight down past her waist.

"Yes, it is very lonely. I have never been away from England before." Walking to the young woman, she put out her hand to her. "I am Katrina Easton. It seems we are to share this hole for the trip to Mexico."

"I am Chin Li." As she raised her eyes to meet Katrina's, a tear slipped down Chin Li's satiny cheek. Pulling her into her arms, Katrina held Chin Li, comforting her, easing her fear. They sat huddled together for a long time. With a bit of prodding from Katrina, Chin Li soon began to speak and they both began to relax.

Her family, like many in China, were poor farmers, barely able to hack out a living to feed their large family. When she was thirteen the crops had all been destroyed by a drought, and in order to survive, the oldest daughter, Chin Li, had been sold to a traveling merchant. After being sold from one master to another, Chin Li ended up in one of the finest brothels in London. Her life there was better than it had ever been in China and with her oriental beauty, Li was very valuable to her mistress. It had been six years since she had been sold into slavery, and once more she was to face a new world and a different master. Unsure of her future and fate, Li was frightened and unhappy. England had more or less become her home in the last four years, and there was also a young man, Yee Ling. A free man, he had worked in the kitchen of the brothel, and they had fallen in love. When her mistress, the madame, found out, Li had been immediately sold to Grant Walker, who had been trying to buy her for over a year.

Bursting into tears, Li hung her head in misery. "I shall never see Ling again. I fear this more than anything. I cannot bear it!"

Katrina's heart went out to the young girl. "You must not give up, Chin Li. I have no intention of being a slave to anyone, and neither shall you. We must be strong."

As Li looked at Katrina, her head held high and a fire in her blue eyes, something told her to trust and believe in this woman. "Yes, I will be strong and believe, my friend."

Sadly, Katrina thought of Blake. She wondered if Mack and Ralph's cruel plan had been successful. It had surprised even her how far they would go to collect the rest of the money Lawrence Langsford had offered them. If they had succeeded in their ploy, everyone would think she was dead and end all attempts to find her. Grimly, Katrina realized she was totally on her own. Exhaustion finally brought sleep; her last thoughts were of Blake.

As the days went slowly by, their lives settled into a pattern. They received two meals, if they could be considered that, of coarse bread and something resembling a stew. Their water was rationed. Once a day, they were allowed to exercise on deck, watched closely by the men. It seemed quite silly to Katrina, for where could they go? Everywhere she looked was only the greenish blue of the ocean. Li experienced some seasickness but it soon vanished. Two weeks passed without incident.

Slowly, Katrina began to speak of her life, and soon the two women knew each other as well as if they had been friends since birth. Their bond grew and Katrina realized how much she had missed by not having a close female companion. She confided her own heartbreaking longing for the man she loved, and the pain that her sudden marriage to another man caused them. Rina even confessed that she often wondered if she should have run away with Blake when he had asked her to. They would be together now, if it hadn't been for her stubbornness, her determination to fulfill the promises made to her father. Instead of being alone in a dark, dank hold of a slaver's ship, shivering from cold and hunger that gnawed painfully at her stomach, she could be curled safe and secure in his arms, warmed by his ardent lovemaking. These thoughts plagued her as much as the haunting nightmares. How could she let him know she was alive? More difficult still—how was she going to get out of the mess she found herself in? She had told Chin Li to have faith and be strong, yet, at times, Rina felt like giving in to the overwhelming despair that battered constantly at her determination and will. What was she to do? Then, when all seemed lost, Katrina would feel the ever-present anger well up inside of her, giving her the will to go on. To survive . . . no matter the odds.

Chin Li felt a growing devotion to Katrina as the weeks

passed. It was evident in everything she did that she was a noble lady, but never did it seem to matter to Katrina that her new friend had been a prostitute. Never had Li felt such warmth and kindness from a woman, especially one so grand. Katrina always had the right words of encouragement, and her faith never seemed to falter. Her admiration grew that morning as they took their morning walk. They tried to ignore the stares of the men and their lustful looks. Most of the men knew enough to keep their actions to looks and wishful dreaming, for Captain Walker made sure he was present on deck during their strolls. Only Willy seemed unafraid of the Captain's retribution. When he could, Willy would make lewd gestures to Katrina or whisper crude remarks to her. Chin Li was frightened by him but Katrina ignored Willy, irritating him further. He sought every chance possible to be near her, to make certain she was aware that he wanted her and intended to have her.

That morning was just like so many others, except that Grant Walker was needed below to settle an urgent matter. Willy took the opportunity at hand and followed the women until they were out of sight of the others on deck. Suddenly, they found their passage blocked as Willy jumped out, a wicked grin spread across his face.

"Well, well, our li'tle darlin's are out for their mornin' walk."

"Yes, and our little shipmate is stepping way out of bounds. Best watch yourself, Willy." Katrina's words dripped with sarcasm.

"I'm no' afraid o' Captain Walker, witch!"

Katrina only smiled, unconcerned, unafraid. "I see."

Chin Li gasped at Katrina's nerve and Willy turned red from fury. Grabbing her roughly by the shoulders, he started to pull her to him, but Katrina reacted instantly, bringing her knee up into his groin. As Willy doubled over, she pulled his knife from its sheath and laid it across his throat, the sharp edge biting into his flesh, drawing drops of blood. His eyes widened in surprise, the pain between his legs forgotten.

"It is not Captain Walker you need worry about, Willy, but me. Touch me again, and you will most certainly die!"

Willy grinned lecherously at her, his voice seemingly unconcerned. "It may be worth the risk, bitch! If ye fight nearly as well in bed as ye do out, it would be well worth the price. Never 'ave I met such a gutsy wench as yerself. I'd take on the devil himself to 'ave ye, and mark me words, I'll enjoy the sweets between yer legs yet."

Katrina started to speak but was cut off by the appearance of Grant Walker. In seconds, he was beside her, his eyes angry and grim. "What the hell is going on here?"

Calmly, she stepped back, freeing Willy from his precarious position. Turning to face Grant's anger, she merely shrugged her shoulders nonchalantly. "We are taking our morning walk, Captain."

Grant's jaw twitched as he ground his teeth in vexation. Never had a woman tried his patience as much as Katrina had since he bought her. Turning to Willy, Grant grabbed his shirt and pushed him away in disgust. "Get out of my sight, you bastard!"

His gaze flew back to Katrina as he fought back the urge to drag her to his cabin and take her himself. Holding out his hand, he demanded in a harsh voice, "Give me the knife."

Katrina bit her lip thoughtfully, as she considered his demand. "You would take my only means of protecting myself?"

"Your tongue is sharp enough, woman, you need no knife." Reaching out, he wrenched the blade from Katrina's small hand and, grabbing her wrist in a painful grip, pulled her after him. Cruelly, he shoved Katrina down the ladder.

An involuntary moan escaped her as she fell and crumpled to the floor in a heap. Leaping down the ladder, Grant knelt beside her, immediately sorry for his anger.

"Are you hurt?" Grant's voice was filled with concern, but Katrina's own anger was to the breaking point.

"Yes!" she snapped, "thanks to you!"

Grant reached out to help her up, but Katrina slapped his hand away. "Do not touch me," she hissed, "just leave me alone!"

Grant's concern immediately disappeared. Standing, he started to leave, his face a cloudy mask of anger and confusion. When he reached the ladder, he turned to Li, who had crept down behind them, her eyes wide with fear. "Take care of her, she is a valuable piece of merchandise!"

At that comment, Katrina's control fled, and she leaped to her feet angrily. A pain shot through her foot, but she felt nothing but the unbearable rage ripping at her mind.

"Merchandise! You are a fool, Grant Walker! I belong to no one but myself! At the moment I have chosen to bide my time, but be warned . . . I have no intention of letting myself be sold into slavery! Not you or anyone can sell me!"

Grant watched Katrina, half-naked, with her hands on her hips, her feet firmly planted. And then he knew—no, this woman would never be a man's slave, she would make men her slave instead. He was silent a moment as he let this thought sink past the red maze of anger. Yes, he knew, but it would not do to let her know she had won. "You have no choice, Katrina."

Katrina's answer was spoken softly, with no doubt as to her meaning, "I always have a choice, Captain."

"Will you always fight and chance death, rather than live a life you do not choose?"

"Yes," stated Katrina simply.

"Why?" he asked, bewildered. "Most women's lives are not to their choosing. Fathers use their daughters as pawns to gain wealth and position. As daughters, you have no choice in deciding your fate, and as wives, you are governed by a husband. You must submit to him since you have no rights to protect you. He can treat you as he wishes. Perhaps even beat you, or kill you, and the laws are on his side. It's no different from being sold as a slave. Chin Li is a slave; she accepts her fate. Why can't you?"

"Because I know what it is to be free and independent. My parents were taken from me as a child, and from that day, I have made my own decisions, I have governed my own life. Chin Li was raised as most women, in a shroud of ignorance, given no freedom to learn who they really are. She knows no other way, but I cannot accept any other way than that of my own choosing."

Katrina paused and turned to look directly into light blue

eyes. "I'll fight you, Grant Walker. I'll fight you every step of the way. Death strikes no fear in me, so I'll stop at nothing to be free of you! I will not be sold!"

Grant stared at her, unable to say anything. Anger, passion, and admiration all played on his features before he turned and silently climbed the ladder. Never before had he wanted a woman as much as he wanted Katrina, but he knew she would fight him, and the thought of rape left only a bitter taste in his mouth. Grant Walker would never know her passion and he would never be able to bring himself to sell her either. What the hell was he to do? These thoughts weighed heavily on his mind as he made his way to his cabin.

Katrina's ankle was only twisted and the soreness disappeared in a few days. It was during the third week out to sea that she began experiencing periods of weakness and vomiting. Mornings became a miserable time for her and soon the greasy stew refused to stay down at all. Katrina could not understand why she would become seasick after so long a time at sea. For two and a half weeks, she ate only bread and water. Though Li often gave her share of bread to Katrina, she continued to lose weight. She refused to let Li tell Grant Walker she was ill, and let him think her anger kept her from taking her exercise and risking an encounter with him.

So far the weather had been calm, but five weeks out the ship ran into a squall that lasted three long days. Katrina was miserable. In her weakened state, with her stomach so uneasy, the storm kept her bedridden. Even Li found it difficult to stand without being thrown to the floor. Katrina never knew it was possible to throw up so much, and after being slammed against the hard crates they slept on, her body felt as if it had been beaten. It was cold and wet in their hole, and the storm left their nerves raw as it tossed the small ship about. Chin Li feared they would be swallowed up by the sea as the thunder deafened them and the lightning streaked through the black night.

Chin Li covered her ears as she huddled next to Katrina, but it seemed to help very little to block out the rumbling that surrounded them. She silently prayed to every God she knew of, hoping that one would be merciful and hear her. Katrina had a fever now, and Li prayed for her friend, too, as she watched her toss and turn fitfully on the mat. What little sleep Katrina had had was filled with terrifying dreams, nightmares that left her trembling with fear. Awake, Rina was strong and unafraid, but as fevered sleep took her, she saw all the horrifying memories she struggled constantly to forget.

In the middle of the third day, the storm ceased its violent attack and left the ship in one piece. A calming rain, warm and sweet, continued to fall, filling the barrels with fresh water. Katrina awoke as the ladder was lowered into their hole and Captain Walker climbed down. He found the two women huddled on their bed and as he looked at Katrina, all the color drained from his face.

He sloshed through the six inches of water that had leaked through the tarp covering the grating. The room smelled of sickness and both women were covered with grime. Gently, Grant lifted Katrina, noticing her grayish coloring. Her hair was matted and dirty. Dark smudges lay beneath her eyes, and when she opened them, he saw no sparkle, only pain. Bruises covered her pale skin, and he tried not to hurt her as he carried her to the ladder.

Looking at Chin Li, he murmured angrily, "Why was I not told of this? How long has she been ill?"

Li's own worried eyes met his, but it was Katrina who weakly snapped, "No one has bothered with us for three days, so stop your barking!"

Ignoring her remark, he climbed the ladder and took her to his own cabin. As gently as possible, he laid her onto his bunk and once again spoke to Li. "She couldn't have gotten this bad in three days."

Li looked timidly at her feet, fidgeting with her hands nervously.

"Well?" asked Captain Walker patiently, knowing she feared his anger.

"Leave her be, Walker! I have been feeling sick for three weeks, seasickness, I guess. This storm made me worse." Sitting up slowly, Katrina tried to get up.

"Stay there!" ordered the Captain. "You look like you're already dead and you smell even worse!"

Even though she felt sick enough to die, Katrina's anger flared. "Well, if you would provide decent food, rather than that grease you call stew, I wouldn't have gotten so weak that the storm would have bothered me! As far as my personal hygiene is concerned, you would smell, too, if you had been stuck in a hole for six weeks that isn't fit for a pig to live in!"

Standing on shaking legs, Katrina moved for the door. Instantly, Grant blocked her way, his face unyielding. "Li, go to the cook and get some decent food! And order some water heated for a bath!"

After Li had scurried out to do as he bid, he picked up Katrina and carried her to the bed again, this time dumping her carelessly on it. He instantly felt bad as she grimaced from pain and he saw her bite her lip to keep from moaning out loud.

"Take off your clothes!" he demanded.

Katrina looked shocked and only stared at him.

"As lovely as you are, Katrina, at this moment you evoke no desire in me. You cannot bathe with your clothes on; besides, they should be burned!"

"I have no others! Those two bastards left me only this chemise and slip!" Katrina blurted out in alarm.

"Then they will have to be washed. Here," he said, throwing her a blanket, "wrap up in this."

Feeling dizzy and weak, Katrina submitted and peeled the filthy clothes from her body. It didn't even matter that Grant Walker watched her every move. A bath! God, it had been so long!

In no time at all, a tub was set up and filled. What seemed a banquet to the women was set up on a table, and they ate their fill. For the first time in weeks the meal stayed in Katrina's stomach, making her feel a bit better.

Gently, Li washed Katrina's hair, soaking away the grime and filth, gently massaging her bruised flesh in the warm water. Once Katrina was comfortably tucked into the bed, Li washed herself. After sleeping a few hours, they ate again, and Katrina was feeling stronger by the minute. That night she slept soundly, no dreams disturbing her slumber. She awoke with most of her old color in her cheeks and without being sick to her stomach, feeling only a gnawing hunger that was soon satisfied. Li and Katrina washed again, putting their clean clothes on, giggling and feeling like schoolgirls as they delighted in brushing each other's shining hair.

Katrina still felt weak but could not believe how fast she was recovering from her seasickness. They spent the day eating and sleeping and took a walk before dusk, enjoying the fresh air and exercise. With another good night's sleep, Katrina awoke with much of her old sparkle and spirit. Li worried over her like a mother, concerned with the warmness of her skin. Katrina shrugged it off, as she dismissed the nausea she was still experiencing. It soon passed, and she nibbled a piece of bread as Li brushed her long, golden hair.

"Captain Walker has certainly been generous, allowing us to stay in his own cabin." Li's voice was soft and appreciative.

Katrina smiled to herself. "He didn't want his valuable merchandise dying on him. I suppose we cost him a lot of money, and we will bring him a fortune in Mexico."

"No," disagreed Li, "I saw more in his eyes than fear of losing money. He cares for you."

This time Katrina laughed outright. "Don't be silly, Li. There is no telling how many women he has sold before us, why should it be different for us?"

"Not us . . . you," said Li matter-of-factly.

Shaking her head, Katrina stood. "You're imagining things." Cocking her head to listen, she heard the ship suddenly come alive with men scurrying across the decks, yelling in excited voices. She tried the latch but was not surprised to find the door locked. She listened intently, trying to learn the reason for the commotion on deck. Within minutes, an explosion sounded, and a cannonball pierced the air and shattered into the side of the ship. Running to the small porthole, Katrina spotted another ship as it bore down on theirs, its cannons blasting. Wood splintered around them and Li, frightened, ran to Katrina's side, fear etched on her delicate features.

"It seems we are being attacked." Katrina's voice was calm and soothing to Li, who was trying not to be afraid of the sudden turmoil blasting about them.

"Don't worry, Li, there is nothing we can do but wait."

Katrina continued to talk to her, but it was difficult to ignore the screams of men as they fell to the deck, dying. They could smell the smoke as the ship burned where the cannonballs had demolished it. Soon the other ship came alongside. The scraping of the wooden timbers was deafening. They could hear the men as they boarded; then came the sounds of hand-to-hand combat above them on deck.

Suddenly the door flew open and Willy filled the doorway, a bloody sword in his hand. Li screamed and the vision before them sent a chill through Katrina. Willy's eyes were wild and glittering. His shirt was covered with blood, whether his own or another's, they could not tell. Standing in front of Li, Katrina warily watched the man as he closed the space between them in long strides.

"What do you want, Willy?" asked Katrina cautiously as she searched for something to use as a weapon.

Waving the bloody blade in the air ominously, Willy sneered at her. "Ye know damn well wha' I want, bitch!" Looking at Li, he screamed, "Get out!"

Confused and afraid, Li turned to Katrina, who nodded to her, giving her a shove toward the door. "Go on, Li."

Seeing her hesitate, Katrina repeated firmly, "Go on!"

Deciding it best to seek help, Li carefully slipped past Willy and out the door. Slamming it behind the girl, Willy locked it, throwing the key across the room, where it disappeared beneath a chest.

Katrina looked at him calmly as she faced the deadly sword and the even deadlier man wielding it. "So, you are using swords now to subdue your victims. Not man enough to take me unarmed?"

The sneer in her voice hit its mark, and he tossed the weapon aside carelessly. "I need no help, witch!"

Leaping at Katrina, Willy managed to grab a handful of hair as she dodged away. At his cruel yank, she fell back onto the floor at his feet and he wound the length of her hair around his hand, pulling her head back, his knee holding her down. With his free hand, he removed his shirt, ripping it from his body, then loosened his pants, freeing the hardness within. Moving on top of Katrina, he pulled up her petticoat, baring her hips. Willy's lips came down hard on hers, bruising and demanding, his hand tearing at her chemise, baring one tender breast to his roaming fingers.

As his tongue probed her mouth, Katrina's hand seized a bottle lying nearby, and as she brought it down on his head, she also bit his tongue, drawing blood and nearly gagging as it flooded her mouth. When he pulled back in pain, she shoved with all her strength, throwing him off her. Quickly, she scrambled to her feet, but Willy reached out and grabbed her slender ankle, stopping her, pulling her down on top of him. Willy found a wildcat in his hands as Rina scratched and bit, her small fists smashing painfully into his face and stomach. Rolling over on the floor, Willy managed to land on top once again and raised his hand, striking Katrina hard across the face. The blow would have crumpled most women, but it barely dazed her as desperation gave her amazing strength and stamina.

Neither of the two people struggling on the floor heard the door crash in. Suddenly, Willy was lifted from Katrina and thrown across the room. She looked up to see Grant Walker looming over her, his face a mask of rage.

"Get out of here! I'll take care of that bastard!"

Katrina had no desire to argue and fled. Li was waiting fearfully outside the door. The two women carefully made their way up to the deck, the sight before them causing Li to blanch, sickened by the scene of violence and death. Smoke filled the air, hanging heavy around them as it mixed with the acrid smell of gunpowder and blood. All about them men fought to protect their ship, or to take it over— it was hard to distinguish one from the other. Katrina knew if they were to escape, it would have to be now, for there would be no chance later.

Chapter 20

Rebecca felt proud as she stood between Ryon and Blake. She ignored the staring eyes and gossiping mouths around them. It had been two weeks since Blake had come home with his arm bleeding and hurt, with no explanations to offer. The only thing Rebecca knew was that he had stopped his excessive drinking and appeared to have come to terms with his overwhelming grief. Blake seemed to have control of his life once again.

Dressed soberly in black, Blake stood out from all the others dressed more colorfully. Rebecca saw the envious eyes of the women as two of London's handsomest and richest men walked into the ballroom. Across the room, Catherine's green eyes narrowed as she spotted Blake, her lips curving into a wicked smile.

So . . . thought Catherine to herself. Now that that little golden-haired bitch is out of the way, he's all mine.

Excusing herself from the two men who were boring her terribly, Catherine Ramsey made her way to Blake Roberts. By the time she reached him, David had joined them. Blake saw Catherine heading his way, and from the look in her eyes, he was sure it would not be a pleasant encounter.

"Blake, darling! It is so nice to see you here. These affairs are not the same without you." Catherine's cooing grated on Blake's nerves but he did not show it. Instead, he flashed a smile that caught everyone's attention. Taking heart, she pressed on.

"I have saved the first dance for you." Catherine fanned her eyelashes shyly, her head tilted slightly to show off her flawless features.

Blake found her game amusing, at least for the moment. This sudden shyness was so unlike her he almost laughed outright, but he bowed elegantly to hide the twinkle in his eyes. When he once again looked at Catherine, he had control of his emotions.

"I would be honored to have this dance, Lady Ramsey." Blake's voice was smooth, almost melodious. Only his friends noticed his slight slurring of the word "Lady."

In her moment of victorious joy, Catherine did not catch the contempt in his voice; in fact she found him to be quite agreeable tonight. As Blake whirled her onto the dance floor, she bestowed on him what she considered to be her most becoming smile. She leaned closer, giving him a full view of her ample, creamy breasts, and allowed them to rub enticingly against his chest.

"You have been ignoring me terribly, Blake," pouted Catherine prettily.

Blake looked unconcerned, his golden eyes remaining unreadable, his voice sounding almost bored. "Have I really?"

Biting her lip in annoyance at his lack of concern, Lady Ramsey continued, "Yes, you have, but I forgive you, darling. We have all the time in the world now."

Blake stiffened slightly, but just as he was about to question her, Catherine spoke again. "I really could use a breath of fresh air, Blake. Don't you find it stifling in here?"

Blake was suddenly tired of her manuevering, so he guided her toward the balcony doors and out into the night's fresh air.

Watching him from under lowered lashes, Catherine waited for him to say something, but nothing came. Taking his silence as agreement with her ploy, she became bold.

Blake could see the changes in her features and that knowing look in her emerald eyes. She was up to something, and he was patient enough to find out what. Pressing her body against his, Catherine ran her long, tapered finger along Blake's jawline, noticing the twitch there as she did so. She attributed it to pent-up desire and moved closer.

But Blake felt only repulsion, and it took every bit of control he had not to throw her from him in disgust. Standing on her toes, she pressed her lips hungrily to his, her mouth parted and eager.

Slowly, Catherine began to realize Blake was not responding, and that hit her hard, like a slap across the face. Color flooded her face and neck, reaching clear down to her breasts as her eyes narrowed wickedly. She stepped back, anger flooding through her, but Blake only cocked an eyebrow in amusement.

When Catherine's hand snaked out, ready to slap Blake's arrogant face, he caught it easily, causing her to gasp in pain. "B-Blake . . . you're hurting me," whined Catherine, her anger tinged by fear as she saw the fire in his eyes.

"Have you no pride or shame, Catherine?"

His question surprised her, and she retorted, her voice loud and grating, "What do you mean?"

A sneer crossed Blake's lips, and he dropped her hand in distaste. "You know what I mean. I have always made it clear I have no wish or desire to bed you, and yet you persist in throwing yourself at me, like a bitch in heat. I know what kind of woman you are, and there is no passion to blind me to the facts. Give up, Catherine. You will never have my money. You had better find some other fool to take you to his bed; it will not be me."

His words stung her, hurting even her cold, cruel heart. Tears sprang to her eyes, not from pain but from anger that he knew her so well. "You loved me once, long ago!"

"And I was young and foolish! I have always been grateful that you were cruel enough to deny my proposal, and greedy enough to go after another poor soul!"

"But I love you, Blake!" lied Catherine, desperate to hold on to him any way she could. Blake Roberts could give her everything she wanted in life; she would not give in.

"You love only yourself and money. You have no idea

what love really is." Pulling her clinging arms off him, Blake started to leave, but her next words stopped him.

"And I suppose you know what love is?" snapped Catherine waspishly. "Did you love that little bitch Katrina?" When he stopped abruptly, Catherine knew she had hit a tender spot and recklessly pressed on. "Is that why you tried to drown yourself in drink?" Her laughter filled the air, bringing a deadly look to Blake's golden eyes. "You mean the infamous Lord Roberts felt more than lust for a woman? You *are* a fool, Blake; she was nothing but a whore, and you couldn't see it!"

In two long strides, Blake was beside Catherine, his hands grasping her shoulders painfully. "What do you mean, witch?" Blake shook her hard, causing Catherine's head to snap back and forth, but she was blind to his rage. She was determined to destroy his holy image of Katrina, and so she lied, for it was Katrina's fault that Blake did not want her.

"She was a whore! Plain and simple. Everyone knew it but you. Why do you think the King married her off so quickly? While you were away, she was sleeping with everyone in court, even your good friends and dear brother! I even heard she had a taste for men in uniform. Especially a certain Lieutenant Greerson! She told me once that she owed him a great debt and could think of no more pleasant a way to repay it. She should have died that day in the forest. Lawrence and Randolph were fools to have let her go!"

Catherine's eyes widened in fear as she realized what she had just said, but there was no backing out now.

Blake gritted his teeth as his emotions played havoc inside of him. "What are you talking about?"

Catherine had no way of knowing how close her lies had come to the truth concerning Katrina and the Lieutenant; she had only known the jealousy Blake possessed for his little darling. The lies all seemed to fall so easily in place as she rushed on. "Didn't that slut tell you about the fall that brought back her memory?" She was groping, but Blake was too upset to see it, and Catherine's courage was fed by the confusion and pain she read so clearly in his eyes.

"Well, we were out on a fox hunt and we ran into your

golden-haired girl, all by herself in the forest. I must say, Lawrence and Randolph seemed to enjoy her very much, such an obliging little strumpet. She even tried to get me into the fun, but I like men, not bitches. Why do you think they did not object to Katrina marrying Randolph? They were both looking forward to more of the same."

Catherine's evil words twisted in Blake's already tender heart. His mind whirled as he considered beating the wicked smile from her face. It had to be a lie . . . but why did he have doubts eating at him, gnawing at the last threads of control? He remembered Katrina's reluctance to talk about what had happened after her fall. He had known she was lying when she denied knowing who had chased her. And hadn't there been obvious tenderness and affection between David and Katrina? Did she promise him something to let the Angel go? Even his own brother, always there for her, just as his grandfather had been.

What else had she kept from him? What other lies had she told? How many other men had heard her whisper words of love into their ears? If she had truly loved him, she would not have married another man! How could he have been so easily duped by her treachery! So many lies!

Suddenly, Blake turned and disappeared, leaving a shaken Catherine Ramsey staring out into the darkness alone. A smile slowly curved her red lips, and disappointment was quickly replaced by satisfaction, for Blake obviously believed what she had said. Why else would he have been so upset? Catherine knew she could not battle a ghost, but she had succeeded in destroying her cherished memory. Patting her hair into place and smoothing her velvet gown, she started back inside, an evil twinkle lighting her hard green eyes and a wicked grin on her face.

When she disappeared inside, Ryon and David stepped from the shadows, shock and disbelief registering on their faces. Quite by accident they had witnessed the whole scene between Blake and Catherine. Neither moved, still unable to understand fully that Blake was gone and that he had actually believed Lady Ramsey.

Finally, David gathered his wits about him and turned

questioningly to Ryon. "He believed her lies? Surely, Blake would not."

A tremendous sigh escaped Ryon as he shook his head. "You saw the look on his face. I am afraid he did and Katrina's not even here to defend herself."

They both knew what Blake had been through. Perhaps he had chosen to take her lies as truth because it was less painful to hate Katrina than to cope with loving her and live with the constant grief. Shaking their heads in concern, they walked around the gardens, unable to face the gaiety of the party.

The ship slipped from the harbor, her sails filled with the early-morning breeze as she skidded gracefully across the glittering blue-green water. The sun inched its way above the horizon to spray its golden rays on the earth below. Bringing his hand up to shield his sensitive, bloodshot eyes, Blake turned away from the light in annoyance. A moan escaped him as he felt a severe pounding in his head; his mouth was dry and cottony. Slowly, his mind began to clear, bringing with it rememberance of events from the night before.

Catherine Ramsey's words had been like a sharp knife plunged directly into his heart. His grief and sorrow had devoured her words as truth, allowing no room for reason or trust to enter. Unable to control his tremendous anger Blake had left the party, ending up on board one of his ships, a bottle of brandy close at hand. He wasn't even certain where he was going, but that didn't matter either. Nothing did.

Pulling himself up, Blake swung his long legs over the edge of the bunk and hung his head in his hands. A knock sounded at the door, taking his attention away from his aching head, and through red-rimmed eyes he watched a young cabin boy enter the room.

"Cap'n said ye might be up, sir. Would ye like somethin' t' eat now?"

Blake nodded his head painfully and the boy disappeared. Slowly, he stood, feeling the swaying of the ship beneath him, and carefully made his way to the washstand. Pouring some cold water into the bowl, Blake stripped off his rumpled shirt and washed his face and body, feeling somewhat better when he was done.

Soon the boy was back, bearing a large tray filled with good-smelling food. He placed it on the table and turned to Blake. His eyes widened in surprise as Blake straightened from leaning over the washstand. Instinctively, the boy took a step backward, awed by the tall, hard-muscled man looming over him.

Blake let out a laugh at the boy's startled look and sat down at the table. "What is your name, lad?"

"Thomas, sir," he replied meekly. "Me frien's call me Tommy."

Looking up from his food, Blake smiled. "All right, Tommy, tell me, where is my ship going?"

"Ye don't know where we're bound, sir?" asked the lad, confused.

"No," stated Blake patiently. "I would not have asked if I knew."

Looking down sheepishly, Tommy answered. "We're 'eaded fer India, sir." He looked and watched Blake hungrily attack the food before him. "This 'ere is yer ship, gov'na?"

Nodding, Blake took a drink to wash down a bite of food. Unable to control his childish curiosity, the lad asked another question. " 'Ow many ships do ye 'ave?" His voice was filled with admiration.

"Too many to count, Tommy. Now, enough of your questions." Blake tried to make his words stern, but Tommy smiled as he scuttled away, leaving Blake to eat his meal alone.

When he had eaten his fill, Blake pulled on a fresh shirt and left his cabin to walk on deck. The wind felt good, clearing his mind of the lingering effects of the brandy he had consumed the night before. As he leaned on the rail he gloried in the feel of the sea beneath him, a sensation he always missed when on land.

As his mind cleared a bit, his thoughts once again returned to Catherine's words—"She was sleeping with everyone in court, even your good friends and dear brother! . . . Especially a certain Lieutenant Greerson! . . . owed him a great debt . . . pleasant way to repay it . . . obliging little strumpet . . ."

"You're a fool, Blake Roberts!" his mind echoed, filling him with rage and hatred. "She was a clever whore, but you could not see it! A fool!"

Hatred wove its way firmly into the threads of his consciousness, and as time passed, it began to fill the empty recesses left by Katrina's death. Grief and sorrow no longer remained, their haunting agony replaced by that of bitter betrayal and an ever-present anger. Blake cursed her memory and himself for being so blind and foolish.

Once he even pulled the ring from his finger, ready to toss it into the sea, but instead he replaced it, swearing it would be a reminder of Katrina's treachery.

As the weeks wore on, the sea in its magical way began to ease the tension from Blake's body and mind, and his mood lightened. During the day, Blake learned to empty his mind of all thoughts of Katrina. It was at night that her memory would slip unheeded into his dreams. In his sleep, he dared to remember her sweetness . . . her love. Like a gentle ghost, she haunted Blake, working her sorcery on him, teasing and passionate, leaving him weak and shaken. In these dreams they made love, just as they had in real life. Blake saw her beauty as if she truly lay beside him. He felt the softness of her skin and touched the silky golden curls of her long mane. He kissed her delicate nose and sensual lips. His hand slid along a curving hip as the other reached to cup a rosy-tipped breast, the nipple taut between his fingers. He could smell her sweet fragrance, always of roses, as her body molded so perfectly against his own hard, muscled one. He could hear her loving words as her breath tickled his ear. Blake even felt the warmth of her body as he gently buried himself deep inside her, bringing them together as one, and taking them to the spiraling heights of passion.

Blake would awaken, calling out Katrina's name, only to find himself alone. It disturbed him greatly that even in death she could arouse him so. Would he ever be able to exorcise his golden girl from his mind? No answer came and he expected none.

Once in India, Blake immersed himself in work at his office there. It had been some time since he had visited the East, and many things needed to be done and looked over. Time helped Blake as he fought to rid himself of Katrina's memory, but it didn't ease the hatred that grew in his heart. Nothing could rid him of that, except Katrina herself, and she was gone.

Chapter 21

Li smiled happily as she watched Katrina come out of Walker's cabin. She ran to her friend and hugged her, glad to see her safe. But Katrina knew they had little time for rejoicing. She sent Li below to get some food while she slowly made her way to one of the skiffs. Quickly, she uncovered it and found some water jugs to take with them, along with some other supplies.

She should be back by now, thought Katrina. Making her way back to where she had left Li, Katrina noticed for the first time that most of the fighting had stopped.

"God," whispered Katrina. "Are we too late?"

As she walked past a couple of dead men Katrina stopped to pick up a sword and a pistol, smiling to find the gun still loaded. A sudden, high-pitched scream startled her. Quickly, she looked about, then made her way down the deck, where she froze in horror.

The deck was swarming with men—not Captain Walker's crew but the pirates who had attacked them. Walker's men were rounded up together at gunpoint, but everyone's attention was on Willy.

He stood in the center of the deck with Li in his steely grip, a knife held to her throat. His eyes were crazed and one leg was bleeding badly. Katrina inched closer so she could hear what was being said.

"I want tha' bitch! I want 'er or this one dies!" Willy screamed at a tall man who seemed to be in command, his hold on Li tightening.

Katrina could see that Li was choking for breath as she clawed helplessly at Willy's sinewy arm. It was then she saw the captain of the pirate ship as he faced Willy, trying to decide on a course of action.

"Who are you talking about, man? I don't see any other woman here." His voice was smooth and soothing, but his eyes were angry and hard.

Willy watched him carefully, his desperation apparent in his voice. "I want that she-cat and a boat. She is mine! Do ye hear? I'll make 'er regret tha' she fought me!" Glancing about him, he continued to scream crazily, "Where are ye, bitch!? Come t' ol' Willy!"

The taller man took a step forward but stopped when Willy turned back. "I'll kill 'er! Stay back, or I'll kill 'er, jus' like I killed the Cap'n. No one'll keep 'er from me!"

Katrina gasped in horror. Silently, she laid down her sword and hid the pistol in her petticoat, then, stepping forward, she drew all eyes to her.

"I'm right here, you bastard!" she yelled.

Willy whirled about, letting go of Li, and as she crumpled to the ground, Katrina brought her pistol up and fired. The ball pierced Willy's head and the shot echoed over the silent deck as everyone watched him sink slowly to the floor, a look of surprise etched on his face.

It took a few seconds for everyone to realize what had happened, and in that moment, Katrina once again armed herself with the sword and faced her new enemy.

The pirate commander bent over Li, but when he was satisfied she was all right, he turned his attention to the other woman. Taking a few steps toward her, he took in every detail. Warily, he noted the sword she held menacingly in her hand. She looked straight at him, and he saw there was no fear in her. He had seen few women as beautiful and fewer with so much courage. The chemise and petticoat were worn and ripped, leaving no doubt about her lovely body. Barefoot, with a cascade of golden hair about her shoulders, hanging past her waist, Katrina made a most tempting picture.

"Trevor Wilde, madam"—the tall pirate bowed rakishly—"at your service."

Now the eyes of the whole crew were on her, but Katrina saw only the look in Trevor Wilde's eyes.

Have I escaped one lecher, just to be raped by another? Katrina thought grimly as she stood her ground. The man she faced was tall and lean, his muscled body bronzed from the sun, his open shirt revealing dark curly hair covering his broad chest. Hair of the same color contrasted sharply with intense green eyes that sparkled like emeralds.

"So you must be the valuable merchandise Grant Walker was carrying. I should have guessed it would be a woman; he could have gotten a fortune for you in Mexico." Slowly, Trevor stepped closer but paused when he was within striking distance of the sword Katrina held. "Why don't you lay that down, you may get hurt."

Katrina did not move.

Trevor held out his hand and repeated, "Give it here," more firmly this time.

"Go to hell," answered Katrina, her voice low and menacing.

As he watched her closely he felt a mixture of anger at her arrogance and passion for her lovely body. He felt a fire building inside of him, and slowly he felt it consuming him, blinding his reason.

"This ship and all on it belong to me now! You had best put that down before I lose my patience. You will not be harmed, I promise that."

"You lie!" yelled Katrina, her nerves frayed as she steadied her shaking legs. She felt hot and feverish; her weakness was returning. Seeing the anger flare in the man's eyes, Katrina went on. "You lie, for I see the lust in your eyes. Are you so ignorant of women that you do not consider rape to be harm?"

"I have never raped a woman!" bellowed Trevor indignantly.

"Then I want your promise that Li and I will not be touched by you or any of your men."

Trevor stood and stared at her, amazement showing clearly on his face. "And if I don't give that promise?"

Katrina's eyes flared determinedly, and her chin raised proudly as she gave her answer. "Then I will fight you."

The words came out so matter-of-factly that Trevor in no way doubted her. "There are many of us, and only one of you. You cannot hold us at bay forever."

"I will do what I must," came her reply.

Confused, Trevor lowered his voice, so only Katrina could hear. "Is the thought of my lovemaking so repulsive?"

"No," whispered Katrina. "I only wish for the same choices that you have. Is it so hard to understand that I wish to choose my lover? Just because I am a woman, must I endure every lusting male's desire to bed me?"

Silently, he stood watching her, conflicting emotions playing across his handsome face as Trevor considered her question. Torn between the truth of her words and his first instincts of lust and passion, he felt momentarily off balance.

"Good God!" he swore to himself. "This little bit of a woman has made me look the fool!"

As the truth dawned on Trevor, his anger returned, blocking out both the lust and understanding. The only thought registering through the red haze that now consumed him was that no man or woman had ever kept him from what he wanted!

Katrina saw the change in his eyes but firmly stood her ground. She knew she could not last long against him, for as each moment passed she felt her strength waning. Taking a deep breath to steady her nerves, she grasped the sword she held with both hands, finding it extremely heavy to lift.

Suddenly, Trevor stepped forward, his own sword drawn for protection, his intent clear in his mind, but he had not expected it to be difficult for him to disarm the girl, and most of all, he had not expected the assault she threw at him. Surprise registered on his face as Trevor fought off the flashing sword and its sharp edge.

Katrina pressed on, knowing she had the advantage of surprise, drawing on the last of her strength. Her concentration was intense as she allowed only one thing to enter her conscious mind. Survival! Katrina could no longer feel the pain in her arms as she continued to swing her deadly blade, just as she was unaware of her rasping breath tearing through her burning chest.

It was then that a movement caught her eye, and when she glanced up, she saw Captain Walker being carried to the deck by two men. A bloodstain covered his belly, and a knife stuck out grotesquely from the deadly wound. Katrina stopped dead in her tracks, her guard dropping as a small gasp escaped her, the shock of his death reverberating through her dulled mind.

In seconds Trevor expertly disarmed her, leaving her standing in a daze. The knowledge that Grant Walker had given his life in defense of hers left her numb, a sadness twisting deep in her heart. Standing only a few inches from Katrina, Trevor seized her shoulders roughly, but she made no attempt to move.

Chin Li twisted away from the man who held her and ran to Trevor, grabbing his arm in desperation. "Please, sir, please, do not harm her!"

Trevor's patience had long since run out and he turned his anger to the Chinese girl. "I should beat her soundly for her foolish stubbornness, and if you do not stop your whining, I shall beat you, too!"

"Beat her?" Li cried, alarmed. "Beat me if you must, but surely you would not beat a sick woman! It would kill her!"

Something in her voice, the fear in her eyes, made Trevor turn his gaze back to the woman he held firmly in his grasp. For the first time, he became aware of the deathly pallor of her skin and the glassy eyes that stared blankly at him. His strong hands could feel her shaking violently, and instinct told him it was not from fright. A small fear began to nag at him as he turned back to the other woman. "What is wrong with her?"

Chin Li blinked at the fierceness in his voice and hesitated a moment. Trevor released Katrina quickly, turning to Li.

"She hasn't got the plague, has she?" he whispered fearfully. "Tell me, girl!"

"No," answered Li, her eyes widening with fear. "No, she is with child!"

Katrina felt her world swaying about her as she fought to maintain consciousness, a black void easing its way into her mind. A cold clamminess washed over her, and slowly, Katrina gave in to the darkness that enclosed her, but as she sank into oblivion, Chin Li's words echoed in her mind— "She is with child!"

Chin Li sighed contentedly as a bird cried in the sky above. The sun was warm and bright as Li thought of joining her friend walking along the beach but, feeling wonderfully lazy, decided to stay where she lay in the soft sand.

Katrina lifted the hem of her colorful cotton dress, like the ones the natives wore on the island, and waded deeper into the blue-green water. She considered a swim to cool off, but decided against it, knowing Li did not like her to swim alone. Looking down at her swollen stomach, she tenderly ran her hand over it, feeling the baby kick inside her womb. It would not be long before she would give birth to her child, and then, she could return to England. And to Blake.

God! How she missed him! Briefly, she wondered if John had received her message and told Blake she was alive. How he must have suffered. Sadly, she stared into the waters swirling about her legs. The thought of their secret pond flooded into her melancholy mind as she remembered all the times they had argued. Then just as suddenly her memories of loving, tender moments overwhelmed her. How she longed for his touch! Reeling from suppressed desires and shaken from the painful longing in her heart, Katrina tried to draw her mind to other things.

Shielding her eyes against the sun, Katrina could see some children playing along an old wooden dock not far from her. With a smile, she waved at her friends, their cries of greeting echoing back. Just then, a spasm ripped across her belly, bringing a gasp of surprise from Rina. The noise and her apparent discomfort were immediately noticed by Li, who quickly scurried away to get Trevor Wilde.

Katrina still could not believe how kind Trevor had been

to them. He had brought Katrina and Li to his home on a secluded island right after he had taken them from Captain Walker's ship, insisting they stay as his guests until after the baby was born. Trevor had been a perfect host, and as the months had rolled languidly by, he and Katrina had become good friends. He was a wonderful man, kind and generous. He had seen to it her message was carried to John in England, and he extended all the comforts of his home to ensure that Katrina and Li enjoyed their stay in the Caribbean.

Katrina had barely had a second contraction when Trevor met her and whisked her into his strong arms. "What is it, Katrina? Are you all right?"

His face was pale, concern furrowing his handsome brow. "It is all right, Trevor. I just think the baby is anxious to be born. It's going to be a boy, Trevor. I just know it."

Almost four months had passed since Blake's sudden departure, and Ryon had received no word of his whereabouts. He and Rebecca had remained in London as long as possible, hoping Blake might contact them, but now they prepared to leave for Windsong. Sitting alone in the library, Ryon once again felt the twinge of pain left by Blake's actions. He felt so helpless and frustrated, wishing for his return. Even a terrible argument would be better than this waiting and not knowing where he was or if he was all right. If he were here, Ryon could at least attempt to explain and make things right. Sighing helplessly, Ryon stood, intending to seek out Rebecca and his daughter. They always eased the pain and sorrow.

Just as Ryon reached the staircase, a knock at the door took his attention from his wife. Answering it himself, he was surprised to find John standing there.

"John! Come in, come in." Reaching out to grasp his extended hand, Ryon greeted his friend happily. "What brings you to London?"

"I've come to see Blake. Is he here?"

John had not seen the Robertses since the funeral, so he did not know of Blake's disappearance. "He is gone, John. I don't know when he will be back."

At John's look of concern, Ryon took him into the library and explained all that had happened since Katrina's death. When he had finished John stood, furious at what he heard. "How could he possibly believe such slanderous lies about Kat? She did nothing but love him! Is he such a bastard he would accuse her of such things?"

Ryon knew how John must feel but tried to explain his brother's actions. "He nearly went mad with grief at her death. Blake has not been himself since. Catherine's lies were too much for him. He loved Katrina—we both know that, even if he did not fully realize it himself. He is not a man who gives love easily, and when it was taken from him, he could not cope. For whatever reasons, Blake believed that lying bitch and now he is gone. I fear he may never return."

Pouring two whiskeys, Ryon sat across from John. "Why did you need to speak with Blake? It must be quite urgent to make you ride straight to London."

John ran an impatient hand through his unruly hair and, coming to a decision, answered, "She is alive, Ryon. I received a brief message from her three days ago. I came right here."

Pulling a paper from his pocket, he handed it to a confused Ryon, who unfolded it immediately, his hands trembling.

Dearest John,
    I pray that at least you are waiting for this word. I am not dead but alive and well. I cannot explain now and no one must know I am alive, except for Blake. You must tell him. I will be unable to reach London until spring of next year. No one else must know. . . . Love, Kat

"Katrina is alive?" The words came out in a whisper, "But we saw her, she was dead!"

Shaking his head, John said, "I don't fully understand what happened. But this note proves that it wasn't Kat! She is *not* dead, Ryon, but her life must be in danger, so no one must know of this note. No one!"

"God," sighed Ryon. So many questions to be answered. "I will pray that Blake has returned by spring."

"Yes," agreed John sadly, "it would be disastrous if she returned and he was not here."

"And we have no way of telling Blake that Katrina is alive." Ryon closed his eyes wearily, the months of worry having taken its toll on the young man. "What else will go wrong, John? They love each other, and yet they have had no happiness together. If she does return, what of Randolph?"

John slumped in exhaustion. "I don't know, Ryon," he whispered. "I just don't know!"

Chapter 22

Katrina's gaze took in the lush gardens below as she thought of the months that had passed so quickly. It had been almost a year since she had left England. The events that had taken place in that time cast a veil of sadness over her beautiful face.

A baby's cry made Katrina smile and she bent down to gently kiss her son's head. She felt a tremendous joy as she watched his smiling face. Jason gurgled incoherently to his mother as she carefully lifted him into her arms.

"Would you like to go out to the garden, Jason?"

Jason's answer consisted of a happy shriek and a small fist waved about in the air. His baby-fresh smell pleased Katrina, as did the feel of him in her arms and his gleeful chirps and squeals.

Katrina remembered little of the pain this cherished child had brought her three months before. It had been forgotten the very moment she first held Jason in her arms. The time since his birth had been devoted to Jason, and Katrina passed through it in a blissful daze, unaware of many things, one of which was her own blossoming as a mother, which made her even more beautiful to those around her. Katrina's figure was slender and firmly muscled just as it had always been, but her breasts were fuller and there was a rosy tint to her cheeks and a sparkle in her eyes. A lovely smile graced her lips most of the time, especially when Jason was present.

Unfortunately, the other thing Katrina was unaware of was how much her beauty was affecting Trevor Wilde. As each day passed he found it more and more difficult to deny the feelings he had for her. It grew harder for him to remember that she was married and was planning to return to England as soon as possible now that spring was here and Jason was big enough to travel. Jason aroused feelings he had not known existed—the baby was like his own son.

Unbeknown to Trevor, Katrina counted the days until she could return to her home. She knew it would be hard to leave Trevor Wilde. He was a wonderful man, but her heart belonged to another.

Sometimes she worried about Blake's response to having a son. But when she looked at Jason's face, she could not believe any man would fail to love such perfection.

Jason squealed his delight as a colorful bird flew by the window they stood near. Kat brushed her lips against the baby's soft curls, turned from the window, and left the cheery nursery. Trevor had had the suite redecorated just for Katrina and her child. Adjoining the nursery was her bedroom and smaller sitting room.

In the sitting room, Katrina paused by the chair Li sat in and cheerfully asked, "Would you like to join us for a walk in the garden?"

Laying aside the needlework she had been working on, Chin Li smiled and happily agreed, as she, too, was anxious for some fresh air and sun. "Do you think Mr. Wilde will be returning from New Orleans soon?"

Nodding, Katrina answered, "Perhaps today, Li. He didn't plan to be gone long."

The two women and the child had barely reached the bottom of the stairs when Trevor burst through the front door; a delighted grin spread across his tanned face when he saw the small group descending the stairs.

"Trevor!" cried Katrina happily and quickened her step to greet him.

Overwhelmed by the beauty before him, Trevor could

not resist leaning down and kissing her tempting red lips. The passion of Trevor's kiss caused Katrina to blush a brilliant red, and suddenly, she became embarrassingly aware of his true feelings for her. The shock of it left her dumbfounded as she searched for the right words.

Seeing her confusion and discomfort, Trevor immediately cursed himself for his stupidity, and he, too, felt at a loss for words as they silently stared at each other. But the person standing in the background saw it in a different perspective. Shock flooded over him as he stood in the doorway, unable to believe what he saw before him.

She's alive! his mind screamed through all the numbness and haze, but anger began to seep in as he witnessed the passionate kiss. It was then that he became aware of the small baby that Katrina held—Trevor Wilde's baby. Betrayal and hatred hit him so hard, he felt breathless and shaken, but by the time Trevor and Katrina pulled themselves together, Blake had managed to compose himself.

Turning to Li, Katrina handed Jason to her, and as she turned back to Trevor, her eyes fell on the man standing in the open doorway. The sunlight filtered into the hall behind him and made it impossible to see his face, but Katrina froze, her face paling to a deathly shade.

Seeing her reaction, Trevor held out his hand, fearing she would faint. "Katrina are you ill? You look as if you have seen a ghost!"

Stepping forward and shutting the door clamly, Blake added casually, belying the tremendous turmoil inside him, "Actually, it is I who have seen a ghost, Trevor. After all, you are supposed to be dead, aren't you, little one?"

Katrina fought to maintain control of her speeding heart and found it difficult to breathe as waves of extreme heat flushed over her, causing her knees to shake weakly. Her dry mouth could not form words and her tongue seemed thick and heavy as she swallowed nervously.

Trevor looked about in total confusion, aware of Katrina's discomfort and shock, but when he met Blake's gold eyes, he saw hatred burning in them. Trevor's words were uncertain and broken as he spoke the question he dreaded to ask. "What are you talking about, Blake? You know Katrina?"

"I am talking about a grave with a marker stating, 'Here lies Katrina Easton'!" sneered Blake with contempt. "I am talking about a woman who was murdered, beaten, and raped beyond recognition, a woman dressed in your clothing, who until now, I believed to be Katrina Easton! Who was she?"

Blake's eyes burned into Katrina's round blue ones. The hate and anger she saw in them added to her whirling emotions, leaving her unguarded and distraught. "I don't know her name. I . . . she was . . . a p-prostitute on the docks . . . that is all I know," she whispered, still unaware of Blake's train of thought. What made him think she would know who she was?

"You vile bitch!" spat out Blake, his fury complete, causing all caution to flee, only a red haze remained.

Katrina's head snapped up at his vicious words. Why was he so angry? Hadn't John gotten her message? Why hadn't he known she was alive? Blake stepped forward, his face so near Katrina's she could feel his breath on her face and the heat from his body. The smell of him was intoxicating. It was all happening so fast, she could not think. In a daze, she stood mutely, unable to believe what she was hearing as he continued his ugly assault.

"Couldn't you find some other way out of your marriage? Tell me, Katrina, how did you arrange it all so cleverly? How did you get Mack and Ralph to go along with it all? But then, I suppose enough money would get men like that to kill their own brothers! And I'm certain you gave them plenty of what they had wanted in the first place! They did mention what a good whore you were!"

Blake's mind snapped, the words pouring from him in a torrent. Whether he believed what he was saying, even he did not know. There was no rational thought left, only a deep searing pain, ripping at his heart and soul. Turning to an astounded and mute Trevor, Blake laughed, cruelly. "So you, too, my friend, have found out what a good whore Katrina really is! I hope you are not too disappointed to find out that she has been shared by *many* others, right down to the vermin that crawl about London's docks!"

He turned his hate-filled eyes back to Katrina and continued his attack, enjoying the shock and pain mirrored in her eyes. Blake had gone too far to stop, driven mad by the months of torment and grief mixing with the hate and anger that had smothered the love. "I am sure those two bastards enjoyed what they did to that unfortunate prostitute, and it is because of her I do not regret killing them. It makes my stomach turn to think I originally did it to avenge what I believed to be your death! I was such a fool to believe all the lies you told me! Catherine Ramsey told me of your whoring! How many were there? Besides Ryon and David, of course! I should kill you myself for all your treachery and deceit, you whoring little bitch!"

Blake reached up and slowly wrapped his strong hands around Katrina's throat, the feel of it good, glorious, as his fingers tightened their grip. Trevor stepped forward, his own anger welling up dangerously.

"Take your hands from her!"

But it was Katrina who answered, holding up her hand to stop Trevor, who was about to strike Blake. "No!"

Both men looked at her in surprise and were stunned by the flash of anger in the sapphire eyes. Looking directly into Blake's crazed eyes, her eyes narrowed menacingly. When she spoke her voice held a note of viciousness that both men felt as well as heard.

"If you truly believe me to be such a 'whoring bitch' as you say, then kill me! Take your hands and squeeze the breath from my body until there is no more!" Taking her own hands, she grasped Blake's own, as if daring him to let her go. The violence of emotions she felt inside her caused her to tremble uncontrollably, her voice rising until she was screaming at him. "If you think me so vile a creature, then for God's sake, kill me! Kill me and be done with me, once and for all! You have always believed the worst of me and nothing I can do will ever convince you otherwise, so kill me! Kill me! . . . I do not want to live knowing you believe such things! . . . Kill me!"

Blake's grip tightened with deadly peril, but Katrina made

no move, her eyes almost pleading with him to do it. Blake would never know whether he would have indeed choked the life from her or not, because Trevor jumped him, knocking him away. Katrina was thrown from the two men, and seeing the cold fury between them, she reacted quickly. Running into the library, she retrieved a pistol from Trevor's desk drawer and returned to the hall. There was no doubt in her mind that they would kill each other, so lifting the pistol steadily, Katrina aimed it toward them.

"Stop it!" she yelled, her voice breaking through their haze of anger. When they saw the pistol bearing down on them, they quickly parted and faced her fury, neither misinterpreting the look in her eyes.

"Blake Roberts, leave this house, for if you had wished to hurt me, you have done so, more than you will ever know! You are right to say you are a fool, because I know no bigger one than you, but for other reasons that you are too stupid to realize! Now go!"

Blake felt an urge to take the pistol from her and slap her silly, but suddenly, he felt disgusted with the whole scene and was sickened by the sight of her. Without another word, he turned and left, slamming the door behind him. The noise echoed about in the entryway as the two people left inside stood frozen in place, uncertain of what to do.

As Katrina stared at the closed door, it was as if in that same moment, another door inside her heart was slammed shut. She felt tired and drained, but most of all, she felt an emptiness that had not existed only moments ago. Numbly, she walked to the stairs and started up them, but Trevor's hand pulled her to him. She saw the questions in his eyes, but still she said nothing.

Trevor guided the listless Katrina away from the stairs and into the library, closing the door behind them. Taking the pistol from her hand, he gently pushed her into a large chair, then poured some sherry into a glass, pressing it into her cold hands.

"Drink this, Katrina. You are still terribly pale."

It was more an order than a request, but Katrina did as she was told, grateful for the burning sensation that spread through her.

Satisfied to see a small flush returning to her cheeks, Trevor took the seat across from her, his voice sad and strained. "Katrina, I wish you would explain what has just happened. I believe I have the right to know. Blake Roberts and I have known each other a long time, but I had no idea when I ran into him in New Orleans that he knew you. I asked him here, thinking your gentleness would ease the pain I saw in his eyes. I thought to surprise him with the special woman in my life. I guess I played the fool."

"I am so sorry if I misled you, Trevor. I was unaware of any feeling other than friendship between us."

"It was not your doing, but mine," sighed Trevor. "Katrina, I wish you would explain."

Katrina's eyes darkened with a sadness that tore at Trevor's heart.

"What is to explain?" answered Katrina, her voice strained. "Blake Roberts believes I am so wicked and depraved that I arranged my own kidnapping, even agreeing to murder an innocent woman to take my place among the dead, so that I might be free of a husband and marriage I detest. He believes me to be a sluttish whore who sleeps with his friends and brother, or anyone else I wish to coax to my bed. He believes that you are my latest lover and perhaps even the father of my bastard child. Blake Roberts and I were lovers, but now he loathes my very existence and nothing I can say will possibly change his feelings. He would never believe that Jason is his son."

Katrina laughed strangely, but to Trevor it was like a sad and bitter cry of pain. "It's funny, Trevor, really it is . . . for I have done nothing but love him from the very first. I have fought against all odds, even against death itself, just to be with him again! I have tried many times to convince myself that I didn't need him complicating my life, and yet, life without Blake would be so empty I could not bear it. Even now, when I should return the hatred he feels, I cannot. I love him, Trevor, and I will never stop! I can no more remove him from my mind than I could my heart and soul from my body! There is no hope for us, but there can never be another man in my life. I have only Jason, who is a part of Blake Roberts, and I will always have that to comfort me."

Trevor stood, his own agony apparent as he paced back and forth. "How can he believe those things about you? You are all that is good and kind; never have I seen you be otherwise!" Kneeling before Katrina, he took her soft hand into both of his and lovingly kissed her palm tenderly. "He must be blind not to see you as you really are!"

Gently, Katrina removed her hand and lifted his face to look into hers and stated softly, almost urgently, "No, Trevor, I am not perfect. I make mistakes . . . too many! You and Blake have no right to judge me, one way or the other, there are too many things that neither of you know, and I cannot tell!"

"No!" yelled Trevor angrily. Exasperated, he threw his hands up in the air as he stood. "I see tremendous love in your heart for even the lowest of persons!"

"I also carry hatred that you cannot even begin to understand! I thirst for revenge like a person thirsts for water. It drives me, it possesses me! Do not burden me with your angelic talk, for I cannot live with that! I am me! Good and bad! And until you or Blake accepts both parts of me, you do not know me!"

Katrina was nearly hysterical; her nerves were shattered and she could no longer control her emotions.

"I love you, Katrina!" pleaded Trevor. "Stay with me, I'll see that you have everything you'll need in life. Stay, Katrina, please!"

Standing, her anger subsiding at his tender declaration, Katrina took his face into her hands as she looked up into his startlingly clear, green eyes. "I cannot stay, Trevor. I cannot love you as you love me. I am so sorry. I never meant to hurt you, for you have been nothing but kind to me. But Blake is a part of me, he is in my mind, he is in my blood, he is in my heart! Blake Roberts is my very soul! He is my very life!"

"You are right, Katrina," Trevor agreed sadly. "It just would make things so much easier if you could forget him."

"Life is never simple," stated Katrina, her own hurt and

pain taking over. "I want to leave for England, Trevor. I want to go home."

Startled, he started to object but decided it would be unwise. "When?"

"Tomorrow, if possible."

Sighing, Trevor nodded. "There is a ship leaving from a nearby island tomorrow evening. We will leave in the morning."

"Thank you," mumbled Katrina. "I had better see to my packing. I will see you at dinner, Trevor."

By the time evening came, Katrina felt weary down to her very bones, and yet she knew sleep would be difficult to come by. If only her mind would cease reliving every moment of what had happened that day. If she could but blot out her memory, if only for one night, so that peaceful sleep could overtake her. Suddenly, her eyes fell on a crystal decanter filled with red wine, sitting on a small table across from where she sat.

Why not? thought Katrina, rising from her chair. Filling a glass, she quickly drained it. Taking the bottle and glass, Katrina left her sitting room and entered her bedroom. It was a beautiful room, done in lavender and blue. But it held no appeal for her that night. Her only thoughts were of Blake and how he had looked. Had his shoulders really been so broad and his waist so narrow and lean? She had seen his muscles ripple beneath the linen shirt he had worn and had ached to touch the fine brown hair revealed by the open front of his collar. Katrina could remember every inch of his sun-bronzed face. It had been so long since she had gazed upon it, she wanted to caress it, to feel every line, to feel his eyes, cheeks, and lips. To feel the bristle of his neatly trimmed mustache and his soft brown hair curling at the back of his neck. Even though his touch was painful, it still had caused feelings to stir deep within her that had long been dormant.

"Dear God," mumbled Katrina, "even as he attacked me with his vile accusations and his eyes showed me the hatred he felt, I felt desire. What manner of woman am I to feel passion when I should feel anger? Why must I love him instead of hating him? Why?"

Katrina shouted her questions to the silent walls, then giggled at her own foolishness, setting the empty decanter aside. How easily the fiery liquid had gone down. When she stood, Katrina felt light-headed and giddy. Feeling much too warm, she crossed the room, weaving slightly, and opened the double doors leading out onto her balcony. A cooling breeze filled the room, soothing her warm skin and gently blowing her long silken hair back from her flushed face.

Closing her eyes, Katrina felt the liquor slowly relaxing her tired muscles, and her nervousness disappeared. Removing the silk robe and gown she wore, she lifted her heavy mane from her neck and allowed the wind to flow over her naked skin. The lamplight cast shadows about the room, bathing Katrina's flawless skin in gold and bringing out flashes of red and copper in her long tresses.

Silently, Blake stood in the shadows of the balcony, his eyes drinking in the sight of her loveliness. She was perfection! He felt the stirring of desire as he watched her, the tightness in his loins undeniable. Even the large amount of whiskey he had consumed could not dampen the passion she had aroused in him. Blake could think of nothing else since seeing her, and nothing could stop him from seeking her out.

"I see having that brat of yours has not ruined your beautiful body, little one." As he stepped forward into the room, Katrina opened her eyes, startled by his sudden appearance. "If I am not mistaken, you are even lovelier than before."

His words were soft and husky, leaving no doubt in Katrina's mind of his reason for being there. Blake's eyes burned like liquid fire as they roved boldly over her naked body and she made no effort to cover her nudity.

"Get out, you son-of-a-bitch!" Her words were slightly slurred as the wine began to numb her lips and impair her reflexes.

With deliberate slowness, Blake closed the doors, his eyes never leaving hers, giving her an answer without words.

Katrina raised an amused eyebrow, then lifted her delicate

shoulders nonchalantly. "I would offer you a drink, but it seems that I am out of wine. You *will* forgive my rudeness, I'm sure."

"Ha!" laughed Blake, causing Katrina to jump at the sudden noise. "You are drunk!"

"As you are, sir!" Another giggle escaped Katrina and she tried to stop it by covering her mouth with her hand. Then turning serious, she glared at him. "What do you want? Didn't you get enough satisfaction in hurting me this afternoon? Or do you wish to twist the knife you plunged into my heart some more?"

Blake began to move toward Katrina. "You know very well what it is I want."

"Yes, I suppose I do," whispered Katrina weakly.

When Blake stood before her, strong and virile, she thought she might actually swoon from the overpowering maleness of him. A wicked smile crossed her sensuous lips as she looked up into Blake's lust-filled eyes. Slowly, seductively, she began to remove his shirt, arousing Blake's desire even further.

"No matter how much you hate me, no matter how loathsome you think me to be, you still come to me. You want to kill me, and yet, you want to love me. You are mine, Blake Roberts! Mine!"

Her deep voice, almost purring with sensuality, was more intoxicating than the whiskey, but her words angered him and he grabbed her hands in a brutal grip, muttering through clenched teeth, "I don't belong to anyone, most of all you! I just thought to ease the pain in my groin between the legs of the biggest whore on this island. You definitely fit that description!"

Katrina's laughter filled the room, angering Blake even further. "You know I am right! Tell me, darling, did you forget me when you thought I was dead? Did other women ease your passion as I have?"

The wine was making Katrina say things she would not have said if she had been sober, but it did not matter. Nothing mattered but the longings inside her. From the look on Blake's face, she knew the answer to her questions. "Yes, Blake, even in death you will be mine, just as I am yours!

We are both slaves to the passions we arouse in each other. Slaves to each other forever!"

"You are a witch! A witch that casts spells that a normal man cannot fight!" His hand snapped up and wrapped easily about her slender neck, the temptation to break it overpowering. As the pressure increased, Katrina only smiled and stared into his golden eyes with her probing blue ones. Her hands quickly released his hardened member from the confines of his breeches, and a low moan escaped him as his pants slid down his muscled buttocks, dropping to the floor. Stepping from them without releasing his painful grip on Katrina, Blake now stood as naked as she was.

"You are mine, as I am yours . . . say it!" choked Rina, uncaring of the pain, only aware of her overwhelming needs. "Kill me! Love me! It doesn't matter! You are mine!"

Blake closed his eyes, trying to fight against the reality of her words. Slowly, his hold on her throat eased, and without even realizing it, his hand began to caress her cheek, gently, tenderly. Pulling her to him, Blake leaned down, but paused, his lips almost touching hers. "I am yours, you witch!"

Then his lips took hers, possessing her passionately, hungrily. He devoured the sweetness they had to offer as he plundered her juicy mouth, his tongue tasting the wine she had drunk earlier. They were like animals, fierce in their passion as the loneliness of the past year descended upon them. Blake crushed her to him, bruising her tender flesh painfully, but it didn't matter to Katrina, it only added to her own uncontrollable desire. An all-consuming fire exploded in them, taking their near-frenzied lovemaking to heights neither had ever dared dream of.

Blake lifted her easily to him as Katrina wrapped her strong legs about his waist. As he carried her to the bed, her fingers ran through his hair and then moved to feel his face, leaving no feature untouched. When Blake's lips left hers, Katrina bit and nibbled, nearly driving him mad as he tortured her delightfully in return. His tongue teased her sensitive nipples, and the fullness of them made him wild. She arched against him, pleading with Blake to take her, his hard shaft rubbing along her delicate flesh, teasing and arousing her beyond endurance.

Grasping his back, Katrina pulled Blake to her, nails digging deep into his warm flesh. Unable to hold off any longer, he plunged deep within her soft moistness, the warmth of her sending chills through his body, the tightness nearly causing him to lose his control too soon. Katrina gasped as Blake filled her completely, giving her pleasure beyond description as she raised her hips to bring him even closer, plunging him even deeper within her body. Nothing in the whole world existed to them but each other. Blake's rhythm increased as he drove further and further into her, bringing them both to the point of fulfillment. Katrina dug her nails into his already bleeding back as she felt the explosion in her body. Waves upon waves of pleasure shattered through her, causing her to moan in ecstasy as every part of her body trembled from the ultimate passion. As Blake felt her climax, his own release flowed from him. He felt his whole body shake uncontrollably as he strained against Katrina's warm, glistening body, filling her with his seed.

Both of them lay weak and shaken, each wondering at the ultimate lovemaking they had just experienced. Violence, desperation, hate, and anger, combined with passion, love, tenderness, and desire, had created a joining that neither Katrina nor Blake would ever forget.

"Oh, God! I love him! How can I face a life without him?" Katrina cried silently just before sleep overtook her as she lay tucked lovingly in Blake's arms, his own even breathing mixing with hers.

It was still dark when Blake woke up, his mind muddled by the drink he had consumed, but somewhat clearer than it had been earlier. He quickly slid from the large canopied bed. Looking down at the sleeping Katrina, his lips curled slightly in distaste as he mumbled to himself, "You look like an angel, little one, with your hair spread about you like a golden halo, your face so sweet and innocent, but we both know different, don't we? Tonight you played out the whore so well, I find it difficult to leave your pleasurable body, but I must."

After he had silently dressed, Blake started to leave but

paused at the balcony doors. Turning, he walked back over to the table by the bed and, taking out several coins, tossed them onto it. Then, taking the ring Katrina had given him from his finger, he laid it next to the money.

"Good-bye, witch! I pray that we never meet again!"

Chapter 23

Trevor walked into his bedroom already feeling lonely. Visions of Katrina waving good-bye to him were imprinted vividly on his mind; the feel of her soft lips still lingered on his own. Trevor had wanted to go with them, but she had insisted she must return to England alone, with Li as her only companion. He conceded, for he knew he had no right to interfere in that part of her life. Because he loved her, Trevor had let her go, hoping that she would find happiness.

Pouring himself a drink, Trevor wearily walked to his bed, its comfort inviting him to sleep. It would be dawn in just a few hours, but he felt too tense to sleep. As he set his empty glass on the nightstand, he spotted the note sitting on it. Picking it up, Trevor saw that it was from Chin Li and began to read.

"Oh, my God!" muttered Trevor in the silence of his room. "What have I allowed you to return to, my dear Katrina?"

It took him several minutes to read the carefully written pages and with each passing moment, Trevor felt more afraid. In the letter Chin Li wrote of all the things Katrina had spoken to her about, explaining about Katrina's tortured past. He understood now the hatred she had spoken of and the revenge she sought. Now he knew of the secrets Katrina had kept inside of her.

He reread the last lines of the letter, his hand running worriedly through his tousled hair.

> You must find Blake Roberts and tell him what I have just told you, Trevor. Make your friend understand how wrong he has been about Katrina and how much she needs him. Katrina may never forgive me for what I am doing, but if it keeps her from danger I will have no regrets. Please, I beg you, go to Blake. Katrina and her son need him.
>
> —Katrina's friend and yours, Chin Li

Carefully, Trevor refolded the letter and placed it inside his shirt. Grimly, he stood and left to find Blake.

It was a balmy night. The stars flickered bright and shiny against the ebony sky. The moon was a pale yellow, almost colorless, lighting the darkness with a soft glow. Trevor rode up to the tavern nestled among other buildings that made up the small village on the island. He reined his horse in front of the inn and slid off, looking carefully about him.

When he entered the inn, several men hailed Trevor merrily, inviting him to share some ale. After declining politely, he quickly looked about, searching for Blake Roberts, his green eyes stopping when they clashed with Blake's hard gold ones. Slowly, he crossed the room and sat down across from Blake, who sat with his feet up, casually puffing on a cheroot. Trevor felt the smoldering anger that surrounded Blake, an invisible screen swirling about, like the smoke that hung heavily in the air. He could see from Blake's glazed eyes that he had been drinking heavily and when he spoke, his words were slurred and clumsy.

"If you know what is best for you, you will leave now, Trevor."

"I have come to talk to you, Blake," said Trevor calmly. Though Trevor appeared unconcerned with Blake's drunken state, he was acutely aware of the fury Blake barely held in control.

His voice angry, Blake sneered, "I have nothing to talk to you about!"

"Well, I do!" yelled Trevor, his patience gone. "I have some important facts you're going to listen to whether you want to or not, you bastard!"

Blake let out a furious cry and leapt at the other man. As he flew across the table and crashed against Trevor, all men in the room turned cautious and curious eyes to the spectacle. Both Blake and Trevor fell heavily to the floor, table and chairs thrown about like pieces of kindling, as they scrambled about among the filth and dirt.

Trevor staggered back from Blake's crashing blow to his chin, then, like a bull, he charged, catching Blake in the midsection with his shoulder, lifting the taller man from the floor and slamming him against the wall with force. They hit so hard that anything that had hung on the wall came tumbling down along with Blake and Trevor as they once again rolled about on the floor.

Those who watched saw how evenly matched the two men were, even though the stranger had consumed quite a bit of ale before Trevor had come in. Many took bets and each began to root for his favorite, enjoying the fracas that had joyously interrupted an otherwise boring evening.

Blake grabbed Trevor, easily throwing him over the bar, sending him headfirst into several barrels of ale and wine, scattering them in all directions. Picking himself up, Trevor then lunged at Blake, all reasoning gone. The cruel words Blake had yelled at Katrina echoed in his mind, adding fuel to his fire. Trevor saw again the pain in her eyes, and each time his fist struck Blake, he felt a wave of joy and satisfaction.

A different emotion ruled Blake as he struggled with the man he had always considered to be a good friend. Visions had been haunting him since he'd found Katrina, visions he could not cope with rationally. In his mind, he saw Trevor and Katrina, their bodies entwined as they made love. It was the worst form of torture for Blake, and it tore at him, ripping and clawing like a vicious cat, shredding his vulnerable heart and soul into pieces to be slowly and agonizingly devoured. As he struck at Trevor he cursed the lying whore that possessed him, as if in some way this burst of violence would exorcise her from his mind.

The two men began to grow weary, their movements slow and clumsy, both breathing heavily as they labored to stay afoot. Facing his opponent, Trevor grabbed hold of Blake, reason beginning to return as his fighting anger eased.

"You're as stubborn as you are foolish! I should just leave you here and go after Katrina myself!"

This made Blake pause, a feeing of dread seeping through the haze of fury. "What do you mean, go after her? Isn't she at your house?"

Trevor shook his head and remarked, "I think we should go there now. We have some talking to do, Blake. It's time you listened for a change!"

Without waiting for an answer, Trevor turned and walked away. Blake followed him home in sullen silence.

Trevor walked into his house, barking orders to the servants, who had waited up for his return. Taking the stairs two at a time, he reached the second floor landing before Blake burst into the hall, his annoyance apparent. When Blake finally reached Trevor's room, he found two tubs set up. Already half-stripped, Trevor struggled with his leather boots. Something like a growl erupted from Blake, causing the servants who had been heating the water to scatter nervously, then quickly disappear from the room.

"You had best start explaining yourself, Trevor. My patience has run out!"

Seeming not to have heard him, Trevor pulled off his breeches and stepped into the tub of steaming water. Once he had settled back, the warmth easing his strained and bruised muscles like gentle, massaging fingers, Trevor motioned to the other tub.

"You are filthy, Blake. I will explain as we wash. The *Sea Hawk* will be ready to sail by dusk."

Suddenly, Blake felt tired as he ran his hand through his damp curls. Seeing Blake's uncertainty, Trevor spoke again. "You trusted me once, my friend, trust me now. The truth is that Katrina was not my mistress, she never thought of me as anything more than a friend. I was foolish enough to hope for more, but her heart belonged to someone else from the first time I set eyes on her. Katrina thought of no one but you, Blake; I never had a chance."

Blake was stunned for a moment. Perhaps Trevor was right—he had to trust in someone. The least he could do was listen to his old friend. So, stripping down, he, too, climbed into his tub, then waited for Trevor to continue.

"Katrina is on her way back to England. It seems she kept a few things from both of us, but Chin Li had the sense to write me and tell everything. She *was* kidnapped, Blake, and by the same two men you thought had taken her, but they were paid by her uncle, Lawrence Langsford and his son . . . her husband."

Blake became confused and demanded, "Langsford! Why the hell would he do that?"

"Langsford wanted her out of the way. The man Katrina seeks revenge on for the death of her parents *is* Lawrence Langsford!"

Trevor stopped, feeling hurt, realizing that Katrina had never felt she could confide in him. She'd allowed him to believe that the father of her child, and the man she longed to return to, was her husband. But when he glanced at Blake, his own self-pity was forgotten as he saw the pain Blake was feeling at that moment, for she had never told him her darkest secrets either. Trevor read the shock, fear, and horror on Blake's face as Trevor's words soaked into his muddled mind. Trevor went on with his story.

"Katrina is a threat to his sole possession of Camray, so he hired two goons to take care of her who wanted her dead for reasons of their own. . . ."

Blake listened mutely as Trevor repeated all he had learned of Katrina's past. He told Blake about Walker, about Chin Li, about Willy. And then he told him about himself. Trevor's voice became gentle, almost caressing, the tenderness in his eyes making Blake clench his teeth angrily. "The first time I saw her, it took my breath away. Never had I seen such enchanting beauty mixed with spirit and fearlessness. I will not lie to you, Blake; I wanted her from that first moment. I was blinded with such desire I lost control. I acted the fool, my friend, putting her life in danger. I can never forgive myself for that! She was with child and I nearly took her like a common strumpet!"

Blake's head snapped up, surprise registering on his tired face, his eyes asking the question Trevor answered, "No, Blake, the child is not mine. Katrina and I were only friends, just as I said. I will admit to my disappointment, but there is nothing more to tell. You hurt her terribly with all your accusations and insults. She deserves much better than that. Never in my life have I seen a woman with such strength and perseverance."

"And who is the father, Trevor? Did Chin Li bother to enlighten you as to who he is? Or does Katrina even know?"

Trevor flushed at Blake's ugly words. "You are, you bastard! Katrina has always been faithful and true to you, but you are too goddamned stubborn to realize that! We may not think much of Grant Walker's morals when it comes to selling women as slaves, but I do know the man protected his women. He even went so far as to give his own life protecting Katrina from that bastard Willy, so use your head, man! Katrina has been untouched by anyone except the man she loves more than life itself! For the love of God, Blake! That man is you! You are the father of her son!"

Chapter 24

Katrina felt her heart race wildly as they neared England's shrouded coast. Home! The word sounded dear and echoed warmly in her mind. Through the sad bitterness and hatred that had clung to Katrina during the voyage, a sparkle of new hope began to emerge, making a weak appearance through the haze of numbness that had surrounded her for weeks.

Chin Li had grown frantic when Katrina withdrew inside herself, forcing all the painful thoughts and memories into a dark place within her and figuratively locking the door on them. Katrina became a stranger to her friend, but most of all, she had become a stranger to herself. She had willed Blake Roberts from her mind but, in doing so, was left empty of feeling and hope.

Jason became her life during the day, but when he slept soundly in his crib, memories haunted Katrina's own slumber. The nightmares returned along with the feelings of anger and betrayal. She turned all her pain and bitterness into fuel for her hatred of Lawrence Langsford. When she was not occupied with Jason, Katrina's mind would turn to her enemy.

In the privacy of her cabin, she exercised, toning her

muscles and reflexes, preparing, as she had for years, for the final confrontation. It had to come to an end once and for all; she could no longer bide her time patiently. Lawrence Langsford would pay for slaughtering her parents.

Perhaps if the years had dulled her memory of that night, if she had been able to forget, to recall little—and then only with a child's vague memories—her hatred would not have been so obsessing. But even her tremendous love for her son could not blot out the ugliness inside of Katrina. When Li tried to talk some sense into her friend, she found no logic or caution in her, only grim determination to face Langsford and kill him. Unable to do or say anything to stop it, she saw Katrina change, slowly, before her very eyes. It was as if there were only two things in her life— Jason, her son; and Langsford, her enemy.

"You must learn to trust in me, Li. I know you cannot understand my reasons for what I do, so you must not worry and simply trust me."

Katrina's words echoed in Li's troubled mind, bringing pangs of guilt to her heart. Had she betrayed her friend to the very man Katrina wished to leave behind? Was she right to ignore Katrina's wishes? She had witnessed Katrina's skills with weapons and knew her courage to be great, and yet Li feared for her.

Jason stirred, bringing Li's thoughts back to the present, his movements also catching his mother's loving eyes. "Here, I'll take Jason for a while. You must be getting tired of holding him."

Li shook her head and smiled reassuringly. "No, Katrina, I'm doing fine. I'd rather take charge of Jason and let you take charge of all of us and our baggage. The docks look like a madhouse."

Madhouse was an understatement. The London docks crawled with people of every description. Cargo crates were stacked everywhere, some filled with live animals, which added to the noise and confusion. Smells of every sort drifted to their noses as Kat and Li made their way carefully through the crowds.

The two women and child attracted much more attention than Chin Li was comfortable with. The whistles and catcalls brought a dark blush to her face, but Katrina seemed to be oblivious to the throngs of men surrounding them. After what seemed to be an eternity, their luggage arrived, and Katrina left Chin Li with Jason and their trunks to find a carriage to take them to an inn. Briefly Li had wished Katrina had sent a message of their arrival so someone could have met them, but she had said there was no time. Li was frightened to be left alone but relaxed as the attention they attracted was focused elsewhere for the moment. Had she thought on the matter a bit, she would have realized that as Katrina had left, the men and their attention had followed her.

Katrina carefully weaved in and out of the stacks of cargo, dodging people along the way. Spotting a line of carriages, Katrina stepped forward to wave one down but found her way blocked by a huge bulk of a man dressed in seaman's clothes. He looked as if he hadn't bathed in quite some time; his smell confirmed the notion. His lopsided grin revealed a nearly equal number of tobacco-stained teeth and holes left by the ones that had already rotted out. Stubble covered his face, not quite a beard, but rather just enough to show he shaved once in a great while. Glossy, almost colorless eyes stared at Katrina rudely, the whites no longer clear, but bloodshot and yellow. When he spoke, the slurred, rough words completed the picture of dissolution.

"Looky 'ere, mates! I found me a pretty li'tle lass. Yes, I 'ave now!"

Katrina found her way blocked by men and crates, her only avenue out was past the man who had spoken. "If you will excuse me, I need to pass."

Katrina had hoped to avoid any trouble and prayed he would step aside; after all, there were people swarming all around them—certainly they realized that.

" 'Ow 'bout lettin' me buy ye a drink, 'oney?"

Thinking of Chin Li and Jason, Katrina bit back the sharp retort she had been about to blurt out and instead smiled becomingly at the fat, ugly man. "Perhaps some other time, sir. I am really in somewhat of a hurry. I thank you for your kind offer, though."

Once again, Katrina tried to pass, but a pudgy hand

snaked out and grabbed her arm, stopping her. Anger welled up in her, causing all caution to flee as Katrina's head snapped up, her cold blue eyes filled with fury as she met faded gray ones.

"Take your hand from me, you fat son-of-a-bitch, or you'll lose it at the elbow!"

Surprise registered on the sailor's face as she hissed the words at him, the venom in her eyes warning him to heed what she said, but it was the flash of metal in her hand, partially hidden among her skirts that made him drop her arm and step back, more from shock than fear.

Another voice from behind Katrina sounded. "I do believe the lady said she was in a hurry."

Looking past her, the obese man saw a Lieutenant standing just behind her, his arm resting ready on his sword, his jacket pulled back to reveal a pistol as well. Mumbling some incoherent words, the fat man disappeared, the others following him into the shadows.

Once they were standing alone, Katrina turned to see who had stopped to help her, and incredibly, found herself facing David Greerson.

"David," she whispered.

Stunned for a moment, David stood staring at her, then suddenly came alive, grabbing her in a tremendous hug, lifting her completely from the ground and whirling her about joyfully.

"My God! I don't believe my eyes!" Laughing, David finally set her down as people continued to stare in curiosity. Noticing the attention they were attracting, David pulled her back into a pile of crates for more privacy. Once out of reach of prying eyes and ears, David gave her another quick hug.

"God, have you got a lot of explaining to do, Katrina. Why . . . why, you're supposed to be dead! I saw you myself! . . . or . . . rather, someone we all thought to be you. Dear God! You're alive!"

Katrina reached up and laid a finger on David's lips, stopping his chatter. "There is much to explain, I know, but I cannot right now."

David started to object, but Katrina's pleading eyes

stopped him. "Dearest, David, I must ask you a very large favor."

"Anything!" he exclaimed readily.

A sigh escaped Katrina, a sadness showing in that moment that David was keenly aware of. "Promise me, no questions."

Confused by her manner, David objected, "But, Katrina..."

"No questions!" she interrupted. "Promise me!"

David hesitated only a moment, then reluctantly nodded his head.

"Thank you," muttered Katrina, relieved. "And thank you for your help just now."

A pleased smile crossed David's handsome face as he shrugged. "If I had known it was you, I would have allowed you to handle the matter. I could have been hurt crossing such devious characters as that! I am certain the Angel in Black could have carved that blubber up quite well."

Seeing the teasing glint in his eyes, Katrina smiled. "You scoundrel!" she cried good-naturedly, then more seriously added, "I am grateful David, and very happy to see you."

Suddenly, David thought of Blake, an awful uneasiness descending on him. Clearing his throat, he tried to explain. "Ummm... Blake is not in London, Katrina. He... is..."

Seeing the sudden change in him, Katrina broke in, relieving him of an unpleasant task. "I know, David. You need not be concerned about him."

Looking away so David would not see the pain on her face, she changed the subject. "I have someone waiting with my things. I must return."

"I have my carriage over there. I will take you wherever you want to go."

As the two walked to David's landau, they were unaware of the woman standing in the shadows, who had been listening to them closely, a murderous gleam in her green eyes. As soon as they were out of sight, Catherine Ramsey ran to her own waiting coach and followed them. She had come to the docks to see her latest lover off—back to France and to his wife. The shock of seeing Katrina alive left her weak with anger and rage. As she fought the hot tears and jealousy, Catherine nearly fainted when she saw Katrina take Jason and introduce him to David as her son. Trembling from the force of what she saw, she could not deny the truth. Jason was Blake's son! Then, slowly, the rest of what she'd heard sank in.

Katrina Easton was the notorious Angel in Black!

A plan began to form in her devious mind, and she smiled in satisfaction. Perhaps she would be rid of her yet!

"Yes," she murmured contently to herself, pleased by her thoughts. "You will not spoil my plans for Blake Roberts! Not this time, you bitch!"

Purring like a contented kitten, Catherine pulled on her gloves and slid further back into the plush seat, letting the curtain on the window fall back into place. She had seen enough.

At David's insistence, he drove Katrina, Li, and Jason to Ryon and Rebecca's townhouse. Their homecoming was filled with much joy and happiness. Rebecca cried openly as she hugged Katrina; she hadn't been able to believe what Ryon had told her about Katrina's being alive until that very moment.

David was a bit hurt when he found out that Ryon had known Kat was not dead, but he managed to overcome his reaction. All that mattered for the moment was that Katrina was home and well.

Chin Li stood back shyly, her own eyes misting from the touching scene played out before her. Jason woke up at the noise and giggled happily as he watched his mother. Rebecca sniffed, having brought her tears under control, and turned to see Katrina's friend and the child she carried. A small gasp escaped Rebecca as she saw the baby's golden gaze.

Katrina walked over to Li and lifted the happy baby into her arms. "Ryon and Rebecca, may I present my dear friend, Chin Li." Turning her gaze to Li, she continued. "Li, this is Ryon and Rebecca Roberts, Blake's brother and sister-in-law."

After they had acknowledged the introductions, Katrina's eyes fell on Rebecca and Ryon. "This is my son, Jason."

Once more Rebecca began to cry as she hugged both

mother and child, then tenderly took Jason to her. Ryon stood awkwardly, with his mouth still gaping open in surprise.

"J-Jason!" he finally stuttered, tears filling his own brown eyes as he closed the distance between himself and Katrina.

"Yes," stated Katrina, keenly aware of the delicate situation. "Your grandfather, Jason Roberts, was very dear to me, Ryon. I hope you do not mind me naming my son after him."

Ryon grabbed her in an affectionate bear hug. "Mind? I am filled with joy, Katrina! He would have been proud that his first great-grandson was given his name!"

It had slipped out before Ryon had had a chance to think of what he was saying and his blunder brought a crimson flush to his cheeks. Seeing everyone's discomfort, Katrina smiled warmly.

"Jason *is* Blake's son, I am not ashamed of that, nor should any of you be. He is a beautiful boy, with his father's looks, his father's golden eyes. I cannot hide his identity from anyone who knows Blake Roberts, nor would I want to. If you have any problems or reservations accepting Blake's bastard son in your home, I will undersand and leave."

Rebecca ran forward, her eyes filled with pain as she answered for Ryon, too. "Katrina, I'm hurt that you would think any such thing. You will stay with us for as long as you wish, you are considered a member of this family and always will be! And since when do any of us care what others think? Besides, when Blake returns, I am certain you two will work out your differences."

"Rebecca!" cried Ryon, uncertain of what Katrina knew about Blake's sudden departure, and from the look on her face, he became quite alarmed. "He has been gone for quite some time, Katrina. I have not been able to let him know that you are alive."

Then Rebecca added, "I am sure he will be thrilled to see you and his son."

Katrina's sad, bitter laughter took them all off guard. "Thrilled?" Her voice cracked with suppressed emotion. "It's not the word I would use to describe his reaction when we last saw each other."

Everyone seemed to chime in at once, all saying the same thing. "You've seen Blake?"

"Yes," answered Katrina, her voice becoming hard and unfeeling. "On a South Sea island at the home of Trevor Wilde. I don't think he will be coming home soon. It seems he believes certain lies fabricated by a red-haired bitch! He made it very clear exactly what he thought of me and my son! I will not speak of the matter again!"

Katrina turned, walked stiffly across the room to a small table, and poured herself a liberal amount of brandy. Anger bolted through her so fiercely, she shook from the force of it. Closing her eyes, she gulped the liquor down; the burning sensation eased the terrible pain in her heart. She concentrated on replacing the visions of Blake with Langsford's evil face, turning her anger and pain to him. Immediately, she felt some relief as hatred began to bubble inside of her. She could almost taste the sweet revenge she had waited so long for.

Everyone watched Katrina, unable to say or do anything but stare. They saw the subtle changes in her, but only Chin Li knew what they meant. Katrina understood the hatred and anger inside of her, it was something she could live with, but the pain and sorrow Blake Roberts had inflicted was something she could not live with. They threatened to take away the very things her hatred had kept alive all of these years. Blake's betrayal was the one thing Katrina feared to face, knowing she was not strong enough to defeat her bitterness and loneliness. So she chose to put it from her mind, to ignore its existence and instead replace it with something she knew and did not fear, her hatred of Lawrence Langsford!

When Katrina faced her friends again, her face showed none of her emotions. "Forgive me, I must be tired."

Rebecca wrapped her arm lovingly about Katrina's shoulders, her voice sad and sympathetic. "No! Forgive us, we—"

Katrina held up her hand, stopping Rebecca. "It is nice to be home again."

"I'll take you to your rooms." Rebecca smiled warmly.

David stepped forward and took her hand. "I will say good night then. I will see you tomorrow, Katrina." He placed a light kiss on her cheek and left.

When Rebecca started to leave the room, Katrina said, "I have a few matters I wish to discuss with Ryon. I'll be up shortly."

When they were left alone in the room, Ryon felt uneasy, not quite sure of what to say to her, but Katrina spoke first. "I have two favors to ask of you, Ryon."

Ryon was surprised and answered happily, "Anything, Katrina. Grandfather always said should you need help we would always be here for you."

Swallowing hard, Katrina smiled in return, her nerves barely under control. "Thank you, Ryon. First of all, I would like you to locate a man, Chin Li's love. They were separated about the same time I was kidnapped. I would like to see them together again; she is very dear to me."

Katrina gave Ryon the information he would need to locate Yee Ling, then made her second request. "I plan to leave in the morning. I would appreciate it if you would look after Li and Jason for me."

"Leave!" shouted Ryon in shock. "What do you mean, you just got here. What is going on, Katrina? You are kidnapped, then found dead. A few months later, John receives a note that explains nothing, except that you are alive and will return. After a year, you are here, with no explanations offered. What the hell has happened to you?"

Katrina felt angry at his questions, and yet he had a right to know. Frustration and impatience, combined with her frayed nerves, caused her to snap back, "I cannot explain! Not now! You will have to accept that, for that is all you will get! I need to return to Tattershall for some time alone!"

Ryon did *not* understand, and her reasons were not enough. "You can be alone here. Why go to the village?"

Katrina drew a deep breath. "I need time to think, to sort out the mess my life is in."

Cleverly, Katrina sought to appeal to his sense of pity. "I still have a husband, or have you forgotten that? Everyone believes me dead, including Randolph. A year has gone by and everyone will want to know what has happened. I do not know if I am ready to face all those explanations, Ryon. It has all been so difficult and not so easy to explain."

She paused a moment, the lies falling into place easily. Her hesitation played on Ryon's imagination as he tried to figure out the horrible things Katrina must have faced alone and suffered through in the last year.

"I am married to a man you know I hate. And now, I have a son that is undeniably Blake's and not my estranged husband's! The father of my child thinks me a whore and anything else his depraved mind can think of that is foul enough for me to deserve. When he saw me, Ryon . . . he tried to kill me!"

"Oh, Katrina! I *am* so sorry." Ryon sat down, the impact of what she was saying ripping him up inside.

Katrina hated what she was doing, but knew she had to continue. "Ryon, I just need some time alone, before it is known that I am alive. I need to know that Chin Li and my son will be taken care of in my absence. Please, Ryon. I need some time to myself."

When she saw him hesitate, Katrina added her last plea in desperation. "There is so much pain inside me and an anger I cannot control. I must come to terms with it; surely you can understand that! Do not cross me, Ryon. I will do it, with or without your help."

Ryon could see her determination, and yes, he could even understand her reasons for wanting the time alone. Blake was hurting them all, but Katrina had to be experiencing the most pain. "All right, I can't stop you. Chin Li and Jason will be well taken care of, so you needn't worry about them."

Relief flooded through her as her plan began to fall into place. "Thank you, Ryon."

It was dark by the time the coach lumbered into the quiet village. It had been too long since her eyes had rested on the crowded cottages and the narrow streets of Tattershall, but they looked just the same. She was home at last! The dear little cottage she had slept in for most of the last ten years, with its sparse furniture and drafty walls, looked wonderful as she made her way down the cobbled streets

to its familiar worn door. For a few seconds, she merely
stood there, taking in the smells and sounds she had longed
for. Inside she heard Jake's familiar cackle and Jenny's
merry laughter as they shared their meal, its aroma teasing
her nostrils as the lights inside flickered, casting shadows
in the darkness. Her heart was pounding hard as she reached
out for the knob, and it nearly stopped when John's deep
voice protruded through the silence. Dear John! Closing her
eyes, Katrina tried to calm her racing heart, then slowly,
she turned the handle.

A bowl fell from Jenny's hand as she stared at the small
figure standing in the doorway. For a few brief seconds, no
one seemed capable of movement, everyone frozen to the
spot.

"Oh, my God!" muttered John as he stepped forward,
wrapping her in his large arms and twirling her about the
room in happiness and relief. When at last he let go and
Katrina turned to Jake and Jenny, tears were streaming down
their wrinkled old cheeks. Grabbing them both, she soothed
them, reassuring them that she was all right. It was some
time before any of them were calm enough to speak.

During the commotion, no one had heard the noise out-
side, until a thunderous crash resounded against the door.
Everyone looked around in bewilderment; then suddenly,
Katrina's face lit up and she ran to open the latch.

Blackstar stood outside, his head bobbing up and down
wildly as he shook with excitement. Katrina squealed in
delight, wrapping her arms lovingly about his neck, letting
him lift her from the ground as he snorted loudly in her ear.

"Oh, Blackstar! How I have missed you!" Taking him
back to his shed, Katrina calmed him, her voice and presence soothing the black beast. When she returned, they all
sat at the table and she related all that had happened to her
in the last year. Jenny cried many times during her tale but
the news of Jason's birth brought tears of joy, then anger
that she had left him in London. But when the story was
complete, they all understood Katrina's reasons and knew
the danger she and her son were in. Lawrence Langsford
had failed once again to rid himself of Katrina, and they
all knew he would try again. Now she had a son, a new

threat to him, one he would not abide with grace. At least he did not know Katrina was alive, and for now she would be safe.

At that very moment, Lawrence and Randolph's coach pulled into Camray with a third passenger aboard. Catherine Ramsey stepped gracefully from the luxurious interior, her gloved hand resting on Lawrence's. A flicker of emotion crossed her eyes as she thought of Katrina. The look of a cat about to pounce on a defenseless mouse lit her green eyes as a smile of immense satisfaction curved her lips. Had someone besides Langsford seen that look, he would have fully expected her to lick her lips hungrily.

Chapter 25

Impatiently, Blake waited for Trevor to board the longboat that would to take them ashore. Once on the dock, Blake quickly found out when Katrina's ship had arrived, nearly panicking when he learned he was a full two days behind her.

"She could still be in London, Blake," suggested Trevor as they made their way to Blake's townhouse. "Katrina hasn't had time to get into any trouble, I'm sure."

Blake's cold amber eyes flashed at Trevor, his lips curling into a sad smile. "You certainly don't know Katrina as I do, Trevor." Looking away, Blake paused a moment. "Katrina *is* trouble! I saw it the first time I laid eyes on her, riding that beast of hers."

"You're being unfair. Katrina does not look for trouble, I know her well enough to realize that!"

Blake noted the slight agitation in Trevor's voice as he rushed to Katrina's defense.

"She does not have to look for trouble, it finds her. Katrina's beauty has a tendency to bring out the worst in men. I can certainly attest to that! When I am around her I lose all control!"

Trevor cleared his throat, nervous at the turn the conversation was taking, but Blake seemed to feel the need to talk. "Is that how she affected you when you first saw her?"

"Ahhh . . . yes, very much so. I have never lost my composure so quickly. She is truly beautiful."

Blake saw only understanding in Trevor's sharp green eyes. "You love her very much, don't you?" asked Blake bluntly.

Trevor knew he could not lie and answered, "Yes, I do."

An uncomfortable silence descended on them. Trevor felt wary and Blake sought the right words to explain what he felt. "Katrina is very fortunate to have so many people who truly care for her, Trevor. It is so difficult for me, because I feel a jealousy that tears me apart when I think of others' loving her. I want to be the only one to feel that way about her, the only one so privileged!"

"You are privileged, Blake! Katrina has chosen you to love in return. I don't mean the love you have for family and friends, but the passionate love that you both have shared. The love that created your son! The kind of love that allows you to forgive one another and to feel each other's pain and sorrow. Katrina's love for you is faithful and true, of that I have no doubt. I consider you the luckiest of men—do not be a fool and risk losing her. No one has loved her as you have, and strangely enough, I don't think anyone else ever will."

Just then, the carriage pulled up to the townhouse, and Blake jumped from it before it had completely stopped. Taking the front steps two at a time, Blake burst through the door, his hollering taking everyone by surprise and sending the servants scurrying.

"Ryon! . . . Ryon! Where the hell are you?" Blake nearly collided with his brother as he walked into the hall, the look of shock and surprise clearly showing on the younger man's face.

"Blake!"

Suddenly, the two brothers were in each other's arms, laughing and hugging their greetings. "God, I was beginning to fear we would never see you again!"

Blake held Ryon at arm's length, his eyes sad and tired.

"I have been the biggest of fools, Ryon. Can you and Rebecca ever forgive me for the pain I have caused you?"

"Of course we can." Rebecca's voice broke into the intimate scene, and in seconds, Blake found himself surrounded by his family. "All that matters is that you are home and safe once again. The past and all pain shall be forgotten."

Blake's expression became grave at her softly spoken words, and he gently touched her face, wiping away the tears that streaked down her cheeks. "The past is like a shadow. It has no substance, but is always at my heels. And there is some pain that cannot be forgotten. I doubt others will be as forgiving as you two are."

"Come and sit, Blake. We have so much to talk about."

Just then, Trevor walked in, drawing everyone's attention to him. "Damn it, Blake! Is this any way to treat a guest?"

Having heard the great commotion, Chin Li left the salon and now stood in the doorway leading into the hall. "Mr. Wilde! Thank God you are here!"

Blake whirled about, his face paling as he saw Chin Li, Jason squirming impatiently in her arms. "Katrina is here?"

It was more a statement than a question, and relief flooded through him. Turning toward the stairs, looking to the second floor, he asked, "Is she upstairs?"

As Blake started toward the staircase, Ryon grabbed his arm, stopping him. "Katrina is not here, Blake. She left yesterday morning for Tattershall."

If Ryon had meant to say something more, he did not, for the stricken look on Blake's face stopped him.

"Gone?" His look of fear turned to anger as he bellowed his rage at his confused brother. "Gone! Why did you allow her to leave? Dear God!" His golden gaze fell on Li. "Why didn't you stop her?"

Ryon looked about in total bewilderment. "All you need to do is follow her to the village. Two days will make no difference! Then you can settle your argument, or whatever the hell it is that you two seem to be continuously doing."

Blake tried to control the feelings inside him, his teeth grinding together impatiently. "What reason did she give you for leaving, Ryon?"

Holding his own anger in close check, he answered his brother's question. "Katrina felt she needed some time alone to sort out a few things. I don't know exactly what happened between you two, but I do know she was very upset. I had no right to detain her, Blake."

"Chin Li, you know why she left. Why didn't you try to stop her?"

Surprisingly enough, Chin Li faced Blake's anger with no fear, answering honestly, "The letter I left for Mr. Wilde has brought you here; there was nothing else I could do. What guides her now has influenced her life for many years, much longer than you or I. She is unable to deny the overpowering feelings of hatred inside of her. I fear that there is no one who can stop her, even you, Lord Roberts."

Ryon frowned uneasily. "I don't understand what is going on here."

Trevor grasped Blake's arm and motioned toward the salon. "I believe we have some explaining to do, but please, let us do it sitting down."

Rebecca, embarrassed at her lack of consideration, rushed forward to see to everyone's comfort and soon they were sitting, drinking tea.

Blake sent two servants off with messages as Trevor explained their reasons for concern to the others. Blake continued to pace the floor as the story unfolded, his anxiety increasing with each moment.

"Blake," started Ryon, his own features grim, "I had no idea! I assure you, I would not have let her go—"

Blake interrupted his brother, "I know, Ryon. Katrina has kept her secrets well. We would all have done things differently, had we known what we do now."

One of the servants returned and spoke with Blake, the others anxious to know what he was about. "He has just returned from Langsford's townhouse here in London."

Turning to Trevor, Blake almost whispered the words. "It seems Langsford has suddenly left his residence and gone to Camray. He, too, left two days ago, his son and Catherine Ramsey with him."

Ryon jumped up, concern straining his voice. "But he

couldn't know she has returned! How could he? We all agreed to say nothing!"

"Damn it, he knows! I don't know how, but he knows and has gone after her!" Blake slammed his fist angrily against the wall, causing the hangings to rattle and move precariously.

"I will leave within the hour!"

Trevor stood, "I will be ready!"

"Not this time, Trevor. I need you here. I've sent word to Lieutenant Greerson; he will accompany me."

His gaze fell to Ryon, Rebecca, and Chin Li. "And I expect you four to take good care of my son until I return with his mother. Don't underestimate Langsford. If he has found out about Katrina, he will probably know she has a son, and that means Jason is not safe, either. Ryon, you and Trevor must protect him. I am depending on you both."

They all nodded solemnly, tension filling the room. Walking over to Li, Blake lifted Jason from her arms. "He is absolutely beautiful. Katrina has given me more than I ever dreamed of."

Kissing the soft golden curls, Blake handed him back to Li. "Thank you."

Li nodded, instinctively knowing the thank-you was for much more than letting him hold his son. It was Blake's way of acknowledging many unspoken things.

David Greerson waited impatiently in the library, his curiosity driving him wild as his imagination worked overtime, his mood as sober as the room he stood in.

"David, I am glad you came." Blake entered the room, closing the door behind him, his riding clothes on.

"So you have come home. I was quite surprised to receive your message."

Blake noted the stiffness in his voice and could not blame him for his coolness. "I need your help, Lieutenant. Katrina is in trouble."

Seeing the expression in Blake's eyes, David knew it must be serious. Curious, Lieutenant Greerson did as Blake suggested and sat in the leather chair, accepting the drink he was offered. Then Blake sank into the matching seat, opposite David's, and related the tale.

When he had finished, David felt numbed by all he had learned. "Where is she, Blake?"

David dreaded the answer, wanting desperately to hear that she was upstairs and safe. But Blake was unable to give that reply.

"Katrina has gone to Tattershall. She left yesterday morning."

David blinked, trying to think clearly. "Then as long as Langsford is here in London, she is safe."

"Langsford has gone to Camray! He knows she is here and alive. I think Catherine Ramsey is involved; she left with Lawrence and Randolph." There was a note of desperation in Blake's words; his eyes filled with silent suffering.

Lieutenant Greerson stood. "We had better go. How long will it take you to get ready?"

"Everything has been prepared; the horses are waiting."

David shook Blake's hand warmly. "Thank you for calling me, Blake. We'll find her and she'll be all right. I am certain of that. Katrina's one tough little lady."

"Yes, I know," muttered Blake. "We had better go."

The night was clear and warm, the stars sprinkled across the sky in random patterns, their brightness sparkling against the blue-black background. The moon hung just above the horizon as the two men began their trip across country, and as the hours raced by, it climbed its way into the heavens. It was almost dawn when they finally stopped to eat and allow the horses to rest. A kaleidoscope of soft pastel colors began to spread across the eastern sky as they shared a moment of peace, their thoughts of Katrina keeping them company.

David remembered the night, long ago, when he discovered that the Angel in Black was Katrina Easton. His life was devoted to his career in the service, his loyalty to the King of England, but he had gone against this King and country, allowing her to go free. As he thought of that, David knew without a doubt that if it were to happen again, he would do the same. He hadn't known it then, but when Katrina spoke of her hatred that night, she was talking about Lawrence Langsford.

He wondered what he would feel and do if he were in her shoes, then he asked himself a very important question: Wouldn't he kill Langsford, too?

The answer was clear. Yes! He would hunger for revenge. It would be a pleasure to see Langsford die by his blade. Could they deny Katrina the very thing that they themselves would seek?

Then he thought of the danger she was in, and he no longer considered what she might want or need. They must find her before Langsford and Randolph did.

David Greerson glanced at Blake, who lay sprawled out, his back leaning against a large oak tree. Would he and Katrina ever straighten out their differences and be happy together?

Blake noticed the curious look David was giving him and wondered at his thoughts. It would have amused Blake to know that David's thoughts were much like his own.

Watching the sun make its way into the grayish sky, he longed to have Katrina by his side, safely watching the new day arrive. How he prayed for her safety! She would not expect Langsford to know she was alive and in England, and this terrified Blake. The wily bastard would definitely take advantage of that and surprise her. Katrina had escaped his murderous attempts twice; Langsford would take no chances this time. Blake shuddered in horror.

"Dear God! What kind of sunrise are you facing today, little one? I have this dreadful feeling that you need me and I cannot help you. Lord, do not forsake her now!"

With this last thought, Blake rose, and grimly the two men mounted their horses and, like madmen, raced over the miles, untiring, unbending in their mission.

Chapter 26

Katrina opened her eyes, blinking, until the room, shrouded in darkness, came into focus. Something had roused her from a deep sleep, her mind slowly clearing as she tensely listened to the silence around her. Then she heard it again. It was the sound of horses and they were very close.

Sliding silently from the bed, Katrina crossed over to the window and pulled the worn curtain back to look out. A chill ran over her, and the hair on the back of her neck stood on end as she watched a large group of men riding down the darkened streets, straight for her cottage. A cloud passed over the moon, shadowing the faces of the nameless figures cloaked in black.

"It couldn't be!" whispered Katrina to herself. But she knew the answer to the nagging question inside her, and quickly she ran to the bag she had brought with her, withdrawing a pistol from it. She jumped slightly when the door downstairs was kicked open; then, with quick, agile steps, Katrina ran to the ladder and dropped down to the bottom floor. Jenny's scream echoed in the small house as she and Jake were dragged from their bed, Jake's curses mixed with Jenny's frightened cries as he knocked one of his captors onto the floor, preparing to take on the rest.

Katrina watched as one of the men raised his pistol to
club the old man and halt his stubborn resistance. Before
he could strike, Katrina's own pistol barked, dropping him
where he stood. Reacting as quickly as his aging bones
would allow, Jake grabbed the gun from the dead man and
tossed it to Katrina who placed herself between the men
outside the door and her family. Jake tended to the terribly
frightened Jenny, trying to quiet her sobbing, knowing Rina
needed no distractions.

"Katrina!" Lawrence Langsford's voice rang out. "It is
best you come with us now. We have too many men for
you to resist for long. Your friends could be hurt!"

Katrina's anger was coursing through her like a fiery
potion, giving her strength and courage, leaving her torn
between logic and the tremendous need for revenge.

"This is between just you and I, Langsford! Do you
always hide behind your hired help?"

Lawrence's jaw twitched angrily as he warily watched
the town wake up around him. Damn! They had hoped to
get in, catching everyone asleep, and take Katrina without
alerting the whole town. How the hell had she known he
was coming?

The sleepy-eyed Father Murray shoved his way into the
crowd, scowling with disapproval. "What is going on here?"
he shouted, his face showing surprise when he recognized
Lawrence and Randolph Langsford. "Sir! I demand an explanation!"

Lawrence stepped forward in an attempt to maintain control of the situation. "There is no need for concern, Father,
it is really quite a simple matter. I have come to take my
son's wife home."

Father Murray's knees nearly buckled as he struggled to
comprehend the man's statement. "But . . . I . . ." Swallowing hard, he started again. "Katrina is dead, you will not
find her here. You know that, Mr. Langsford."

Randolph replied calmly, "Katrina is inside the cottage
and very much alive! The reasons she is not dead are still
unclear, Father, but she is, indeed, inside."

Then, taking advantage of the crowd that had gathered
about them, Randolph played the hurt husband to his au-

dience. "It seems my wife was not happy with the marriage that the King himself arranged, so she sought a way out of it. I have learned that it was her own treachery that created her kidnapping and so-called death. This debauchery put us all through much sorrow and grief, just so that she would be free to satisfy her sluttish desires. All know of her sinful affair with Lord Roberts, blatantly flaunted before the King and all his court and, most distastefully, before me! It is not enough that she is a whore, and cuckolded me, but now she has returned from God knows where, with a bastard son, bearing no shame or remorse for her actions. Father, it is my right, as her husband, to deal with her as I see fit, and there is no one here that has the right to stop me!"

Father Murray turned livid with rage, his round face red as a beet as he stuttered unintelligibly. The people began to argue angrily, their contempt for the two men obvious.

"I have the right to stop you, you bastard!" John stepped out of the crowd, a pistol in each hand, leveled at the two men. Katrina's mouth went dry as she watched John facing all of Langsford's men. Then to her horror she saw Tom and Charlie moving forward to back John up.

At that very moment, several men broke the windows at the back of the small cottage, drawing her attention for a second; then, slowly, her world began to fall apart. John fired when he heard the noise inside, one ball barely grazing Randolph's arm, the other missing Lawrence as he dove for cover. Katrina fired, killing one man that aimed his pistol at John but another got off a shot and John crumpled to the ground, grabbing his side. Other shots were fired to ward off the crowd, sending people scurrying for cover. Tom and Charlie's actions were quickly halted by the several pistols aimed their way.

"No!" cried Katrina as she shook her head in disbelief. Jenny's scream diverted her attention, and she whirled about to find three men in the room and Jake lying facedown on the floor, moaning, bleeding from a blow to his head. Jenny sat on her knees beside him, crying as she hugged him to her full bosom. Katrina threw the empty pistol at the intruders, her fury overwhelming her as she screamed.

"You son-of-a-bitch!" Then, pulling her knife out, she ran out the door, nearly insane with hatred.

"You gutless bastard! You never had the nerve to face me alone! It seems to be your style to have others help you do your dirty work!"

Lawrence and Randolph slowly inched toward her, their eyes on the knife she held tightly. Father Murray shook his head in shock as he watched Katrina, her eyes filled with hatred and fury, waiting like a wild animal, surrounded by violence and death. Those villagers who had not fled crossed themselves, fearing the sight before them was a ghost and not really Rina.

Randolph walked in front of her, drawing her glassy blue eyes to him, but careful to stay out of reach of the blade she wielded so menacingly. Crazed beyond control, Katrina hissed her contempt.

"You are just like your father, you bastard! Evil and cowardly."

"Drop the knife, Katrina!" ordered Lawrence, drawing her attention back to him. "Drop it or I will kill him!"

Going numb, she stared, horrified, as Lawrence stood over John, his foot cruelly laid on his bleeding wound. She watched as he put weight on it, making John scream in pain, the noise ripping through her like a bolt of lightning. Then Lawrence lifted the pistol he had and aimed it directly at John's head.

"Drop it, or he is dead!"

Katrina blinked, unable to think clearly. But one thing shattered painfully in her mind, making its way through the confusion. John would die! If she did not go with them, he would die! She made her choice. The knife dropped with a dull thud to the soft earth.

Father Murray had finally gotten his tongue and called to Langsford. "You have no right to take Katrina! She will remain with me!"

Turning toward his voice, Katrina muttered unfeelingly, as if in a daze, "No, Father, you must not interfere. I will not be responsible for anyone else being harmed. Go, and take care of John and Jake. I beg you, do as I say."

Seeing him hesitate, she pleaded with him. "Please, Father, you must see to John . . . now!"

Reluctantly, he did as she said, not knowing what else to do. They had no means of stopping Randolph from taking his wife. Carefully, they lifted John and took him to his cottage, and to Katrina's immense relief, she saw Jake wobble along with Jenny's help.

Katrina was suddenly aware of the men that now surrounded her.

"I knew your compassion for these people would get you to come willingly! But remember, fight us and I will change my mind and burn this whole village and the people in it to the ground!"

Katrina said nothing and allowed Randolph to tie her hands in front of her, the rope cutting into her tender wrists.

"Now, that isn't too tight, is it?" asked Randolph sarcastically, giving the ropes a cruel jerk. His laughter stopped and changed to anger as the pain he inflicted elicited no response from his captive. It infuriated him to see her shoulders pulled back and her chin tilted arrogantly as if she hadn't a care in the world.

"You will change your tune when I am done with you. You will show fear then, I guarantee it!"

Katrina only smiled, aggravating him even further by her calmness and lack of fear. Suddenly, he struck her full across the jaw, knocking her to the ground.

Pain shot through Katrina as her head snapped back from the harsh blow, the world tumbling and crashing in on her as she fell to the hard ground, bruising and cutting her arms and knees on the rocks. Slowly, fighting off the threatening blackness, she dragged herself to her knees and squatted on all fours, trying to maintain her balance. When her world stopped whirling about, she got to her feet, her lip split and bleeding.

"Get her on a horse!" bellowed Lawrence to his son, a pleased look crossing his face when he saw her mouth. But it soon turned to displeasure when he met her icy, hard gaze. Kicking his horse, Lawrence headed back to Camray, the vision of her hate-filled eyes clearly imprinted on his mind.

Mounting his own horse, Randolph pulled Katrina roughly

in front of him and followed his father. He took immense pleasure in telling Katrina exactly what he had planned for her. His hands busily prodded and pinched her freely, hurting and bruising her flesh, but Katrina put it from her mind. She allowed none of his sick words to penetrate her wall of numbness, allowed no fear or desperation to seize control of her. Pure concentration put her into a world that Lawrence and Randolph could not enter. And that very distant look in her eyes and chilling smile nearly made Randolph lose what little control he had.

Katrina remained meek and uncaring, giving Randolph a false sense of security when she made no attempt to struggle. When they were a good distance from the village, she made her move, surprising her captor. She brought her elbow back with tremendous force into his ribs, knocking the breath from him and very nearly unseating him. His yell of pain caused his already nervous horse to rear, and in his attempt to stay in the saddle, he let go of Katrina's waist. In a flash, she was off the horse, landing nimbly on her feet, even with her hands awkwardly tied. Confusion erupted as other horses stamped about tensely at their sudden and abrupt halt, one nearly running into her as she fought her way out of the mess. Quickly, she dashed into the cover of the woods and ran as fast as she could go. Stones and brush cut her feet and legs, bruising exposed flesh, but Katrina continued to run, ignoring the pain.

In the distance, she heard Lawrence's shouts and then she heard the horses making their way through the foliage after her. The mounts and men quickly covered the short distance she had managed to gain. One of the men tried to catch Katrina, but just as he leaned down to catch her, she stopped and turned, ducking out of his reach. Randolph was right behind him, and took off after his wife, who was once again running in another direction. When his horse overtook her, Randolph slid out of his saddle and tackled her, throwing her roughly to the hard ground, his own heavy body slamming on top of her.

Katrina's flimsy chemise was ripped away, exposing her shoulder, and the slip tore to her hip as twigs and rocks scraped her arms and legs painfully. Randolph quickly rolled off her and stood, pulling her up by a handful of golden hair, yanking her head back dangerously.

"I should kill you now!" yelled Randolph, breathing heavily from exertion and anger. "But it would be a shame not to enjoy your charms before I kill you. It *is* my right as your husband!"

His free hand shot up to caress her bruised and scraped chin, but Katrina bit it and held on. She could taste the blood that ran in her mouth as he cried out, trying to free his hand from her vicious grip, but, like someone possessed, she refused to release him. Randolph pulled back even farther, forcing her head to a painful angle until she was forced to let go of his hand.

Calmly smiling, ignoring the blood that ran from her mouth, Katrina hissed, "I do not consider you my husband and no power on earth can change that!"

"Well, do you think you two could stop your quarreling long enough to reach Camray?" Lawrence drawled, his impatience apparent on his face.

Randolph reddened at his father's insolence but said nothing, dragging Katrina to his horse roughly. To make certain she did not try to escape again, he tied her to his saddle horn, cutting off the circulation in her hands, the ropes burning and cutting into her wrists until she could feel the trickle of warm blood running down her fingers.

As the group of men and one woman entered the long drive to Camray, Katrina experienced a twinge of sadness, thinking it a strange homecoming indeed. Looking to the east, she saw the beautiful sunrise, the colors, awe-inspiring and tranquil, spreading across the dark sky. At that very moment her thoughts were of Blake, his face clear in her mind, and she was suddenly sure Blake was thinking of her too.

Randolph slid from his mount, then untied Katrina and jerked her off the horse. She fell to her knees on the rough ground. A smile twitched across Randolph's thin lips as he looked down at her, anticipation lighting his eyes as they roved over her supple figure.

"You look good on your knees, bitch! It is time you learn where you belong. On your knees or beneath a man!"

"Well," began Katrina, a smirk on her face, "since there are no *men* here, I will just have to stay on my knees!"

Randolph nearly choked with fury, the muscles in his neck distended as he clenched his teeth, a low growl escaping from deep within him. He brought his fist up to strike Katrina, but she continued to stare boldly, unflinching as he slapped her face, then backhanded her.

"Is it a sight that pleases you?" asked Lawrence, entering the sitting room at Camray. Standing at the large double windows, Catherine Ramsey continued to watch the scene outside, a satisfied smile on her face and the glimmer of joy sparkling in her eyes.

"Yes," she giggled happily. "It pleases me very much, indeed, to see Katrina Easton groveling on her knees!"

"On her knees . . . yes. Groveling . . . no, not Katrina."

A dismayed frown puckered Catherine's face, her lower lip pouting like a child's. "What do you mean, not Katrina? Just look at her!"

Catherine was tired and cranky from the long ride to Camray, and her anger surfaced easily. "Look at her! Her face is already swelling from where she's been hit and she's covered with bruises and scratches. She looks positively horrid! No one could bear up under such a beating, not even that bitch!"

Lawrence lifted an eyebrow in amusement, knowing the jealousy and hatred Catherine bore Katrina. "I must admit, I have never known a woman with so much courage. It is a shame she must die."

Catherine rushed over to stand in front of him, her face fearful. "You are not going to back out, are you?"

"No, never!" yelled Lawrence, the force of his answer causing Catherine to jump and instinctively back away a few steps. "I have more reasons to want her dead than you, my dear. Her existence is a continuous threat to my own. No one . . . I repeat, no one, will take Camray from me!"

"Are you certain no one will question her untimely death?" Catherine asked, uncertain about her part in this whole affair.

Lawrence sighed and once again explained to ease her fears. "Of course not. She is legally wed to Randolph, and it is his right to bring her home, even by force. Katrina made it quite clear to everyone, including the King, that she was not a willing participant in the marriage. Add that to the gossip you spread about her many affairs and her torrid relationship with Blake Roberts, and it's easy to prove she has humiliated my son to the point of disgrace. It is only natural he would be angry, and we are witness to her own prodding, taunting him unwisely. It is not surprising that he would beat her. No man would tolerate her whoring ways, and it will be terribly unfortunate that when he attempts to finally, and rightly, consummate the marriage, she is accidently killed. A man can only take so much from such an insolent wife."

Catherine smiled sweetly again, almost purring in contentment. "You are so right, Lawrence, darling. Who would possibly question such a wronged husband?"

Another thought occurred to her; her forehead wrinkled in perplexed thought. "What about her bastard? Surely, you cannot allow him to live?"

"He will be taken care of in time. First, we must take care of Katrina Easton, once and for all!"

At that moment Randolph came crashing through the front door, literally dragging Katrina behind him and swinging her off balance onto the floor near Lawrence and Catherine, who were standing in the doorway to the hall. Sprawled in a heap on the floor, her chemise barely covering her breasts, Katrina looked at them, cool amusement in her blue eyes.

"Well, well," drawled Katrina, sarcasm dripping heavily from her words. "I am not surprised to see you here, *Lady* Ramsey. After all, I have always considered you the lowest of vile creatures, much like the Langsfords. I guess it is right to say that animals do seek their own kind."

Catherine screeched her anger, her face as red as her hair as she made a leap for Katrina, her nails ready to claw her smiling face. Reacting quickly, Katrina rolled at the same time, and Catherine landed awkwardly on her back. Lawrence grabbed for Catherine and dragged her off of Katrina, but she managed to dig her sharp nails across Katrina's bare shoulder.

"You little whore!" screamed Catherine in fury, trying to free herself from Lawrence's steely grasp.

Katrina scampered to her feet just as Catherine twisted free and stepped toward the woman she hated so much. Katrina clasped her tied hands together and brought them up, clipping the unprepared Catherine on the chin, sending her flying back into Lawrence's arms. Randolph's fingers wrapped around Katrina's elbow like a vise, whirling her around to face him, his anger out of control as his hands clamped about her throat, his face twisted and distorted in an ugly grimace.

"Kill her!" screamed Catherine hysterically.

Katrina felt his fingers digging painfully into her flesh, blocking her breathing. Bringing her knee up into Randolph's groin, she broke his deadly grasp as he doubled over in pain. Katrina attempted to get past him and to the door, but his hand snaked out, wrapping about her tiny waist, pulling her off her feet. With her hands tied and her feet dangling off the floor, locked in his crushing hold, Katrina was unable to move. Frustrated, she stopped struggling, trying to conserve her energy.

A low rumble of laughter tickled her ear as Randolph whispered to her, her back stiffening against his chest. "Shall we go upstairs to the privacy of our room?"

Keeping an unyielding grip on her, Randolph climbed the stairs, his laughter ringing throughout the house. When he entered his room, he finally let Katrina go and hurriedly locked the door. Carefully watching him, she stepped out of his reach, calculating her chances of escape.

As if reading her mind, Randolph sneered, "There is no way out, witch!"

Slowly, he began to stalk his prey, taking pleasure in the chase. Katrina put the bed between them, but he easily leaped across it, wrapping his hand in her long hair and yanking her painfully back to him. Throwing her onto the bed, Randolph landed on top of her, knocking the breath from her.

His lips ran over her bruised neck and scratched shoulder, sending shivers of revulsion through her. Grabbing her tied hands, Randolph yanked them above her head, and held

them with one hand while the other roamed her body freely.
When his lips took her own, she twisted and wriggled, her
legs kicking and thrashing about. Once again, Katrina bit
as hard as she could, capturing his lower lip in her sharp
teeth. Letting go of her hands, Randolph yelled angrily and
struck her a hard blow to the ribs. Bellowing in pain, he
rolled off of her, holding his bleeding lip. Katrina immediately brought her elbow around, landing a blunt blow to
the middle of his chest, knocking him from the bed. In
seconds, she was up and running for the door, her numb
fingers trying to unlock it. Just as she succeeded and pulled
the door open a few inches, Randolph's arm shot out and
slammed it shut. Then Katrina was lifted from the floor and
thrown violently against the wall, her head slamming into
the fine wood with stunning force.

She saw stars and streaks of light, blackness threatening
to overtake her. Her knees went weak, and slowly, she sank
to the floor, Randolph's angry words filtering in through
the haze that engulfed her, the pain shooting like daggers
in her skull.

"You're going to die, bitch, but first I'm going to have
you! And in ways you have never dreamed of!"

Katrina heard her chemise ripping, the sharp intake of
his breath as his hungry eyes roamed over her naked body.
Katrina's vision began to clear as her anger surfaced through
the blackness. He casually opened a nearby drawer and
retrieved a long, narrow leather strap from it. Randolph
smiled in anticipation, an evil glint lighting his dark eyes.
As the strap snaked out, Katrina tried to crawl from the
onslaught, but the blows fell again and again. There was
no escaping his cruelty and she huddled on her knees as he
continued to beat her unmercifully. Then, finally, he threw
the strap aside, grabbing Katrina and pulling her to him.

"No!" screamed Katrina, coming alive once she realized
his intentions as he attempted to mount her from behind.
Snarling and kicking like a wildcat, she forgot all the pain
and fire burning her lacerated skin. One slender foot landed
squarely in the middle of his chest, sending him sprawling
on his back.

On her knees, she scampered away from Randolph, but

he managed to grasp one foot in a steely hand. Katrina felt herself being pulled back and desperately she felt about the floor for something, anything, finding a handful of ashes from the fireplace. She could hear Randolph's cruel laughter as he slowly, agonizingly pulled her to him, working his way up her leg and thighs until he could grasp her shapely hips and pull her beneath him. Then, Katrina twisted and threw the ashes in his face, temporarily blinding him. He released her and she shoved him from her, stumbling clumsily to her feet. Feeling as if she had run for miles, she breathed raggedly as her eyes searched the room for a weapon, her gaze finally resting on the fireplace poker. From the corner of her eyes, she could see Randolph clearing his eyes of the ashes and turning toward her, only a few feet away. She made a dive for the poker at the same time he jumped for her, his hand catching her leg as Katrina felt the coldness of the iron in her hand, the weight of it giving her a surge of strength.

Swinging the weapon with deadly accuracy, she landed a blow across his temple, and slowly, Randolph crumpled to the floor. Trembling with pain, Katrina could not move, she only stared at the lifeless form at her feet. His hand was still wrapped about her ankle. Finally, when her breathing became more even, she moved, shaking the hand free from her foot, dropping the bloody iron with a thud. He was dead!

Squeezing her eyes shut, Katrina tried to think, but her head pounded fiercely and there was no part of her body that did not ache. She must get away.

Her thoughts began to race as she came up with a plan. Lawrence would follow her. He'd want to kill her even more now. Looking down at the dead body of his son, her husband, she came to a decision. She needed a few days to regain her strength. That she knew as pain shot through her. Then she would be ready.

"If I ride north, away from Camray, Langsford will follow," she whispered aloud, the sound of her own words calming her frayed nerves. "It would get him away from the village, and, most important, further away from my son.

I will lead him away until I feel strong enough to face him, and then he will die!"

Quickly, she rummaged through the drawers until she found a knife to cut the ropes that still bound her wrists. The process was awkward and slow, but finally she was free. Walking to the large wardrobe, she took a shirt from it and pulled it on, wincing from the pain rippling across her back. Silently, Katrina left the room and made her way through the halls that were so familiar to her, memories floating in her dazed mind. Using the servants' back entrance, she made it outside unseen, and she went directly to the stables.

Unbeknown to Katrina, she had indeed been spotted by a young servant girl working in the hallway outside of Randolph's door. Quickly the girl ran to the stairs and signaled to the butler, then returned to her work. Carefully, the word was passed among the small group of servants that had originally been employed by Lord Easton, that Katrina was free. Like guardian angels, they diverted any eyes that might betray her flight and kept an eye on Lord Langsford and Lady Ramsey, who had each retired to separate chambers for some needed rest. Orders had been given for no one to disturb them or Randolph until late afternoon, no matter what they may hear or see. So obeying their orders, they did not bother to inform the master of Camray of Katrina's disappearance. What may have happened to Randolph, no one really cared to know.

As Katrina stood in the darkness of the stables, she carefully looked around her, surprised to see no one about. She started for one of the stalls to get a horse. Just then, a wagon rattled out into the yard and rambled over to the stables, stopping directly in front of where she was concealed in the shadows. Holding her breath, she waited for the wagon to leave.

The driver stepped off the wagon, went to the back and fiddled with the baskets and tarp thrown in the back. Katrina heard him speak, without turning in her direction.

"Ye 'ad best get in, Missy, I will be takin' ye 'ome t' Jenny now. Be sure an' cover yeself wi' the tarp, so as no one will see ye."

"Missy?" Katrina muttered in disbelief, the gray head bobbing in a familiar way. It was Sid! Only Sid and Margo had called her Missy when she had been young. Margo, her nanny, and Sid, the stable master. Quickly, she crawled onto the bed of the old wagon, covering herself as he said. The wagon slowly rumbled out of sight of Camray, and Lawrence Langsford.

Once out of hearing, Sid hollered back to his charge, "Are ye all right, Missy? 'E did no' 'urt ye too badly, did 'e?"

Katrina noted the trembling in his voice and was touched by his concern. "No need to worry about me, Sid. I'll be fine."

Sid nodded. "I 'ope ye killed 'im, Missy! No' jus' fer wha' 'e 'as done t' ye, but fer wha' 'e 'as done t' many an innocent lass. 'E is a cruel one, Lady Katrina, the devil 'imself! Bu' I suppose ye already know tha', don' ye?"

Katrina had heard of many cruelties that both Langsfords had inflicted, and her heart went out to all the good people at Camray, who had no choice but to bear it.

"Randolph Langsford will not hurt anyone again, Sid." The words were reassuring to the old man, but Katrina knew there was still another Langsford to contend with.

Sid drove as fast as he could, without jolting Katrina too terribly. She often bit her lip to keep from crying out, not wanting to alarm the older man, but he knew how badly she hurt. Once they neared Tattershall, Katrina asked him to stop.

"I will walk the rest of the way, I do not want to be seen with you. I want as few people involved in Langsford's anger as possible. I'm only sorry you have endangered yourself, Sid, by bringing me this far."

A loud "Humph" escaped from Sid as he helped her from the wagon. "Ye needn't worry 'bout this ol' man, Missy. 'E will never know it was me who 'elped ye. We were all careful."

"So"—Katrina smiled—"you all made sure I didn't blunder into someone. I thank you all, and someday, I hope to repay you for your kindness."

A tear slipped down his tanned, wrinkled cheek as he

climbed back onto the wagon seat. "Ye take care o' yerself. Tha' is all we want of ye. God bless ye, Missy!"

He slapped the reins lightly, and the horses continued down the road, the dull, even plodding of their hooves growing quiet in the distance. Careful not to be seen by anyone, Katrina made her way to her cottage, knocking softly on the door. Jenny opened it, and anticipating her reaction, Katrina quickly muffled her scream and slid into the house. Immediately, she was smothered by the portly woman's affectionate hug. As Jenny pulled her into her warm arms, she could not stop the cry of agony that escaped at the old woman's embrace.

Jenny pulled back fearfully, and her lip trembled as she looked at Katrina's swollen and bruised face, traces of blood still on it.

"Oh, me God!" muttered Jenny, close to hysterics as tears ran freely down her face.

Putting a sore hand on her friend's shoulder, Katrina pleaded with the woman. "Please, Jenny, I need your help and we have no time for tears and pity. Do not break down on me now!"

Taking a deep breath, trying to calm herself, Jenny nodded, pulling herself together as she asked, "Wha' must we do?"

"I have killed Randolph." The words were so calm, but they struck fear in Jenny as she listened to Katrina. "Lawrence and Catherine Ramsey will call it murder, so I must go away. I cannot stay here."

Confusion and fear battled inside of Jenny as she trembled from emotion. "I don' understand. 'E did this t' ye?"

Katrina nodded and Jenny exclaimed, "Then 'e deserved t' die! It was no' murder!"

"He claimed the rights as my husband. Lawrence will make it look as if I deserved to be beaten, since everyone knows I've denied Randolph my bed. You heard him, Jenny! I still have no proof to claim he murdered my mother and father, then arranged my kidnapping. To a court, what I have done will be murder!"

Wringing her hands in distress, Jenny agreed. "Then I will get Jake."

"No, wait!" cried Katrina. "Jake mustn't know I am here.
You must help me, Jenny. No one else must know." Katrina
paused, then lifted saddened eyes to Jenny. "John?"

"Achh! 'E will be fine, Katrina, 'oney. Ye know it would
take more than a bullet t' stop 'im, but 'e is no' goin' t'
like wha' ye are doin'!"

Slowly, Katrina lowered herself tiredly onto a chair. "I
think it would be best if he did not see me this way."

Understanding what she meant, Jenny busied herself with
preparations, then turned to Katrina, who sat at the table,
her head lying on her arms. "I'll brook no argument from
ye, Rina, bu' if ye are t' be leavin' quickly, I'll be needin'
'elp. I'll be right back wi' Maggie and Rita. Ye know they
will say nothin'."

Before she could object, Jenny was gone, and in minutes
she bustled back with the other two women. Together they
set about preparing Katrina for her long trip, neither woman
saying anything about her obvious beating. A bath was
prepared, and Jenny started to remove the shirt, turning pale
as she saw the rest of Katrina's body. Never before had the
woman seen such a battered and bruised body, cuts and
scrapes covering her delicate skin, but it was her back and
buttocks that nearly caused one woman to faint. Jenny stood
back, covering her mouth in shock, the tears starting once
again.

"Ohhh, me li'tle girl! Wha' 'as tha' devil done t' ye?"
Then her eyes rounded in fear as she attempted to ask the
question that was in her mind. "D . . . did . . . did 'e?"

Instinctively, Katrina knew what Jenny was trying to get
out. "No, Jenny. I became his widow before I became his
wife."

In less than an hour Katrina had been bathed clean of
the dirt and blood, and a soothing salve had been massaged
into the many cuts covering her body. Her hair was brushed
and washed, then twisted into one long, neat braid. After
a warm, filling meal and a couple of cups of herbal tea to
ease her pain, she felt somewhat better. A bag was prepared
containing food, water, and medicines, along with another
containing oats for Blackstar. When Katrina had dressed
and pulled on her black boots, the stallion was ready, com-

plete with a sword and two pistols. The three woman had done what would have taken Katrina hours to do alone. It was still midmorning, and Katrina hoped to get a good head start on Langsford, who must still be asleep at Camray.

Looking at the three women, Katrina said her good-byes. "Jenny, make them understand why I had to leave and tell them that I love them both. When I can, I will send word to you and perhaps you will be able to bring Jason to me."

Jenny knew whom Katrina referred to, and nodding, she wondered what Jake and John would do when they found out she was gone. Jenny could not speak for the lump in her throat, so she gave Katrina a gentle hug, her eyes saying everything for her.

"May God be wi' ye, lass," muttered Maggie as she and Rita put their arms about Jenny in support.

As Katrina rode away she felt a twinge of guilt for not explaining the whole truth to her friend, a woman who had been like a mother to her. But it was best she did not let Jenny know that she planned on Langsford's following her, planned to lead him to his death. No, Jenny would not have allowed her to go alone if she had thought Lawrence would go after her.

Turning for one last glimpse of the village, Katrina mumbled to herself, "Take care and forgive me."

She nudged Blackstar and he galloped into the forest, disappearing into its denseness, Katrina's black clothing blending with his dark coat, melting into the darkness around them.

Chapter 27

The clouds rolled in, dark and ominous, making the day gloomy and dreary, much like Blake's mood. He and David had ridden hard all day and reached the village just as the muted sun was setting. As he slid off Hera Blake looked at the sky, and the first drops of rain began falling on his uplifted face.

Blake pounded on the door loudly, bringing Jenny's tear-stained face to the door. This time it was too much for the old woman and she fainted dead away. Blake was barely able to catch her as she withered to the floor. Jake looked around, confused, a white bandage wrapped securely about his head. But relief and happiness showed in his eyes as he greeted Lord Roberts and Lieutenant Greerson.

"I did no' think ye would be 'ere so soon, Lieutenant. We jus' sen' someone t' get ye early this mornin'."

Dragging Jenny's heavy, lifeless form to a chair, Blake tried to revive her as he questioned Jake. "Why did you send for the Lieutenant, Jake? Where is Katrina?"

The distraught look on the old man's face nearly panicked Blake as he left Jenny and roughly grabbed her husband by the shoulders. "Where is Rina, Jake? Is she all right?"

Jenny finally recovered and, seeing Blake shaking the

old man, spoke up. "Lord Roberts! Please! Please let 'im go!"

Realizing what he was doing, Blake stopped and forced himself to be calm. Lieutenant Greerson tried to make some sense of what was going on. "I would suggest we all sit down and allow them to explain what has happened."

Slowly, the whole story came out and Blake continued to sit perfectly still, staring into the fire, his face shadowed in the candlelight.

"It was late this afternoon when Lawrence Langsford came 'ere. 'E was insane wi' fury an' threatened t' kill us all if we did no' give 'im Kat. She was right, yes she was. 'E accused 'er of murderin' 'is son!" cried Jenny dabbing at her reddened eyes. "Oh, Lieutenant, if ye 'ad seen 'ow 'e 'ad beat 'er, ye would no' be thinkin' it murder. They were goin' t' kill 'er! Ye must believe me! She 'as every reason t' fear the man."

David patted Jenny's hand in a comforting gesture and smiled. "I believe you and I know the complete story about Lawrence Langsford and his reasons for wanting her dead. Katrina had no need to fear accusations of murder."

"Oh, dear," wailed Jenny, "I should no' 'ave let 'er go! 'E 'as gone after 'er!"

"It's what she wanted," stated Blake, finally speaking. Everyone looked at him curiously, not understanding. Turning his dark golden gaze to David, he continued.

"Katrina knew Langsford would follow her to the ends of the earth, and that is exactly what she wants him to do. She is leading him away, and when she is ready, she will face him and try to kill him. He may have surprised her this morning, but she has turned his advantage into her own."

"It seems we 'ave been two blunderin' ol' fools!" sniffed Jake, wiping at the tears welling up in his eyes.

Blake felt his heart go out to these two people who had cared for and loved Katrina like their own. "You did the best for everyone concerned, even Rina. I have learned one thing since she came into my life, and that is, she will do as she damn well pleases! God help anyone who tries to stop her!"

"I believe that is exactly what we intend to do, stop her," David said, smiling.

Blake, too, smiled and nodded. "Then may God help us!"

"She's a 'ell of a fighter, Kat is!" Putting his arm about his wife, Jake reassured her. "She will be fine, deary. Ye will see, an' maybe our Kat will be free, once an' for all."

David looked confused and asked, "Free? I don't understand what you mean?"

Blake understood and explained to the Lieutenant. "Free of all promises that hold her; but most of all, Katrina will be free of the anger and hate that have burdened her for too many years."

Blake looked out into the dark night, the rain falling in a steady stream as the lightning streaked across the black sky, thunder following loudly. "We will wait until morning to leave; we can't get far in this storm."

"I think we could use some sleep, anyway, Blake," agreed David. "At least we know they can't get far either."

"I'll be back later," said Blake absently, his mind elsewhere as he walked out the door.

Blake pulled the collar of his redingote up around his neck as he walked through the darkened streets, his hat pulled low on his forehead to shield his face from the falling rain. When he came to a small cottage, he stopped and pounded on the door. Father Murray answered it and greeted Lord Roberts warmly.

"I have come to see John," explained Blake.

John spoke out from across the small room. "It's about time you got here. Come, sit down. You will forgive me if I do not get up."

Blake crossed the candlelit room and pulled up a chair beside the bed where John sat, propped up by pillows, his chest bare except for the white bandage. Blake noticed two more men sitting near the fireplace and John explained their presence.

"They are watching me to make certain I don't go after Kat." Looking at Blake's disheveled appearance, he sighed, relieved. "Well, you are here now, and I do not have to worry anymore. I'm not so sure I could have made it."

Blake wasted no time and asked, "Where is she headed, John?"

"North," he stated simply and then elaborated when Blake looked annoyed. "I've been thinking about it for hours. If I know Kat, she'll head for an old hunting lodge her father owned. It'll give her shelter, a place to prepare an ambush. Lawrence has never bothered to go up there. A bit too rustic for a dandy like him. Kat and I used to go there, every once in a while, when she felt a need to get away from here. It will take her about six days to get there. She will wait for Lawrence there."

"If he doesn't catch up to her before then," murmured Blake worriedly.

John grinned, much like a proud father. "Not a chance! Kat will know exactly where she is going and can move fast, but Langsford will be trying to follow her. He will do well not to lose some hours, rather than gain some on her."

Frowning, Blake questioned John further. "Can I catch up to her before Langsford?"

"Yes." John nodded. "There is a shortcut I'm certain Kat won't take. Given her condition, she'll most likely stay close to the main roads."

"What makes you think that?"

John explained, "If she keeps to the roads, Kat will find help along the way. We know several families between here and the cabin; they will see she is taken care of. It would be too dangerous for her to go cross-country alone. Even Kat is not so foolish. She will keep to the roads."

John gave Blake directions to the lodge and added, "I have some cousins that live about an hour from the lodge. Kat will most likely stop there before going on. You may catch up to her there."

John paused for a moment, then added, "Kat is not going to be happy to see you, Blake. She will probably be madder than hell."

Blake's laugh was more like a snort. "That's an understatement! God knows I've given her reason enough to be angry."

"She is hurting inside, Blake, really bad! I have never seen Kat run away from anything before, but she is afraid to face the pain you have created. Instead, she has turned all her concentration to Langsford. Try and understand, Blake. Kat will not be the person we are most familiar with. She is like a wild animal that has been wounded and backed into a corner. Kat will be fighting for her life, and she wants ... no, she *needs* to kill him! Revenge is everything to her now, and she will not listen to reason. Only one thing is in her mind—Langsford must die!"

Blake covered his face wearily with his hands. "Are you telling me to let her fight the man? To stand back and possibly watch her get hurt ... or even die?"

John saw the turmoil in Blake's eyes as he answered. "I don't know! I only know the pain and anger that has built inside of Kat for ten years! You and I, we can sit here and say we understand, but we really don't! We can claim to know the right thing to do, as long as our decisions are made for a woman and not for ourselves. We preach two standards! One for men, the other for woman. If we were in Kat's place, wouldn't we do the same thing she is? Wouldn't we want revenge as much as she does?"

Angry at how close John's words were to his own thoughts, Blake yelled, "I don't know! I just know one thing ... I can not let Katrina fight him. It scares the hell out of me when I think of losing her. I could not bear it again! No ... not again! And no matter how skillfull she is, if she fights Langsford, she may die! There are never any guarantees when you are fighting for your life. So I cannot allow her to seek her revenge! I cannot!"

Sadly, John muttered, "She may never forgive you."

"I can live with that," sighed Blake. "But I cannot live without her."

The water was hot, its steam drifting in wisps around Katrina as she luxuriously relaxed in the old wooden tub. The warm, soothing liquid worked its magic on her tired and bruised body, easing the soreness of her muscles and burning of her cuts. She sighed in contentment. It felt good to have clean hair again, she thought, feeling the weight of it piled on her head. She touched her face gently.

"At least the swelling has gone down. I couldn't see

much from this eye with it swollen shut." Katrina smiled as a woman several years older than her poured some more hot water into the tub. "I am sorry if I frightened you, Meg."

"Don't ye be worryin' 'bout me, Kat. It was just a shock t' see ye, especially in such a condition. Why, it still makes me blood boil when I think o' a man doin' t' ye wha' 'e did! I sure do no' know 'ow ye rode tha' beast so far wi' yer back in such bad shape."

Katrina began soaping her body, controlling her features to show no pain. "Now, Meg, I will be fine, really! This bath alone is working miracles. I just look worse than I feel."

"Humph," retorted Meg, "that's for sure. Yer plumb black n' blue."

Katrina listened patiently to Meg's kind chastising, aware of the sight she presented. But she did feel much better, for the first three days had been terrible. The pain had eased and the soreness was slowly disappearing, but the bruises were at their ugliest in various shades of black, red, green, and blue. The lacerations on her back and buttocks were beginning to heal, along with the various other cuts and scratches on her body. She was beginning to feel like her old self again.

Yes, thought Kat to herself, I feel like I am ready to face you, Langsford! I will be waiting! Tonight you will die, Langsford!

"What is that?" Katrina jumped, hearing a noise in the other room.

Meg listened a moment, then answered, puzzled, "I do no' know, Kat. It sounds like someone at the door."

Katrina suddenly tensed, the voices drifting to her ears and she rose quickly from the tub. "My God, it can't be him."

Meg quickly grabbed the large cotton towel and wrapped it around Katrina's dripping body. "Wha' is it, Kat?"

Just then the door burst open and Blake's large form loomed frighteningly in the room, his face an angry cloud. Meg's mouth dropped open in fear, she nearly swooned as she trembled from his overbearing presence.

"Wh-wha' are ye doin', sir? This is me house ye be bustin' into."

Katrina cut off any further protests. "It's all right, Meg."

Meg's frightened eyes met Katrina's cold gaze, and chills went down her spine. "Kat . . . 'e's no' the man who did ye 'arm, is 'e?"

"No, Meg, he is not. This is Lord Blake Roberts of Windsong. You have no need to fear him."

Blake stepped forward, sincerely ashamed that he had frightened the poor woman so terribly. "Ma'am, I am here to help Katrina, not harm her. Please forgive the sudden intrusion, but I must speak with the lady."

Confusion overwhelmed Meg, who was uncertain of what to do. "The lady is no' presentable, Lord Roberts!"

Seeing Blake's patience was wearing thin, Katrina gave Meg a small shove to the door. "It *is* all right, Meg. Leave us."

Not wanting to interfere any longer, Meg ran into the other room, and Blake closed the door behind her.

"What are you doing here?" asked Katrina, her anger bolting through her with tremendous force.

Blake did not answer, he merely walked toward her, slowly. He heard the fury in her voice but shadows covered her face. Once he stood before her, Katrina turned away, but he reached up and turned her face to him.

Carefully, Blake examined her bruised face, not missing one small detail, his own face giving away none of the torment going on inside of him. It was the hardest thing he had ever done not to reveal the hot fury that boiled through him or the pain that nearly broke him.

"Dear God," he whispered, his voice finally betraying his feelings to Katrina.

Twisting away from his grasp, she closed her eyes, feeling a strange flush of shame washing over her. "I asked you a question!" she yelled, her voice rising with her fury.

Suddenly, Blake ripped off the towel covering Katrina, revealing the rest of her abused body. Both Katrina and Blake gasped, she from surprise at his sudden action, and he from the shock that shot through him with such intensity he could not breathe. The look on his face hypnotized Katrina; she was unable to move away from his scrutinizing gaze. Slowly, he turned her around, his hands trembling as they touched her shoulders.

As Blake stood staring numbly at her back, he actually felt sick, the bitter bile rising in his throat. Taking a deep breath, he closed his eyes to block out the horror before him, trying to bring his turbulent emotions under control.

As she stood, her back to Blake, Katrina finally came alive, reacting to the anger and humiliation his silent examination aroused. Whirling about, she brought her hand up hard against his face, the slap echoing in the silent room. Instantly her anger was gone.

Staring down at her stinging hand, Katrina saw and felt the wetness on her palm. Raising her eyes, she met Blake's angry look, the trace of his tears still on his face where the imprint of her hand reddened his cheek.

"Blake," mumbled Katrina weakly. Questions tore at Blake's heart, but his anger was stronger.

"Get dressed!" he ordered through clenched teeth as he shoved her from him.

Why had he done that? he berated himself silently. He'd wanted only to hold her, to comfort her, but instead, he had pushed her from him. He looked away as she dressed.

David was waiting outside when Blake pulled Katrina from the house and lifted her like a child onto Blackstar's back.

"David," cried Katrina.

Nudging his horse closer, David, too, could not believe how terribly her face had been beaten.

"Dear God, Katrina." Tenderly he reached over and caressed her bruised face, a motion that was not lost to Blake as he fumed jealously.

Reaching up and squeezing his extended arm reassuringly, Katrina smiled warmly. "It is not nearly as bad as it looks, David. I'll be fine."

"She is lying, David. The rest of her is worse than her face. That bastard took a strap to her back!"

Blake felt like a child itching to throw a tantrum. Why was she so soft and tender with David and only hard and cold with him? Grabbing the reins from Rina, he kicked

Hera into a run, forcing Katrina to grab onto the saddle horn to keep from falling off at the suddenness of the start. Confused by Blake's actions, David followed.

Blake refused to give the reins to Katrina as they made their way to the lodge. By the time they arrived, darkness was settled around them and Katrina's anger was nearly out of control.

She knew they intended to stop her from fighting Lawrence, and she desperately sought a plan, but none came. Intentionally, Katrina said nothing, her silence grating on Blake's nerves.

"Why didn't you tell me about Langsford?" Blake finally burst out, unable to stand it any longer.

Calmly, Katrina looked at Blake and answered, "You would only try and stop me, as you are doing now."

Blake slammed his fist against the door he stood near. "You can't fight him, Katrina! I cannot allow it!"

Angry now, she stood her ground. "*You* cannot allow! Just who the hell are you to stop me! You have no right!"

"But *I* do," interrupted David, the only one to remain calm. "Revenge is wrong, Katrina. It is a matter for the law."

"The law!" screamed Katrina, surprising both men with her fury. "And tell me, David, what can the *law* do to Langsford? You have no evidence he has committed any crimes! Only my word against his!"

Knowing she was correct, David found it difficult to meet her angry eyes.

"Neither of you has the right to stop me! He slaughtered my parents and three times has tried to kill me! Tell me, David! Tell me that revenge is wrong!"

He did not answer.

Katrina's anger was prodigious, and she trembled from emotion, her voice loud and strained. "Tell me, Blake, how many men have you killed for less reason than mine? How many died in the name of honor and pride? I know for a fact, if either of you were in my place, you would thirst for revenge as I do! But because I am a woman, you say I cannot do this, I cannot hate the man that has made my life a living hell! Am I to be meek and frightened by him and forget what he has done to me?"

Blake reached out and grasped Katrina by the shoulders, her eyes wild as her chest heaved with each deep breath. "Katrina!" yelled Blake, trying to calm her down. "Listen to me! You're acting crazy!"

Katrina felt her sanity slipping, and indeed, she was a bit crazed. The one thing she wanted more than anything in this world, they were trying to take from her.

"You bastard! I hate you!" Katrina started striking Blake with all her might, all the pain and anger surfacing that had been smothered since their meeting on the island.

Trying to fend off her blows, Blake remembered John's words: "She is like a wild animal that has been wounded . . ." Indeed, she was hurting, and Blake saw the pain and anger, the hatred spilling from her like blood from a wound.

"Kat! Please understand! I can't let you do this! I could not bear it if you were hurt!"

Twisting away from him, Katrina turned vicious eyes on Blake. "You son-of-a-bitch! You've hurt me in every way you possibly could! I can take no more! Tell me, which do you want? Last time we met, you wanted to kill me! Which is it? Kill me! Or love me! Am I your whore, or your lover?"

Blake tried to step toward her, but out of control, Katrina picked up an object and hurled it through the air at him. "Control yourself, Katrina! You're hysterical!"

"No!" Katrina smiled strangely, shaking her head back and forth. "I am anything but hysterical! I am angry, so angry I can hardly stand it! I am hurting! Not from the bruises and cuts on my body, but from the terrible hatred inside me. I hate Langsford!"

Her agony was so apparent, Blake was unsure of what to do or say. "I know you hate him, Katrina. It is only natural after what he has done to you."

Katrina felt light-headed and warm. Her voice rasped hoarsely as her body trembled from emotion. "This hate inside me . . . it's evil, I know. But it's powerful and con-suming . . . possessing me! For ten years I have lived with it!"

Closing her eyes as if to block out the visions before her,

Katrina whispered, "The nightmares . . . they're so real . . . there is no peace . . . no silence!"

In a trance, she continued, her eyes glazed and unseeing. "I can hear my mother's screams!" Katrina put her hands over her ears as if to block out the noise, but the noises inside her head continued.

Dry-eyed, she stared at them beseechingly. "Oh, God! I cannot wipe the memory from my mind! Every detail! . . . I . . . I can smell it! . . . Did you know . . . that death has a smell? . . . I can feel the warm stickiness of my father's blood on me . . . turning my white party dress red . . . seeping through to my skin. . . ."

Katrina fell silent for a moment as she stared at her hands, as if seeing the blood staining them. Then she went on, her words whispered so softly David and Blake could barely hear.

"I remember the fear! . . . I ran as fast as I could, just as I promised my mother. . . . I ran until I thought my lungs would burst . . . but he came after me. He found me so easily. . . . I had nowhere to go. He was like a giant, standing over me, his sword raised in the air. . . . I knew then, I was going to die. I was so afraid . . . but so was he. Then . . . I wasn't afraid any longer."

Drawing a ragged, weary breath, Katrina ran her fingers through her hair, pushing it from her face. "I have no fear inside me; he took it from me on that night long ago. Just as I've had no tears to ease my pain since then. There is only hate. . . . Blake, I cannot live with it any longer! It will destroy me!"

"I won't let it destroy you, little one." Blake was tremendously shaken by what he had just heard, his own heart tormented by her pain.

Silence engulfed the room as Katrina stared into the fire. Blake was silent, unable to find the right words. David felt they needed some time alone and left the lodge.

Confused and aggravated at his own ineptness, Blake turned away and looked out the window into the darkness outside. Immersed in his thoughts, Blake was unaware of Katrina's movements as she lifted a stick of wood from the pile near her and crossed to stand behind Blake, bringing it down on his head.

Blake crumpled to the floor as Katrina dropped her weapon and knelt beside his unconscious form. "I am sorry, Blake, but no one can stop me. Not even you!"

Acting quickly, she dragged him into a small room. The windows had been boarded shut long ago. Then, carefully, she tied him up and gently put a rag in his mouth. Just as she finished, David entered the outer room.

"He's coming, Blake! I can see the signal John's cousins were going to light when Langsford passed them!"

Looking about, confused by the empty room, David called out, "Katrina, Blake!"

Running into the room where David stood, Katrina cried, "Quick, David, he has hurt himself!"

As David ran into the dark room, Katrina stepped up behind him, a pistol in his back. "I am sorry David. Really I am."

Looking down at Blake's still form, David realized what Katrina was doing "It's not right, Katrina."

"It is what I *have* to do. There is no other way."

Turning his head to look into her darkened eyes, he asked, "You wouldn't shoot me? Would you, Rina?"

"I wouldn't kill you, my friend, but I would shoot you. I'm sorry, but my need for revenge is much stronger than any feelings I have for you. Even my love for Blake cannot stop me. Langsford is coming and I will be the only one waiting for him. I will not be denied my revenge!"

"It is wrong!" he shouted.

"No! It is *right!* . . . So very right!" cried Rina, raising the pistol to deliver a stunning blow to the back of David's neck, sending him into oblivion.

"It is time, Langsford! And I shall be waiting!"

Chapter 28

Katrina waited patiently in the shadows, alert and ready. She could hear some scuffling in the other room and knew Blake and David must be awake, and most likely, fuming angrily. By the time they freed themselves, it would be too late.

Leaning her head back, she closed her eyes. Her breathing was ragged and heavy, but she could feel her heart beating in her head, a strong, steady beat, loud and constant. Suddenly, she heard a noise and her heart skipped a beat. Her cold, hate-filled eyes flew open. A shadow moved across the window, silently stealing its way to the doorway in the dark. The door slowly creaked open and Lawrence edged his way into the lodge, a pistol in hand. Spotting the bed in front of the fire, he quietly walked across the floor to the sleeping figure.

Pointing his weapon at what he thought to be Katrina Easton, Langsford kicked at the bundle of blankets.

"Looking for me, Langsford?"

Katrina stepped out from the shadows, her own gun leveled at his back. He stiffened and cautiously turned around to face her, his hands reaching into the air as he spotted her weapon.

"Where are your men, *Uncle?* You usually travel well escorted," sneered Katrina.

Lawrence's eyes were dark and ominous, his lips set in a thin, grim line, his jaw muscle twitching in barely suppressed fury. "I wanted the pleasure of killing you myself, bitch!"

"So, you thought to catch me asleep. Perhaps dreaming sweet dreams . . . but you've made too many mistakes, Langsford. That is *really* too bad!"

Katrina's voice was sharp and sarcastic, nettling Lawrence's own anger.

"What mistakes were those?"

"First of all, I don't dream sweet dreams anymore." She walked forward slowly, her pistol steady and deadly, the shadows dancing around her. "I dream only nightmares. Nightmares of that night you murdered my parents. You do remember that night, don't you?"

Katrina was baiting Langsford. Gritting his teeth, Lawrence answered her question, his eyes evil and dangerous as he played her game. "Yes, it was one of my better moments, at least I thought so, until you suddenly appeared from the dead. Not once, but twice. What kind of witch are you, Katrina? You are not easy to kill."

"I'll not die with a sword in my back, not like my mother. And unlike my father, I know better than to trust you." Rina's voice was filled with disgust and hatred, her eyes mirroring what her words said.

"Your father was a fool! Weak and honest, but Camray was his, until I took it from him . . . and from you!"

Lawrence was nervous under the point of her gun, sweat popping out on his forehead and upper lip.

"And now"—Katrina smiled wickedly—"I am taking it back. Camray will be mine again, as it should be."

"No!" screamed Lawrence angrily. "It should have been my son's, but you killed him, you bitch!"

Laughing, Katrina nodded. "Just like I am going to kill you now."

Terror began to seize him as he stared down the barrel of her pistol. "So, you are going to shoot me. That is rather cold-blooded, even for you."

"I am not in the habit of slaughtering helpless people. That's your game, not mine. Put your gun on the table . . . over there."

Langsford did as she told him, laying the gun down. "What now?"

"You and I . . . we have a score to settle, but I've waited too long for it to end so quickly, with the pull of a trigger. No . . . I want to see your fear as I drain your life away." Katrina's pulse was racing wildly, power surging through her body, giving her strength and control. "You have a sword—defend yourself!"

Setting her gun aside, Katrina picked up her own blade.

"You're crazy," cried Lawrence, noting the evil glint in her blue eyes.

Katrina's casual, uncaring smile was unnerving. "Perhaps."

Nimbly, she lunged forward, taking Lawrence off guard, neatly slicing several buttons off his coat, then bringing her blade across one cheek, drawing blood. Surprise and anger lit his face as his hand dabbed at the drops of blood dripping down his chin.

"Bitch!" sneered Langsford, drawing his own sword in fury. "You stupid bitch! I am going to kill you, just as I should have long ago. I should have never depended on someone else to rid me of your presence. Even my son could not kill you!"

"Those were your other mistakes," goaded Katrina. "As you have found out, you bastard! I am not so easy to kill!"

"I am going to kill you now!" yelled Lawrence as he charged at her, no longer in control of his fury.

His blows fell with full strength on Katrina as he struck again and again. Toying with him, she held back, allowing him to think she was on the defensive, barely able to keep up her guard. She intended to draw it out, enjoying the elation of her ultimate revenge to its fullest extent.

"You should have shot me when you had the chance. Now you will die." Lawrence smiled, confident of his swordsmanship. But as he pressed his advantage, he felt a strange sensation as deadly, calm, blue eyes faced him. There was no fear or desperation, only cold-blooded calculation. "I must admit, you do handle a sword quite well. I *am* surprised, but unfortunately for you, your ability is not enough."

Smiling smugly, Lawrence made his move to disarm and kill his opponent but instantly found himself outmaneuvered. Swiftly, Katrina turned the tables on him, and he found himself besieged by a hell-cat.

"Another mistake!" yelled Katrina, her laughter grating on Langsford's nerves. "You have underestimated me once again."

Her sword was quick and accurate, drawing bits of blood wherever it grazed his flesh. Slowly and deliberately, Katrina slashed again and again. Langsford backed up against her onslaught, but she continued, untiring, her hatred fueling her strength.

Lawrence felt surprise mixed with fear at her physical abilities; her slender arm wielded the sword expertly, never showing signs of weariness. As they continued to fight, he began to feel the terror of death as she dominated, cutting and slicing him at every turn. Like a deadly snake, her blade struck its victim, almost hissing as it cut through the air. Sweat rolled into his eyes as his breathing became ragged and his arm began to ache wearily.

"What's the matter, Langsford?" taunted Katrina, her ever-present smile widening. "Getting tired?"

Her sword came down on his left arm, rendering it useless. Numbly, Lawrence stared at her, disbelieving.

"You are going to die, you bastard!" Promptly, she brought her blade around and gouged his leg cruelly. "I promised my dead father I would kill you . . . and tonight I will finally be free of that promise."

Again, she drew blood, and Langsford attempted to defend himself, futilely, as Katrina continued her deadly game. Seeing the end drawing near, she disarmed him, and he fell to his knees, blood covering his entire body, the tip of her blade at his throat.

"Oh, God!" cried Lawrence in horror. "Don't kill me, Katrina! I don't want to die!"

Finally freeing themselves, Blake and David broke through

the bolted door. Seeing Langsford at Kat's feet, Blake yelled, "Katrina! Look at him! You've won. Isn't that enough?"

Katrina looked at Langsford. The sight of him sickened her as he continued to cry and beg for mercy.

"Shut up!" she screamed. "You can't even die like a man! You son-of-a-bitch!"

David and Blake eased toward her. "Don't kill him, Katrina. Look at him. He's not worth killing."

Blake's words seemed to have no effect on her, so David tried to get through. "We heard every word. He will hang for the murder of your parents. That is what you want isn't it?"

"No!" Katrina cried. "I *want* to kill him myself. That is what I *want!*"

David inched nearer. "Let the law do it! There has been enough killing, Katrina."

Then Blake was next to her, his hand clamping onto hers. Their eyes met and Katrina whispered hoarsely. "No! . . . Please! He deserves to die!"

Slowly, Blake forced the sword away from Langsford's neck, and he crumpled to the floor trembling, his cries loud in the silent room. "He is pitiful, little one. Leave him be."

Katrina turned and walked away, leaving Blake standing near Langsford. She felt tired and, suddenly, for the first time, realized that pains were shooting across her back, blood soaking her shirt from the newly opened wounds. Silence filled the room, except for Langsford's sniveling, and disgusted, she glanced his way.

Terror struck her as she saw Langsford's hand snaking out for the pistol he had discarded. Blake's unguarded back stood before him. Katrina screamed and ran just as Lawrence brought the loaded pistol up.

"Blake!" she yelled, fear twisting her heart as Katrina shoved Blake out of the way the same second the gun was fired. The bullet ripped into her shoulder just as she thrust her sword straight out with tremendous force. The blade plunged deep, piercing Langsford's chest as the tip bit into his heart. Katrina stood in front of him as he slithered lifelessly to the dirty floor.

No one seemed able to move. Katrina continued to gaze

at the dead man; the two men were in shock at what they had just witnessed. Blake was the first to move, realizing with astounding clarity that she had just saved his life. Reaching out, he touched her shoulder tenderly. "Katrina."

She seemed unaware of him. "Katrina, it's over. It's all right now."

Katrina continued to stare at the dead man, her lips moving soundlessly; finally they formed intelligible words. "He knows . . . see . . . he is smiling because he knows."

Glancing down at her feet, Blake felt a chill rushing over him, for indeed, Lawrence Langsford was smiling, blood trickling from his gaping mouth. Looking back to Katrina, he became alarmed by the paleness of her face and gently turned her to face him. "What does he know, little one?"

Katrina swallowed and licked her lips, her mouth dry as she mumbled. "He knows that he has killed me, too."

Fear pricked Blake's mind as he looked into empty blue eyes, and grabbing her shoulders, he started to question her further, but stopped, horrified. Beneath his hand he felt the warm, dark blood, and glancing down, he saw the wound in her shoulder.

"He has killed me, too," Katrina repeated before she collapsed into Blake's strong arms.

Lifting her gently, he cried, "No, Katrina. I won't let you die." Hugging her to him, Blake kissed her softly. "I won't let you die!"

Katrina opened her eyes, unaware any time had passed, conscious only of the pain in her shoulder, shooting down her arm and across her chest. Blake removed her bloodied shirt as gently as he possibly could, but a moan escaped her lips with the movement of her arm.

Confused, she looked about her to see Meg's worried face.

"'Tis all right, 'oney," cooed Meg comfortingly. "We will take good care of ye, so don' ye be worryin' 'bout anythin'."

After Katrina had passed out at the cabin, Blake had bundled her up and ridden like a demon down to the village, rousing Meg and her family. As Katrina's eyes moved back to Blake, she noticed the lines of worry etching his pale, drawn face, his eyes bloodshot and tired. She continued to study him as he washed the blood from her body and cleansed her wounded shoulder, his touch gentle on her tender skin.

"B-Blake," cracked Katrina, her throat dry and parched as her bloody finger reached out to touch his cheek.

Blake grasped her hand in his and whispered, "What is it, little one?"

"Why did ... ?" Katrina swallowed hard, pain shooting through her like a bolt of lightning, but she bit her lip to keep from crying out. Catching her breath, she tried again, aware of Blake's intense golden gaze on her. "Why ... did you follow me?"

Perspiration covered Katrina's face as a fever took hold, working its way through her frail body. Blake felt fear prying into the agony he felt at watching the pain on her face. Katrina had lost a tremendous amount of blood. Wiping her forehead, he answered her question. "I have a lot of explaining to do, Katrina, but it will have to wait until you are better. David has gone to get a doctor and will be here soon. Now you had better sleep."

Reaching up, Katrina pulled Blake closer, her lips seeking his in a weak kiss; then she whispered softly, "I love you, Blake ... even when I wanted to hate you, I loved you. ..."

Closing her eyes, her strength gone, Katrina felt the darkness closing in about her, Blake's words distant and vague. "Sleep, little one ... sleep. I will be here when you wake up. I promise."

"Where the hell have you been?" yelled Blake as David walked into the room. He stopped halfway across the floor when he realized David was alone.

"Is the doctor still outside?" he asked weakly.

David sadly shook his head in answer to Blake's question and nearly fell when his friend lunged at him, grabbing him by the collar.

"Where is the doctor, David?" Panic seized Blake as he shook David fiercely and screamed, "Where!"

Seeing the fear in Blake's eyes, David tried to explain.

"He was gone, Blake. The doctor won't be back for several days."

Blake let go of David, his mind reeling uncontrollably.

"Oh, God," he moaned, his heart constricting painfully. "She's nearly dead from the loss of blood and the bullet is still in her shoulder."

David walked over to where Katrina was lying, sleeping fitfully, fever raging inside of her. "We will have to remove the ball."

Blake ran his hand over his face and through his hair, feeling helpless and frightened. "I know," he answered, "I know."

Standing next to David, Blake tried to wake her. "Katrina! Wake up, little one."

Finally, she opened her eyes, their blue depths large and glazed with pain and fever.

"Listen to me, Katrina. The lead ball is still in your shoulder. You know it has to come out."

Nodding to Blake, she smiled weakly at him. Her lips moved, but nothing came out, so Blake leaned over to hear her better. "Do it," she said.

The look of trust in her eyes caused Blake's breath to catch as his heart raced wildly.

David handed Blake a bottle of brandy and said, "Give her some of this."

Carefully, Blake lifted Katrina's head and poured some brandy into her mouth, forcing her to swallow the fiery liquid. She could feel the warmth spreading through her numbed body, her mind slipping in and out of reality, trying to escape the pain and agony. Sweet ebony engulfed her once again.

"I will cut the lead ball out, Blake, but you will have to hold her down." David's face was grim.

As they prepared to do the surgery, each man silently prayed for her. Meg held a lantern so David could see better, his knife glinting in the golden light, his hand shaking slightly. He looked at Blake, insecurity in his green eyes.

"Do it!" cried Blake, repeating Katrina's own brave words. "She is depending on us."

Taking a deep breath, David began to dig into the bloody

wound, Katrina immediately rousing from her unconscious state. Blake held her down, whispering comforting thoughts into her ear, but she was beyond hearing them.

Pain wracked her body as she moaned, her mind delirious from the burning fever. Her blue eyes, glazed and unseeing, blinked as she tried to focus on the faces before her. A tortured scream escaped from her as David went deeper, finally touching the ball embedded in her shoulder. Blake ground his teeth in anguish at her cries but held her immobile so David would not hurt her even more. Blood gushed from the wound, causing him to fear she would bleed to death. Finally, David pulled the small ball from her body, a sigh escaping him when he laid the knife aside.

Katrina was still, unconsciousness finally releasing her from the excruciating pain. Quickly, Meg and Blake applied bandages and pressure to stop the dangerous flow of blood. Long, arduous hours ticked by as Blake fought to save Katrina's life, his determination unending. She had stopped bleeding, but her fever was high, sending her into another world filled with pain, visions, and nightmares. Blake sat by her side, bathing her continuously in cool water, softly stroking her fevered brow.

Refusing to leave her, he continued to nurse her through the long days and nights, never ceasing to speak comforting words of love to her. During the long vigil, she relived many memories, and Blake's heart broke as he listened to the agony she had kept inside of her for so long. Blake felt his blood run cold as Katrina's screams filled the silent room.

Never before had Blake understood Katrina's feelings and thoughts so well, her fevered mind taking them both into her private world of nightmares and dreams. He became acutely aware of how delicate a balance there was between love and hate in her difficult life.

To Katrina, time did not exist; only the endless pain held any reality. Many faces floated before her tired eyes, she couldn't tell the reality from the dreams.

She was a child again ... no ... it was too hard to remember.

"Papa," cried Katrina. "Papa!"

Blake roused from his fitful sleep and stroked her cheek tenderly. "Ssshhh . . . little one, I am here."

Smiling, feeling relieved, she muttered, "Papa . . . I am so tired . . . very tired."

"Then sleep, little one. I will not go anywhere."

Closing her eyes once again, Katrina fell into a feverish slumber, a kaleidoscope of visions and memories. Cradling his head in his arms on the side of her bed, Blake listened as she mumbled incoherently.

"Oh, Katrina. I should have known the very first time I saw you that I would lose my heart to you." His mind wandered back to the time he first saw her riding Blackstar, leaving Windsong. So much of their past had been filled with anger and mistrust. But there had been moments of happiness and immense passion. Never before had a woman aroused him so.

A low moan brought him from his dreams, and when his eyes flew open, he saw Katrina as she was now, feverish and near death, her body bruised and slashed from Randolph's brutality. Anger filled him again as he thought of what that bastard had done to her. Had he not been dead already, Blake would have moved heaven and earth to kill him.

Revenge! Hadn't that been exactly what Katrina had wanted? Hadn't she been willing to move heaven and earth to see Lawrence destroyed?

Thoughts continued to resound in his mind, colliding with one another as he stared at her sleeping face.

"You would have faced the devil himself to see Langsford dead," cried Blake, understanding shattering through him. "You did fight the devil, little one, and because of my interference, you lie here, near death, taking the bullet meant for me!" Tears choked Blake, misting his eyes until he could not see. "Don't die, Katrina!"

Katrina's eyes fluttered open, a faraway look glazing them as she spoke in her dreamlike state. "We live in fear of the pain in death, but we were born to die."

She looked into Blake's golden gaze, filled with pain, then continued, "I am not afraid, so you needn't be. . . . Do you think they were afraid?"

Confused, he asked, "Who, Katrina? Who was afraid?"

She spoke so calmly, but he could tell she was still in a feverish delirium, unaware of what she was saying. "The men I have killed. Do you think they were afraid of death?"

Not really expecting an answer, she kept talking, more to herself than to Blake. "I killed the first at the inn.... They were going to hurt me. I could not bear to have him touch me.... I knew the second man's name, Willy...."

Blake listened quietly as Katrina chattered on. "I felt nothing when I shot him, no regret... just nothing. The third... Randolph, my husband... he deserved to die and I felt pleasure as I struck him with the poker! He would never beat and rape another woman again, I made certain of that!"

Something gripped Blake's heart at her words, fear creeping into his weary mind, his voice speaking the thoughts he had been terrified to acknowledge. "Did he rape you, Katrina?"

Shaking her head, she answered, "No... but... but he tried... he beat me... my hands tied... he hurt me!"

Katrina shook violently, chills beginning to wrack her frail body, her teeth chattering as her face perspired heavily from the fever. "I killed Lawrence... Langsford... the only one I had... I had wanted to kill.... He is dead... isn't he?"

A look of panic crossed her haunted blue eyes but disappeared quickly. "Y-Yes! I remember... dead!... Good! ... yes, his... body at my... feet!"

She continued to babble hysterically as Blake wrapped blankets around her to stop her shivering, pulling her into the warmth of his arms.

"Papa!... I... killed him... just as... I... p-promised."

Katrina was shaking so hard, Blake feared her wound would start bleeding again, so he laid on the bed, covering her small form with his own body. Slowly, he warmed and calmed her. They fell asleep wrapped in each other's arms.

The sun was shining in the small window, the light filtering across the room shedding warmth on Katrina's ashen face. Blinking open her eyes, she immediately saw Blake slumped in a chair next to her bed, his face unshaven and ragged. The fever had finally broken, leaving her mind clear but tired. She made no sound and continued to watch him sleep, realizing he had stayed by her side during the recovery. Lost in thought, it took a second for her to realize he had opened his eyes and was returning her gaze, his eyes worried.

Smiling shyly, Katrina whispered hoarsely, "You look exhausted. And in dire need of a shave."

A sigh of relief escape Blake as he closed his eyes a moment in thanks, his hands grasping her smaller ones and pulling them to his lips. "Oh, little one, you have had me scared to death for over a week. Thank God the fever is gone."

His soft lips sent shivers through Katrina, and her heart beat faster. Unable to think of anything else to say, she mumbled, "I'm sorry."

Surprised, Blake glanced up. "Sorry? God, Katrina! Sorry? Because of me, you were shot. You saved my life!"

"I owed you that, Blake."

"You have never owed me anything, Katrina," said Blake, kissing her slender fingers. "You have given me so much and I have given you nothing but pain in return. Can you ever forgive me my foolishness?"

Confusion welled up inside of her. "Forgive you? No . . . I cannot. There is still too much pain inside of me to forget and forgive." Katrina's voice was strained, her eyes reflecting the turmoil she felt inside. "I love you . . . I always have, I cannot deny it, no more than I could deny the hate I felt for Langsford!"

Blake felt helpless as he pleaded, "You say you love me, yet you can't forgive me. What do you want from me, Katrina? I've admitted how wrong I've been. Isn't that enough?"

"No!" she cried. "No, it's not enough. It's too easy. You must show me you really care. You must prove you are worthy of the love I have given you."

Stunned by a sudden surge of frustration, Blake looked away. "What is this? A test? What the hell must I do?"

Katrina felt dizzy from weakness and hunger as her head pounded fiercely. "It is all so simple to you." Closing her eyes, she moved her hands to her temple and whispered, "All I have to do is say 'I forgive you' and everything will be all right again. No, Blake, there is too much separating us, too much unhappiness. Three simple words will not make it right. That is for us to do by actions, not words, and only time will heal the wounds you have inflicted."

Seeing her pain and weariness, Blake was immediately contrite and changed the subject. "You're tired. Rest, and I'll bring you something to eat. You must be starved."

Before she had time to answer, Blake left, and Katrina felt the twinges of regret. "Why couldn't I just say the words he needed to hear?" she asked herself, but her tired body won out and sleep overtook her before she could consider an answer.

They avoided the subject during the next two days; Katrina spent most of her time sleeping and eating. It wasn't until the third day that she even felt like sitting up in bed.

"You are looking much better today."

Katrina turned and smiled happily at David as he stood in the doorway to the room she occupied. Patting the side of the bed, she said, "Come, sit and visit a while. Everyone else seems to be occupied."

Happy to see the color returning to her cheeks and the sparkle to her eyes, David laughed. "How can I resist such a tempting offer?"

The sound of Katrina's laughter drifted to Blake as he entered the small cottage. Thinking how nice it was to hear her laugh, he crossed to the bedroom door but halted just as he opened it a crack, seeing David sitting close to her.

"Tell me, David, what have you been doing in the last year?"

Smiling handsomely, he answered, "I have what I consider to be wonderful news! I've been waiting until things calmed down to tell you."

David's words were lost on Blake as he chided himself for the jealousy growing inside of him and turned away from the tender scene.

"I have met a wonderful woman, Katrina, and we plan to get married soon," David announced happily.

Surprise lit Katrina's face. "Oh, David!" Her hand caressed his face tenderly.

Katrina's cry caused Blake to turn back, and as he saw her loving gesture, his gut tightened painfully.

"Married! . . . That is wonderful! How soon?"

Delighted by Katrina's reaction, David kissed her hand, as Blake stood mesmerized by what he was hearing.

David answered, "We will be married as soon as you are well!"

A roaring in his ears kept Blake from hearing what David said next. "You will come, won't you?"

"Yes!" she cried joyfully. "Yes, I will!"

David leaned forward and kissed Katrina ever so tenderly on the lips and whispered, "You showed me that sometimes we must allow our hearts to rule our lives. Had I not met you and learned that, I may not have listened to my heart when I met Elizabeth. I would not know the happiness she has brought into my life and is yet to bring to our future. You are a very special lady, and I will always love you as my friend."

"And I will always love you as mine," replied Katrina.

Blake could not hear their soft words, but he could certainly see the gentle kiss and Katrina's cry still echoed in his mind. "Yes! Yes, I will!" He turned and left, slamming the door behind him.

It couldn't be! he cried to himself. Katrina said she would marry David!

Anger and pain flooded over him, choking Blake as he walked to Hera. It was true! He had seen and heard it with his own eyes and ears.

It was true!

Chapter 29

Five weeks had passed since Blake's sudden and unexplained departure. Katrina tried to hide her emotions, but no one could help seeing her pain and confusion. She knew she should be happy. David had corresponded with the King, explaining everything that had happened to Katrina Easton. Camray was returned to her, along with all her properties, making Katrina a very wealthy woman. She had finally achieved what she had promised her father over ten years ago, but there was no joy in it. She could think of nothing but Blake.

David finally consented to her returning home, after four weeks of convalescing, but Katrina remained at Camray only one night. After taking care of the most urgent matters at hand, she left Jake, Jenny, and John in charge and started for London and her son. It was late when she and David arrived, so they got rooms at an inn, waiting until morning to go to the Robertses' townhouse.

When the carriage pulled up to the house, Katrina felt giddy from excitement. She'd missed Jason so terribly. She had been told that Blake had been staying at Windsong since his return, so Katrina knew she would not see him, though she could not tell if she was thankful or disappointed by the reprieve. But her thoughts were on Jason now. She wanted to take him to their home. Perhaps later, when she was settled, she would know what to do about Blake Roberts.

When the door opened, a smiling butler led her into the large sitting room and left to tell Lady Rebecca of Katrina's return. Large double doors stood open, allowing a gentle breeze to fill the room, delicate scents from the garden teasing Rina's senses as her eyes took pleasure in the well-groomed flowers and shrubs outside. Stepping out onto the patio, she carefully examined a perfect red rose but was distracted as the front door opened, then slammed shut.

When Blake entered the room, Katrina froze, unprepared for his presence, her heart racing wildly in her chest. Unaware that she was just outside the doors, Blake walked across the room and poured a cool drink from a pitcher sitting on the table. He was dressed handsomely in brown doeskin riding breeches and jacket, and a snowy white shirt open in front, showing the fine curly brown hair covering his chest. It was apparent he had been riding; his hair was mussed and eyes sparkled like the sun. As he stripped his jacket off and carelessly tossed it on the settee, Katrina caught a hint of his masculine scent. She was aroused by the mere sight of him! The realization brought a blush to her cheeks.

Just then, someone pounded on the front door. The butler hurried down the stairs to answer the summons, and Catherine Ramsey rushed in, also dressed in riding clothes, her face flushed and angry.

"Where is he?" she asked impatiently.

The butler remained stiff and aloof. "To whom are you referring, Lady Ramsey?"

Her temper flaring, Catherine narrowed sharp green eyes and snipped, "You know damn well to whom I am referring, and don't tell me he is not here, because I followed him on his morning ride!"

Blake stood in the open doorway, his face grim and taunt. "What do you want, Catherine?"

Whisking past Blake into the sitting room, she smiled wickedly. "I thought your seclusion at Windsong would come to an end, so I have had your place watched. I knew you came home yesterday and followed you on your morning ride. You really are very predictable, darling!"

Blake felt his control slipping and slammed shut the door that led out into the hallway. "I would think you would be bright enough to avoid me; I may be tempted to strangle your scrawny neck for your collaboration with Langsford."

An innocent look carefully played on her face as Catherine cooed, "Oh, Blake, I was only trying to help poor Randolph find his wayward wife. After all, we all thought she was dead and buried. Surely you cannot blame me for what happened!"

"I can and I will," Blake growled, his eyes a dangerous fiery gold. "You almost got her killed!"

"Well," huffed Catherine, feigning a hurt expression. "What do you care, Blake Roberts? You certainly wasted no time in leaving her up north, so I don't understand this sudden concern for her welfare! She is nothing but a lying little whore and you're still hot for her bed!"

"Shut up!" yelled Blake, his outburst causing Catherine to step back in fear. "Don't you dare speak that way about Katrina ever again, or I swear, I will shut your lying mouth for good! My concern for her is none of your damned business and you had best remember that. Now get the hell out of my house!"

Catherine's eyes sparkled angrily and narrowed to small slits as she gathered her courage, speaking with much more calmness than she felt. "I *think* I will stay, and if you are really concerned about that witch, you *will* listen to what I have to say."

Licking her lips nervously, she went on, seeing she had gotten Blake's undivided attention. "You see, darling . . . I know about Katrina's little secret."

"What are you talking about?" asked Blake directly, annoyed beyond endurance by her obnoxious attitude.

A calculating gleam entered her eyes, and her voice rang with sudden confidence as Catherine boldly laid her cards on the table. "I know that Katrina is the Angel in Black. Now . . . I am sure the King would find that very interesting, indeed."

For several minutes Blake did not move, the look in his

eyes murderous, his hands clenched in a hard fist as a muscle jumped in his jaw. He felt the urge to kill her and be done with it, but Blake still had a sliver of reasoning in his muddled mind.

"What do you want?" he demanded.

Catherine walked over to him, her face soft and flirtatious as her fingers moved over his chest provocatively. "You know what I want, darling!"

Her voice was whispery soft and husky, but it irritated Blake enormously. Her touch repulsed him. "Be specific," he snared, grabbing her wandering fingers in a painful grasp.

Pulling away, a pouting look on her lips, Catherine hissed, "I want you, Blake Roberts! You *will* be mine, or Katrina will hang for her crimes. You will make me Lady Catherine Roberts, wife of Lord Blake Roberts of Windsong, or . . ."

Catherine didn't finish, her meaning quite clear as she smiled smugly, aware of the power she now had over Blake. "Don't look so forlorn, Blake. I will make you a wonderful wife."

Catherine felt victory surging through her. Her laughter filled the room, grating against Blake's raw nerves and drifting out to where Katrina stood, hidden by the shrubs, stunned beyond belief. Silently, she left through the garden gate to where her carriage still waited in front.

Catherine took Blake's speechlessness as consent and continued to outline her plans. "Now, dear, there is a costume ball at the palace tonight and you will be my escort. Then we will announce our plans to be married. The quicker the better, don't you agree?"

Blake felt a sick tightening in his gut, his mouth suddenly dry. Rage shook him so violently that he feared to speak, his control was strung so thin he was near giving in to his impulse to strangle the life from Catherine's corrupt body.

Feeling encouraged by his silence, she assumed he had accepted the idea of their marriage, a thrill of victory making her bolder. Catherine leaned forward and kissed him hungrily, her lips moving seductively on his own. Blake fought the urge to throw her from him but willed himself to be still as he tried to gain some semblance of control over his rage.

Catherine pulled away, her eyes flashing angrily at his

stiffness. "You really must do better than that, darling. Not only must you *marry* me, but you have to keep me *happy*. Now . . . you wouldn't want me to be unhappy, now would you?"

She affected the tone of a mother scolding her errant child, filling Blake with an unreasoning rage that broke his restraint.

Gripping her wandering hands painfully, Blake growled through clenched teeth, his eyes smoldering with golden fire. "Now, you listen to me, Catherine Ramsey, and you listen carefully. I'll not stoop to your blackmail, for there is no way in hell that I would marry you!"

His words were angry and insulting as she retorted unwisely, "Then I shall have to make a visit to the King, now, won't I, Blake?"

"No," he muttered, hurting her with his strong grasp. "We won't be seeing the King, not now, not ever! Unless, of course, you do not value your worthless life, bitch!"

Her green eyes widened in shock. Drawing a calming breath, Catherine charged on, not willing to give in just yet. "You are threatening me, Blake? You would not dare!"

"Believe me, I dare!"

"You're lying!" cried Catherine, panic seizing her. "You wouldn't kill a lady!"

A slow, evil smile crossed Blake's lips, his eyes clearly showing he would. "We both know *you* are not a *lady!* If you *ever* threaten Katrina again, I will not only see you dead, but I will enjoy it immensely."

Fear pricked her; at that moment she believed he would carry out his threats. He was playing a better hand than the one she had, and Catherine knew she had lost.

Shoving her away from him in disgust, Blake pointed at her as she trembled and cowered away from him. "Now, get out of my house, and don't you dare to ever step foot in here again!"

Scurrying from him, she stopped suddenly when she heard him shout, "Remember! I'll not let anything or anyone harm Katrina or my son in any way! Forget that, bitch, and you will live only long enough to know regret!"

Catherine ran from the room in tears, not even aware of

the woman descending the stairs. Rebecca watched curiously as Lady Ramsey rushed out onto the street and to her waiting carriage. When she entered the sitting room, she found Blake looking furious and unhappy. Jason squirmed in her arms, drawing his father's attention to them.

"Where is Katrina?" asked Rebecca, looking about the empty room.

His mind on what had just happened, he answered vaguely, "Catherine just left."

Frowning, Rebecca walked over to him. "No, not Catherine, I saw her leave. Where is Katrina? I was told she was waiting to see Jason and take him with her."

Blake's face fell. "You mean she was here?"

The butler entered, a sad look on his face. "She is no longer here, sir. I saw her getting into her carriage just a few moments ago, before Lady Ramsey left."

"Now, why would Katrina leave without seeing Jason?" asked Rebecca, glancing at Blake in confusion.

No one answered.

The evening passed agonizingly slowly for Blake, his mind wandering to Katrina's appearance and disappearance time and time again. He came no closer to understanding her. And why had he received a message for him to meet Katrina here at the palace? It was late and still she had not come. Needing a moment to himself, he took another glass of champagne and walked out into the fresh air. After a few moments, he felt somewhat revived.

Catherine Ramsey was also at the costume ball, deliberately avoiding any contact with Blake. Obviously, he had gotten through to her. He felt somewhat sorry for the poor fellow who had escorted her. She clung to him as she fawned over his every word, and Blake could see the fool was unaware of the trap being so carefully laid for him. Catherine's costume was colorful and flamboyant, feathers adorning it everywhere. Blake laughed, thinking her endless chattering nature suited the bird costume she wore.

His own attire was simple but drew everyone's gaze. Dressed as a buccaneer, Blake was extremely dashing, the fawn-colored breeches showing off his hard-muscled legs and tight buttocks, while the snowy white shirt, open in front, drew the women's eyes and the men's envy.

"I was beginning to think I would never find you!"

Blake turned around to find himself face to face with a worried-looking David Greerson.

"What do you need?" asked Blake cautiously, his emotions in careful check.

"Katrina has disappeared!" shouted David, concern filling his voice. "She went to your townhouse this morning to get Jason but never returned. I became very worried and went to your house but was told she had arrived but left, very suddenly, without her son. I have looked everywhere with no luck, and she has yet to return to the inn."

Blake kept his face blank and unreadable, his voice calm and unconcerned. "I have not seen Katrina, David, but she did send me a brief message asking me to meet her here. I really don't know why, we have nothing left to say to one another."

Blake's manner was the last straw for David, who had nearly gone mad trying to locate Katrina. "You bastard!" he cried, grabbing Blake by the collar. "Just what the hell went on at your townhouse? Katrina's been upset enough by your untimely departure—how dare you treat her so badly!"

Unable to control his anger any longer, Blake shoved David back, his golden eyes dangerous. "Why should she be upset by my leaving? She's marrying you!"

David's mouth fell open, his shock written clearly on his face. "Marrying me! What made you think Katrina and I are going to be married?"

"I heard your touching words of love and saw your tender kiss! I heard you declare that you would be married as soon as she was well, and I heard her agree! You cannot deny it!" yelled Blake, his hurt apparent in his trembling voice.

Enlightment dawned on David, and carefully he tried to explain. "Blake, I did not ask Katrina to marry me. I merely told her of my engagement to a very fine lady, and as my dear friend, she was delighted by the news. I had intended to tell you that same day, but you had disappeared so suddenly, without any explanation. The kiss was an innocent gesture of a love shared by good and dear friends. Katrina is my friend, Blake! I had hoped you understood that!"

Blake paled as David's explanation sank in. It was true, he had not heard everything that had been said, only bits and pieces. "It seems I have allowed my jealousy to rule me once again, something I swore not to do. Will I never learn?"

"Your disappearance hurt her much more than she let any of us know. We had no idea you had overheard part of our conversation and misunderstood."

Blake stiffened. Seeing the sudden change in Blake's manner, David asked, "What is it?"

"I think I may know why Katrina has disappeared," mumbled Blake, his mind quickly going over that morning's argument with Catherine.

"The patio doors were open!"

Confused, David shook his head. "So?"

It all fell into place. "When I entered the sitting room this morning, the doors leading to the gardens were open and the room was empty. I remember noticing the vague scent of roses, Katrina's favorite perfume, but I shrugged it off. She had been there and must have gone onto the patio. Katrina must have been just outside the room when Catherine burst in."

"What has Catherine Ramsey to do with all of this?"

"Well," continued Blake seriously, "Catherine knows that Katrina is the Angel in Black and threatened to use this knowledge to blackmail me."

Surprised, David questioned, "Blackmail for money?"

Blake smiled sadly. "Not exactly. She is demanding I marry her or she will tell the King everything."

Shocked, David cried, "And you intend to marry that witch?"

"No! Of course not! I told her to go to hell, and if she even dared to think of threatening Katrina with her knowledge ever again, she would regret it." Blake's voice was hard and deadly, and David knew, without asking for details, what must have gone on.

"But that still does not tell us where Katrina is. And what

about her note asking you to come tonight? If she was to be here, where the hell is she?" asked David warily.

Blake sighed in frustration. "I don't know, David. I just don't know."

Just then, a commotion inside drew their attention, as excitement rippled over the crowd. Both men worked their way to the center of the ballroom, stopping dead in their tracks when they spotted the reason.

Dressed as the Angel in Black, Katrina sat proudly on top of Blackstar as he pranced nervously in the crowded ballroom. In unison, David and Blake broke through the tight circle that had formed around the impressive figure. Katrina's eyes locked with Blake's and she casually threw him a kiss and winked boldly.

Fear gripped Blake, twisting his stomach into knots as he realized what she was doing. A screech penetrated his numbness as Catherine Ramsey ran out into the open space the crowd had fearfully given the black beast and its mysterious rider.

Her breasts were heaving angrily, her ample bosom almost spilling from the low cleavage of the costume she wore. "You! . . ." she spit vehemently.

Unconcerned, Katrina gracefully slid from Blackstar, handing the reins to a stunned David. Just then, the crowd parted to allow the King himself to approach the curious rider. As he reached Katrina, she dropped into a flawless curtsy, kissing the King's hand.

"I must say, this is the most exciting entrance we have ever had at one of my costume balls, and to come as the famous Angel in Black! Quite enchanting! If the criminal herself is as shapely as you, my dear, I can understand why she is spoken of with such admiration." His laughter echoed in the now deathly silent room, as everyone waited for the mystery lady to speak.

"You are too kind, Your Majesty." Katrina smiled warmly. "But you are indeed speaking to the criminal herself. I am the Angel in Black."

A murmur spread across the room and the King stepped back instinctively. Catherine stepped forward, in a frenzy. "You bitch! What are you doing?"

"I have just played the winning hand and you have lost."

"Lost!" screamed Catherine uncontrollably. "It is you who have lost, you fool. You are wanted for your crimes against the Crown. You will hang!"

"But you will not have Blake," Katrina reminded her quite calmly.

Catherine laughed wickedly and sneered, "But neither will you!"

Shaking her head, Katrina whispered huskily, "Blake will always be mine. Even in death!"

"No!" shrieked Catherine, leaping at Katrina, her claw-like hands reaching for Katrina's beautiful face.

Reacting quickly, the Angel grabbed Catherine by the wrists and easily forced her to her knees. "I would just as soon hang for murder as for thievery! Do not tempt me!"

When Katrina let go of Catherine, the woman sank to the floor, sobbing uncontrollably. Katrina felt pity rather than anger and stepped past her to the King, who stood transfixed.

"I am surrendering to my King and freely confess my crimes!"

Katrina pulled her sword from her side, causing gasps of fear from the court as guards stepped forward, drawing their own weapons in defense. Carefully, Katrina stepped forward and laid the blade at her King's feet, followed by her two pistols.

Two men stepped forward and grasped Katrina by the arms. Blake rushed to her aid, panic clearly written on his face.

"No!" cried Katrina, stopping him before he struck a guard. "Blake, please, no!"

"Wait," demanded the King, everyone freezing. "I would know who you are. Remove her mask!"

A hand reached out and pulled the Angel's hat and mask off, releasing her golden hair to tumble down her shoulders to her waist.

"Katrina!" cried King George in surprise. "What manner of joke is this?"

Looking straight into the King's sad eyes, she answered, "It is not a joke, my lord. I am the Angel in Black."

"It can't be," he muttered.

"It's the truth." Her grim words echoed in the large room. "I have no reason to lie and most assuredly, much to lose."

Feeling betrayed and made the fool before all his kingdom, the King turned scarlet with anger. "Take her to the tower!" he yelled. "I'll not abide such treasonous behavior! Take her away, so I do not have to look upon her face again!"

As the guards started to lead her from the court, Blake started forward but was stopped.

"Katrina!" he cried in agony.

Looking back, she felt her heart lurch painfully as she saw the suffering in his eyes.

"Why?... Dear God, why?" he yelled agonizingly as he struggled against the men holding him back.

Pausing a moment, Katrina tried to speak, her voice trembling with emotion. For the first time in ten years, tears spilled onto her cheeks, blurring her vision.

"Because I love you! I love you, Blake! Even more than life itself!"

As they pulled her from the room, she cried over her shoulder, "Blake, take care of our son!"

Blake sank to his knees in defeat, the vision of her tears breaking his heart.

"Katrina!" he bellowed, his cries echoing in her heart as she was taken away, her tears flowing freely now.

"Katrina!"

Chapter 30

The sun sank slowly in the western sky, melting shades of rose and purple against the azure sky, a very peaceful, soft sunset. But the peace did not enter Katrina as she stood at her only window in her chamber high in the tower. She felt heavy with a melancholic longing, unable to forget Blake's heart-wrenching cries as she was taken away. She closed her eyes against the visions haunting her, but his cries echoed again and again. Frustrated, she covered her ears to close out the noise.

"Katrina!"

Blake called her name softly as he entered the cell. When she did not seem to hear him, he gently caressed her shoulder and whispered, "Are you all right, little one?"

Whirling about in total surprise, Katrina threw her arms about Blake's neck, and he pulled her into his arms, lifting her from the floor. "How did you manage to get in?" she asked, hugging him tightly.

"It took a lot of talking, but the King finally agreed to let me see you. . . ." Blake kissed her ear, sending shivers through her, then whispered softly, his breath tickling her, "We have all night."

Suddenly shy, Katrina moved away, a flush staining her

cheeks. Feeling awkward and uneasy, she turned to sarcasm to hide her vulnerability. "One last night of love for the condemned prisoner!"

Seeing the fear beneath her facade, Blake scolded, "You little fool, you should not have done this."

"I suppose you would have me meekly stand by and watch that blackmailing bitch trap you into marriage! I do not need you sacrificing yourself for my sake, Blake Roberts. I knew what dangers I faced when I first rode as the Angel, and I am not afraid of the consequences now."

Katrina faced Blake's angry glare head on, her own fury igniting emotions that had been building for some time.

Hurt by her stubbornness, Blake stated frankly, "It was all for nothing, Katrina! Had you waited only a minute longer, you would have known there would be no blackmail! You sacrificed *yourself* for nothing! Did you never stop to think of our son, Katrina! What is to happen to our son, Jason? Am I to raise him with no mother?"

The shock brought tears to her eyes and a choking pain to her heart. "Y-You believe me? You truly believe he is our son?"

Nodding, he pulled her into his arms once again, stroked her head comfortingly while his own tears blurred his vision. "When Trevor and I found out about Langsford, I was finally able to start seeing things more clearly. Oh, Katrina, can you ever forgive my foolishness? When I look at him now, I don't know how I ever could have doubted you. Thank you for our beautiful son, little one. I am so sorry I could not be by your side when you brought him into this world. You have suffered so much pain, and I have caused much of it."

Blake felt Katrina's shoulders shake as a sob tore from her. It was more than he could bear. Lifting her, he carried her to her small cot, then cradled her in his arms as she sobbed for all the years of pent-up emotions. Pain, rage, fear, agony, grief, love . . . Katrina sobbed with them all. She was finally able to cry again.

Rocking her like a small child, Blake pulled his hand-kerchief from a pocket and wiped her tearstained face, looking into her watery blue eyes. "I love you, Katrina," he murmured. "I have done my damnedest to fight the feelings you have aroused in me, but to no avail. Never has any woman affected me so. I love you and want to spend my life with you, little one. And nothing and no one will ever come between us again! Not even the King can take you from me!"

Suddenly afraid, Katrina stuttered, "B-Blake, you mustn't do anything foolish! Please—"

Blake stopped her words with a finger to her soft lips. "I did not come here to argue.... I came here to tell you of my love, and ... to show you."

Bending his neck, Blake captured Katrina's red lips, soft and delicious, his kiss tender at first, then deepening with passion. Pulling away, Katrina asked, "Why did you leave me so suddenly, with no explanation?"

"Later"—Blake smiled—"I'll tell you all about it later. Now..." With deliberate slowness, he nibbled along her neck, and quickly all her questions were forgotten; only their lovemaking was important.

It was a sweet and tender moment as the dark gloomy cell became their chamber of love. Blake made love to every inch of her body, gently at first, building their passions with each deliberate movement. Katrina returned every caress and Blake's moans of pleasure mixed with hers.

The bruises and cuts had healed on her body. Only a red scar on her shoulder remained, and it, too, was almost healed. Carefully, he kissed it, remembering the pain and fear he had felt during her fever. Blake's hands ran along her body. She was so lean and strong, yet so softly sensuous. Her breasts were full, firm orbs, and he delighted in teasing their rosy tips to hardness with his tongue, loved to feel Katrina squirming in delight. Her movements aroused him further, the evidence hard between his legs. Katrina's small, slender fingers explored and massaged, driving him insane with ecstasy.

Every minute, every second, every inch of their bodies was treasured as they climbed to spiraling heights, bringing lust and love into their ardent lovemaking. As Blake entered Katrina, driving hard into her moist softness, she felt a frisson of satisfaction and possession, her long nails digging into Blake's hard-muscled buttocks. Slowly, he pumped deeper and deeper as a fine sheen of perspiration covered their entwined bodies, the scent of their lovemaking an aphrodisiac. Words of love were spoken, words that were for so long left unspoken. No more! Nothing was left untouched, no emotion or thought. Theirs was a night of love and joy, so pure and meaningful, a night that would forever be preserved in their memories.

Afterward they lay in silence, their bodies as one. Katrina was lying curled up on top of Blake, her head resting on his wide chest, a shapely leg thrown over his thigh. One of Blake's arms was wrapped about her waist, his hand resting lightly on her rounded buttocks. His other hand held on to Katrina's. Together they drifted off to sleep, each dreaming of the other. When they woke, they made love once again and afterward finally spoke of many things that had kept them apart, clearing the air once and for all of the misunderstandings and distrust that had come between them. As the sun rose high into the sky it brought a new beginning for the lovers, and the past assumed its proper place as they thought only of the future.

Another day passed as Katrina waited in her isolated cell, hearing nothing and seeing no one. The night was lonely, and she wanted desperately to feel Blake in her arms again, but she had only her dreams as comfort. Morning came and with it a summons from the King, so Katrina prepared herself. After bathing with a bucket of cold water, she dressed in a soft white cotton dress from the bundle Blake had brought to her. Carefully, she brushed her long hair and left it unbound to flow about her shoulders and down to her waist. Then she patiently waited for them to come for her.

Less than an hour later four yeomen warders came, taking her to a wagon for the trip to the palace. As the rickety cart left the protective high stone walls of the prison, passing into the streets of London, soldiers on horseback immediately surrounded them as an escort. The sight that met Katrina's eyes was astounding.

Hundreds of people lined the crowded, narrow streets, each hoping to catch sight of the famous Angel in Black, crying out their devotion and love. Slowly, the group of warders made their way into the cheering crowd, the guards keeping the people away from Katrina. She was touched to the core by their loyalty. A young woman carrying a small babe ran past the men on horseback, keeping pace with the slow-moving wagon as her words drifted to Katrina over the noise.

"God bless ye, Angel! 'Ad it no' been fer the coin left on our table one night, me babe would no' 'ave 'ad the milk she needed to survive the winter! God bless ye and keep ye!"

Reaching down, Katrina took the object from her outstretched hand, before losing her in the crowd. Looking down, she gently fingered a delicate brass cross and chain, then tried to put it around her neck but found it difficult in the rocking cart.

"Allow me, Lady Katrina."

Surprised, Katrina glanced up into the sympathetic eyes of a guard, and lifting her heavy gold hair, allowed him to place the cross about her neck.

"Thank you, sir." Katrina smiled as the young man blushed proudly.

Mumbling, he turned away shyly, "My pleasure, ma'am."

It took them a long time to make their way to the palace gates. Quietly, Katrina was ushered into a private room and left totally alone. A door opened and the King walked in, his face grim.

Katrina bowed low as the King reached out to touch her head gently. "Rise, my child, we have much to discuss."

He indicated two chairs in a corner of the large room, and Katrina sat, waiting for him to speak, surprisingly calm and at ease.

"You have angered me, Katrina."

Looking innocent and pure, dressed in white, she asked, "In what way, Your Majesty?"

Scowling, King George reprimanded her, "By your foolish escapades as the Angel in Black! I just don't know what you had in mind riding about robbing people! Just what did you hope to accomplish?"

Trying to control her anger, Katrina answered, her voice

smooth and soft. "I think you know my reasons for doing what I did."

"Ah!" cried the King. "You came to the aid of the poor. Much like Robin Hood, centuries ago. There are other ways, Katrina. It was not a matter to take into your own hands!"

Katrina stood stiffly, her fury finally apparent in her eyes and voice. "For me, I saw no other way, Your Majesty! I saw only the need to help those I love, to keep them from the greedy claws of people like Langsford and his son! Perhaps someday life will be better for the poor, but I cannot be wishful of the future and expect that to help them now, so I took the only action I knew would work. Now! Not tomorrow!"

King George sighed deeply as he noted the fire in her eyes and acknowledged the honesty in her words. His anger with her ebbed. "I would choose your painful honesty over another's soothing deceit any day."

Katrina was silent.

"Your sudden confession the night of the ball shocked me. And I was angered by your deceit. I hope you were not terribly uncomfortable in the tower?" The King's words were tinged with guilt, and Katrina turned curious eyes to him, realizing he had just come close to apologizing to her.

"I have been in worse places, my lord."

Her answer did nothing to ease the guilt he felt, not just from allowing his anger to control him and send her to the tower, but for making her marry Randolph Langsford. His decision had nearly cost Katrina her life, something that did not rest well on his conscience. Silent a moment, he pondered these notions, then voiced his next question out loud. "You married Randolph, knowing the danger it would put you in. Why?"

Blue eyes as dark as the night sky looked up at the King. "I gave you my word to abide by your decision. I could not go against my given word."

"You are an honorable woman but a foolish one," mused King George sadly.

"What am I without honor?" questioned Katrina evenly.

The King knew what he must do, his own guilt for his part in her nine years of suffering leading him to be merciful.

"Come!" he demanded, and Katrina followed him to a large adjoining room. It was crowded with people, each bowing low as their King made his way to his ornate throne. A hush came over the people as they waited for his judgment of Katrina Easton and her crimes as the Angel in Black.

Clearing his throat, he began.

"It seems I am faced with a grave decision. Katrina Easton is charged with crimes she has committed against the Crown as the Angel in Black. Since her sudden confession a few nights ago, London has been besieged with people coming in support of their lady. They crowd the streets and chant her name, claiming her crimes were committed for their sake. In addition to the obvious support of the people, I have had a barrage of confessions from others who have admitted to knowing her identity and being accomplices in her crimes."

Katrina was shocked, her eyes meeting Blake's as he stood next to many people dear to her. Trevor Wilde, David Greerson, Ryon and Rebecca, Chin Li, John, Jake and Jenny had all come forward. In the crowd she spotted many other familiar faces from Tattershall, including those of Father Murray, Tom, and Charlie. Turning to face the King, she pleaded desperately.

"They had nothing to do with my actions, except to try to dissuade me from my purpose! And you know I do as I please, so I beg you, do not consider their foolishness, Your Majesty!"

"I see you are willing to beg for their sakes, but not for your own."

Unblinking, Katrina answered, "They are innocent, I am not."

Considering this, the King spoke again.

"The situation is this. . . . I have a beautiful, headstrong lady who has robbed my subjects, and yet, even the officer who sought to capture her has asked for the lady to be pardoned. Then I have numerous accomplices, including a priest. And last, but not least, I have throngs of people surrounding me that love and cherish this woman . . . and I, too, have developed a fondness for her that cannot be denied. Considering all of these things, and most importantly, what I feel in my heart, I have come to a decision. Katrina Easton, you are given full pardon for your crimes and shall be free to go. But I warn you, do not ever make me regret my decision today, for I shall not be so merciful again!"

A cheer went up in the crowded room and Katrina bowed graciously to her King. "I thank you for your compassion."

Smiling, he replied, "And I thank you, child . . . for your honesty."

Turning around, Katrina ran to Blake's arms and laughed as he twirled her about joyfully. Then he kissed her, long and passionately, the crowd cheering as feelings of elation vibrated throughout the streets of London.

It was a time for joy and celebration in Tattershall. Blake and Katrina stood together, hand in hand, accepting the best wishes of the people. That day, with all their dearest friends and family present, Katrina Easton and Blake Roberts were married in the small church by Father Murray. Dressed simply in a gown made by the women of the village, Katrina looked more beautiful than ever. Happiness and love shone in her blue eyes as she looked into Blake's golden gaze, seeing her joy mirrored there.

Squeezing her hand, Blake leaned down to whisper in her ear as Jason squirmed happily in his father's arms.

"I love you, little one."

Smiling up at him, Katrina answered, "I love you, Blake. More than life itself."

Their lips met in a soft, delicate kiss, the tenderness reflecting all that had passed between them, their love bringing them together at last.